WHISPER

They listened to a skylark high above the fields behind them, filling an empty sky with its song.

'I do want to make love to you,' Marius said quietly.

'Yes, I know.'

'You—have strong objections to that?'

'I suppose I should. But I don't. I haven't ever . . .' Libby's voice trailed away.

Marius said, 'Ah . . .,' sounding depressed.

'Do you mind, about that?' she asked, squinting at him in the sunlight.

'No, I don't mind.' He rolled over and pushed himself up on his elbow again so that he stooped over her. Her chestnut hair glowed and her slightly parted lips were very kissable. He ran an exploring finger across them, and said softly, 'Of course, I should like to be the first. What worries me is—something else.'

'Because you'll go away again?'

He looked relieved that she had spoken the words. 'Because I must. Probably quite soon. And the likelihood of my coming back is slight. I don't want to just "love you and leave you". It hardly seems fair.'

Ann Hulme was born in Portsmouth and educated at the Royal Holloway College—part of the University of London—where she took a degree in French. She has travelled extensively, and it was the fascination of the various countries in which she made her home—France, Germany, Czechoslovakia, Yugoslavia and Zambia—which made her begin to write. She now lives in Bicester, Oxfordshire, with her husband and two sons.

WHISPER IN THE WIND is a sequel to THE FLYING MAN which is also published by **Worldwide**.

WHISPER IN THE WIND

ANN HULME

WORLDWIDE BOOKS
LONDON · SYDNEY · TORONTO

All the characters in this book have no existence outside the imagination of the Author, and have no relation whatsoever to anyone bearing the same name or names. They are not even distantly inspired by any individual known or unknown to the Author, and all the incidents are pure invention.

First published in Hardback in 1989 by Worldwide Books, Eton House, 18–24 Paradise Road,
Richmond, Surrey TW9 1SR

This paperback edition published in 1989 by Worldwide Books

ISBN 0 373 57446 0
09/8906

Set in 10.5/11 Times
Made and printed in Great Britain

CHAPTER ONE

GRACIE FIELDS's unique voice, that curious mixture of natural vocal gift and exquisitely artificial soprano, was borne on the breeze from some open window. Having put the cover tidily over the ancient typewriter, Libby took a last quick look around her improvised office at the back of the Red Cross hut, glared at the telephone, daring it to ring, picked up her gas-mask case and thankfully let herself out at the end of another week. She locked the door, rattled the handle to check it, and made sure the emergency telephone number was pinned to it, just in case some child—Tommy Ryan, for instance—should decide to do something really dreadful over the weekend. Most of the evacuee children had settled down and now behaved fairly well. But there was a hard core of malcontents, and Tommy was their undisputed leader.

'Why worry about Fifth Columnists,' Dr Greaves had asked wearily, 'when we've got Tommy Ryan undermining our entire community?'

The arrival of the evacuees in this quiet coastal village had caused considerable upset, even though the number had been limited to a dozen youngsters and three pregnant women, all from the East End of London. Adjustment had been difficult for the newcomers and their hosts. Country children were accustomed to roam freely, but not to run wild in the manner of these city-dwellers. Country children all understood how important it was to close gates.

The newcomers, pallid-faced and with rickety limbs but boundless energy, found it amusing to let Mr Harris's dairy Jerseys out into the lane, and thence into Miss Biddle's back garden to destroy an entire vegetable crop, 'dug for victory'. Local children climbed trees. The newcomers swung on branches until they broke. When pursued and cornered, they defended themselves stoutly with a stream of verbal abuse couched in the sort of language no one in the country expected to hear from children.

'Little devils . . .' said Farmer Harris, out of breath from fruitless pursuit and purple in the face with rage. 'Right little demons, that's what!'

However, despite all the initial problems, the evacuees had settled in gradually, and a few had even taken to country life with relish. But Tommy, a child of the brick jungle, was different. Tommy hated them all, the entire village, and wrought his vengeance whenever possible.

Libby's job, as billeting officer, was to co-ordinate efforts to settle the evacuees and deal with any problems which arose. Every second problem seemed to concern young Master Ryan, or one of his faithful band of followers. This week, however, had been reasonably peaceful on the Tommy Front. He had done nothing worse than cut out pictures of plump ladies modelling fearsomely boned salmon-pink corsets from a catalogue, and post them through Miss Biddle's door. Miss Biddle had caused some consternation by descending on the village bobby and declaring herself to have been the recipient of obscene literature. It had all been cleared up quickly and painlessly, except for Tommy, who had been clipped severely round the ear by Constable Burrows. Life went on.

Life did go on, that was the strange thing about it all. They were in their third full year of war, and it had become a way of life. Gas-masks, clothing coupons, food rationing, black-out, how easily they had all accepted these things not only as necessary, but natural. Just now, war or no war, it was Saturday lunchtime, the sun shone warmly from a cloudless blue sky, the corn stood ripe in the fields, and Jamie had a week's leave and would be home when she got there.

Libby threw her gas-mask into the wicker basket on her bicycle and wobbled off down the road. No one seriously thought clouds of poisonous gas were about to envelop the village, but as Aunt Jennie firmly insisted, if people in charge did not observe basic procedure, it was no use asking anyone else to do so. She would have to do something, however, about getting a new bike. This one had been unearthed in the vicarage potting-shed (the verb was apt), and donated for public use, i.e. Libby's, as part of the vicar's war effort. It was kind of the vicar, but she had twice taken nasty tumbles because of the bicycle's eccentricities. Miss Biddle had a bicycle, relatively new and in first-class working order, but she was unlikely to offer it to Libby. Somehow, Miss Biddle managed to blame Libby for the presence of the evacuees in their midst, and Tommy in particular, who was Miss Biddle's sworn foe.

Libby herself was not a true villager, which was another reason why Miss Biddle mistrusted her. A Canadian, with both her parents far away in Canada, she lived here, for the duration, with Aunt Jennie and Uncle Gerard. They were not, technically, quite uncle and aunt. Gerard Daventry was a cousin of Libby's mother. Libby missed her parents very much, but was determined to see out the war in Europe. Most of her childhood had been spent in Europe, largely in France, where, perhaps unusually for a Protestant child, she had been educated at the hands of nuns. Though they had stood no nonsense, those Norman Benedictines, they had been of a jolly disposition and lived in a fairly relaxed community. 'Mother Superior doesn't open our personal mail,' had confided one young nun to Libby once, 'but over at the Carmelites, Mother Superior reads everything.' Libby had often envied the sisters their blend of simplicity, innocent joy and capacity for sheer grinding hard work. But though attracted by the faith which sustained them and the discipline and routine which in some measure protected them from life's uncertainties, she had always known she could never join them.

The summer of 1939 had seen her on holiday in England with her mother's relatives, the Daventrys. When war signals were made, it was at first suggested she return at once to Canada and safety. But everyone had thought it would all be over by Christmas, and anyway, Libby was inspired by the example of Jennie Daventry with the idea of doing war work. Perhaps her training at the hands of the Benedictines also influenced her not to shirk what appeared to be her duty.

Jennie Daventry was a formidable woman, one of the first to sit in Parliament. No longer an MP, she was still prominent in public works, and the war had given her unprecedented opportunities to display her organising skills. She spent a great deal of time in London, commuting down to the country at the weekends.

Her husband, Libby's beloved Uncle Gerry, had

been a successful solicitor. However, a severe heart attack had led to his early retirement and to the selling of their London home. They had sought a secluded country retreat and found it here. He seemed content to let his wife pursue her wide-ranging public career. Libby thought he was rather a remarkable man in his quiet way. Yet she also sometimes asked herself if Aunt Jennie's busy life outside the home, and Gerard Daventry's unprotesting acquiescence, did not conceal a basic failure in their marriage. Her own parents were bound by a passionate and deeply-rooted attachment which no one could fail to sense. They operated in every way as a team. In the Daventrys' marriage, there was much affection, respect and tolerance—but the fire, if there had been one, had gone out.

The love in Gerard Daventry was directed towards his son James, a little older than Libby, and known in the family as Jamie. She had always called him 'cousin', even if the cousinship was once removed. Jamie was currently a flight-lieutenant, and based in Kent. His father's days were made or marred by the arrival or non-arrival of letters from Jamie. Libby knew that if anything ever happened to his son, Gerard Daventry would not survive it, and the real possibility remained a constant, haunting fear.

The bicycle jangled and protested as it bumped through the village. Libby rode past the last houses and turned into the long, winding lane which led to Merriton House, about three miles distant. After a few minutes she passed the entrance to the RAF camp. The sentry recognised her, grinned and saluted. Libby gave him a cheerful wave, and nearly fell off the bicycle.

‘’Ere!’ he shouted. ‘You want to be careful on that heap of scrap!’

Libby rode on, past Harris’s fields. Besides farming, the Harris family owned the local butchers. The same cattle browsing peacefully in the meadows would turn up later as Sunday casseroles and best mince. Bert Harris always reckoned his animals were bred for their table qualities, though unkind local gossip said his meat came from worn-out dairy cows. She came to where the main road crossed the lane and saw that the bus had just stopped to let someone alight. It roared off, Mavis, the clippy, giving her a wave from the back platform.

Libby found herself alone at the crossroads with a stranger. He stood on the grass verge, grasping a suitcase in one hand and rubbing the other thoughtfully across his chin as he glanced mistrustfully about him. His attitude was not altogether surprising. All signposts had been taken down to confuse any enemy paratroopers who might choose to descend on them . . . successfully confusing any other visitors as well.

Abruptly he looked across the road, directly at her, and she became aware of scrutiny from a pair of shrewd, critical eyes. To her alarm, he stepped off the verge, obviously with the intention of seeking directions. The familiar country lane had never seemed so lonely. Libby gripped the handlebars tightly with palms which had become moist with sweat. He stopped a few feet away, as if he realised he made her nervous, but the sound of his voice still made her jump.

‘Perhaps you can direct me to RAF Merriton?’

The accent was faint, but clearly discernible. The voice itself was not unpleasant, but a little too curt for true politeness, and he emphasised the word 'you' in a slightly superior way which ruffled Libby's transatlantic independence of spirit.

Free Pole, Free Czech, Free something-or-other, she thought. But he spoke better English than these usually did. Propaganda films shown in every cinema constantly warned people about giving directions to well-spoken foreigners who appeared from nowhere. Admittedly, this one hadn't leapt out of a plane at twilight; he had descended sedately from a No. 54 bus, but one never knew. He was not in uniform, which was odd, and the suit he wore, with a slightly creased elegance, was so well cut that it would have caused comment in the village even in peacetime.

Her hesitation must have become obvious, because he added less brusquely, 'I didn't mean to frighten you—I only want the camp.'

'If people in charge don't observe the rules . . .' echoed Aunt Jennie's didactic voice in Libby's head. Aloud, she said firmly, 'I hope you don't mind, but I'd like to see your identity card.'

She was afraid he might object, but he nodded, as if she had done the right or expected thing, and putting down the suitcase, hunted in his inner breast pocket. Again she felt a prickle of irritation. He made her feel as though she were successfully passing a series of tests, yet he was the one to justify himself. Now he produced an identity card, which he handed to her.

Libby blushed, suddenly embarrassed at her own suspicions. Her imagination had run away with her. The poor man was completely *bona fide* and only wanted to get to the RAF camp to which, no doubt, he had been posted. He was a gallant ally, not a disguised enemy agent. There could be any one of a dozen reasons why he was not in uniform.

She glanced quickly at the card: Marius Velden. Returning it, she said, 'I'm sorry, it's just . . .'

He was putting the card back in his pocket and shaking his head. He had very straight, thick dark hair, parted on one side with a tendency to fall forward over his forehead. She judged him about thirty or thirty-one. Not particularly tall, just above middle height, he was nevertheless chunkily built. Beneath that well-fitting suit was all solid muscle, no fat. He was certainly physically very strong, and an inner strength, of character or will, was reflected in his face. It was well shaped, with good features and slightly prominent cheekbones. The lines engraved on either side of a wide, straight mouth might have been laughter lines but for the expression in the otherwise very fine hazel eyes, which were unusually watchful. She could not tell whether this indicated a natural arrogance or an acquired defensiveness. But she remembered how her father had once described someone he had met as a 'lone wolf'—and somehow the description seemed to fit this man very well. Yet, she thought uneasily, wolves, like men, live in a structured society. It is for that reason the loner, the outsider, the renegade, is always to be feared.

'You're right to ask. Everyone should be careful.' He sounded faintly reproving, like a schoolmaster with a pupil disposed to carelessness. 'I'm Belgian,' he added suddenly, and the freely-offered explanation was so unexpected that she was startled.

'Your English really is very good,' she mumbled, still apologetic and starting to flounder, because she felt that now she sounded condescending. 'That's what made me hesitate. I mean, some of the Free

Poles and so on speak a most peculiar English that is quite distinctive. Yours is, well, too good.'

He smiled, much to her relief. The lines either side of his mouth were indeed laughter lines. With the smile, he looked more human and approachable, and she wondered if, after all, he was only shy.

'I was a student here in England, for a little while before the war.' He raised his eyebrows. 'The camp?'

'Oh, yes.' She twisted on the saddle and pointed back down the lane the way she had come. 'About a mile, I'm afraid, and you'll have to walk it.'

He grimaced and picked up the suitcase. 'The exercise will do me good.'

Rubbish, you're as fit as a fiddle . . . she thought, eyeing him appraisingly. Not an ounce of spare flesh, a natural athlete, who probably did weight-training to build up the muscle. For what purpose? A keen sportsman? Out of the blue, perhaps instinctively wanting to compensate for her earlier unfriendliness, she heard herself asking, 'Do you play tennis?'

Now he looked startled. 'Yes, a little.'

'Only on Sunday afternoons, in summer, we usually have a kind of a tennis party. The court isn't very good—it needs repairing—but it's quite fun, and any of the officers from the camp who can play usually come over. It's all very informal.' She pointed across the intersecting main road and down the continuation of the lane. 'Merriton House. You can't miss it. It's a big, old manor house with a gravel drive and huge rhododendron bushes. The name is Daventry. That is, my uncle owns the house, Gerard Daventry, but I'm living with them. You'd be very welcome. My own name is Sherwood,' she added. 'Libby Sherwood.'

He was studying her carefully. 'Thank you, Miss Sherwood,' he said politely, but it seemed to her, a little stiffly. Perhaps he thought her forward. 'If it is possible . . .' He hesitated. 'If I can, I'll come.'

Libby said, 'All right, then, come about three.' She pushed the right pedal of the bicycle down with a determined thrust, and the chain came off. 'Drat it!' she exclaimed crossly.

Marius put down his suitcase and offered, 'Let me . . .' in a brisk tone of authority. He turned the bicycle on to its side, took off his jacket and hung it on a nearby gatepost, and settled down on his heels to repair the mishap. He worked quickly and efficiently, a man who knew what he was doing. His hands were square and strong, but the lean, sunburned fingers were very well shaped, not only capable and dextrous, but moving with a certain instinctive grace. Libby thought he would get on well with her father, who was obsessed by all things mechanical, but at the same time she felt her unease return. Not even the arrival of one of Harris's Jerseys, which put her head amiably over the gate and, chewing placidly, watched them with her lustrous eyes, could rid her of a curious sensation that all was not well.

There was something different about this man, and it was not simply his foreign nationality, his accent—which was rather attractive—or his expensive suit. It was something more elusive, and she could not make up her mind what it was. It seemed almost as though he were altogether too capable, as if someone had trained him, and trained him well.

Perhaps he sensed the thoughts flickering through her brain, because he glanced up, and said, 'I know about bicycles. I used to ride one around Oxford, about the same age and condition as this monster. Anyway, every Belgian knows about bicycles. We have a great love of cycling as a sport.'

'Why aren't you in uniform?' she asked curiously.

He smiled politely, but his eyes grew vague, and he turned his attention back to the chain. He was not going to discuss that. 'I had quite a job, you know, finding this place,' he went on conversationally. 'I got to Southampton all right on the train, but had trouble at the bus station, and the girl on the bus pushed me off by this lane without a word of explanation.'

'That's Mavis,' Libby said. 'She probably thought you knew where you were going. Where had you come from?'

'From London. I've been staying with friends.'

'English friends?' So what if she sounded too curious for normal politeness. He puzzled her, and she wondered if he would pretend not to understand this question, too.

But he shook his head. 'Belgian. Count van Malde(eren. He was, still is, an important Flemish political figure.' He nodded towards his case. 'Sit on that while you wait. It won't give way.'

Libby perched on the suitcase, frowning. Exiled Belgian dignitaries . . . The plot thickens, she thought. She was addicted to the writings of Mrs Christie, but this was hardly a Hercule Poirot. Altogether different, in fact. Too tough, too direct, and too athletic. Also Flemish, which was probably why she had not identified his accent earlier. Most Belgians she had met had been French-speaking, and their English had sounded different from his. Who *was* the wretched man?

She had no time to pry any further. He had

mended the chain and was straightening up, wiping the grease from his hands casually on a cambric handkerchief.

'It should get you home, but you need a new machine.'

'Yes, I know. That one belongs to the vicar. I mean, it used to belong to the vicar's wife.' Libby remounted and pushed a stray lock of chestnut hair from her eyes. 'Thanks. See you tomorrow, maybe?'

She rode off, wobbling slightly and not looking back, but she knew he was standing in the middle of the lane and watching her critically. When at last she reached the turn and did glance back, Marius had picked up his suitcase and was walking away towards the camp. He was still in his shirtsleeves and carrying his jacket slung nonchalantly over one broad shoulder and hooked on his finger. He moved with controlled power, light on his feet and slightly hunched, like a prowling tiger. She bit her lip, and pedalled on beneath the canopy of overhanging branches, trying to rid herself of the feeling that something was—what?: Not exactly wrong, but out of true. She found herself musing: It's like finding you have been dealt a wild card. We didn't expect him, he doesn't fit in, and we can't know what he'll do . . .

The stone pillars to either side of the gate to Merriton House appeared on her left. They still called it the 'gate', although the wrought-iron railings had gone, donated to the last metal collection on behalf of the war effort. Even the old and damaged saucepans had been taken, although quite how many it took, melted down, to make a tank, Libby was not sure, nor was anyone else. She whizzed, free-wheeling, through the empty gate-gap, and was halted by a voice calling, 'Caught you speeding!'

'Jamie!' she cried, and let the bicycle fall to the drive with a clatter as she leapt off and ran into the arms of James Daventry.

'Hold on!' he said, when he had swung her round, feet off the ground, and kissed her warmly. 'I thought I was going to be run down by a demon cyclist. Now I'm afraid I'm about to be raped by one.'

'You are an idiot!' she told him happily. 'How long have you got?'

'Till Friday, and then I'll have to start back. It takes such a dickens of a long time travelling, especially if one has to cross London.' He righted her bicycle and retrieved her gas-mask case and began to push the machine towards the house. 'You keeping all right?' When she nodded, he added abruptly, 'Father's looking his age.'

'He worries about you,' Libby told him soberly, 'although he'd never admit it. You probably notice more change in him than I do, because I see him every day. He keeps pretty fit, on the whole. He'll take on the vicar at tennis tomorrow, you'll see.'

Jamie grimaced. 'Not those ruddy tennis parties with the vicar in tropical shorts and Doc Greaves with that old racket shaped like a snowshoe?'

'All the regulars. It suits your father, or his health. You know how keen he is—was—on tennis. Since his heart attack he can't play much but Doc Greaves believes ex-heart patients ought to take regular gentle exercise, so a sedate game of Sunday afternoon tennis is quite in order. Of course, sometimes, we are graced by the presence of a couple of officers from the camp. They're generally young and fit and altogether too fast about the court, so Doc Greaves won't allow your father to take them on. Much to Uncle Gerry's annoyance, I may say! They paste the poor old vicar into the ground instead.'

'What about you?' Jamie asked wickedly, with a sidelong glance. 'Do they get you down on the ground as well?'

'Shut up, James! They're always very pleasant and nice, but they're like all Englishmen. I mean, they always seem at a loss what to say to me.'

'Don't bounce in like some of your transatlantic hearties and make themselves instantly at home?'

'We don't behave like that. Not in Canada, anyway. I'll have you know you can't beat Canadian small-town society for gentility! Mother wrote me that she has become caught up in a round of charity tea-parties—war funds, you know. Every function is duly reported in the local press the next day, the write-up finishing with the words: "Mrs Sherwood poured." Beat that, Jamie Daventry!'

'Can't. So these Englishmen are just socially gauche, is that it?'

'No! But anyway, I'm sacrosanct. Mr Daventry's niece, you know. I've a sort of notice tacked on my back which says "Don't touch"!'

'Good!' said Jamie abruptly, the laughter vanished from his voice.

'Evangeline Watts turns up occasionally of a Sunday,' Libby informed him, not without malice.

'Oh, well, they won't have any trouble getting her flat on her back,' was the ungallant comment.

'Um, she is a trifle obvious, but she is a very well-meaning sort of girl . . .'

A snort of merriment from Jamie greeted this.

Moved to a spirited defence of her own sex, Libby demanded, 'What about you? Are you still seducing Kentish maidens?'

'Not a chance. The Free Poles got there first. You should see them work. Talk about sweeping a girl off her feet! The sight of our dashing Polish allies in full cry among local womanhood is something, I can tell you.' Jamie chuckled. 'Add to that the fact that they each have such an unpronounceable name that the poor girl can never remember it the next morning, and you'll understand that they have the field to themselves. But it doesn't bother me, because I'm keen only on *you*. You know that.'

'You can't be; I'm a cousin,' she said firmly.

'You are not. Not a first cousin, anyway. Even they, first cousins, aren't in the Table of Kindred and Affinity. People marry cousins all the time.' Jamie's chin had taken on an argumentative thrust. This was an old dispute, and they had been through it many times.

'Yes, the Habsburgs did, and had dotty children. And the old planters did, in the Southern states before the Civil War, and had mad grannies locked in every spare bedroom.' Libby put her arm through his, partly in consolation, and partly because she wanted to ask something. 'Jamie—serious matters. I've asked someone to come tomorrow afternoon, and I don't know whether I should have. I met him just now, by the bus-stop in Lower Lane. I wonder . . . You have friends down at the camp, and perhaps you could check on him? His name is Marius Velden—at least, that's the name on his identity card. He's Belgian, and he was on his way to the camp.'

Jamie gave her a quick, searching look. 'Think he's a fraud?'

'No—o . . .' Libby said slowly, 'not exactly. Nor do I think the identity card was a fake. It's all genuine. But if there isn't something rum about him, I'll eat my hat. I don't know if he will come tomorrow; he was rather stand-offish when I asked him. He mended my bike in double-quick time, so he knows something about mechanics, but he's definitely well educated and well connected.'

'In air force uniform?'

'No, in civvies . . . and expensive ones. Nothing off the peg. Savile Row, I bet. For the better sort of country gentleman, and tailored before the war. Not the sort of thing you buy with clothing coupons! It's all a little odd, Jamie, and don't say I've been reading too many whodunnits.'

He squeezed her arm. 'Don't fret. If he turns up tomorrow, I'll interrogate him, and demand to know his intentions. I don't want you falling for some continental Casanova!'

'I'm not going to fall for him! He—made me a little nervous. Yet he was very nice. He said he had been staying in London with a Count van Malderen, an exiled Belgian VIP. Someone could check on that.'

'Mmm.' Jamie scratched his tousled brown hair. 'All right. How are all those lads of yours?'

'Not bad, except Tommy Ryan.'

Jamie groaned. 'Not the terrible Thomas? Is he still here? What's he done? Set fire to Bert Harris's barn? Stolen Miss Biddle's directoire knickers off the washing-line?'

'Poor Miss Biddle.'

'Old dragon! The kid is unhappy. If she left him in peace, he'd tire of ragging her.'

'He makes everyone else unhappy,' said Libby with feeling.

'Forget about him,' ordered Jamie, gesturing widely as he ushered her through the front door. 'Forget sinister Belgian double agents. I'm home for a week, and *nothing* is to go wrong, do you hear?'

In the room they had given him, Marius put his case on the bed and unlocked it. His spare shirts, neatly folded, lay on the top. 'Try and look inconspicuous,' his controller had told him, 'although one foreign civilian among all those Brylcreem boys is going to stick out like a sore thumb. It's only a small village, and the camp is small enough for any oddity to be questionable. But it's secure. Anyone following you down there would be spotted at once. Just remember, you're there to give a course of lectures. Just another backroom wizard. They'll be polite to you and despise you, and that's fine.'

'Aren't they going to find it strange when I start jumping out of aircraft?'

'It's your hobby.'

'Like hell!'

Marius took out the shirts and hung them in the wardrobe. He had already failed to achieve anonymity. He should have arrived down here wearing gardening trousers and gumboots. He took out the folder of notes for his lecture, hoping that no one in his audience proved to have more information on the subject than he did. Beneath it, lying on the top of the remaining contents, was a photograph in a leather folder. He picked it up, almost reluctantly, and opened it.

Every time he looked at it he remembered that day, and Annette laughing and tossing back her thick chestnut hair. They had ridden out, up into the forest, along a narrow bridle-track. She was an excellent horsewoman, moving as if one with the animal, endowed with a natural grace, balance and rhythm, responding to the movement as if by instinct. Perhaps that was what had made her so good in bed. In a grassy clearing they had tied up the horses and lain down to make love under the open sky. He could recall the scent of the pine needles and the perfume in her hair. Afterwards, he leaned back against the trunk of a tree and lit a cigarette, and she rested against his shoulder with her eyes closed and let a ray of sunlight play on her face. He had been in love, and he had thought she was, too, so he had proposed, making quite a speech about it, all correct and by the book.

She had turned him down in the same way. *Noblesse oblige*. Aristocratic families always did things in the right way. They even did the wrong things in the right way. She had thrown his love back in his face, but she had been so cool, logical and polite about it all, so damned well bred.

'We can be lovers, Marius, that is all right. But marriage, you know, is altogether another matter. It's serious, perhaps boring, but serious. It's not enough to be good together in bed. There are other things.'

'But I love you!' he had protested.

'Dear Marius,' she had laughed her low, throaty chuckle. 'You don't love *me*, you love my body.'

'To me, that's the same thing!' he had shouted at her, growing angry.

'Because you are a man. Men don't think clearly

enough at times like this. Their brains are located in their pants; it's not their fault. Let me think for both of us, darling. Believe me, you'd hate to be married to me. And I'd hate to be married to you, although of course I love you.'

'You go to hell!' he had told her viciously. 'You ice-blooded little bitch!'

He had pushed her away with all the violence at his disposal, and she rolled over and over on the turf, half frightened and half mocking him.

Now Marius closed the folder that held the photo. He ought to have put Annette completely out of his mind by now. He didn't know why he carried the wretched photo around, except that it was a memory of days before war came to the home he loved. He had got over her, even though not easily. At first, hatred had replaced the love, because it sometimes is love in a warped way, being, as it is, an obsession without rhyme or reason. Now the hatred was dulled, like the love, and nothing was left but an emptiness. It had taken a long time, but he was cured. Now he looked back and saw it as one of those bitter-sweet passions of youth which linger in the memory with affection and pain, but hurt less as time goes by. Sometimes now he went whole days at a stretch and never thought about her.

On other days, the cure seemed worse than the disease. Like today, for example, when he had met a girl who had reminded him of Annette so forcefully that it had struck him like a blow to the chest. A girl with the same glossy chestnut hair and clear, crystal-bright eyes, only blue, not green as were Annette's. This one had been perched on a bicycle, a terrible old boneshaker quite dangerous to take out on the road. She was dressed in a serviceable linen skirt and hand-knitted sweater, and a blue paisley head-scarf had slipped off her hair and lay loosely knotted round her neck. She had been so suspicious of him. Smart girl. A good mark for her, and a bad one for him. He was not supposed to be as obvious as one of the conspirators in *Julius Caesar*.

He carried the photo to the window-sill and set it up, as a gesture of defiance, but he was still thinking of the girl on the bicycle. Miss Sherwood had been intelligent and pretty and, unless he was much mistaken, no local. There was a frank self-assurance in her manner and warm tones to her voice, which indicated North America. Yet, lurking in the depths of those puzzled blue eyes studying him so intently had been a hint of bubbling fun. That was what had recalled Annette and what had made him so loquacious. He had virtually talked his head off. And if one slip of a girl could throw him off course so easily . . .

He walked across to the window and peered out, up into the clear sky. The cord of the rolled-up black-out blind swayed in the breeze and knocked against the pane. He was here for a purpose and could not afford to lose sight of it. 'Some hopes,' he thought ruefully. He needed to keep his head clear and his heart unencumbered. No time now for the sweeter pleasures of life. Forget the girl on the bicycle, even if she had had marvellous legs.

He scowled. Yet, for practical purposes, he couldn't forget her. She had been clever enough to check on him. He had to appear no more than he seemed to be. What would Marius Velden, that dry-as-dust lecturer, do if invited to a tennis party? He would go, because he would have no reason not to do so. That other Marius, he had to go, too—and take the opportunity offered to allay suspicion all round and appear another pleasant, well-meaning, slightly peculiar foreigner.

Anyway, he wouldn't mind a game of tennis. Standing in the middle of the room, he made a practice swing round with his arm, as if to serve. He had been Belgian junior champion one year—a long time ago, longer than he cared to remember. Still, he could probably beat the local club players around here. 'Matter of honour,' he said severely to himself, and went off to see if he could borrow a racket.

CHAPTER TWO

JENNIE DAVENTRY also arrived home late that afternoon, for the weekend. She marched into the house in her usual no-nonsense fashion, clad in an unglamorous tweed costume which made no concession to the warm weather, and sensible shoes. Her hat, despite being pinned to her hair by an assortment of pins, managed to be askew. She embraced them all heartily, greeting the dogs with much the same sort of enthusiasm as she greeted the humans, and demanded to know if Jamie was eating properly.

'Yes, Ma,' he said in suitably serious tones.

'Good boy!' said Mrs Daventry, but as she was patting one of the dogs at the time, it was not clear whether she meant her son or the spaniel.

After dinner, it proved such a beautiful evening that Libby and Jamie took the dogs for a last run before nightfall, along the seashore. The gardens of Merriton House ran down to the beach, although to reach the pebble-strewn shore one had to scramble down a rough path carved out of a high bank, and flanked by bramble bushes. The two spaniels negotiated it easily. Jamie went down ahead to catch Libby if she slipped, but in trousers and flat shoes she slid and scrambled down it unaided to land breathless at the bottom.

It was familiar territory to the dogs, which scampered away full of canine enthusiasm. The tide was in, and the water unexpectedly clean and clear. Across it, in the distance, the Isle of Wight seemed almost close enough to reach out and touch, the buildings distinguishable along its shore. A pleasant, cool, salty breeze blew in their faces and everywhere was quiet.

'No seaweed or anything,' Libby observed. 'It must be calm out at sea.'

'In more ways than one.' Jamie pointed. 'Look, a tanker.' The dark functional outline of a ship was steaming purposefully towards the Solent. 'She made a successful run for it, anyway.'

They both fell silent for a moment, thinking of the dangerous journey the ship had made across U-boat and mine-infested waters. Then Jamie stooped and picked up a piece of driftwood tossed high up above the tidemark by last winter's gales, and threw it for the dogs.

'Libby, I want to talk to you, and seriously. Don't try to stop me. I'm going to say it all, and you are going to listen.'

Libby's heart sank. She glanced surreptitiously at his grimly-set profile. He was not so much older than she was, but just now he looked a good deal older. Even in repose, his features, square and uncompromising, tended to have a truculent look, so that nervous strangers sometimes wondered what they could have done to offend him. At the moment he looked positively ferocious, so she knew he was going to say what was on his mind and she couldn't stop him, even though she knew what it was, and what the answer would be from her.

'I want to marry you,' Jamie said bluntly. 'I always have. What's more, you know it.' He glared at her, defying her to deny it.

She nodded, not trusting herself to speak. One of

the dogs had disappeared around a loop in the shoreline, and could be heard barking.

Jamie stopped and turned to face her, blocking any further advance on her part. 'What's more, I'm pretty sure you'd marry me if it wasn't that you've got this bee in your bonnet about our being related. It doesn't *matter*. At least, not a one-off marriage of relatives such as ours would be. All those mad Royals you're always telling me about, they married cousins generation after generation, so no wonder they got inbred and loony! That couldn't happen to our children.'

'It might,' said Libby obstinately. 'I asked old Dr Greaves, and he said it was always a risk.'

'Life is full of risks!' Jamie said sharply. 'Hell's teeth, don't you think I take risks, all the time, up there?' He pointed skyward. 'Look, if it's only the child problem which is worrying you, we needn't have any children. I don't care. All I want is you. Anyway, talking about raising families is looking ahead, and, don't you see, no one can do that now. It was all right before the war, long engagements and a girl asking a chap to give her time to think it over. The same goes for planning a family. But now no one has any blessed time. Here today—gone tomorrow. I'm not trying to be morbid, just realistic. We haven't got the time, you and I, to worry whether we're doing the right thing. Can't we just get married, Libby, and hang all the pros and cons?'

'No, we can't, Jamie!' she burst out. 'Although I love you dearly, I honestly don't love you in that way.'

'Serve you right if I got blown out of the sky,' he

said sulkily. Then, seeing her pale, he added immediately in a contrite voice, 'Sorry, that was petty.'

'I do think about you, Jamie, all the time,' she murmured, 'and pray for you, but I'm not going to marry you.'

Jamie stooped again and scooped up a handful of pebbles. He began to toss them out across the water, one by one, skimming them across the gently-rolling, blackish-green waves. 'Do you want to marry someone else?' He sounded obstinate, resentful and hurt, all in one.

'No! Look, I have my job, and it keeps me busy. Also there's Uncle Gerry. I look after him when your mother is away.'

'Yes, I know,' he said soberly and more calmly. 'The old boy is devoted to you, Libby, and I can tell you it puts my mind at rest, when I'm away, knowing you're here with him. I wish Mother . . .' He broke off, not wanting to be disloyal, and kicked a large pebble out of the way. 'Mother is a good sort, you know, but I just wish she'd direct a little of her good works towards Dad.'

Both the dogs were barking furiously. 'What's the matter with those brutes?' Jamie asked crossly. He put his fingers to his mouth and whistled sharply. 'Here, Spot! Lady! Come back here!'

The two dogs reappeared, bounding round the headland, followed by the solid figure of a man in flannels and a well-worn, crumpled corduroy jacket. At the sight of him, Libby gave a little gasp.

'Who the devil is that?' Jamie asked crossly. 'There's a notice down there which clearly says this piece of shore is private property.'

'Perhaps he didn't see it,' Libby said, watching

Marius approach. 'Jamie, it's Velden, the man I told you . . .' She broke off as Marius reached them.

'Good evening,' he greeted them affably.

'Good evening!' Jamie replied stiffly. 'I'm afraid this strip of shore is private. There is a notice-board.'

'Yes, I saw it,' Marius told him in a kindly fashion, as if assuring Jamie that he need not worry. Jamie's face took on a dusky pink hue.

'Jamie!' Libby interrupted hastily. 'This is Marius Velden whom I met on my way home at lunchtime. My cousin, Mr Velden—Flight-Lieutenant James Daventry.'

Inwardly she was thinking: He's changed his clothes. He must have realised he looked altogether too elegant. Continentals never understand the English obsession with old clothes.

'I'm pleased to meet you,' Marius said courteously. He held out his hand and, after a moment's hesitation, Jamie shook it briefly. Marius gestured at the land atop the steep bank. 'Up there is the back of Merriton House, is that right?'

'Yes,' Jamie said coldly. 'Why should that interest you?'

'I was thinking of walking over tomorrow afternoon.' Marius shrugged. It was a purely continental gesture; a slight, elegant expressive hunching of his broad shoulders. 'I'm glad I've met you again, Miss Sherwood. I was thinking about your kind offer, your invitation to play tennis tomorrow afternoon. If you have no objection, I should like to accept.'

The 'if you have no objection' was addressed to Jamie, who said awkwardly, 'Yes, come. We can lend you a racket, if you haven't one.'

'Thank you, Flight-Lieutenant, but someone at the camp has offered to lend me his.'

Jamie's eyebrows shot up. 'Libby said you were asking for the camp, but as you weren't in uniform, she wasn't sure whether you were RAF personnel or not.'

The same vague look entered Marius's eyes that Libby had seen before. He definitely didn't like questions, even oblique ones, and chose not to hear. One of the spaniels loped up and sniffed at his trousers and he bent and scratched its head. 'I've come down to give a couple of lectures, that is to say, to be very boring. Perhaps you'd care to sit in on one of them, Flight-Lieutenant?'

'I'm on leave, or I should.' Jamie's manner had thawed out considerably but he was still ready to revert to instant hostility. 'I understand you're Belgian.'

'Yes; not too many of us about. We've all suffered greatly from comparison with a certain fictional detective. We're not all like that, believe me!' He glanced up from petting the dog and smiled at them both, but Libby knew the smile was meant for her. As a smile, it was best described as a pleasantly disarming grin. But, instead of disarming her, it made her feel nervous and think: The smile on the face of the tiger . . .

As before, she felt there was something about this agreeably-spoken unusual man that was faintly, indefinably dangerous. Something about the way he carried himself, and moved, lightly balanced on his feet, outwardly relaxed. Yet one could not but feel that, inwardly, every sense was alert, and the compact, well-muscled body could spring into action at any moment. A man who spent his life in a lecture-hall? Like heck, thought Libby inelegantly.

'I was always rotten at languages,' Jamie was saying frankly. 'Your English is very good.'

'He was a student here, before the war,' Libby said, breaking her silence.

'Oh?' Jamie was curious. 'Where?'

When Marius named one of the Oxford colleges, Jamie's curiosity turned to open surprise. But, Libby was thinking, he must be genuine. All this—his college record, and the rest—can be checked: he can't tell lies about things like that. The poor fellow probably has to keep explaining himself like this. Everyone is so suspicious of foreigners.

Without warning, Marius was taking his leave of them. Jamie started to suggest they walk back a little way with him, but this offer was rebuffed very politely yet decidedly. The newcomer had a way of rolling over possible obstacles. He just said what he was going to do, and he did it. Just as he had seen the 'Private Property' notice, and chosen to disregard it. As if he were lord of the manor, coming and going as he pleased, and it didn't apply to him, Libby thought. At one time, lords of the manor had other rights, too, like the virginity of comely peasant girls. She found herself speculating idly as she watched him walk away, his feet sinking into the loose shingle and crunching it underfoot.

When he had disappeared round the headland, she said to Jamie, 'I was right, wasn't I? He is different.'

Jamie was chewing his lower lip thoughtfully. 'Oh, all these foreign chaps . . .' he said vaguely.

That night they were got from their beds by the air-raid siren and tumbled downstairs in dressing-gowns and hastily donned overcoats. They gathered together, dogs included, in the tiny shelter in the back garden, which probably would not have withstood a well-directed hail of stones, and listened to the sinister droning noise in the night sky. It was followed by the familiar dull crump in the distance. Libby put her nose out of the doorway. Outside it was as light as day, and she could see every leaf on the nearby laurel bushes. The sky was lit by a beautiful orange-red glow that had its origin some fifteen miles away as the crow flies, on the horizon, as if someone had lit a giant bonfire.

It *was* a giant bonfire. The docks and centre of Southampton were burning. She wondered if that was the sole target of the raid, or whether the plant a few miles along the coast from them was also intended, but had been missed. She remembered the tanker she and Jamie had seen enter the supposedly safe haven of port after a hazardous voyage, and wondered if, after all the trials and dangers at sea, she had succumbed at her berth.

'Come inside, Libby!' Aunt Jennifer called.

'It's all right,' she called back. As she said it, she thought what a stupid remark it was and how heartless, because just over there was a raging inferno, but all she had meant was that *they* were all right, sitting here, like so many gnomes in their garden shelter, half-underground. She went back inside, and found Aunt Jennie purposefully unscrewing a Thermos flask. The tea had been made and put ready in the kitchen before they all went to bed, just in case. They had all become very adept at staring up at the sky and judging whether tonight was likely to see a raid. Jamie was sitting in the far corner, scowling in the shadows, and refused tea. Every time a dull distant explosion shook the air, he twitched, and sometimes he muttered, 'Bam!' as though he were encapsulating the sound in a balloon, like a cartoonist. She knew he felt he ought not to be here with them. They were civilians, but his place was elsewhere. Yet the world was in the grip of total war—there were no civilians. They were all in the front line.

After the All Clear had eventually sounded, they tramped back indoors and bade each other goodnight all over again. Libby went back to her bedroom, but, not hearing Jamie's door shut, went out again after a moment's hesitation, and creeping along the landing, peered over the top banister. He was sitting on the stairs in his dressing-gown, in the shadowy moonlight, his arms on his knees, not moving. She redescended the stairs cautiously until she reached him and squeezed in beside him on the stair-tread.

Without any preamble, he said quietly, 'You see, I sometimes think it isn't that I might not come back—but that I might return, and find you gone.'

'He would have to be hopelessly off course to drop a bomb on Merriton House,' she said lightly.

'No, he wouldn't.' Jamie's voice was cold and matter-of-fact. 'Very little—and it happens more easily than you imagine. I know a chap who . . .'

He broke off and she put her hand on his arm. 'You hate it, don't you?'

'I don't drop bombs, thank God. Libby, that chap Velden . . .'

Her heart sank. 'You don't think this raid had anything to do . . . ?'

'No, no!' he interrupted. 'Well, I can't say I liked him prowling about on the shore. He must have seen that tanker. We did. The thing is—and it's difficult to explain—we all kill people. That's what war is about, in the end.'

'I thought we were defending civilisation?'

'Yes, we are, but to do it you end up doing the sorts of things you've always been taught are wrong. But there's killing and killing. I mean, I've pressed the button and sent a chap down in flames more than once.'

'I suppose you have, but you're not a killer, Jamie!' she said fiercely.

He turned his head towards her in the shadow. 'But that's what I'm trying to explain. No, I'm not. But Velden is.'

Libby shivered as if a cold draught had invaded the hall, and pulled her dressing-gown more closely round her. 'How do you know?' Her voice sounded unnatural, almost a croak.

'Met 'em before, chaps like that. Decent enough fellows, a lot of them, but got the mark of Cain on them, if you like. I'm not talking about homicidal maniacs, Libby; I'm talking about brave men, heroes . . . I bet you he's got a medal or two stashed away. Don't ask him how he got them, though.'

'But now he's just a backroom wizard, lecturing on his subject.' Her voice sounded unconvincing to her own ears. For some reason she began to feel cross, and to blame Jamie for it. She asked almost brusquely, 'Do you think he's grounded, or whatever the equivalent is for whatever he does?'

'Not for a minute,' Jamie said in a flat voice.

Jamie had expressed a wish that nothing go wrong during his short leave, but, reflected Libby, even if things had not gone wrong, they showed every sign of working out differently from what might be expected. They had started to do that when she saw Marius step off that bus.

After such a disturbed night, she fell into a deep slumber, and awoke to hear the throb of a car engine. She put her head out of the window just in time to see Jamie drive off in the Daventrys' elderly Riley. She squinted at the alarm-clock and wondered where on earth he was going so early on a Sunday morning. Not to early church, because they were scheduled to go all together at eleven.

She dragged on her dressing-gown and made her way to the bathroom. Gazing into the mirror as she brushed her teeth, she thought: I'm so unsettled, I really don't know how I shall get through today. I don't know if I feel this way because of that raid. Or because of what Jamie said afterwards. Perhaps just because Jamie is here. Maybe it's just that wretched Belgian, if he *is* Belgian, and if he *is* named Velden and is what he says he is . . .

Yet, despite everything, he held a fatal fascination for her. She wanted him to come this afternoon, to be able to talk to him again. She wanted to know. She stopped brushing her teeth and scowled fiercely in a way guaranteed to give her wrinkles. She smoothed them away with her fingertips, and found herself thinking, almost incongruously, of Marius squatting on his heels to mend her bicycle. Perhaps they were all of them suffering from too much war. Perhaps Marius was just a very nice man, a long way from home and in exile, and shy. A lot of people hid shyness beneath a brittle façade of self-assurance.

Jamie was back at breakfast-time, a little breathless and with an enigmatic look on his square, honest face. He said 'Good morning!' and sat down and took a piece of toast. 'I see old Mrs Hills is still burning the toast to a crisp.' He began to scrape at it energetically.

'Can't get help these days,' said his father from behind his Sunday paper. 'All the young girls are working in the factories or are in the Forces. We're lucky to have Mrs Hills.'

Libby leaned forward and hissed across the table, 'I saw you slipping out secretly like that. What's up?'

Jamie looked faintly disconcerted. 'Didn't mean to wake anyone. The fact is, I went to see a chap I know. I wanted to check on your friend Mr Velden before he turned up here this afternoon, merrily asking: "Anyone for tennis?"'

'And what did you find out?' she asked eagerly.

Her cousin avoided her eye. 'Oh, it's all right. He is who he says he is. Some kind of backroom expert, boffin, come down to give a talk. They were expecting him.' There was something more, but he was not going to tell her. Probably Marius's expert knowledge carried a secret label.

'I shall be glad when this war is over,' muttered Libby, 'if only because we shall not have to creep about being so secretive all the time and afraid to open our mouths.'

'Did you say he was an Oxford man?' asked Gerard Daventry unexpectedly.

'Yes, Uncle Gerry. His name is Velden. I suspect he's going to turn out to be a first-rate tennis player, so beware!'

As it turned out, tennis was very soon put out of their minds. They had come out of church and were standing by the ancient lich-gate, chatting. Suddenly Jamie exclaimed, 'Hullo, here comes George Evans. He looks a bit put out.'

A stout, red-face figure was puffing determinedly towards them, and Libby's heart sank at the sight of him because it was with the Evanses that Tommy Ryan was lodged. It was clear from the expression on George's face that young Master Ryan had been up to his tricks again. But what on earth had the child done now? Poor George looked really upset.

Evans came huffing and puffing to a standstill before them and took off his battered green trilby. 'Morning, sir. Morning, Mr Daventry. Morning, ma'am.' These greetings were addressed to Gerard Daventry, his son and his wife in that order. George now turned his attention to Libby. 'I'm sorry to bother you like this, Miss Libby, on a Sunday morning and all. But the missus said you should be told and I saw you standing here and thought, well, best let you know.'

'What has Tommy done?' she asked resignedly. She hoped George was not going to demand Tommy's removal. To find Tommy an alternative billet would not be easy. The whole village knew about Tommy Ryan.

'He's gone,' said George flatly. 'Up and gone, run off. Last night we had a bit of a barney, the lad and I, on account of his language. Bad language I won't stand for, and certainly not in front of my wife. So I made that clear to the boy and sent him off up to bed. Then come that blessed air raid. We all got up and went down to the shelter. Then I notices that the boy has got all his outdoor clothes on under his dressing-gown. "What's all that about?" says I. "Reckoned we was going to have a raid," says he. Smart as a new shilling, he is, never at a loss for an answer. So I let it go, my wife being bad with her nerves on account of the raid. I should have guessed what the young imp was up to! Of course, this morning we find he's gone, taken all his stuff. Sorry to trouble you, miss,' he added again in conclusion.

Libby sighed, and Gerard said in his lawyer's way, 'You did quite right to tell us, Evans. Where have you looked for the boy?'

'Just about everywhere, sir. And I've been over to see Bert Harris, and he's looked in his barns and his cowshed. Thing is, mild nights like we've been having, the kid could sleep out under a hedge somewhere, no need to seek shelter. Blessed if I know what to do.'

'Have you told Constable Burrows?' Libby asked.

'Not yet, miss. Think I should?'

'Kid is bound to get hungry,' Jamie offered. 'He'll turn up at lunchtime.'

Libby shook her head. 'No, not Tommy.'

'Think he might be trying to get back home, back to London?' her uncle asked in a low voice.

'I don't know, Uncle Gerard. He might. But the family was bombed out and his mother is living with relatives somewhere. Perhaps, if Tommy doesn't turn up by this afternoon, we should let the police know. He is only twelve.'

Jamie glanced at his wristwatch. 'It's only an hour till lunch. I'll take a walk over Bert Harris's fields and see if I can turn anything up.'

'I'd better go and have a word with Mrs Evans,' Libby said. 'I expect she is very worried.'

'The wife's fond of that boy, you know,' said George unexpectedly. 'It would be kind of you to drop by, Miss Libby. Little brat!' he added with feeling. 'Tan his hide, I will, when I get my hands on him!'

Libby, knowing George to be the mildest man

alive, was not perturbed by this threat. 'Don't worry, George. I'm sure he'll turn up safe and sound. He's a very capable sort of child.'

'I'll take a walk up around Long Wood,' Gerard offered. 'Plenty of places for a boy to hide up there. Might have built himself a camp, like boys do.'

Rather unexpectedly, his wife, who had been listening closely, announced, 'I'll come with you.'

So, instead of going home for a peaceful pre-luncheon sherry (all the more savoured for being hard to get), they went their separate ways to hunt for Tommy Ryan.

Marius had walked across Harris's fields and over the rough area of heath down to the shore. He liked walking out in the open like this, with the salt breeze from the sea blowing in his face. These moments of freedom and safety meant a great deal. Just being able to stroll along, not having to hide. One of the worst times of his life had been the week spent shut in what had been little more than a large cupboard. He had learned then what claustrophobia meant. Loneliness he didn't mind. He was a lonely person.

Things here were progressing pretty much to plan. They'd shown him the aerial photographs and he'd studied them that morning, printing them on his memory. He had a good memory, but the country-side in the photographs had been familiar territory. Hang it all, he was going home. He laughed aloud, struck by the ironic humour of it all.

He was due to give his lecture tomorrow morning, just to keep the record straight, and he had better take a look at his notes or even he wouldn't know what on earth he was talking about. Thank goodness for that reliable memory! Tomorrow afternoon he would make a practice parachute jump. He had jumped out of aeroplanes before, and never liked it. Some people did, but they must be mad. It went against every human instinct to launch yourself out into the void. Jumping at night was marginally easier, because then he felt like some kind of night predator, an owl or a bat, swooping down. He still didn't like it.

Marius pulled out a pocket diary and riffled through the pages, studying the phases of the moon. He had ten days. At this time of year there was little trouble with cloud or mist. On the other hand, that made him vulnerable. He could smell the sea now, strongly. The shore must be just over that hillock. He turned his steps towards it. The ground under his feet felt soft and peaty. Heather sprouted in irregular clumps and the gorse bushes were ablaze with yellow. He liked this kind of countryside. It had none of the magnificence of the Alps. It wasn't spectacular like the Rhine Valley. It hadn't the sturdy dignity of the Ardennes. But it was tough and resilient. Its dark colours were muted and yet beautiful, and it supported an abundance of wildlife of one kind and another.

Marius scrambled up the rise, his feet making no noise on the dry, sound-absorbing turf. He topped the swell of land and slid down the other side, and found himself face to face with a small boy in a darned pullover and faded shorts.

'Don't run!' he said quickly. 'It's all right.'

The child obviously had been going to bolt, and still stood tensed and ready to run. He was not a particularly attractive little boy. He had a pinched, wary, but alert little face, untidy hair, and his socks had concertinaed down round his ankles. His bare legs were thin and crooked, a sign of rickets in babyhood, and plentifully scarred with bruises and scratches. He stood watching Marius with sharp, shrewd eyes.

'Not like a child, but like a man,' thought Marius. 'Young in years and old in experience.'

''Oo are you?' demanded the boy suspiciously in an unmistakable Cockney accent.

'Marius,' he told him. 'What's your name?'

The child shuffled his feet on the loose shingle and avoided his eye. He was a child who gave away no information. 'You could do my job . . .' thought Marius wryly.

'Seen any snakes?' he asked amiably, not pressing the request for a name.

'Ain't none,' said his companion scornfully.

'Wrong. The heath round here is well known for them. There is a sloughed adder's skin back there.' He pointed over the rise towards the heath behind them.

'Go on!' But the boy was interested.

Marius turned and wandered back the way he'd come, his hands in his pockets. After a moment's hesitation, the child followed. They stood before the sloughed snakeskin and studied it.

'Cor!' said the boy at last, and his whole expression brightened. He crouched down to gather up the trophy carefully and tucked it away in his mended pullover.

'I don't live here,' said Marius. 'I'm a visitor.' Sometimes if you want any information, you must first offer a little, bargain.

'I don't live here neither,' said the child. 'I'm a 'vacuee.'

'A what?'

''Vacuee. Come down from London.'

Marius said, 'Ah, I see. Do you like it here?'

'Not much. Nothing to do.' He kicked his sandalled foot against a clump of heather.

'There are two kinds of heather growing here,' Marius pointed out. 'That sort with the little pink flowers, and the larger, purple sort. It's a very tough plant. It grows on poor soil and in bad weather. If you keep a piece, it will bring you luck.'

'Is that true?' The old-young wary eyes peered at him suspiciously.

'The gipsies say so.'

'They don't know nothing! Seen plenty of 'em hop-picking, before the war. My grandma always said they made it up, what they read in your hand.'

'Your grandmother is probably right.'

'She's dead now.' The child eyed him. 'Got any fags?'

'Cigarettes? No, I don't smoke.'

The boy sniffed his disgust. They walked back to the seashore and sat down side by side on a patch of coarse dune grass.

'Is your mother evacuated with you?'

'No, she's gone to live with Fred.'

Who was Fred? Probably a man-friend, thought Marius; someone casually acquired and not likely to be permanent. The child had probably seen a succession of Freds pass through his short life, and had been brought up by the grandmother. He asked, 'What about your father?'

'Don't know nothing about *him*. He went off.'

Marius picked up a handful of stones and began to toss them into the sea. The child, beneath his tough exterior, was lonely, and by nature gregarious. The urge to talk would be too strong to resist.

Provided Marius said nothing, the child would begin to talk his head off. He was obviously in some sort of trouble and, at a guess, had run away.

'I live with old Evans,' said his young acquaintance with a touch of gloom.

'And you don't like him. Is he unkind?'

'No, he just keeps jawing at me. Do this, do that, don't swear, wash yer hands . . . His old lady is all right, but she's as bad as he is for washing.'

'It's nearly lunchtime. Won't Mrs Evans expect you back?'

'I ain't going back!' said the child fiercely.

'I see. All right. Only, I thought, you know how women are . . .'

'I ain't afraid of women!' said his companion stoutly.

'Then you should be,' Marius said softly. 'They can do a lot of harm.'

There was a pause in the conversation. The child extracted the snakeskin from his pullover and examined it.

'You can see where all the scales are,' he observed, not particularly to Marius, but to the world at large.

'They worry,' said Marius, 'women. Mrs Evans, she'll be thinking about you and worrying. A man ought not to let a woman worry like that.'

The argument, man to man, impressed his young friend, who said, 'I s'pose so.'

'I'm going back to the village and, actually, I'd be glad if you'd show me the way. I'm a little lost.'

'All right,' said the child. 'I'll show you.' He set off briskly. 'Me name is Tommy!' he threw over his shoulder.

'Do you want me to come and have a word with Mr and Mrs Evans, Tommy? To explain?'

'No. It's Miss Sherwood you got to watch out for,' said Tommy.

Marius was surprised enough to let it show in his voice. 'What does she have to do with it?'

'She's billeting officer. Looks after all the 'vacuees. Old Evans will have been to see her and told her I'm gone.'

'Ah, so perhaps we should first call on Miss Sherwood.'

They cut across the heath, and before they quitted it, Marius stooped and broke off two sprigs of heather. 'Here you are. I'll keep one and you keep one, and if we have any luck, we'll write it down, with the date. Scientific experiment.'

'That's not science! Science is mixing up things in bottles.'

'No, scientific is making a proper study and using your eyes. Then writing it down carefully, and not jumping to any conclusions until you have proof. Never mind what you think *ought* to happen. Just observe what does happen. Do you understand?'

Tommy nodded, and Marius wondered if it was worth warning the child to adopt the same attitude towards people. Never assume. People can always behave differently from what you expect. Perhaps Tommy already knew that. He said, 'I'll give you a notebook and pencil, and next time you come up here on the heath, write the date and the weather and how many different plants you can see, or insects or birds, that sort of thing.'

'Aeroplanes?'

'If you like. But aeroplanes are big things. Train

yourself to notice small things; it might save your life one day.'

Especially if you end up with a job like mine—which, God forbid, you ever do—Marius added mentally by way of reservation.

'She's all right, is Miss Sherwood,' said Tommy, out of the blue. 'She nags, but she's all right.'

'Yes, I believe you,' Marius said.

'She ain't 'alf pretty,' said the gallant Thomas with some condescension, since womenfolk were clearly not truly worthy of his consideration.

'Yes,' Marius said seriously. 'She ain't half pretty.'

CHAPTER THREE

GERARD DAVENTRY had found no sign of Tommy's presence in the woods; Jamie had tramped all over Harris's fields in vain; and Mrs Evans had quoted scripture at Libby. By the time they reassembled, late, for lunch, they were all tired and irritated. In the kitchen, Mrs Hills, presiding over dried-out brisket and solid gravy, was on the point of walking out.

Libby pacified Mrs Hills with some difficulty and now stood staring out of the drawing-room window, down the length of gravel drive leading to the denuded gateposts. She pushed back a lock of chestnut hair from her perspiring forehead with a sigh. Wherever the wretched child was, he would have to stay there for the next hour or so. Jamie still maintained hunger would bring the errant Thomas home, and Libby, tired and fed-up, was prepared to give the theory a try. If lunchtime passed with no news, Constable Burrows would have to be informed.

'And very pleased he'll be, on a Sunday afternoon,' she muttered to herself. He would be in his garden behind the police house, would old Cyril Burrows, hoeing his vegetables. Taking him away from his garden was a worse crime than any on an official charge-sheet, as far as Constable Burrows was concerned. She gave a start and blinked in disbelief. Two figures, both dishevelled, had appeared at the bottom of the drive. One was already a familiar figure, solid, dark-haired and self-possessed. The other was very small and scruffy and trailed along beside the taller, evidently offering some objection and being reassured.

Libby's first emotion, after initial surprise, was one of relief. Then annoyance took over, because they had wasted so much time, apparently for nothing. She exclaimed, 'Excuse me!' to the others, and hurried out of the front door to intercept Marius and his young companion before they reached the house.

'Tommy!' She stooped over him. 'We've been so worried about you! Where have you been?'

'I can look after meself!' said the culprit stoutly.

'So he can,' said Marius firmly. 'Don't fuss. Tommy looked after me as well, and guided me home.'

Libby turned her attention to him, peering up at him through a fringe of chestnut hair. He grinned down at her disarmingly, but she was not in the mood to be cajoled. 'Where was he?' she demanded suspiciously and with suitable grandeur. She straightened up and consciously adopted her best official manner, though well aware that it cut no ice with Marius, and probably amused him.

He gave her a somewhat old-fashioned look. 'We met by the shore. I am something of an amateur naturalist, and so is Tommy here. We had an interesting talk.' He raised his eyebrows. 'I understand you are billeting officer. Perhaps you would explain to Mrs Evans?'

Libby abandoned the official manner, as it was unnatural to her and she was finding it hard to conceal her annoyance with Marius. 'If you found him, you should have brought him back immediately. We've wasted a great deal of time. You didn't need to encourage him to wander about as he pleased . . . He does it all the time.'

'Now you're a very fortunate young woman,' said Marius softly.

It stopped Libby in mid-speech, and she flushed deeply. This is an unfortunate and very miserable little boy, he was reminding her, and that's what matters most here. She rubbed her hands through her hair so that it tangled wildly. 'Yes, of course. I'll get the Riley out of the garage and drive Tommy home straight away. You had better stay to lunch. I mean,' she corrected herself, 'I'm grateful that you brought him back, and we would be delighted if you would stay to lunch.'

When she came back from the Evanses', Libby found, rather to her surprise, that Marius was getting along very well apparently with both Jamie and his father. Jennie Daventry—and this surprised Libby even more—seemed to be made a little nervous by their guest. Mrs Daventry fidgeted with her sherry and finally went to supervise Mrs Hills in the kitchen, leaving Libby to make conversation with the three men.

Conversation turned at first on Oxford, but then on Belgium, which the Daventrys had visited before the war. When Marius spoke of his own country, she could not help noticing the change that came over him. The wary, defensive manner thawed and was replaced by a buoyant enthusiasm, which increased his boyish appearance and made him look younger and altogether more likeable. She was struck by the way he spoke of small villages and isolated hamlets. It seemed to her that he was motivated less by any kind of conventional patriotism, as she had always been taught it, than by a real, deep and committed love for patches of ground which he knew—an area, a district, a corner of the landscape: its people, its wild plants, its customs, its cooking.

Reference to the last was perhaps unfortunate in the circumstances. When they eventually assembled round the table, a sullen Mrs Hills slapped down an assortment of tureens with a clatter. In a loud voice, she informed them all that it was not her fault if folk couldn't get themselves to the table on time, and if the meat was tough, they might remember it had stood waiting over an hour, and anyway, Bert Harris was selling all sorts these days in that shop of his, with the excuse of it being wartime.

Libby hardly needed this reminder of the failings of Merriton House's cuisine. It seemed only fair to apologise to the guest. 'She's a competent enough cook in her own way, but a little heavy-handed, and has a tendency to burn things.'

'She's a diabolical cook,' said Jamie, taking the lid off the nearest tureen, and grimacing. 'But we're all used to it.'

'Do you cook?' Marius asked Libby.

'Bacon and eggs and that sort of thing. I'm not much of a cook, and shouldn't criticise Mrs Hills, I suppose. My sponge cakes go flat and my pastry is hit or miss.'

'Patisserie,' said Marius in that admonitory way he sometimes had, and which annoyed her, 'is an art in itself. A great many very good cooks never attempt it.'

'We can't get the eggs to make sponge cakes,' said Jennie Daventry. 'That dried egg the Americans send us makes very good omelettes.'

'Dried eggs . . .' said Marius thoughtfully, considering this curious notion.

'If you take my advice,' said Jamie to him, 'and want to play any decent tennis this afternoon, eat as little of this lot as possible.'

'Now then, James!' said his mother sharply. 'We mustn't waste food, not in wartime!'

After lunch, Libby took Marius outside to inspect the tennis court. She found herself apologising again for its state of disrepair. 'There's a war on,' she said defiantly.

'Why should you apologise?' Marius asked her. 'Have you picked up that habit in England? The English never tell you anything or explain anything without apologising first.'

'Oh, really?' She sounded nettled.

'Yes. And they always apologise if they win, at tennis or anything else. "I'm sorry, I seem to have won"' they say. Why don't they shout, "Look, I've won, good for me!" mm?'

'You know,' Libby said slowly, 'I am never sure if you're laughing at us or not. I even suspect you don't like us very much.'

'You have been very kind to me, all of you,' Marius said reproachfully.

'I don't think you want anyone to be kind to you.' She stared at him, her forehead crinkled against the sun which shone into her eyes, and studied him, squinting. 'I think you want to stay in your own self-contained box. Do you just not like people? Or is it the war, and you don't want . . .' Her voice trailed away uncertainly, as she became aware that she might be about to say something which could not be taken back, however disastrous it might prove. 'Do you not want to be hurt?' she had wanted to ask.

'Are you afraid of caring about other people?' She bit the words back in the nick of time.

Marius was standing by the sagging net, leaning against the netpost, his hands in his pockets. He was watching her and listening carefully, as if weighing her words. But the wary look was back in those fine hazel eyes. Libby felt herself thrown on to the defensive, but while she sought to justify herself, he spoke.

Unexpectedly, he said very quietly, 'You are wrong in thinking I don't like you, all of you. But I suspect that you, Libby Sherwood, don't like me very much.'

She knew she had turned crimson. She could feel the blood rushing into her face. 'I don't know you.' She fiddled uselessly with the net. 'Actually, I'm glad you decided to come today. I think I was rather rude to you, in the lane. Asking to see your identity card and so on. The thing is,' she hesitated, and then plunged on determinedly, 'You make me want to ask questions, and I know I shouldn't, and can't, and you wouldn't answer them.'

'May I ask one of you?'

'What's that?' she asked suspiciously.

'I would like you to explain your accent.'

'Oh?' She was startled. 'I didn't think it was so obvious, at least not after all this time in England. My father is Canadian, my mother English-born. I was born in Paris and brought up between Canada, France and here.'

'You're quite a League of Nations,' he said. 'Where are your parents now?'

'In Canada. Don't ask if they are worried about me. People always do. Of course they are; any parent would be. But they know I'm perfectly capable of looking after myself, and I'm living with Mother's relatives. Besides, my parents are rather unusual people themselves. My mother is an artist.'

'And, I suspect, a great beauty in her youth.'

'Yes, she was—still is. Why do you ask that?'

'Because you are a very pretty girl, and looks tend to run in families.'

'Thank you,' she said cautiously, not sure whether this was a compliment or not.

He pushed himself away from the netpost and wandered off a few steps. 'You remind me of someone,' he said, sounding a little moody and, briefly, less sure of himself.

The chink of vulnerability encouraged her. 'Are you married, or engaged, or—anything?' she asked hesitantly. 'It's so awful for refugees. I chose to stay here during the war. People like you, I suppose, have it forced on them.'

Marius said sharply, 'I am neither married nor engaged, nor was I forced to come to England. I also chose to come here—because that was how I could help my own country!' There was an awkward pause, and he went on more mildly, 'Speaking of engagements, do you have some kind of understanding with your cousin?'

Within himself, he was hoping that she would answer 'Yes', that she and that pleasantly aggressive youngster were engaged. He knew he stood on the edge of a precipice. He could not afford to start anything now which had any real meaning. If he had not met this girl, it wouldn't have been even a possibility. Perhaps it was that chestnut hair, so like Annette's. Perhaps it was something else, that elusive chemistry which makes a nonsense of reason and logic.

This girl sets old Adam stirring in me, he told himself, that's the trouble. It was made worse by the reason he was here in the first place. Within a very short time, he was going into action. His own sort of very specialised action. He was like a cavalry charger which scents battle. He was pursuing his own lonely, dangerous war, and the approach of an engagement with the enemy stirred up the senses, set the nerves tingling and, as always, affected not only the heart-beat and the pulse, the brain and the senses—but the loins. What he needed now was an excuse in order to protect himself—and her.

It was with a bitter-sweet mixture of pleasure and despair that he heard her reply, 'No, I haven't. You're wrong to imagine it.' She tossed back her hair in the way which made him feel he had been struck in the diaphragm. 'It's only Jamie . . . He has a bee in his bonnet, I mean, he's taken the idea into his head that he is in love with me, but he isn't really. He's just being silly.'

Marius asked, 'A man is foolish, is he, if he allows himself to fall in love?'

His voice was unexpectedly cold, and she realised she had touched on some unhealed wound. She also suspected that to him her words sounded not only priggish but foolish.

'No, of course not! Only I've known Jamie all my life; he's a relative; I know how his mind works.' In increasing embarrassment, the words stumbled off her tongue.

'Do you, indeed?' Marius asked softly. 'I wonder.'

Libby flushed angrily. 'I certainly know him better than you do!' she said sharply.

'True.' He shrugged and began to wander about the court, making a tour of the worn patches in the asphalt, examining them. She wondered if this was so that he would know better how to avoid them later, when playing. Was he so thorough in everything? Yes, if anything he means to do depends on it, she thought. After a moment, he glanced up, towards her, and said, 'Life is short, especially nowadays. Do you think of that? Pilots like your cousin get shot down all the time. You don't think you're being a little hard-hearted?'

'I don't think Jamie would want me to get into bed with him if my only object was to console the condemned man, if that's what you mean!' Libby retaliated.

'Why the hell shouldn't he? It's the best consolation I can think of. Don't put noble ideas into his head which he doesn't have. He's a human being.'

She now looked so angry that he thought she was going to stalk off the court back to the house. But an obstinate expression had crossed her face, too. She meant to argue that out with him. He walked back towards her briskly and came to a stop. She looked as if she really would like to bolt, but she stood her ground, glaring at him with snapping blue eyes.

'Men and women view sex differently,' he said reasonably.

Libby gave a little hiss. He was speaking quite objectively, as if the subject were perfectly innocuous and quite a normal topic of conversation between people who had barely met. She did not know whether to feel insulted, or whether what she felt was alarm, because she was about to be told something she did not want to hear.

'You mean,' she said in a brittle tone, 'that women get foolish and emotional.'

'Men get emotional, too. Perhaps not so often, but when they do, they are very vulnerable.' He sounded so serious that she glanced at him nervously. 'Be careful what you say to your cousin. Don't be misled by an old friendship, or kinship, into thinking that what you say can't hurt him.'

'I don't mean to hurt Jamie, and I shan't. Please let me handle my own affairs,' she said firmly.

He seemed not to have heard her, but continued talking, in that calm, objective way, setting it out for her so that she should not misunderstand. 'Action—I mean, combat or the prospect of it—often affects a man sexually. He is . . .' He made a wide all-embracing gesture. 'You understand?'

Libby flushed.

'If a man lives all the time in the shadow of battle, then—how shall I say—the natural balance of the body is upset. His senses are heightened. They become super-active. *All* his senses: sight, hearing, nervous and muscular reaction, sexual potency. A woman should realise that. She should not expect a man to behave in wartime as he would in peacetime. Not even old friends and cousins.'

'What about you?' Libby asked before she could stop herself.

He chuckled unexpectedly. 'Nor me,' he agreed, and grinned at her ruefully.

To her immense relief, the sound of voices cut through the air. The other players were coming out. One voice rang louder than the others, clear to the point of being penetrating, and female. Evangeline Watts had chosen today, of all days, to grace them with her company.

Evangeline was known in some quarters as 'the Hunt Trophy'. She was a tall, bosomy girl with rather protruding teeth, a great deal of untidy ginger hair and a hearty laugh. She appeared now, waving at Libby enthusiastically, and bouncing down the path towards them.

'Hullo, hullo!' she shrieked, her large bosom marking time with the syllables. She was bursting out of a skimpy tennis dress and when she sat down, as now, to tie up a loose lace of a plimsoll, she stuck her foot up in front of her on a garden chair with cheerful unconcern, displaying serviceable beige interlock knickers.

With a sinking heart, Libby introduced Marius to her. Evangeline stared at him with round eyes and exclaimed, 'Golly!'

The vicar arrived, smiling vaguely, and clad in his usual yellowing voluminous knee-length shorts, beneath which his legs protruded like the wooden legs of a puppet. Dr Greaves, on the other hand, who followed him, was short, stocky and grey-haired. He wore cricket whites and was clearly still the keen amateur sportsman of his youth. Marius went indoors to change into borrowed whites, and Jamie drew Libby aside.

'I say,' he whispered, 'ought we to warn him about our Eva? Before she drags him kicking and screaming into the rhododendron bushes?'

'If he goes into the bushes with Evangeline,' Libby said bluntly, 'it will be because he wants to.'

'I saw you chatting earnestly to him just now.' Jamie scowled ferociously. 'He wasn't putting immoral proposals, was he?'

'No!' she snapped a little too vehemently. 'He was lecturing me on war and peace, like some sort of modern Tolstoy. I think . . . I think there is a woman somewhere in his past. He's very edgy and fends off personal questions, but he's hiding something. Jamie, do go and help them wind the net up before the vicar breaks an arm.'

'I'm going to play with Marius!' said Evangeline loudly, when the former reappeared.

'Don't you dare, Jamie!' Libby threatened. 'Don't you dare say a word!'

As she had suspected he might be, Marius proved an excellent tennis player, and in partnership with Evangeline, soundly thrashed Jamie and Libby into humiliating defeat. Evangeline squealed with delight and flung both arms round her partner's neck in an unabashed way.

'That was a very good game,' he said politely, detaching himself from Miss Watts's ardent embrace, and shaking hands with Jamie and Libby in a formal way.

'Nothing like animal sweat,' muttered Jamie to Libby, mopping his brow. 'Or animal spirits.' He grimaced towards Evangeline. 'Watch our Eva go to town on the poor fellow now!'

'I'd rather not!' Libby said crisply. 'I'll go and make the tea.'

Mrs Hills went home for the rest of the day after lunch on Sundays. Alone in the large, tiled kitchen, Libby pottered about, making tea and cutting paste sandwiches. Aunt Jennie was haranguing the vicar on social welfare, and it was unlikely that Evangeline would come in to help. Eva had other prospects in view. She is so obviously man-mad, thought Libby crossly. Not even the vicar's presence would hinder her, and Marius can't be blamed if he takes up the offer being made so blatantly. She felt out-of-sorts and resentful. It was being trounced at tennis in such a humiliating way, she told herself. But she knew that was not the reason. It was Evangeline's behaviour. On the one hand, it let the side down. Good heavens, surely a woman didn't have to throw herself at a man like that? Couldn't Eva Watts manage any dignity? On the other hand, there was a nagging feeling that Evangeline was poaching.

'Oh, ridiculous!' muttered Libby, spreading paste as thinly as was humanly possible. 'There is a war on . . . Am I being quite childish? The next thing, I shall be marching up to Eva and declaring, "I found him first!"'

She paused, knife in hand. However, Marius was her guest. She had invited him, and she ought to protect him from Eva's advances. On the other hand, if the legend surrounding Eva's activities was even half true, men did not usually mind. Even Jamie, Libby suspected, had fallen into her snare at some time in the past. There had been that Christmas party when a game of 'murder' had led to both Jamie and Evangeline hiding in the broom-cupboard, and when Libby opened the door, they fell out, entangled and breathless, mumbling unconvincing explanations.

A step behind her made her look up, and she saw to her astonishment that Marius had come into the kitchen and stood, arms folded, by the door, watching her quizzically.

She brandished the knife, and said crossly, 'I don't need any help. Go and talk to—to the others!'

'It's hot out there, and I am reasonably competent in the kitchen. Give me that,' he walked over the took the knife firmly out of her hand, 'before you cut yourself or stab me.'

Libby propped herself on the corner of the table

and glared at the kettle which, true to the proverb, reacted to being watched by refusing to boil.

Marius, setting the sandwiches on a plate with mathematical precision, said quietly, 'I don't care for your friend Miss Watts. She is like some sort of large puppy, affectionate and untrained.'

'Most men like her,' Libby muttered. 'I thought you were getting on quite well together.' She did not mean to sound so resentful, or to allow her heart to give a little leap at being told Evangeline didn't matter, after all.

The kettle rattled its lid and emitted angry puffs of steam. Libby lifted it off the hob carefully with a knitted holder, glad to have something practical to do.

He watched her make the tea in silence, before asking, 'Are you angry about something?'

'No!' she said with unnecessary emphasis. It was warm in the kitchen, steamy from the kettle, and her body still perspired from the tennis match. She blinked and put her hand to her face to rub away the pearls of sweat which escaped from her hairline and threatened to trickle down her nose.

Without warning, she found her wrists gently but securely imprisoned in Marius's fingers. He pulled her hand away from her face, and when she looked up, she saw that he was frowning. 'But you're upset about something?'

She shook her head uneasily. 'No, only very warm.'

So close to him, she was uncomfortably aware that he, too, was flushed from the heat and his exertions. His dark hair was damp and ruffled, and his borrowed tennis shirt clung to his skin in flesh-coloured patches of sweat.

'Horses sweat, gentlemen perspire, ladies glow . . .' Libby said aloud, quite without meaning to, or knowing she was going to say it.

'What?' He looked puzzled, and the wary look was back, as if this was some riddle he ought to have understood but had not.

'Oh . . .' She was embarrassed, the flush deepening to a rosy pink, and she wriggled in her sticky tennis dress. He still held her wrist, and she did not know whether this was an oversight on his part or deliberate, and short of dragging her wrist forcibly from his grip, she did not know how to make him let go. To ask, 'Kindly release me!' would sound unbearably prim. 'It's just something my mother always says she was taught as a girl. Ladies never sweat, or didn't at the turn of the century. It was unfeminine.'

'I don't think it unfeminine. There's something very attractive, even erotic, about a pretty girl with scarlet, glistening cheeks, and the scent of naked skin . . .' He bent his head and stepped closer.

Libby gulped and tried to free her wrist at last. In doing so, she pressed against his chest, and his damp tennis shirt became transparent. Through it, she could see the musculature covering ribcage and diaphragm, and how it flexed and rippled with each intake of breath. He was breathing quite heavily, and the unbuttoned neck of the shirt revealed a tangle of damp, dark hair on his chest.

Embarrassed at seeming to stare at his body and yet too nervous to look up into his face, she mumbled, 'You are very fit, and a first-class tennis player.'

'Mm. I do other things well, too . . .' his voice murmured by her ear, the breath tickling her earlobe and neck. Libby said nothing but fixed her eyes on the middle button of his shirt. 'Look up!' he ordered, not sharply, but firmly.

'W-What?' Startled, she did so, and he kissed her. At the touch of his mouth against hers, she almost jumped out of her skin. It was not surprise, because she had known instinctively that he meant to do it, sooner or later. Yet she was still shocked that he had taken the liberty so boldly and casually, and more shocked by her own reaction, every nerve shuddering, right through to her toes and fingertips.

'You ought not to have done that!' she said shakily.

'Why not? You didn't like it?' He was laughing at her now, not with his mouth but with his hazel eyes, the merriment gleaming in the irises and dancing in and out in gold flecks.

'I didn't expect it!'

'Yes, you did.' The retort was calm, so calm and confident that she lost her temper, and it helped to restore the control she had momentarily lost over her own limbs.

'And I didn't like it!' she stormed at him.

'An untruth, Miss Sherwood,' he said chidingly. 'Tell me you don't like this.'

This time he had given her warning and she attempted to dodge aside, but he moved with unlooked-for speed, deftly catching her round the waist and spinning her so that she squeaked in alarm and found herself pinned against the pantry door.

'Now, then,' said Marius, grinning at her. 'Gentlemen perspire, ladies glow, but when they get together . . .'

'What?' croaked Libby.

He shrugged. 'Steam like rutting stags, I shouldn't be surprised.'

Unwisely, Libby opened her mouth to retort and found she couldn't close it again, because he trapped it with his, and when she squirmed and squealed incoherently, trying to free herself, he grasped a lock of her chestnut hair so that she could not move without it tugging, and was forced to stay still and submit. Several young men, quite aside from Jamie, had kissed her in the past, but never like this, demandingly, harshly, his firmly muscled body thrust against hers, his tongue forcing its way between her gritted teeth. The palms of his hands were perspiring, however, and it allowed her to slip her wrists free and fetch him a resounding box on the ear.

He released her. 'Ouch!' he said crossly.

Blessing her stars, because he had retreated a little and she could breathe again, Libby gasped, half-choking, 'Don't you dare to touch me again!'

He stared at her furious, shiny face surrounded by a mop of tangled chestnut curls. Then he threw out his arms in a gesture of surrender. 'Look, you're free!'

'Thank you,' she said with dignity, straightening her crushed tennis dress and trying to smooth down her hair. A burst of chattering voices wafted in through the open window.

'They want their tea!' she exclaimed, a note of agony in her voice. 'You made me forget all about them!'

'In England,' observed her companion resignedly, 'everything stops for tea; even, I suppose, lovemaking.'

'No one is making love to me, certainly not *you*!' she informed him briskly. She piled crockery and sandwiches onto the trolley in higgledy-piggledy haste. 'Why don't you make a pass at Eva Watts? You can explain your theories about war and male potency. She'll be very interested.'

'Why don't you come for a walk with me tomorrow evening?'

Libby stopped, teapot in hand, and gaped at him. 'Are you completely insensitive? What on earth do you think I am?'

'A very pretty girl, or I wouldn't ask.'

'I most certainly will not.'

'Why not?'

'What do you mean, why? Because . . .' Libby was suddenly unable to think why. 'Because,' she went on triumphantly, 'Jamie is here on leave and will expect me to walk the dogs on the beach with him.'

'I see. Well, what about lunchtime? You do take time for lunch?'

'I eat my sandwiches in my ramshackle little office in the village. Get out of my way, please, or I shall run the trolley over your foot, and I promise it will hurt.'

'Eat your sandwiches down on the shore with me?' He jumped nimbly out of the way as Libby shoved the trolley determinedly towards him.

'I can't. I haven't time.'

'You've a damn sight more time than I have!' he said so fiercely that she looked up in alarm, struck by the vehemence of the tone, and something almost akin to a note of pain.

The mirth had gone from the hazel eyes. Libby felt a shiver run down her spine, as if a cold breeze had blown across her. 'All right,' she muttered unwillingly. 'Twelve o'clock.'

The scrape of a foot by the door made them both look up guiltily.

'I suppose,' Jamie said sarcastically, 'we are going to get some ruddy tea today? We aren't all going to be left to die of thirst out here?'

He stood, blocking the doorway, his head slightly lowered like a steer at bay, glowering at them, and looking from one to the other suspiciously. She had no idea how long he had been there, or how much he had heard or observed.

'My fault,' said Marius easily. He took the tea-trolley away from Libby and propelled it towards the door with such force that Jamie was obliged to jump out of the way. Libby scuttled past in the confusion, avoiding her cousin's eye.

Outside, late afternoon torpor had fallen over the scene. The vicar had fallen asleep in a deckchair, his bony knees stuck out at right-angles. His gentle, discreet snores rose into the still air like the faint buzzing of bees. Gerard chatted to the doctor, and Jennie Daventry read the paper. Evangeline lay on the grass sun-bathing, with the skirt of her tennis dress pushed up round her sturdy thighs, her long legs turning salmon-red.

'She has the wrong complexion to try sun-bathing,' thought Libby. 'Get up, Eva!' she ordered. 'Tea!'

Evangeline rolled over like a large, dozing seal, and sat up. 'What have you two been doing in the kitchen?' she asked tactlessly. 'You've been ages.'

'It takes ages to cut sandwiches. You might have come and given a hand, Eva.'

'Not me,' said Evangeline, opening her round eyes very wide. 'I don't play gooseberry.'

CHAPTER FOUR

MONDAY MORNING proved chaotic, as it usually did. Jennie Daventry had to catch the early train. Jamie volunteered to drive his mother into town, eighteen miles by the road, to the station. They set off, Aunt Jennie's hat as crooked as ever and her arms full of folders and files, as she shouted last-minute instructions to them through the car window.

'Make sure Miss Biddle replaces those black-out curtains at the Red Cross hut, Libby. The air-raid warden has complained twice. Gerry, I think Spot ought to go to the vet. He keeps shaking his ears, and it's probably canker.'

'Come on, Ma,' urged Jamie impatiently. 'Time, tide and trains wait for no one.'

They roared away in a shower of gravel, and Gerard Daventry looked markedly relieved. He took Libby's arm to walk back into the house. His face had a flushed, purplish look to it and he seemed to find breathing a problem. It was probably the strain of the weekend, she thought, and a house full of people. It was all getting too much for him.

'I'll take Spot to the vet tomorrow,' she offered. 'I can't take him today. I've a heap of work down at the office, and there's Tommy . . . I've really no time.'

She felt horribly guilty as she spoke, as if she were being disloyal, but she did not want to tell him about the arrangement to meet Marius during her lunch-time. She was not exactly ashamed, but it would not help to have everyone know it. When she did see Marius—always providing she did—she would make it clear that he was not to presume on a casual lunchtime arrangement to go for a walk and eat sandwiches. This was definitely the first and last time she would agree.

'I'll take the dratted dog,' Gerard said mildly. 'Gives me something to do. You haven't got to rush off straight away, have you, although I appreciate how busy you are? You don't need to tell me.'

'No . . .' Libby looked at him apprehensively. The irrational fear filled her mind that he knew about the proposed meeting with Marius, and was going to object.

'Then come and sit down for five minutes,' he said. 'I haven't had a chance to speak a word to you all weekend, what with that wretched child going missing and your Belgian friend coming to lunch. To say nothing of Jennie full of her latest good works.'

From the kitchen came a distant clamour as Mrs Hills hurled breakfast plates into the enamel washing-up basin and yelled at the elderly gardener, who was refusing to pull up any carrots, and pretending to be deaf.

'Do you mind, Uncle Gerry?' she asked curiously, as they sat down in the drawing-room.

It had an unkempt, Monday-morning look. Sunday newspapers still stuck out of the side of the sofa and Jamie's ashtrays were unemptied. There were dog hairs all over the furniture. Mrs Hills's niece Veronica—a simple girl with a vacant stare and a mind filled with nothing but the latest film she had seen at the cinema—was supposed to come and help clean up on a Monday. But she was late. She was always late. Her name was not really Veronica, of course. It was Elsie. But she greatly admired Veronica Lake, the film star, and lately had taken to wearing her lank fair hair draped over one eye in imitation of her idol. This led to her dropping even more ornaments than she usually did.

'I mean,' Libby explained, 'don't you mind Aunt Jennie rushing off to do good works all the time? I know there's a war on, and everything she does is important and needed, but wouldn't you rather she were here?'

'If she were,' he said calmly, 'she would be fretting at having nothing to do.'

She could try looking after this house, and you, thought Libby mutinously.

Gerard took off his spectacles and began to polish them carefully. 'When you marry, Libby dear, you accept your partner as he or she is. You can't change anyone. That's a fallacy. Young people often think differently, of course; that's why they are often a cause of concern to their elders, who see them getting interested in unsuitable friends. There may be nothing wrong with a fellow or a girl, as such, but as a marriage partner, well, that's rather different. Evangeline Watts, for example, is a nice enough girl at heart, but a man would be a fool to marry her. What she is now, she'll always be: a bit of a tart.'

He put on his glasses with Olympian calm, apparently unaware of the amazement this unexpectedly frank speech on his part had caused his niece.

'You are a very attractive girl, Libby. Got a good deal of your mother in you . . .' He fell silent for a moment, seemingly lost in some private train of thought. Then he resumed with, 'Velden took a bit of a fancy to you, and I'm not surprised.'

Libby, scarlet, made a play of folding up one of

the discarded newspapers. Uncle Gerry was sharp. She supposed it was because he was a lawyer. She wondered how much he really knew or had guessed.

'You know, I expect,' he said, 'that it's been rather a cherished hope of mine that one day you and James would make a match of it. I know James is more than keen. You get along well together. I think your father would like it. James is a pilot, and your father was a flying man in the Great War, as you know.'

'I'm very fond of Jamie,' Libby told him awkwardly, 'but not . . . I don't love him. That is, I do love him, but I'm not *in* love with him, if you understand. I don't think he really is in love with me. It's an idea he has in his head, and he's obstinate. I believe he will get over it.'

'Oh, yes, if you turn him down, he'll get over it,' Gerard agreed. 'One does.' There was another curious silence, in which his thoughts seemed far away. 'I feel a responsibility towards you,' he went on. 'Not only because you are Alix's daughter, and I was always fond of your mother, but also because you are a long way from home. Although you have travelled a great deal and you are a very capable young woman, you are still young—and the world really is not such a very pleasant place, Libby, not even in peacetime. Of course I know love cannot be forced, but at least give James serious thought.'

'I have,' she said. 'It's no good. I'm sorry, Uncle Gerry, it really wouldn't work out.'

He sighed. 'Very well. We'll let it rest at that. I won't bother you about it again.'

He was obviously bitterly disappointed. Libby suspected that his life had been one of continual disappointment. Had he once been in love with her mother? Had he been turned down and married Aunt Jennie on the rebound? She would never know. She got up and kissed him. 'Everything will turn out all right.' It seemed a lame thing to say, meaningless, but she wanted to offer some comfort, and she could not think of anything else.

'Yes, yes,' he murmured. 'Off you go, and don't worry about the dog. I'll take him along to the vet, or Jamie can do so when he gets back.'

Libby collected her belongings, loaded them into the bicycle basket and wobbled off down the lane. She could not pretend she felt like concentrating on work, but work had a way of thrusting itself into the forefront of things. It did so this morning, in the substantial personage of Miss Biddle, not five minutes after she had settled down at her desk.

'Libby!' said Miss Biddle loudly. She appeared in the little cramped room, arms akimbo. She was a stout, short woman with a round, pallid face and dark little eyes like gimlets. Her upper lip sported a distinct moustache.

Libby sighed. 'Good morning, Miss Biddle. I know I've mentioned this before, but I really would be most grateful if you would knock. It may only be the Red Cross hut, but this is my office, and I am very busy.'

As she spoke, she let her eyes roam around the tiny area. It hardly looked very official. There was a battered kettle and a tin mug in one corner, and a stack of old newspapers waiting to be collected for pulping.

'Your office it may be,' said Miss Biddle, as if this were doubtful, 'but I am still caretaker of the hut. I've been with the Red Cross twenty-five years.'

'Yes,' said Libby firmly, undaunted. 'That reminds me. Mrs Daventry particularly asked that you get the black-out curtains mended or replaced. The air-raid warden has complained.'

'Air-raid warden?' snorted Miss Biddle. 'You mean, I suppose, George Evans with a tin hat on, cycling round of an evening and peering into other folk's front windows. He's no better than a peeping Tom!'

'Oh, rubbish!' said Libby crossly. 'And if you have proper black-out curtains, no one can see into your front parlour.'

'Well,' said her visitor vengefully, 'I've got my own bone to pick with George Evans, and with you, miss. That child has been up to his devilment again.'

'You'd better sit down,' Libby said wearily, 'and tell me all about it.'

'Gone!' said Miss Biddle, plumping herself down on a wooden chair. 'Every last one of them. Even the ones which weren't nearly ripe. Vandal!'

'Every one what, Miss Biddle?'

'Strawberries, what else? Cleared the entire bed.'

'When?' demanded Libby.

'How should I know? Got up early this morning and did it, I dare say. The child's a thief. Born and bred in him. Slum child, come from goodness knows what kind of home, and we're supposed to put up with his nonsense here. I don't mind telling you, this was always a respectable community before those evacuee children were foisted on us.'

'Look,' Libby said rather crossly. She did not like Miss Biddle at the best of times, and knew the feeling was mutual. To her, Libby was an outsider. 'If you didn't see Tommy take the strawberries, how do you know he did?'

'Who else?' Miss Biddle leaned forward, her pudgy hands grasping her plump knees. She wore thick peach-coloured lisle stockings, held up by elastic garters above the knee. They were clearly visible, as her plump body inclined towards Libby, and her skirt strained over her ample hips.

'That's not proof, Miss Biddle.'

Miss Biddle rose to her feet, radiating venom. 'I didn't expect any sense or sympathy from you. I knew you'd take that child's part. We'll see what Cyril Burrows has to say.'

'If you mean to go to Constable Burrows, Miss Biddle, I suggest you take some evidence along with you. There's such a thing as false accusation, you know.'

'That brat posted rude pictures through my front door,' Miss Biddle snarled at her. 'Naked women!'

'Corset advertisements, Miss Biddle.'

'A child that age ought not to know such a thing as corsets exist. When my late father was a child, he didn't even know ladies had legs!'

Libby blinked at this late-Victorian titbit. 'I'll talk to George—and to the child, Miss Biddle. I'd be grateful if you'd leave it with me.'

There was no sense in antagonising the woman further. She was more than capable of causing a great deal of trouble.

'I'll be back!' warned Miss Biddle, waddling towards the doorway, and firing the words over her shoulder like Parthian arrows.

'You won't forget about the black-out curtains, will you?' Libby reminded her politely.

When she was alone again, she buried her face in her hands and drew a deep breath. It was going to be one of those days. There had to be some way of stopping Marius from coming at twelve. Libby's hand strayed towards the telephone, with a vague idea of calling up the camp and asking to speak to him. But that probably was not a very good idea. Instead, she rang up the Evanses' cottage. George was out, but Mrs Evans answered, and Libby told her she would call by that evening, 'just to see how Tommy is.'

Then she got up and made herself some tea, spooning it out carefully, because she was running short and there was no way she could get any more coupons this month. She took the tea over to the window-sill to sit in the sun and watch the birds flutter about the waste ground behind the hut. She wondered what Marius was doing. She did not even know how long he meant to stay in their community. He wouldn't tell her, of course. She felt that what she hated most was the impossibility of asking questions. Here was a man about whom she knew nothing, and would dearly like to know a great deal. She doubted very much that she even knew his correct name. He was unmarried, he did something or other which was hush-hush, and even Jamie wouldn't tell her what it was. And he was coming at twelve to spend the lunch-hour with her. What were they supposed to talk about in the circumstances? He might not want to talk . . . she thought uneasily.

Twelve o'clock was upon her before she realised. She pushed all the papers away in a drawer, and collected up her box of cheese sandwiches and an apple. As she locked the outer door, she vainly hoped he might be either late or forgetful. But he was neither, and when she turned round, he was walking towards her.

'Hullo,' he said amiably.

'You do realise, don't you,' she said grimly, 'that the whole village will know about this? You have no idea what gossip it's going to cause.'

'There's no one about. The place is deserted. Not even a cat. Everyone has gone to eat.'

'You don't know Miss Biddle,' she told him.

Sure enough, as they passed Miss Biddle's cottage, a lace curtain twitched. 'She'll tell everyone,' Libby muttered. She became aware that Marius held a paper bag. 'What's that?'

'My contribution to lunch. I shall eat your sandwiches.'

'Will you? Wait until you're asked.'

'I never do that.' He cast her a mocking, sidelong glance.

'That I can believe!' she mumbled.

They walked out of the village and climbed over a five-barred gate into one of Bert Harris's fields. Marius held the gate steady as Libby scrambled over, trying to hold down her skirt and aware that he was studying her legs. There was a footpath running across the field, a short cut to the heath and thence to the shore. A few cows grazed in the distance. Marius handed her his paper bag, and then vaulted athletically over the top of the gate to join her.

'Heavens!' Libby exclaimed, startled. She peered into the bag. 'This is a bottle of wine. Where on earth did you get it?'

'Dark secret. You don't think I can sit and eat stodgy English sandwiches with nothing to help them down?'

She stared at him in dismay. 'But I can't go back to my office smelling of drink!'

He shrugged. 'Then I'll drink it all.'

'You won't, you know!' She hugged the bottle to her chest as if to prevent his wresting it from her and draining it at a gulp.

They strolled across the turf, avoiding the inevitable cowpats and swatting at the buzzing flies. When they were nearly at the far side and the gate out on to the heath, Marius suddenly asked very quietly, 'Libby, can you run—fast?'

'Fairly,' she told him suspiciously. 'Am I supposed to be running away from you, or what?'

'No, a cow.'

'Cows don't chase you. Bulls do that.'

'This one is going to—she's newly calved and she's moving to protect her baby—now!'

Libby had never realised what a very large animal a cow is, especially an angry one. The beast bore down on them like a tank. Marius seized her hand and they made a dash for the heath and safety, scrambling over the gate and falling together on the turf on the further side. Libby found herself sprawled inelegantly across Marius's legs. She recovered herself hastily and scooped up a shoe which had come off. As she pulled it on, the cow blew gustily at them through her nostrils over the gate before trotting off, triumphant.

'You didn't drop that wine, did you?'asked Marius anxiously.

'No . . .' she panted. 'And how about asking me if I'm all right?'

'You look all right.' She looked marvellous. Her hair had fallen all over her face and her skirt was rucked up above her shapely knees. As she bent double to tug on the lost shoe, the neck of her blouse gaped invitingly and revealed a tantalising glimpse of soft white bosom. 'Give me your hand,' he said. He hauled her to her feet and they struck out across the heath to the shore.

There was quite a lot of flotsam cast up on the shingle. Marius hunted among it with a boyish enthusiasm, while Libby settled herself in the sun on the dry grass growing above the shingle on the sandy turf and watched him. After a few moments he came back and presented her with a curious shell, a shilling, a cuttlefish skeleton and a piece of wood with a nail in it.

'Now I know why you got along so well with Tommy,' she told him. 'What am I supposed to make of a piece of wood, for heaven's sake?'

'I don't know. It's curious, and you can see from the nail that it's very old. A piece of old sailing-ship? There must be a wreck out there.'

They ate the sandwiches and drank the wine. Libby knew she was going to be late back to the office, but she didn't care. The sun was warm and she felt drowsy. She supposed it was the wine.

She lay back on the turf and put one arm over her eyes to shade them. 'Can I ask one thing? Not a state secret.'

Marius, lying propped on his elbow, surveyed her. 'Ask away.'

'I do realise your name probably isn't Velden. But is it really Marius? Because, you know, it's a very odd feeling, to talk to a person and think you are always calling him by the wrong name.'

He said, 'It really is Marius.'

She mumbled, 'Thanks . . .' and he smiled to himself and folded his jacket into a pillow for her head. 'I shall fall asleep,' she protested.

'Go ahead.' He threw himself back on the turf

beside her, staring up at the blue sky. 'I'm glad you've come here with me,' he said. 'I thought you might back out.'

'I nearly did,' she confessed. 'I've had an awful morning. Miss Biddle has been accusing Tommy of all sorts of things again.' She turned her head towards him, and saw that he was watching her now. Something in his hazel eyes set her heart lurching painfully in her chest. She flushed, and mumbled, 'Uncle Gerry said you'd taken a fancy to me.'

'He's right.'

'I wish you hadn't,' she told him miserably.

Very seriously, Marius said, 'I wish I hadn't.'

They were both silent for a long time. Then she asked uncertainly, 'Is it just a case of what you were telling me, about comforting the condemned man?'

'No,' Marius said. 'If it were, I'd be sitting here now with Miss Watts.'

There was another long pause and they listened to a skylark high above the fields behind them, filling an empty sky with its song.

'I do want to make love to you, though,' Marius said quietly.

'Yes, I know.'

'You—have strong objections to that?'

'I suppose I should. But I don't. I don't know why. I mean, we've hardly met. And I'm not that sort of girl. I mean, I'm not like Evangeline. I haven't ever—you know . . .' Her voice trailed away.

Marius said, 'Ah . . .,' sounding depressed.

'Do you mind, about that?' she asked, squinting at him in the sunlight, trying to decipher the expression on his face.

'No, I don't mind.' He rolled over and pushed

himself up on his elbow again so that he stooped over her. Her face was very pink with the sunshine and the wine. Her chestnut hair glowed and her slightly parted lips were very kissable. He ran an exploring finger across them, and said softly, 'Of course, I should like to be the first. What worries me is—something else.'

'Because you'll go away again?'

He looked relieved that she had spoken the words. 'Because I must. Probably quite soon. And the likelihood of my coming back is—slight. I don't want to just "love you and leave you". It hardly seems fair.'

Libby, watching his face closely as he spoke, said, 'You're a nice person, very honourable. Jamie thought . . .' She broke off the words, but too late.

'Jamie thought what?'

'That you were, well, not very nice or very honourable. That is to say,' she stumbled on quickly. 'He didn't mean you weren't a very brave man, but he said you had the mark of Cain on you.'

'He thinks I'm what he would call a thug?'

'The word he used was "killer",' she said bleakly.

Marius pushed himself away, and turned on to his back. She was afraid he was offended and angry, and was too nervous herself to speak. But after a while he said, almost gently, 'I don't want to talk about it. I don't want to talk about anything I've done, or anything I might do, or my reason for doing it. I want to keep this moment, these few days, just as a child might keep that shell or the piece of wood. A souvenir. Something you take with you, to remember the good days by, when the dark days come. I want . . .' He closed his eyes briefly, and then opened them and went on in a dogged tone, 'I want something beautiful, because all the rest is ugly. It's whispering in the wind, but I want something to remind me that there is something better than this hell . . .'

Libby rolled over and put her arm round him, and pressed her face against his. 'Yes, I know. I understand.'

His hand traced the soft outline of her breast. 'That's why I want to make love to you. You are beautiful. You are good. You make me want you, very much.'

'Yes . . .' She hesitated. 'But not here. Not just now. I'm sorry. I—I know it's what you want, but I can't, not out in the open like this. Someone could come along, or . . . Anyway, I have to go back to the office afterwards, and I don't think I could, not if we . . . You may think this stupid, but I'd rather we were in a bed.'

'All right,' he said. 'I'll work something out.' He sat up and picked up his jacket. Glancing out to sea, he said, 'I ought to take a dip in the nice, cold ocean!' He grimaced at her wryly. 'Always a problem, a situation like this.'

'Sorry,' she mumbled awkwardly.

He got to his feet and gave her a hand up. 'We'll put a message in the empty bottle and float it out to sea.' He produced a pocket diary and tore out a page. On it he scribbled, 'None but the brave deserve the fair.'

'Why did you write that?'

'Because it's true.' He stoppered the bottle and threw it far out into the dancing waves.

They stood and watched it bobbing about for a moment, and then turned and began to make their way back. At the beginning of the village, they parted.

'I'll phone you,' he said, 'and let you know what I can fix up.'

She nodded.

He looked a little uncertain, as if he would have preferred her to have said something, anything. 'You do know,' he reminded her, 'that whatever we begin now, it's like a candle-flame. It burns brightly, but into its own body. It becomes its own executioner, and is extinguished—' he snapped his fingers—'like that. Beautiful, but brief. You can change your mind, if you want.'

'I understand,' Libby said, drawing a deep breath. 'I accept that.'

After all, wasn't that what Uncle Gerry had said? You accept a partner as he is, you can't change him; you can't change anything.

Jamie had put his mother on the London train and was driving back carefully to Merriton, one eye on the fuel-gauge. With both Libby and his mother engaged in war work, they generally managed to get their hands on just enough petrol, but when he came home, the extra demands on the Riley strained the allowance to its utmost.

The road, empty of other traffic, wound its way between sun-drenched fields. As the Riley idled along, Jamie stuck his elbow through the open window, enjoying the breeze blowing in his hair, and the peace of his surroundings. He wished he could feel an equal peace within himself, but he couldn't. He supposed he was tired, but then, if he was tired, he ought to sleep better than he did. It was becoming increasingly difficult to sleep at all. He lay awake, listening, his body tense, waiting for the warning sirens, the sound of distant engines approaching. In his mind, he flew with the pilots who had been scrambled and fought out their dog-fights. He wished he could face the foe as they did, openly. Not in the hole-in-the-corner way he did. Yet though he no longer experienced any thrill from his lonely missions, he still felt like a watch-spring that had been wound up so tightly that it couldn't unwind itself. The watch was still ticking, but the mechanism was faulty. He had wanted to talk to Libby last night, after the air-raid, when they sat together comfortably on the stairs. But he could not even tell her; that was the worst part of it.

About two miles from home, he was distracted by the sight of a horse and rider ahead. The rider had a mop of ginger hair and a splendid backside. Jamie's grimly-set features relaxed into a grin. He overtook her slowly and stopped the car on the grass verge. Climbing out, he leaned against it, waiting for her to come up to him.

'Hullo, Eva,' he said. 'What's happening to the Women's Land Army these days?'

She slid out of the saddle and slapped the mare on the rump. Jamie resisted the impulse to do the same to her. 'Bert Harris doesn't like women about the place,' she informed him cheerfully.

'I thought he might like *you*,' he said, teasing her.

'Bert's a suspicious old sod,' she said amiably. 'I don't think he likes anyone there. He thinks someone might check on him. Have you any idea what he sells on the black market by way of eggs, butter and cream?'

'No, but I can imagine it. Bert is a businessman. Colonel OK?'

'Daddy?' said Evangeline vaguely. 'Oh, fine, running round organising the Home Guard and having the time of his life. They lie in trenches and practise firing at aircraft with empty rifles.' She burst into a hoot of laughter. She never wore a brassière, and her pneumatic bosom bounced beneath her sweater.

Jamie closed his eyes briefly. 'Lor', Eva, I know you have a magnificent body, but do you have to flaunt it under my nose?'

'If you think it's that good,' she told him with a toothy grin, 'why don't you take advantage of it?'

'You ain't got no morals, my girl. You didn't have to set your cap at our Belgian friend so obviously.'

'I thought he was rather gorgeous.' Evangeline scratched the side of one splendid breast in an absent-minded way. 'Anyway, don't preach at me. There's a war on, and when it's over, what's going to be left? Not much, I can tell you, and there won't be much fun about. Daddy says the socialists will get into government. Your mother might like that—or she says she would. Much she really knows about the jolly old working class! Daddy says he knows all about barrack-room bolsheviks.'

'Your father, with due respect, is a pompous old bore, and soaked in black-market whisky to boot.'

'Doesn't mean he isn't right. Anyway, war or no war, I'm going to have a damn good time *now*.'

'Perhaps you're right,' he conceded.

'You bet I am! And if you're waiting for Libby to fall into your arms, you've got a jolly long wait. Now I, on the other hand, am yours for the taking.'

'Right here in the middle of the road, I suppose?' he retorted sharply, because he didn't like her mentioning Libby.

'Don't be daft,' she said, pointing across the nearby field. 'Old Bert's barn is just over there.'

'You never give up, Eva,' Jamie said in some admiration.

'Oh, come on!' she urged. Her eyes gleamed with excitement and it communicated itself to him, so that his trousers suddenly felt too tight.

He hunched his shoulders. 'Oh, hell, why not?'

He opened the gate for her and they tramped across the meadow to the barn, leading the mare. Evangeline tied up the animal in the shade. Being brought up in the tradition that horses matter more than people, she carefully loosened the girth and folded the stirrup-irons tidily over the saddle. Her father was a past Master of Foxhounds.

Inside the barn was cool and dusty and smelled of tractor fumes and rats. A pile of hay was stacked invitingly in one corner. Evangeline leapt into it with a whoop of delight, seizing Jamie by the arm as she did so, so that he lost his balance and plunged forward to land on top of her. They rolled over in the hay, throwing handfuls of it at each other like children.

After that, things took their natural course, and when Jamie finally sat up, he said, 'You're enthusiastic but exhausting, Eva.'

'Not so bad yourself,' said Evangeline, sprawled in the hay.

'Put your breeches on, woman, for pity's sake. If old Bert wandered in you'd frighten the life out of him!'

Evangeline began to scramble into her clothes. Jamie got up and wandered over to the barn door, where he leaned against the jamb in a shaft of sunlight, and lit a cigarette.

Evangeline, who was nothing if not observant, saw that his hands were trembling.

'Don't give way to a crisis of conscience now!' she admonished him. 'Don't start thinking you've betrayed your true love and fallen into sin with little old me.'

'Shut up, Eva!' he said in a sudden burst of anger. He crushed the cigarette packet back into his pocket.

Evangeline pulled a piece of hay out of her mop of carrotty hair and put it between her teeth. 'You know what I think?' she asked unexpectedly, and a little indistinctly. 'I think you're cracking up, old chap.'

'No, I'm not!' he said sharply.

'I'm not one of your family,' she retorted, unabashed. 'The trouble with them is that they're all too darn clever. Lots of brain and no common sense. You think too much. The war's getting to you.'

'Hardly surprising, is it,' he asked bitterly, 'after all this time?'

'There's another thing wrong with 'em,' said Evangeline singlemindedly. She took the piece of straw from between her teeth and waved it at him. 'They're all so busy helping other people that they ignore each other. Libby's running round all day looking after those wretched kids. I'd drown 'em! Your mother will fetch up as Dame Jennifer Daventry when this war is over, see if she doesn't. Your father's got more sense than both of them put together, but he's a creaking door. Dodgy ticker. Wheezes like a grampus after tennis, and worries Doc Greaves stiff. Now, me—no one is going to give me any medals, but don't worry, Jamie my lad. When she's needed, little Eva will always be there.'

He glanced over his shoulder said quietly,

'Thanks, Evangeline.' He grinned at her and went to give her a helping hand to get to her feet.

They stood for a while picking straw out of each other's hair and clothes. 'Like a couple of perishing monkeys grooming one another,' said Evangeline. Then they went outside to the tethered mare and she pulled up the girth. The mare had disobligingly blown herself up, so Evangeline took care of that with a knee in the animal's belly, and jerked up the girth buckles before the mare could recover.

'Hope to hell you never do that to me,' said Jamie in awe.

'I told you,' said Evangeline, in a matter-of-fact voice and without looking up, 'I'll look after you when the time comes. Give me a bunk up, there's a good chap.'

He cupped his hands and she plonked one booted foot into them and he hoisted her into the air. She stretched out one hand to ruffle his hair affectionately, and then clapped her heels to the mare's flanks and set off across country at a canter.

'She's like perishing Boadicea,' said Jamie to himself, and sighed, because he knew everything she had said had been right. He *was* cracking up. Sooner or later, more important people than Evangeline would notice it. And if he meant to wait for Libby, he was going to have a very long wait. She had been right about that, too.

Still, the encounter in the hay with Evangeline had made him feel a lot better, and he whistled cheerfully as he made his way back to the car.

CHAPTER FIVE

LIBBY CALLED at the Evanses' cottage, as she had promised. Tommy robustly denied going anywhere near Miss Biddle's strawberries, and she believed him. So did the Evanses.

'The boy isn't a liar,' said George stoutly. 'Gets into mischief, yes, but when he's found out, he'll own up. Fair brazen he is about it sometimes. But what he isn't, is a liar.'

Mrs Evans, nodding her head vigorously in the background, added to her husband's defence of young Tom with a strong attack on Miss Biddle.

'Think I don't know Cecily Biddle and how her mind works? She was always a trouble-maker, even as a girl. She was a spiteful child, always telling tales out of school. No one liked her then, and no one likes her now. She's only herself to blame for it all. Mind you, those Biddles were always a funny sort of family—you ask any of the old folk around the village as remembers. Always kept themselves to themselves a bit and fancied themselves. Cecily always gave herself airs. Truth was, you know, the old man drank—people used to see him rolling home from the pub of a Saturday night. Terrible temper he had. So don't you worry, Miss Sherwood, I can take care of Cecily Biddle. I know where the body's buried, as they say.' Mrs Evans nodded triumphantly.

'Wife's very fond of the boy,' whispered George in Libby's ear. 'We'd like to keep him here, after the war is over, if we could. He don't have no proper family. His ma is a bit of a flighty piece, by all accounts, and never so much as sends the kid a postcard. Wicked cruel, I call it.'

Libby left them drawing up their battle-lines. She was afraid one of those fierce feuds was developing which only small and closed communities can really experience. She hoped she was not going to be drawn into it, but was rather afraid that she would.

All next day, she found it difficult to concentrate on anything. Every time a footstep sounded outside the door of her office, she feared to see it open and either Marius appear or Miss Biddle, and she did not know which visit she dreaded most. As it happened, neither appeared. Marius, she supposed, was busy. She did not believe he had forgotten their arrangement.

The more she thought about it, the more she questioned her own sanity. Here she was, Libby Sherwood, always so sensible, such a capable girl . . . and what had sensible Miss Sherwood done but blithely agree to an amorous tryst with a virtually unknown foreigner! 'Getting into bed with a man I hardly know . . .' she muttered. 'And it's not as if I normally do such a thing!' Or had ever done it. Her heart sank. She had not the slightest idea how one behaved on such an occasion. She wondered if Marius fully realised this. One could, of course, lie back as on the altar of sacrifice, with one's eyes tightly closed, and surrender oneself and one's honour as part of the war effort. She had a strong suspicion that that was not what Marius had in mind. Romance was, however, singularly absent from their proposed arrangement.

In despair, she spent the evening hunting through

the novels in Merriton House, seeking out scenes of passion with the the hope of gleaning some hint of just what a woman did. The books were all irritatingly vague. Heroines were forever swooning into the arms of glowing-eyed lovers, but subsequent proceedings were reduced to a row of dots. Would he, for example, expect her to take off all her clothes? Well, yes, if they were to be in bed, and a bed was what she had insisted upon.

Retiring to her own solitary bed that night, Libby stripped off and stood in front of the cheval glass, surrounded by her underwear, and surveyed her naked reflection with a mixture of horror and despair. 'I can't do it!' she announced aloud. 'Not in front of Marius.' She pulled on her nightgown, put out the light and wriggled down under the sheets. She began to pray that something would happen to prevent any arrangement for them to meet. Marius might be posted out earlier than he anticipated. One or the other of them might break a leg. He might decide she wasn't worth it.

Most of the following day also passed without sight of or a message from Marius. Libby really began to hope that the whole thing would come to nothing, after all. She was worrying to no purpose. Marius had been distracted from the idea, or had been sent away at short notice, unable to send her a farewell message in time. Her heart rose, and she began to feel much more cheerful. Even Miss Biddle had not said anything more about strawberries, although she was dragging her feet over the blackout curtains, claiming the material was unavailable. That might well be the truth.

That evening, just before dinner, the telephone rang. She had no way to prove, as she told herself, that it had to be Marius, but she knew it was. Her previous euphoria evaporated and panic returned. First and foremost, she was afraid that either Uncle Gerry or Jamie would get to the telephone first. She raced out into the hall, but as ill luck would have it, Mrs Hills got there before her.

The cook was standing by the hall table, a sturdy figure in a wrap-over pinafore and surgical stockings, holding the receiver several inches from her ear and bellowing into it suspiciously. 'Who? Who? Well, who do I say it is, then?'

'All right, Mrs Hills,' gasped Libby, virtually snatching the receiver from her hand, 'I'll take care of it.'

'Foreign feller,' said Mrs Hills. 'Wrong number, most like.' She stomped off back to her kitchen, whence came strong smells of burning.

'H-Hullo?' Libby whispered into the telephone. She cleared her throat and repeated more loudly, 'Hullo—Merriton House.'

'Libby?' came Marius's voice down the line. A faint crackle overlaid it, and she wondered if he was phoning from the camp.

But no, she thought, he would not break the rules so clumsily. He would be in a public telephone-box somewhere. Disastrously, now that she was required to speak to him, her voice failed her, and her throat seemed paralysed.

'Libby?' he repeated, more sharply. 'Are you there?'

'Y-Yes,' she croaked.

'I'm sorry I couldn't call you before, but I've been . . . busy. Listen, can you take some time off tomorrow, and go into Southampton?'

'Yes . . .' she faltered. 'Yes, I expect I can. I'll

have to take the bus. If I take the car, it will be more obvious.'

'Try and make it at lunchtime. I'll meet you at the bus station.'

'Yes, all right.' The conversation was ridiculous. On her side, it was monosyllabic. Why, oh why, could she not just tell him she had changed her mind? Far better to do that now, safely, at the end of a telephone line, than to make a complete and utter fool of herself tomorrow. She opened her mouth, fired with a resolution to tell him that she could not, after all, come.

Too late. 'I have to go, see you then,' he said quickly, and hung up, the click of the replaced receiver echoing down the line like a harbinger of doom.

Briefly, she stood with the phone in her hand, ruefully contemplating the malevolence of Fate, before muttering, 'Drat it!' She sat down and stared hopelessly at the walking-stick stand opposite. He, or in this case she, who hesitates is lost. She was committed to meeting Marius the following day, and could do nothing now to prevent it. Blind panic swept over her for a moment, followed by an anger directed against herself for being so silly as to get herself into a ludicrous situation.

'I don't *do* this kind of thing!' she told the stand. Well, she was about to do it now. Deflowered, she thought gloomily, in a hotel bedroom, by a man I hardly know. She supposed it couldn't be classed as a fate worse than death. But it didn't come under the heading of a barrel of laughs, either. That was what was wrong. It would be neither a moment of great and mutual passion, nor a bit of fun. It would just be the result of a misunderstanding, and a mistake.

Libby made a valiant effort to pull herself together. 'At this rate,' she told herself sternly, 'you'll arrive to meet Marius tomorrow in hysterics!'

The double-decker bus lurched along the country lanes. Trailing, untrimmed low branches struck the roof with alarming effects, like thunderbolts. Libby was the only passenger downstairs and felt as if all her bones were being shaken out of joint.

'They made our dad cut all his trees back!' yelled Mavis conversationally above the overhead racket. Her face expressed disapproval. She was the elder daughter of Bert Harris, and was married to the driver of the bus. Her husband was medically unfit for the army, but quite fit enough to steer his unwieldy vehicle back and forth on a country route.

Mavis, in her clippy's uniform, her leather pouch of tickets and metal punch slung round her like bandoliers, balanced effortlessly on the swaying platform, one hand grasping the upright pole. She continued her side of the conversation in a loud, cheerful voice, punctuating it by ringing the bell twice at intervals to indicate to Maurice, the driver, that no one wanted to get off at the approaching stop. As no one waited there either, he could drive straight past. Few people travelled at this hour, except when it was market day. Libby found herself wondering whether Marius had taken the trouble to find all this out.

She sat uncomfortably on the long seat facing into the aisle, by the exit, her legs dangling. She wished she had been more prudent and taken a seat up at the front, behind Maurice in his glass tank, so that it would not have been so easy for Mavis to talk to her. Not that the clippy asked too many questions, filled as she was with domestic gossip of her own.

'Goin' shopping in Southampton?' she bellowed affably.

'No, well, yes—only for black-out material. The Red Cross hut, you know.'

Libby reflected ruefully that she was a poor liar, even when the lie was partly founded on truth. She was definitely not cut out for clandestine affairs of the heart. She had no talent for the subterfuge involved. She probably had no talent for the physical side of it, either. That was something they would find out very soon.

The reality of the situation, and what she was proposing to do, swept over her once more. Wretchedly, she thought, 'This is all crazy. I suppose Marius has remembered the necessary precautions and has bought the whatever-they-are. I hope he doesn't expect *me* . . .'

The practical, unromantic problems involved suddenly seemed insoluble. She could hardly suggest, as soon as she stepped off the bus, that they dash, hand in hand, into the nearest chemist's. Or should she make some highly artificial excuse, brightly demanding, 'You don't mind if I just call in Timothy White's and buy a corn-plaster?'

'. . . and so he said he'd take them,' yelled Mavis above the clatter of the bus.

Libby was recalled to her presence with a jerk. 'Sorry, Mavis, I missed that,' she apologised. 'It's so noisy.'

Mavis took it in her stride. 'Them two Germans—from the POW camp—as they sent along to help on the farm. Well, dad said you can't get able-bodied help and the Land Girls is all right, but dad, well, he's used to having men around doing the work. The Land Girls, they make him feel he's got to mind his language, and our dad's language is a bit purple at times, you know, especially when he gets to shouting at the cows, or that old tractor breaks down again. Mind you, one or two of those girls can use pretty ripe language. Anyhow, he never got over what Miss Watts did.'

'Evangeline?' Libby exclaimed in surprise.

'That's her. The tall, horsy one. Colonel's daughter and a lady, she is—and her language turns the air blue at times, I can tell you. Turned up all togged up in a new Land Army uniform, she did, and went and let the bull get in with the heifers. You should have heard our dad's language that day!'

Maurice brought the bus to a screeching halt, and Libby grabbed at the rail for safety. A grizzled man in wellingtons threw a corded box wrapped in brown paper on the platform.

'Sid's,' he said mysteriously.

'All right, then,' said Mavis, apparently understanding. Ping-ping. The bus rattled away again. 'So along come these two German fellows, and there's our dad waving his arms and trying sign language, and bits of French what he remembered from the trenches in the last war, and all sorts. "*Parley-vous English?*" he says. And "*Schnell, schnell!*" and anything else he can think of. Then one of the Germans speaks up in ruddy perfect English, and says, "That's quite all right, old chap, just tell us what you want done . . ." spoke real posh, says dad, just like someone on the wireless.'

Libby smiled, despite her worries. 'Are they good workers?'

Mavis shrugged. 'Spend all their time chasing the

Land Girls, dad says. Catching 'em, too. Those girls don't run that fast. Nothing but giggling and squeaking, and if those two fellows go back at the end of the day wore out, it's not with pitching hay, so our dad reckons.'

Libby reflected, not for the first time, what a peculiar thing war was. She wondered why it happened at all, since ordinary people, left to their own devices, generally managed to get along perfectly well, regardless of language or any other problem. But history wasn't made by ordinary people, or composed of everyday events like a tumble in the hay . . .

'Or a tumble in a borrowed bedroom,' she thought apprehensively.

The bus turned into the station. Mavis picked up Sid's parcel, bade Libby farewell, and jumped off the bus to rejoin Maurice, who was climbing down stiffly from his cab.

Libby descended from the platform. There were one or two morning shoppers waiting with their shopping-bags of purchases to catch a bus back to their villages. Even with rationing and clothing coupons and every conceivable sort of shortage, people still managed to shop. Marius was standing by the newspaper stall. At the sight of his solid, uncompromising form, her heart gave a curious little lurch. He caught her eye, saw her give him a tremulous smile, and came to greet her, grinning broadly.

'Don't kiss me!' she hissed in horror, as he stooped. 'Mavis can see us!'

'Who's Mavis?' He frowned.

'The conductress. Just over there. Walk on round the corner; I'll follow.'

They completed this conspiratorial manoeuvre

and converged outside the bus station on the busy pavement. Here anonymity seemed assured, and Libby relaxed.

'You look petrified,' Marius observed. 'Have you changed your mind?'

He sounded quite calm about it. Now was another chance to say 'Yes, I have,' but she only stammered, 'No, I just feel guilty, like a spy.'

He glanced at her, then chuckled, apparently amused by some private joke. He took her arm. 'Spies work hard at looking innocent. Have you eaten?'

'Yes—thanks.'

It wasn't true, but she couldn't eat a thing. Anything would lie on her stomach like lead. She would probably be sick. She felt almost sick now, and her stomach muscles tightened into knots.

'It's impossible to buy a drink in this country outside your ridiculous licensing hours,' Marius was saying. 'But would you like some coffee?'

She did not want the coffee either, but it seemed a way of gaining a little time, of putting off the fateful moment. 'Where?'she asked.

'Anywhere you like. The coffee is all very bad everywhere.'

'There's a war on,' said Libby automatically.

They sat across the grimly functional table-top in the local British Restaurant, and drank coffee which was not, after all, too bad. Marius was studying the paintings which decorated the walls.

'You said your mother was an artist. What would she make of these?'

Libby glanced round. 'It depends, I suppose. She's an interior designer. She trained in Paris with some very famous French designer.'

'And your father, does he paint?'

'No, but he likes paintings. He collects them. He's a very good pianist.'

'A talented family. And you?'

'Nothing much.' Libby fiddled with her spoon. 'I sketch a little.'

Marius put his hand over hers, stilling her nervous fingers. 'You really haven't done this sort of thing before,' he said quietly.

'No,' she told him honestly. 'Have you?' She bit the words off. 'Stupid of me, of course you have.'

He looked pained. 'I'm not some sort of over-sexed Don Juan. I don't, in fact, do this all the time. I—I like you.'

It seemed an odd, inadequate way to express it, but she understood exactly what he meant. They were neither of them in circumstances which allowed either to talk of love. Love was best left out of it. There was no time for that. It would be a mistake in any case. Love led to broken hearts and memories which tore you apart. Talk of liking, of wanting, of good, old-fashioned lust—but not of love. Love was suspended for the duration of hostilities, like so much else.

Suddenly, Libby felt cool and practical. She pushed away her cup. 'Where do we go?'

'Do they know you at the Black Swan?' he asked, naming an old coaching inn. When she shook her head, he added, 'Good, I've taken a room there.'

'Won't they find it odd? I mean, two people turning up there in the middle of the afternoon?' She knew she sounded naïve.

'No,' Marius said simply. 'Why should they?'

Why, indeed?

* * *

The Black Swan had somehow survived, miraculously intact, despite the ruin all round. Beside it, a blackened, burned-out shell of a building stood as mute witness to the efficacy of the raid on Southampton they had observed from afar a few nights ago. Workmen were busy shoring up its damaged walls, and boarding up its empty, gaping windows and door spaces. The whole thing would have to come down, when they got round to it. In the meantime, they did their best.

The remains of the city's ancient walls about them were a magnificent irony, a testament to the folly of man. Once raiders could be kept out by stone, whether they came from land or sea. But how did one defend oneself against raiders from air? The medieval ferrymen of Hythe, across the water from Southampton, had built the walls. They had been obliged either to pay a tax on every passenger or to give a day's labour. The ferry still plied between the city and the settlement across the water. The walls still stood in places. No matter how much wreckage and ruin man wrought, somehow, tenaciously, life went on.

The Black Swan managed, for all its present sad surroundings, to look better on the outside than it did inside. There the greasy smell of lunchtime washing-up hung in the air, and tired and irritable waitresses were clearing up in the vacated dining-room. The clerk handed over a key, barely looking up from the sporting page of his newspaper.

Upstairs was not exactly quiet, but the noises from below and outside were muted. Distantly, dishes clattered in the kitchens, someone was whistling 'Run, rabbit, run', off-key, and rushing water from an antiquated plumbing system occasionally rattled through the pipes. The little room itself was surprisingly cosy, with chintz curtains, age-darkened rafters and an endearing lack of symmetry. The floor was uneven, the carpet worn, the window set in walls a foot thick. It transported them back to the days of sailing-ships in the port and highwaymen on the road to London. For those who frequented the Black Swan, life had always been risky.

'I know a fine old place, a medieval manor house converted into a hotel, in the Belgian countryside,' Marius said unexpectedly. 'When the war is over, if we're both still around, I'll take you there.'

'Don't talk about that!' she said sharply.

'No, you're right. Sorry, I forgot.' He took off his jacket and hung it on a chair-back. Then he cupped his hands round her face and tilted it up towards his. 'I thought you might not come,' he said, a little huskily.

'And you would have minded very much?' Her voice sounded dry and odd to her ears, unlike its usual self.

'Yes, very much.' He lowered his head and his mouth closed over hers.

She was nervous. He could feel her trembling beneath his hand like a frightened yearling. He had expected that, but what he had not expected was the uncertainty he was experiencing within himself. He was angry with himself, because although it might be the first time for her, it certainly was not for him and he had never given the matter a second thought before. It had always been an animal reaction. You wanted and you took. The building up of desire, the tension, the moment of ecstasy and the release: he knew these things very well. But this was different. There was no pretending otherwise. It was madness, he thought, because for all their sensible words, they were neither of them an emotionless automaton, and both were straying deeper and deeper into the labyrinth of untapped passions from which there was no escape.

They undressed in silence and climbed into the creaking bed. Marius bent over that beautiful, untouched body, and felt like the fisherman who opens up an oyster and discovers nestling in its depths the perfect, lustrous pearl. No man has seen it before, it has lain in the depths of the ocean, waiting for him. He knew that this image, its freshness and its softness, all its perfection, would remain with him as long as he lived. However long that might be. Probably not long.

A pain touched his heart, not of fear, but despair. Because it was too late. He was set on a road from which he could not turn back. But running his hand lightly over the contours of that slim, naked form, it seemed to have that quality the early painters had tried to capture. This was a Venus d'Urbino, the essence of youth and desirability, of sensuality without coarseness, and above all, without the threat of the passage of time. Every curve, every dimple was encapsulated, perfect for ever, in his memory. He would look into his mind, as he might have gazed at a painting on a wall, and always see her thus. A man might dream of such a woman all his life, and seek her without finding her. He had found her, but for a brief moment only.

Libby wondered what he was thinking. He was perspiring slightly and his damp skin clung to hers. She put her hand on his shoulder and felt the tenseness of the muscles beneath her touch, and sensed the power of that fit, sinewy body. The faint, agitated ticking of his watch echoed in the silence which had befallen the room. If she was afraid now, it was a new kind of fear, an anticipation of the unknown, and mixed with curiosity. She felt strangely light-headed, and as though, with her clothes, she had shed the old Libby Sherwood she had always known and emerged as someone else, who had always been hidden within, unbeknownst. The old Libby had been only a chrysalis, hiding the butterfly waiting to emerge and take wing. She felt herself relax, and reached up her arms towards him.

Without warning, Marius pushed himself away, rolling over and jumping up from the bed. He walked away and grabbed his shirt.

'Get up and get dressed!' he ordered harshly, throwing the words over his shoulder without looking at her.

Libby sat up, bewildered and alarmed, her heart pounding. 'What's wrong?'

'Every damn thing. I said, get your clothes on!'

He sounded angry, shouting at her, as he struggled into his own clothes. She began to be angry, too. But she asked, 'Is it my fault?' because she could not think what could possibly have gone wrong, and something had obviously, dreadfully, done so.

'No.'

Her own anger spilled over. 'You asked me to come here! Do you realise what a decision that was for me? Do you think I usually deceive my family, tell them lies? I have never been with any man. I was scared out of my wits when I was on the bus today. Now you just tell me not to bother!'

'I don't care what it was for you!' Marius yelled at her. 'I also had to tell lies in order to come here. I run a risk. You're a free agent. You need not have come. I told you you could change your mind. The same goes for me. I'm not free to disobey orders—which is what I have done, for your sake—but, confound it, I am still free to change my mind, and I have changed it.' He scooped up her underwear and threw it on the bed in a tangled heap. 'Hurry up.'

'Don't treat my stockings like that!' she snapped. 'We can't get them!'

'Is that all you're worried about?' he snarled at her.

Libby got out of bed and dragged on her garments, her face burning and her body trembling with frustration, rage and a sense of insult.

They clattered back down the winding staircase. The clerk accepted the key back again without comment, hanging it up on its hook, and returning to his paper. He had reached the crossword. But as they went out into the street, one of the waitresses was heard to whisper to her friend, with a stifled giggle, 'Blimey, that was quick!'

Libby and Marius walked back to the bus station in sullen silence. When they were almost there, he suddenly spoke.

'It wasn't anything to do with you. I meant what I said to you before. It's just that it would have been a mistake.'

'Took you a while to decide that!' she said briefly.

'All right, so it took me a while to decide, but I have decided it. What's more, I'm right. Listen to me, Libby . . .' He caught at her arm and stopped her, pulling her round to face him. Her face was still flushed and her hair untidy. Her eyes sparkled at him warningly.

'Let go!' she said tightly.

He let go of her, and, for the first time, she

realised how near she was to tears. They welled up and prickled at her eyelids. A sense of outrage alone prevented them welling out and spilling down her cheeks.

'If you were Evangeline,' he said, 'it wouldn't have mattered, back there. But you aren't Evangeline . . . and what you are, is something special. I wish, with all my heart, we could have met at some other time, in some other place. If I still have it in me to pray, which is doubtful, I would pray that we might do that: meet again somewhere, in different circumstances. I . . .'

He broke off, and turned away from her, beginning to stride away down the street again. After a moment's hesitation, she followed, and because he had gained distance on her, was forced to run to catch up with him. She caught at his hand when she did, and squeezed it.

'It's all right,' she said. 'I'm sorry I was so cross.' She paused and then asked, 'When the war is over, if I'm in Canada, would you come and find me there?'

'If I could.' His voice sounded lost, hopeless. He couldn't. The war would never be over for him. He was a man who counted his life's expectancy in days, perhaps in hours. A man without a future.

Libby said, 'Then I'll come and find you.'

He seemed struck by that, and turned and smiled at her.

The bus was not due out for half an hour, so they went and walked in the park. In front of the statue of Palmerston, Marius said, 'I wish I had a camera, then I could take a photograph of you.'

'I have one, if you want it,' she said. She opened her purse and fumbled inside. 'It's just an old snapshot of me, and Uncle Gerry and the dogs, on the lawn at Merriton House. Jamie took it in the summer of thirty-nine just before the war broke out. I'd been in Paris, and I was on my way home to Canada. I only came to stay with them for a week or two, and look at me, still here!'

She handed over the snapshot, with its creased corners, and Marius put it in his pocket. They went back to the bus station. Marius seemed disinclined to join her in the long queue, and lingered discreetly by the news-stand.

Libby asked impulsively, 'Why don't you travel back with me? I don't care who sees us.'

'I do,' he said. 'I'm breaking all the rules.'

'For me?'

'For you, yes, for you, of course!' He sounded rather cross.

He might just as well have said, 'For nothing!', because nothing was what he had got out of it. Responsibility weighed on her heart, and guilt. The bus drew in, not Mavis and Maurice this time, thank goodness, but a harassed conductress with a brittle manner whom Libby didn't know. Probably someone doing war work. Libby got on last, and lingered on the platform to say goodbye, until the clippy demanded snappishly of Marius, 'Are you travelling or not? We've got a timetable, you know!'

Marius gripped her fingers. 'I'll try to be in touch, but time's getting short.'

Depression added itself to her sense of guilt. No time left, and what time there had been, wasted. She wanted to say, 'I'm sorry,' but it was too late for that, too. The bus drew out, and they were parted.

'I always decide what to say too late to say it,'

Libby reflected. 'I don't say the wrong thing. I say nothing at all, and I don't know which is worse.'

The first person she met when she arrived home was Jamie. That was a relief, in a way, because she had been more nervous at the thought of meeting Gerard Daventry and his shrewd gaze. At the same time, the sight of her cousin filled her with a mixture of guilt and resentment. Guilt, for the obvious reason, and resentment because he caused her to feel the guilt.

Jamie was wandering around the drawing-room, scowling, but when he spoke, it was not to ask where she had been or what she had been doing, but to say, 'I've had a message. I don't have to go back to Kent immediately, but I'll have to report to the local camp. I might be around for a few more days.' He looked truculent, his face red with some emotion, and his tousled hair sticking up on end because he had been rubbing at it.

Libby muttered weakly, 'Oh, good.'

It sounded horribly feeble, and he must be hurt by her lack of enthusiasm, she thought immediately. Such an unexpected piece of good news ought to have sent her flying into his arms to hug him in joy. Instead, she shuffled her feet and gave him a wan smile.

Strangely enough, Jamie did not seem as aware of her lack of spontaneous delight as she was. He took out his cigarettes and shook one out of the packet. As he lit it, he mumbled, 'It's only for a short time.'

Libby pulled herself together. 'Even so, Jamie, your father will be so happy.'

'Oh, yes, Dad's pleased.' Jamie drew on the

cigarette nervously. 'Have a good afternoon in town?'

His tone was casual, almost careless, but she felt the blood rush to her cheeks. 'Yes, thanks, I went looking for black-out curtaining. How did you know?'

'I saw you get on the bus here. I was just bringing Spot back from the vet. Ruddy dog had grass-seed in his ears.'

'That's all right, then.' Libby hesitated. 'I'm going upstairs to change before dinner.'

He only nodded, walking to the window to stare out at the evening sky. There was a hint of rose about it. Fine day tomorrow, he thought. Red sky at night, shepherd's delight: Red sky in the morning, shepherd's warning. The spell of fine weather was due to continue, so the meteorological boffins reckoned.

Aloud, Jamie said forcefully, 'Damn!'

They had not said why he was wanted here, but he knew. The odds were that, when he walked through those camp gates tomorrow, the first person he would see would be Mike, his navigator, grinning at him, and saying, 'Well, skipper, here we go again!'

He hated these missions, although originally he had volunteered for the special flight which made tricky night-time sorties to drop agents over occupied territory. Now he did not know quite what had made him want to do it in the first place. Unless, though he disliked to think this might be the answer, he had imagined himself as a sort of Scarlet Pimpernel. What it really meant was dropping some poor devil to contact the local Resistance. He, Jamie, was once again to be ruddy chauffeur.

He leaned his head on the window glass, feeling its coolness. The garden outside was beautiful and unreal. Even vegetables growing where before the war there had been flower-beds did not detract from its illusion of calm, a world without sudden death, without a continual game of Russian roulette.

He could remember how stupidly enthusiastic he had been, the first time he had flown on one of these cloak-and-dagger operations, as Mike called them. So full of *Boy's Own Paper* keenness. The whole thing had seemed an adventure until he had actually set eyes on their passenger, whom they nicknamed a Joe, and realised it was no play-acting, but a game in deadly earnest. The silent man—and once the Joe had been a woman, which was a thousand times worse—was being taken on what might only too well prove a one-way trip. A solitary mission, requiring unbelievable courage. One human being floating down through the moonlit night towards the unknown. Hunter and hunted. Protected by no Geneva Convention if caught. They were often caught. The enemy was not always unsuspecting. Sometimes there was a welcome committee down there on the ground—the wrong welcome. Betrayal was the wild card in the pack.

'Wonder who it is this time?' Jamie murmured, rubbing away the condensation his breath made on the pane. 'Which ruddy hero shall I be piloting to his death on this run?'

CHAPTER SIX

LIBBY SPENT the following day torn between elation and despair. The elation was quite inexplicable, she told herself, and had no foundation at all. The despair was more easily accounted for. She had failed Marius, failed him where it mattered most, in the bedroom. She had been awkward and unco-operative when she should have been warm and tender. It was unlikely, she told herself, that he would try and contact her again, despite his parting words. On the other hand, he had asked for her photograph. He carried it in his pocket.

It wasn't the best photo in the world, she thought gloomily. A slightly tilted, too-far-away snapshot taken with a box Brownie, black and white, and showing a girl in a floral summer dress, looking absurdly young, a middle-aged man and two grinning dogs. Romance was just not working out for her. She seemed doomed to failure. Do other couples have all these problems? she wondered. Few couples, however, found themselves in the peculiar situation in which she and Marius were trapped. Any sensible person would call it a day.

The nuns who had educated her in Normandy had set great store by girls being sensible. Now, looking back, Libby could not help wondering if by 'sensible' they had not denoted a slow maturing of the emotions. Perhaps they were right. Perhaps the flower that blooms too early is struck by frost. She had not been a physically precocious child. Academically, she had been nearly always at the top of the class, less because of natural brilliance than because she was a hard worker, struggling to overcome her weaknesses. Possibly it was that which distracted her from what was happening to her body. She was growing up, but remaining a child.

They were not allowed to go out singly or even in twos into the town. Three was the prescribed number. Any expedition into the life outside the convent walls meant finding two like-minded friends and presenting themselves, all three neatly lined up, before the nun in charge of the door, who had been summoned by a bell. They had to say where they were going, and how long they would be. Eventually, the door was opened—grudgingly.

In the last year of her education, these expeditions into town had been made in the company of two friends, Chantal and Marie-France. Libby and Marie-France were content to potter around the shops, turning over the price-tags on the racks of cheap clothing set out on the pavements, looking at books, wondering whether they dared purchase a fashion magazine. Chantal was different. She was a child of the Mediterranean, and already, in so many ways, she was a woman. She didn't want to look at book titles, or sit in cafés eating ice-cream. Chantal was interested in men. The other two were aware of the difference between their friend and themselves, and it made them uneasy. But, worse, Chantal had a boy-friend in the town and would slip away to meet him. Her friends found her behaviour embarrassing and, somehow, in bad taste. It let the side down, and in addition it involved both of them in unwilling subterfuge.

They would all meet again in good time and

reappear, in a threesome, back at the convent. But the other two spent the entire afternoon fearing that they would be spotted, Chantal's absence noted, and the inevitable questions would be asked. What would they do? Would they lie? Would they say she had gone to the Ladies' Room? Would it be believed? To be caught lying would certainly mean expulsion and shame. Would they, then, meekly own up to the truth, and split on a friend? It involved almost Jesuitical splitting of hairs. Above all, both resented that Chantal had put them in this intolerable position, plunging them into unwished crises of conscience—yet neither had the courage to refuse to cover up for a friend. The two innocents suffered agonies of remorse: Chantal never did. Neither did she ever get caught. Vaguely, Libby felt that a lesson had been learned. You simply have to have the nerve. Other people will follow you. What she did not know was whether she would ever have the necessary nerve, or would just go on failing Marius at the last minute.

Libby cycled home at the end of the following day, meditating on this and on other problems. The one tap in the Red Cross hut had developed a monotonous drip. George Evans had promised to come and put a new washer on it, but he was apt to promise help to everyone, and as a result it was generally some time before he actually got round to each job. On the other hand, if anyone was driven to despair before he got there, and asked someone else or did the job themselves, George was deeply offended.

She had almost reached the junction of the lane and the main road when she saw Marius sitting on the bank with his arms resting on his knees, and obviously waiting for her—unless he was waiting for the bus. She slowed down and got off the bicycle and he stood up, dusting bits of grass from his clothes, and came to meet her. She watched him approach a little nervously, because she was not quite sure what to say, or quite why he was waiting, and in any case, after the episode in the bedroom of the Black Swan, things could not be quite the same again. Looking at him now, fully dressed, she could not help seeing him, in her mind's eye, naked. And that reminded her what a mess she had made of it all. 'Hullo,' she said bleakly.

Marius said, 'Good afternoon,' which sounded very formal for two people who had lain naked together on a bed, and he didn't try to kiss her. The idea sprang into her head that he had come to tell her it was all over and done with. He had, on reflection, decided not to bother with her any more. She could hardly blame him. His voice startled her.

'I've about an hour. I thought we could walk a little way over the fields.'

'I've got my bike,' she said lamely.

'I'll put it over the hedge. No one will see it there—and if they do, I shouldn't think anyone would want to take that.' He indicated the bicycle with some disdain.

The scorn rankled, even though it was founded. 'It might not look much, but it's the only bicycle I have!'

Marius did not bother to reply, but picked up the machine and lifted it effortlessly over the nearest hedge and dropped it down out of sight. They proceeded more sedately themselves, via the gate, and strolled over the uneven turf. He had his hands in his pockets, so the question of holding hands did not arise.

Libby felt struck dumb and sought for some topic of conversation. 'I wasn't expecting to see you. I mean, I thought you'd be busy.'

'I am busy,' came the unpromising reply. 'I told you I've only got an hour.'

An hour or two or three, here and there, it was all he had, and—she thought miserably—not to be wasted as on their previous rendezvous. The field sloped slightly and the warm, late-afternoon sun played on it. There was not a breath of wind. The bramble bushes that lined the perimeter were already in fruit, though a little unripe yet. She and Marius sat down by mutual consent in the shelter of an aged oak tree, near the bushes, and observed the peaceful, rural vista spread out before them.

'You're not mad at me?' Marius asked her quietly.

'Oh, no,' she exclaimed, startled. 'I thought you were probably cross with *me*.'

He laughed and she joined in, and the ice was broken. He put out his arm and she leaned back against the gnarled oak trunk, nestling into his supporting shoulder. 'It's a beautiful day,' she said, 'and it doesn't seem possible that there could be any war or anything bad, anywhere.'

'Sometimes,' Marius said soberly, 'it's harder to believe there is anything good, anywhere.'

She turned her head to look into his face. 'You're thinking of your own country, and your own people, and I'm sorry, because there's nothing I can do or say which can comfort you—or anyone else in your situation. It will all come out right in the end, I do believe that.'

Marius leaned forward and kissed her. 'You almost make me believe it,' he said softly.

'You must believe it already, or you wouldn't fight on.'

'Sometimes there is nothing left to do, but fight. It's not a question of choice.' He ran his index finger down the line of her nose, over her lips and down her chin. 'You are a very pretty girl!' he said, quite practical.

'Thank you, sir. Bit of a disappointment, though . . .'

'Don't say it!' he ordered, putting his finger against her lips. 'Just accept the compliment.'

She smiled at him a little uncertainly, and his heart felt heavy. He had turned over in his mind whether or not to come and meet her, and had still not been sure if he was doing the right thing, as he sat waiting by the roadside. Well, of course he was doing the wrong thing! Getting involved with a woman, any woman, was madness. Getting involved with this one was a refined kind of insanity for which he ought to be locked up for his own safety. And for hers. He could have made love to her in the Black Swan, and still regretted with a part of his mind and being that he had not. He still wanted to make love to her, and even sitting here with her set the old physical reaction stirring to the extent that he was beginning to feel distinctly uncomfortable. But it could never be a casual union of the kind so common in wartime. It would be a commitment. He was not free to make any commitment. But he still felt that urge, and leaned forward to kiss her again, his hand slipping down over her shoulder, feeling the soft flesh beneath the flimsy material of her blouse give under the pressure of his fingers, and the swell of those delicate, perfectly formed breasts yielding to his touch.

Libby turned her face up to meet his, pressing the softness of her lips against his firm mouth, surrendering to a surge of yearning, and pushing herself against him. She twisted her arms round his neck, holding him tightly, as his hand slipped inside her blouse and closed on her breast, and she gave a little moan. Then, suddenly, she saw his eyes look past her, over her shoulder, and his expression change. Instinctively she drew back, and so did he, taking his hand away quickly.

'What are you doing here?' asked Marius, of someone behind her, and unseen by her.

Tommy emerged from the brambles and presented himself before them, eyeing them dispassionately. 'Mrs Evans sent me out to look for blackberries, if they're ripe yet, for her jam and that. You can go on snogging; I ain't going to get in your way!'

'We're not!' snapped Libby, flushing and angrily trying to refasten her blouse.

'Oh, yes?' said the worldly-wise Thomas. 'Anyway, there ain't the right sort of blackberries yet.' He sat down on the turf in front of them and crossed his legs, Buddha-fashion, to contemplate them, rather as a Tibetan monk might gaze serenely upon the image of the Enlightened One.

'It's nice to see you, Tom,' said Marius mildly. 'But you wouldn't like to go and hunt for berries in some other place?'

Tommy was a businessman. 'My mum's boyfriends usually give me a shilling to go away.'

'Unwise of them. Never pay a blackmailer. Good

manners, Tom, should tell you when your company is *de trop*.'

'What's that?'

'When you're in the way,' said Marius firmly.

'All right.'

The boy got reluctantly to his feet. 'Ta-ta.'

He ambled away and could be seen wriggling through a gap in the hedge, leaving it considerably wider than it had been before his passage, so that the next time Harris's cattle were turned out here, they would probably escape the same way.

'I ought to be getting back,' Marius said. He stood up and offered her his hand to rise. They strolled back to the bicycle and he returned it to the road. 'But I'll see you again.' He kissed her quickly on the cheek and turned and walked away towards the camp.

'OK,' she said, striving to conquer her feelings of frustration. She pushed down the pedal with unnecessary violence and set off for Merriton House. For the first time, she felt about Tommy Ryan in much the same way as other villagers felt about him.

Libby was woken up, two nights later, by the rattle of what she took to be hailstones against the window. Then she remembered that it was late summer and unlikely to be hailing, although in England one could never be sure. She scrambled out of bed and pushed open the casement. At first she could distinguish nothing, and then she saw the familiar stocky silhouette of a man standing by the rhododendrons. Her heart skipped a beat and then gave a painful lurch. He raised one arm and beckoned to her urgently.

She pulled on her dressing-gown and crept hurriedly downstairs through the darkened, sleeping house. The back door creaked noisily as she opened it, and she had to leave it ajar, or she would not have been able to get in again. It was a wonder, the state she was in, that she remembered.

At first she couldn't see him, and when his hand came out of the darkness and touched her arm, she jumped and almost cried out aloud. Then she whispered, 'How did you get out of the camp, and how did you know that was my bedroom?'

'If I can't get out of camp at night, I'm not good at the things I'm supposed to be trained for . . . and I know which is your room because I chatted up, as I believe the expression is, a truly terrible girl who works here. She wears her hair draped over one eye and peers at you vacantly with the other. I kept expecting Boris Karloff to lurch in at the door.'

'Veronica,' she said. 'Where on earth . . .?'

'The Black Cat café in the village. She waitresses there on the days she doesn't work here. Didn't you know?'

They moved away from the house, and Libby shivered in her dressing-gown.

'I'm sorry,' Marius said contritely. 'I should have thought you might catch cold.' He put his arm round her and she huddled up against him.

'We can go and sit in the air-raid shelter,' she suggested. 'I just hope there isn't a raid, or everyone else will come charging in.'

The shelter was quite comfortable in a spartan way, and supplied with rugs. Marius tucked one round her knees, as they sat on the bench. It was dark, and she couldn't see him very well. She stretched out her hand and it found his, and he clasped her fingers reassuringly. 'I feel as though I was about fifteen years old and had crept out of the dormitory for a midnight feast,' she confessed.

'I, too, had thought my days of creeping about and throwing stones at girls' windows were over. One likes to fancy one grows sophisticated with age,' he told her.

She giggled, and then said seriously, 'I'm not sophisticated. I'm a bit like Veronica . . . kind of simple.'

'Heaven forbid!'

'No, truly. I mean, where romance is concerned. I'm just not very good at it, I think. Certainly no *femme fatale*.'

His voice, in the darkness, had a barbed note to it when he replied, 'Sometimes, it's better not to be too clever.'

There is a woman or there was a woman, she thought. He was hurt, badly. Is he still in love with her? Am I really just the soldier's consolation? If so, I'm pretty poor consolation. 'I wish I were just a little bit more clever than I am,' she said, a little sadly.

He turned towards her, his voice suddenly urgent and his fingers holding hers tightened their grip so harshly that he hurt her. 'Listen to me, Libby. What you are, that's what I like. I don't want you to be different, just the way you are.' He released her hand and caught at her shoulders. 'The other day,' he said awkwardly, 'in the hotel . . . I'm sorry if I upset you. I'm sorry for this whole mess. I really . . .' He fell silent, and then finished, 'I really do mind what you think and what you feel. It matters to me. You matter to me.'

She put out her hand and touched his face. 'Kiss me?' she asked.

He slid his arms round her and she turned her face up towards his. A little later, when they broke apart, she whispered, 'I feel a little like Alice in Wonderland, as if I'm in a different world. It's a little topsy-turvy, and when I try to make sense of it, I come up with such odd conclusions that I'm a little frightened. Do I make sense?' she finished anxiously.

'You make sense,' Marius said, stroking her hair.

'I was so afraid you wouldn't want to see me any more,' she confessed.

'I couldn't keep away.' Suddenly he muttered, 'Oh, Libby . . .' with such despair that she hugged him tightly to her and whispered,

'Don't! Don't, my darling.'

After a moment, he said more calmly, 'I won't come creeping round the gardens another time. I'll find some other way.'

'Marius . . .' she said quietly, 'I should like you to make love to me.'

'It would complicate things too much,' he said obstinately. 'And I didn't come here for that, I'm not asking you. I'm sorry now for a lot of the things I've said. They have rebounded on me, as it were. I never meant you to think you had to . . . I didn't mean to put you in an impossible situation in that regard, where your feelings were disregarded and only mine mattered. Only mine don't matter. I'm sorry. It was selfish of me, and pretty stupid into the bargain.'

'I didn't say I felt I had to,' she said resentfully. 'I said I wanted you to.'

He said sharply, 'Don't!'

Outside the shelter, the trees rustled. Libby shivered. 'Jamie said we ought not to plan for a future, but live now. I suppose that's a counsel of despair. But I can't feel despair. I feel right when I'm with you.'

He twisted his fingers in her hair. 'When I was a child,' he said, 'I made a den in the forest. I took all kinds of bits and pieces up there, secretly. Furnishing it, if you like. Sitting in it was a little like sitting in this shelter. Then, one day, I went up there to find they were clearing the trees in that area, and they had bulldozed my den flat. They never even knew it was there. You can't build yourself a life away from other people, Libby. You can't protect yourself, or your emotions. There is always someone out there with an axe, ready to chop down the tree you're sitting under.'

She said unsteadily, 'Doesn't that make this little time very precious, and not to be wasted?'

She heard him draw in his breath sharply. 'It's not wasted for me.'

He kissed her again, this time a little more roughly. His fingers moved to the buttons on the bosom of her dressing-gown and fumbled with them, until his hand slid inside and closed on the soft flesh of her breast, kneading it gently. She pushed herself against him, wanting him to touch her, her body alive with a dull yearning ache, which finally located itself in the very pit of her stomach, so that she found herself wriggling on the bench. He sensed the growing unrest in her, the heat of her body and the rising desire, and drew his hand back, but she whispered, 'Don't stop, please . . .'

This time, when he returned his hand, he rested it on her thigh and dragged up her nightgown. There was an urgency in his own touch now, and he was breathing heavily. She felt a confusion and a panic, because she did not know what to do next. But he caught at her leg, behind her knee, and pulled her across him, so that she straddled him. He was struggling now, with his own clothing, and then he pulled her down on to him, and she gave a sudden cry.

It was almost dawn when he left. Libby hoped that he had no trouble getting back into camp. Early greyness was stealing across the grass, wet with dew. The door was still ajar, thank goodness, and she closed it carefully. Glancing towards the staircase, she thought she saw a light beneath Jamie's door, which was at the top. But by the time she reached it, the light, if there had been one, had been switched off. She would have liked to slip into the bathroom and wash, but she was afraid the running of the taps would be heard. It would have to wait an hour. Back in her own room, she realised how cold she was. She crept into bed in her dressing-gown and snuggled down into the blankets, and although she meant to stay awake, fell asleep.

She did not see Marius for the whole of the following twenty-four hours. They seemed an eternity. She kept wondering what he was doing, or if he thought of her. Reaction was setting in. She was a twenty-two-year-old girl who had never before given her body to any man, and from her high point of euphoria, panic pulled her down into an abyss. Would he now, after all, forget her, now that he had got what men were all supposed to want? Was it only her inaccessibility which made her desirable? Even if that were so, he would remain a part of her.

She had once seen a film about Catherine the Great in which one character observed that a woman never forgets the name of her first lover. He was more than a name. He had opened out for her a window onto a new world. He had shown her an aspect of her own emotions and of her body of which she had not dreamt. He had both taken her virginity, and revealed to her not only a pleasure in the flesh, but the joy of union with one particular being who was, for her, unique, and always would be. At this, she stopped being afraid, and suddenly felt secure. She was different, too, for him. She was not just like any other woman. No words could explain what they were to each other, but both knew. They were two halves of one creation. Singly, each was incomplete. Only together, united in the flesh, were they one, harmonious whole. Only in each other was there any fulfilment.

The next morning, when she arrived at her office, it was to find that new black-out had appeared as if by magic. Miss Biddle was there before her, busily engaged in putting up the funereal light-proof curtains designed to disguise their presence from prowling enemy night fighters. She was teetering unsteadily on the top of some wooden steps, which were plentifully bedaubed with multi-coloured splashes of old, dried paint. As Libby entered, the steps wobbled alarmingly, and she ran to steady them.

'There you are, Libby,' came Miss Biddle's starchily virtuous voice from above. 'Keep a tight hold on these steps.'

Libby wasn't late, but Miss Biddle contrived to make it sound as though she were. Dutifully she hung on to the steps, although it put her in the embarrassing and ludicrous situation of peering up Miss Biddle's skirt every time she raised her eyes. The directoire knickers hove into view as she stretched, and the garters securing the thick lisle stockings. Libby resisted the urge to snap the elastic with a resounding ping! against Miss Biddle's flabby, mottled red and white thighs. She understood instinctively why Tommy was moved to play so many practical jokes on Miss Biddle, cruel though these often were. Something about the woman invited it.

Guiltily, Libby offered, 'Would you like me to do that?'

'I finish what I start,' puffed Miss Biddle. 'You've no idea what I had to do to get this material.'

'Really?' Libby murmured.

Miss Biddle glanced down suspiciously. 'I was up early to finish stitching them on my old treadle machine. That machine is on its last legs, but you can't get the spare parts.'

'There's a war on . . .' The useful response slipped out.

The steps lurched wildly as Miss Biddle clambered down, out of breath but triumphant. 'Though I do say it myself,' she announced, 'I made a tidy job of those.'

She was right, and Libby agreed with her with unforced enthusiasm. Her genuine tone caused Miss Biddle to mellow visibly.

'If you can lay your hands on a length of material from somewhere, some nice, cosy pattern like flowers—not utility—I'll run up some curtains for your office, Libby.'

'That's very nice of you,' she replied cautiously.

Miss Biddle followed her into the office and stood by the door, watching with her sharp little eyes, like two currants in a lump of dough, as Libby unpacked her bag and set out her lunch box, file of notes, pens and pencils neatly on the table.

'Nice day,' said Miss Biddle. 'You'll be taking your lunch out of doors again, I dare say.'

Libby froze, with one hand still inside her bag. 'I might.'

'You should, young girl like you. It's not good for you to be cooped up in here when all that fresh air out there is going to waste. I get out in my garden on nice mornings like this. Gives me an appetite. I can see people going up and down the street,' she added.

I bet you can, Libby thought. She smiled non-committally.

'I saw you and your young man the other day, setting off. Having a bit of a picnic, by the looks of it.'

'Yes, I saw your curtains move,' Libby replied calmly.

Miss Biddle flushed unattractively, a dull magenta. 'I was watering my geraniums. Dry out on that window-sill in this weather, not but geraniums stand a bit of dryness. He'll be a foreigner.'

'Yes, Miss Biddle. But he isn't my young man.'

'Whatever they calls it these days,' said Miss Biddle, investing the words with seedy innuendo. 'Where's he from, then? Not one of those Polish fellows, I hope? Though the girls do seem to like them.'

'No,' Libby paused, then lied easily, 'Czech.'

Miss Biddle digested this piece of information. As she had no means of verifying it, and had been no further abroad herself than the Isle of Wight, she accepted it at face value. 'There, I thought as much.'

'I am very busy,' Libby said firmly, opening her files.

Her companion moved reluctantly towards the door. 'Your uncle, Mr Daventry—looking poorly these days—does he mind you running around with this Czech fellow?'

'I do not "run around" with anyone!' Libby said with suppressed anger.

'I thought you were walking out with that nice young Mr James Daventry.'

'Then you thought wrong, Miss Biddle!' Libby's temper flared up at last. 'Now will you please go away!'

Miss Biddle left, but not looking displeased. If anything, she looked smug. Libby realised, too late, that the flash of anger on her part was what Miss Biddle had been angling for. Anger, to Miss Biddle, meant confirmation. The woman now felt free to inform the village that Libby Sherwood had thrown over nice James Daventry and taken up with a Free Czech.

Libby worked determinedly all morning, and because Miss Biddle had recommended her to get fresh air, perversely sat in her office, eating her sandwiches from one hand and scribbling on with the other. Authority wanted to send them more evacuees, but it wasn't going to be easy to persuade the village to accept any more, mostly because of Tommy's antics.

Thoughts of Tommy led to thoughts of Marius. Marius hovered, anyway, at the back of her brain continuously. He wouldn't go away and she couldn't dismiss him. Nor did she want to. She thought, half-amused and half-surprised: I suppose I've fallen in love. How very odd it is, and quite unlike I'd imagined. How wrong the books get it. Not so much wrong, perhaps, as inadequate. How would she describe the way she felt? It was impossible. She felt nervous, alarmed, excited, frightened, inattentive, all these things. She had to force herself to concentrate on her letter. In her chest, where popular tradition located the heart and all it symbolised, she felt as though she carried some pulsating, crazy organ which had gone haywire and danced and hopped erratically to its own delirious rhythm. Even her skin felt strange and ultra-sensitive. She was both uncomfortable and happy, and it was a peculiar sensation.

Above all, her love was an armour against which arrows were no more than pinpricks. She could even afford to tolerate Miss Biddle's nosy enquiries. Cecily Biddle was, after all, no more than a lonely, bitter woman who had never known how to form a human relationship with anyone. The shame of the drunken father and the desperate striving for respectability, the conviction of overlooked worth, all had turned to spite, and spite into a prison, through the bars of which Miss Biddle peered resentfully at the world she could not join. A world full of people living out emotions both pleasurable and painful, which she neither shared nor understood.

But I have Marius, Libby thought. And, no matter what happens now, I'm changed. I'm different. I understand.

She got up from her desk and went to perch on the window-sill which overlooked the cluttered yard behind the hut. It was not a beautiful sight. Tattered tarpaulins covered curiously-shaped objects that nobody wanted but for which no one felt himself responsible. There were some ancient planks left by decorators. Those would go for firewood the coming winter, the many knots in the wood spitting sparks out into someone's living-room. Otherwise only weeds grew in a desultory manner around the perimeter of the yard where a fence hung between vertical and horizontal, as if it couldn't decide whether to fall down or not.

As Libby watched, the fence rocked. A head appeared on the top of it, disembodied, like that of an old-time felon displayed on a pike. The head was small and scruffy, and was followed by a wiry and even scruffier body as Tommy swarmed over the fence like a spider and dropped down into the dust.

She pushed up the sash window and called to him.

He scuttled across, bent double, casting furtive looks to either side, as he had seen actors do in the cinema. His pinched little face was full of importance. 'I gotta message!' he announced in a conspiratorial growl.

Libby's heart gave a little hop. 'From Marius?'

Tommy nodded. 'Yus—Marius.' He pronounced it 'Mary-uss'.

'You had better come in,' Libby said, pushing the window right open and stepping back.

He hopped nimbly over the sill. 'Old Biddle looks out for me, so I come round the back. I never took her rotten strawberries!'

'That's all right,' Libby assured him. 'I believe you.'

His brow creased horribly as he struggled to remember the exact words of his message. 'He'll meet you where you went before, down by the shore. He says you know.'

'What time?' Libby asked anxiously, looking at her watch.

'He says three o'clock, and he's sorry fer it being inconvenient.' The last word appealed to Tommy. He repeated it, savouring the syllables. 'Inconvenient, if it is. But he can't come no other time. If it's no good, and you can't come, I'm to go back and tell him. But if it's all right, I'm to do nothing. Marius says he'll understand if you can't.'

Tommy looked relieved at getting this long and involved explanation off his chest. Libby gave him the one remaining cheese sandwich and he sat on the edge of her desk to eat it, breaking the points of her nicely-sharpened pencils by trying to sharpen them again in the sharpener.

It was already a quarter to three. Libby pushed everything together into her bag. 'Tom, can you take my things back to Merriton House for me? Just take them round to the kitchen at the back and give them to Mrs Hills. Say I've been called to see someone about an evacuee problem, and I'll be along later.'

'Right-o,' said Thomas indistinctly through a mouthful of half-chewed bread. He gathered up Libby's bag, made an exit the way he had come, through the window, and disappeared over the fence with the agility, she thought ruefully, of a natural cat-burglar.

Marius was already there, waiting for her. Libby called to him and waved and ran, panting, down the slight incline to the shore, and into his arms. She clung to him, gasping for breath, and he said, 'I would have waited, you know.'

She nodded, and he kissed her before she had properly got her breath back, and she gurgled, and saw stars from lack of oxygen. After that, for no reason other than it was a hot afternoon and they both felt like children playing truant, they took off their shoes and paddled in the edge of the sea. It was icy cold, and bleached their feet, and strands of brown and green seaweed tangled themselves round their toes. Marius had rolled up the legs of his trousers, and she laughed at him and told him he only needed a handkerchief knotted at the four corners on his head.

'I've seen those postcards,' said Marius severely. 'The man with the handkerchief and the rolled trousers always has a very fat lady companion.'

'I'm not fat,' she said indignantly. She stooped and picked a tightly tangled mess of brown strands out of the water. 'This is called "Mermaid's hair", did you know?'

He took it from her and stretched out the dark stringy tendrils. 'And I thought mermaids were beautiful and had long, blonde hair.' He dropped it back into the water, where it floated, more beautiful in its element than out of it.

For some reason, it made Libby think of drowned Ophelia, or Millais' painting of her, with her long locks floating in the water. She shivered, and put her arm round Marius's waist.

He draped his arm round her shoulders, and they walked slowly down the shore. 'You had no difficulty getting away?'

'It was all right, although I suppose Miss Biddle saw me. She saw us the other day, as I told you, and she's been trying to quiz me about you. I said you were Czech; do you mind? I wanted to throw her off course.'

'*Děkuju Vám pěkne*,' Marius said politely. 'If I'm called upon to say no more than "Thank you very much," I shall pass muster.'

They made their way up the stony beach to the turf, hopping over sharp shingle, and sat down to let their feet dry in the warm air. Marius lay back and stretched out one arm and she lay down beside him, nestling her head on his shoulder. The sun shone on their faces, warm and peaceful.

'We might not be able to meet much more,' Marius said quietly.

Libby felt a little stab at her heart. The armour of her love was less perfect than she had thought. It was sadly vulnerable to some attacks. She began to feel uneasy because she sensed an uneasiness in him. All that afternoon, even when he had been laughing, his eyes had remained serious.

'I'll send Tommy again, if I can get away,' he went on. 'He's reliable.'

'He's taken a liking to you. I wish . . .' she paused. 'I wish we didn't need to hide. It makes it look as though we're doing something wrong, and we're not. It's right, I feel it inside my heart.'

'Other people might not agree.' He turned his head to look at her. 'I want you to promise me something.'

'What is it?' she asked uneasily.

'You're young and you're beautiful, but you'll grow old one day. Don't grow old alone.'

'I can't marry James, if that's what you mean.'

'Then marry someone else. That's all.' He turned his head back, to stare up into the sky.

'They shall not grow old, as we that are left grow old . . .' The words of Laurence Binyon's poignant epitaph on the battlefields of the Great War drifted into her head, with a meaning they had not held for her before. Marius was one of those destined not to grow old. He would be forever young. This moment, here on the shore, would live for ever in her memory, just as it was, because there was no future for them together. Their future was as empty and unmarked as that clear blue sky above, and nothing would ever be written on it. She would never see him age. They would never have children and watch them grow. That strong, muscular body would never grow weaker or gain wrinkles. Those whom the gods love, die young, said the Greeks. They die in the full flower of their manhood, young, virile, perfect.

'I shall have grey hair and false teeth,' she said aloud, 'and wear sensible clothes like Aunt Jennie. And keep dogs or cats. Or both.'

'I'm allergic to cats,' said Marius unexpectedly. 'They make me sneeze.'

'You will always be with me,' she said almost inaudibly. 'You'll never leave me.'

Jamie squinted at his wristwatch in the moonlight. His man would be on time. They always were. A date with possible sudden death, and they kept it to the second. They never tried to prolong the departure. Sometimes they almost seemed in a hurry. Beside him, Mike whistled softly between his teeth because he was nervous and, like Jamie, hated the moment when they first set eyes on their passenger.

Jamie moved away from the large bulky form of the Halifax on the tarmac, out into the silver-lit night. His fingers fumbled for his cigarettes and, as he found them, he heard the approaching steps and saw the two black silhouettes appearing and looking sinister against the grey background. That was their man, on the right, his head tilted slightly as he listened to his last-minute instructions. Jamie put the cigarette between his lips and took out his matches.

They had almost reached him, still talking together in low, urgent voices. Radio operator? thought Jamie, speculating idly. Resistance co-ordinator? No, saboteur. Explosives expert. There was something about the quick, neat, sure movements of the man's hands as he gesticulated in answer to some query.

The saboteurs were a race apart. There was a curious hesitancy about even mentioning them. They had no nerves, they were highly skilled, with brains like precision instruments, dedicated and ruthless. Their business was destruction, and they went about it with a thoroughness which tolerated not the slightest error. Yet in a way, because their targets were often roads, bridges, railway lines or installations, their war was waged less against men than against metal and concrete. Men got killed, of course. That's what war is about. The saboteur, primed like a living grenade, was dropped on the unsuspecting enemy to wreak havoc.

Jamie struck his match, not for a cigarette, too late now, but because he was curious to see the Joe. It flared up, and the yellow glare fell on their passenger's face as he stood before Jamie on the runway. The illuminated features smiled at him in recognition.

'Good evening, Flight-Lieutenant,' he said politely.

'Hullo, Velden,' Jamie said wearily. 'I thought it might be you.'

'It's all right,' Marius told him gently, as if he, Jamie, were the one to be encouraged and reassured. 'It's all right. I'm going home, you see.'

They didn't speak again. They had had a relatively peaceful flight. A little flak over the coast, nothing much. Privately, Jamie would have preferred a hotter reception. This way, it was almost as if they were inviting him in, holding open the door and waiting. Mike tapped his arm and pointed below to where the yellow lights of signalling torches suddenly showed. The men on the ground had heard the drone of the engine. Now everything turned on split-second timing. Other people, less well disposed, might see those lights.

Almost without warning, it seemed the moment had come. And almost before he could take account of it, their passenger had left them, and was a dark shape floating earthwards.

The plane banked and peeled away. Mike heaved a deep breath. 'Right, he's away. Good luck to him. Now *we* can make for ruddy home as well. England, Home and Beauty, here we come!'

CHAPTER SEVEN

FOR THE next couple of days, Libby waited for Tommy to bring another message. When he didn't, she sought him out and asked him if he had seen Marius. Tommy hadn't.

The cold hand of fear laid hold of her heart. With it came a cruel certainty: the message would never come. But she had to know. Jamie was mooching about in the gardens, the dogs at his heels. He had been avoiding her these past two days. She had not paid too much attention to it, but now it seemed suspiciously obvious. She followed him down a path between neat rows of vegetables, and faced him across the smouldering remains of the bonfire. The dogs were rooting happily in the bank, scenting rabbits.

She didn't enquire whether he had seen Marius, or if he knew anything. She just asked, very quietly, 'He's never coming back, is he?'

Jamie reddened, but did not try and pretend he had misunderstood. In a way, he was relieved that she had broached the subject. All the same, when he wanted to answer her, he stumbled over the words, afraid to look into her clear blue eyes. The words stuck in his throat.

'Some of them are lucky,' he mumbled. He tossed a piece of dry cabbage stalk on the bonfire, which was a mistake, because it singed and emitted a pungent and unpleasant odour.

'No,' she shook her head. 'Tell me the truth. I won't cry or have hysterics, and I won't blab, either.'

Jamie looked up with haunted eyes. 'These cloak-and-dagger fellows, once they get out into the field, they generally don't last long. He may have been given carte blanche to take out whatever objectives he can before he's picked up. But my guess, and it's only a guess, is that he's been sent in to take out a specific target. Whether he's successful or not, once he's tried, they—the Germans—will know he's there. There will be a terrific hue and cry. Waffen-SS all over the place, sniffer dogs, the lot. Anyone who hides him . . .' His voice trailed away.

Libby looked down at her hands, which she had been twisting tightly together. 'Thank you,' she said in a subdued voice. It was a funny thing to say, in view of his words. But what she meant was: Thank you for being honest, and trusting me.

Jamie understood her. 'He's a very brave man,' he said soberly.

'Yes, I know.'

What she knew was that this was not just a hero, but a man she loved. Someone she had held in her arms, if only briefly, and to whom she had been joined in the flesh, not two beings, but one. Now and for all time. She could recall every inch of that naked body, feel on her damp palms the softness of his skin and the firmness of the muscles, the beat of his heart pressed against hers. She remembered every line on his face, the way his hair fell forward over his forehead. He would indeed never leave her.

Without warning, despite what she had told Jamie, she turned and ran blindly down the path. She could not go into the house, and found herself out in the lane. Blessedly, it was empty. She thrust her clenched fist against her mouth to stop herself screaming.

'It isn't fair!' she muttered. 'It's so soon, too soon. We hardly met. We had no chance at all.' But she knew that this was what he had been trying to tell her at that last shoreline meeting. He had been hinting, as best he could, that the hour had come. He was flying out. He couldn't tell her that, but he could try and prepare her as best he could. At the same time, he had wanted to reassure her, talking of sending a message by Tommy, so that she would not be frightened. Secretly she had known it, too. She had known that she had to remember that moment, to print it on her memory. Her mind would not accept it, but in her subconscious she had bade him a kind of farewell.

Suddenly she became aware that she was not alone in the lane. A small, untidy, dogged little figure was sitting on the grass verge beside the gatepost, patiently waiting for her to notice him.

'Tommy?' she whispered, and he got up and came towards her. Before her he stopped, serious, defiant, worried. He was holding a battered flat tin box that had once held shortbread, with a picture of Edinburgh Castle on it.

Libby asked weakly, 'Would you like to come in and have a cup of coffee and a biscuit?'

'All right,' he said graciously, as a ruler granting audience.

It was Mrs Hills's day off. Libby led the boy into the kitchen and made coffee for them both, glad to have something to do. Her hands shook as she stirred the cups. Real coffee was hard to get and kept for special occasions, so it was Camp coffee from a bottle. Tommy liked the picture, the Highland officer and the Indian syce. He studied it carefully and put the bottle down in front of him, so that he could keep an eye on it. She put down the cups, and sat down opposite him across the scrubbed deal table. He dunked his digestive biscuit in his coffee and watched the bits break off to form islands and float round the top.

'What's wrong, Tom?' She tried to sound nonchalant.

'I was waiting for you, by your gate, because I didn't want to see the other bloke.'

He meant Jamie, and even Tommy called it a gate, although it wasn't there. They all did. There's probably a psychological explanation for that, Libby thought irrelevantly. The gate has gone, but we know it ought to be there, so we talk about it as though it were.

'Sometimes I climb that tree by your gate and watch you all,' Tommy said. 'You don't know!'

'You ought not to eavesdrop!' she said crossly, but then added, 'You get really good conkers off that tree in autumn. Just wait a few weeks.'

Tommy had not come to talk about conkers. He put his biscuit tin on the table, and hesitated. 'If I show you this, you won't tell no one?' He glared at her suspiciously.

'Cross my heart,' she promised, doing so.

He opened it carefully. It held a curious miscellany of things. 'He give me some of this.'

'James did?' she was puzzled. 'The flight-lieutenant?'

'*No!*' Tommy said scornfully. Trust a woman to get it wrong! 'The other one, Marius.'

Libby said, 'Oh.'

'This 'ere,' said Tommy, taking out a notebook, 'is where I makes my scientific observations, like he showed mc. This 'ere is a dead snake, well, not a snake 'xactly.' Tommy made an effort for scientific accuracy. 'Only its skin. They take them off when they get big, and underneath they got a new one. That's heather. I'm to write down if I have any luck, only I haven't had, so I reckon that proves it don't bring you any. Scientific and all.'

Libby stared down at Tommy's precious hoard as it was spread out on the kitchen table, every piece a link with Marius. She coveted it.

'*He* had a piece of heather and all, but I don't know if it brought him any luck.' Tommy stared straight at her. 'Is he coming back?'

'I don't know, Tom,' she said quietly. 'Sometimes, you know, in wartime, people don't.'

'I thought you'd know,' the boy said, 'because he liked you.'

'I—liked him. I'd like him to come back. If he . . . if he ever does, I'll tell you, I promise.'

Tommy was putting everything back in the tin. Over the piece of heather he hesitated. Then he picked it up with grubby fingers and held it out to her. 'You can have that if you want. It ain't no good.'

She took it gently. 'Thank you, Tom. Thank you very much. I'll keep it very, very safe.'

'Might bring you more luck than me. Some people is born lucky, my gran used to say. I got to go.' He scrambled down from his chair, his tin box under his arm. 'Thanks for the coffee, and when you've finished with that bottle, I'd like it, if you don't want it, or just the picture. It'll come off it you soak it in water. Mrs Evans does that with jam-jar labels.'

He vanished with disconcerting speed, leaving Libby alone in the kitchen, holding a piece of dry heather.

For forty-eight hours Libby remained in a daze. She supposed it was a kind of shell-shock. Then she began to think about Marius, and ask herself what he was doing, and where he was and if he was safe, and the 'ifs' piled up until there were so many of them that her head rang with unanswered and unanswerable questions.

When the forty-eight hours were up, she gave herself a shake, and said severely, 'If you don't know the answers, you had better do something about finding them out, my girl.'

Oddly enough, the first person in the chain of discovery was Mrs Daventry. Libby cornered her when she arrived home that weekend.

'Aunt Jennie? Can I have a word, kind of official?'

'Evacuees . . .' said Mrs Daventry briskly. 'You can't be doing with any more. I understand. Don't worry, I'll get the message across.'

Libby shook her head. 'No, not that. You—You have a lot of contacts, don't you? I want to get hold of a Count van Malderen, who is a Belgian in exile, and living in London. He's quite an important man and I'm sure he's active in some political sphere or other. I'd like to go and see him.'

Mrs Daventry looked faintly puzzled, but was used to coping with whatever problem arose. 'I'll see what I can do. How soon do you need to see him?'

'As soon as possible,' Libby said firmly.

Mrs Daventry scratched her scalp with the end of a pencil, disarranging what little hairstyle she had left, and said 'Um . . .'

Trust Aunt Jennie, though, she was reliable, and a born organiser, especially of other people. Early the following week, Libby found herself sitting in the train and chugging up to London.

Smoke from the engine billowed past the windows and made it difficult to see out through the small aperture in the protective netting stuck to the glass. She had brought a book, one of her favourite detective stories, but it seemed artificial and unreal compared with the real-life adventure on which she was embarking. She closed it and thrust it into her bag, and leaned back with her eyes closed, rehearsing over and over again in her head what she was going to say. They might just tell her to go away and not be silly. They would find she was not so easily got rid of!

She had not known what to expect. The house was eminently respectable, in Belgravia, whitewashed and with scrubbed steps. The railings had been taken for the war effort and tape criss-crossed the windows, otherwise it looked rather like a high-class doctor's surgery. She hesitated at the foot of the steps, just as if she were about to consult a practitioner about some disreputable affliction. When she finally summoned courage, darted up the steps and rang the bell, she was admitted by an elderly woman in an apron who led her down an echoing hall to a room at the rear of the house. The woman knocked, opened the door and left, so that Libby was obliged to walk in unannounced, though, she knew, not unexpected.

The man who rose courteously to meet her was middle-aged, but still good-looking. He had thick grey hair, which grew in a disturbingly familiar fashion, and his stocky frame moved towards her in a manner which set her heart pounding even more painfully than it had been doing.

He said politely, and with very little accent, 'Good morning, Miss Sherwood. I hope you had a pleasant journey here?'

She mumbled something and took the chair he indicated.

'You would like some coffee, no doubt?' He reached out and pressed a bell-push. Then he sat back, and placed the tips of his fingers together, steeple-fashion. 'And what may I do for you?' His eyes watched her, not unkindly, but carefully.

She said stiffly, 'I'm a friend of Marius.'

His eyes narrowed slightly, and took her in more shrewdly, but he didn't reply. He only nodded and waited.

'My name is Libby Sherwood,' she went on. 'I'm a Canadian citizen, and I'm twenty-two. I was educated in France and I'm bilingual—I could pass for French, or French-speaking Belgian, without any trouble. I'm perfectly fit and healthy and I don't panic. I want to help.'

'Do you?' he asked softly.

'Yes.' She met his gaze steadily. 'I've come to you, because I don't know any other way of doing it. No, that's not quite true. I could have asked Mrs Daventry to talk to someone on my behalf, but I'd rather not involve my family directly. It—would be better if they didn't know.'

'Yes,' he agreed, 'it would. I am not, of course, the person to whom you should be talking. However, perhaps you would permit me to offer a little advice?'

The door opened and the woman with the apron brought in coffee. She seemed of a silent disposition, setting it down and retiring without a word. The smell of the coffee struck Libby's nostrils.

'It is not a game,' he said gently.

Libby flushed. 'I know that.'

'I wonder if you do.' He pointed at her bag on the floor by her chair. The detective novel was sticking out of it. 'It is not, as in such books, conveniently sorted out in the last chapter. The good do not always triumph. The bad are often successful. There are no rules. No one comes to you with information, or, if they do, that person is to be mistrusted. You may find yourself alone, frightened and injured. You may be betrayed. You cannot change your mind. You cannot turn round and simply come home.'

'I've thought about all that,' she said steadily. 'I've taken it all into consideration. I'm not playing the role of a heroine in a book. I tried to read that novel on the train, and I couldn't. I realised how unlike reality it was. I don't want to escape into a pretend world. I want to be in the real one.'

He said 'Ah . . .,' leaned forward, and passed her a cup of coffee. 'Do you take sugar?' She shook her head. 'I used to,' he said regretfully, 'but with rationing, I have learned to do without. Tell me, from whom did you have my name? From Marius?'

'Yes,' she said steadily, 'from your son.' He looked up sharply, and she added quickly, 'No, he didn't tell me, but just looking at you . . . You're so alike.'

He gave a rueful smile. 'That is a pity, perhaps. You say you are a friend of Marius. You know him, perhaps, very well?'

'Only for a short time. But I *think* I know him well. I'm sorry if that sounds arrogant.'

'No,' he said, 'only young.'

They drank the coffee in silence. He was obviously deep in thought and she did not dare to disturb him. He was making up his mind, and he was not the sort of man to change it. If he decided that she was just a lovesick girl with a head full of dreams of adventure, that would be that. He put down his cup carefully, and she held her breath.

'Come and see me again,' he said. 'I shall telephone you. Leave me a number.'

There was nothing to do but go home and wait, so Libby did just that. They would either contact her, or not. 'If a person comes to you, that person is to be mistrusted'—that's what he had said. It followed from that, that they might very well mistrust her. She fidgeted about the house and her office and tried to concentrate on her work, but it was almost impossible. That was partly why the next thing that happened took her so completely by surprise.

Afterwards, with the gift of hindsight, she could see that it was always going to happen and she should have realised it. They all should. But she had been wrapped up in herself, and her plans, and in worrying about Marius. More fundamentally, she had simply not understood Jamie as well as she had claimed to Marius. Marius had warned her about that, and she should have listened to him.

As it was, when Jamie started to cry, which was the beginning of it, they were all taken completely aback. He started in the middle of dinner. It was the usual disastrous meal. They had been given some trout, but Mrs Hills had contrived to turn the fish into strips of flannel.

'How anyone can ruin trout . . .' Jennie Daventry said resignedly.

And Jamie began to weep, very quietly, in a private sort of way, to himself. For a moment they just stared at him in horror and dismay. Libby even thought mistakenly, for a second or two, that he was laughing. It was when he put his hands over his face, and the tears oozed out between his fingers, that she finally realised the truth.

His father was the first to understand what was actually happening. Perhaps he, alone of them all, had waited for this. He got up and moved awkwardly round the table, still clutching his napkin in his right hand, and put his left on his son's shoulder, murmuring, 'It's all right, old chap, we'll take care of it.'

Over his son's bowed head, his eyes met Libby's frozen face, and he ordered crisply, 'Go and phone Greaves and tell him to come over, double quick.'

Nervous breakdown is an illness, but you can't describe it to people as you can other illnesses. So Libby ruminated, as she trudged towards the garage to get out the Riley. The air buffeted her face. There was a nasty wind. It was an autumnish day. Dry leaves crunched under her feet and there were rain-clouds hovering on the horizon, sulking. She dragged open the doors and wedged them. It isn't like flu or lumbago. You can tell people about those afflictions, and they say, 'Oh, yes', and happily begin to tell you about when *they* had it, and what *they* did for it. There's an end, as the Bard put it. But not with nervous breakdown. You can't see it. The sufferer doesn't come out in a recognisable rash, or even necessarily look pale and wan. Jamie looked much as he always had done, a picture of health, even in a hospital dressing-gown.

She had tried telling kind enquirers what ailed

him, and they only looked bewildered, and asked, 'But what is actually wrong with him?' as though they couldn't imagine an illness without a temperature or aches and pains. Some comments were extraordinary. They ranged from the brutal and stupid, 'He must pull himself together'—as if poor Jamie wouldn't like to do that, if he could—right down to a whispered, 'Is it in the family?' as if he had gone mad.

Miss Biddle had come to the Red Cross hut expressly to ask after him, and to say, smiling spitefully down at Libby, 'I dare say the poor boy took it very hard, you giving him up for that Czech.'

The awful thing was, Libby was haunted by the possibility that she had contributed directly to Jamie's condition. Miss Biddle's words hit hard. At the very least, she ought to have seen what was happening to him, but she had thought of nothing but herself and Marius. How could I have been so selfish? she reproached herself.

She did not like hospitals of any kind at any time. She hated the sweet-sour smell of disinfectant and the polished floors, the clinical white linen and the notices requesting silence. She and Gerry Daventry both moved awkwardly, he breathing heavily, and looking far from well, more as though he ought to be a patient, not a visitor. They clasped flowers and fruit from the garden, and Libby's shoes squeaked noisily on the linoleum.

Jamie was in his dressing-gown, but sitting by a window, and staring out at the whirling leaves picked up by the freakish wind and tossed high in dusty clouds. He looked very young, and very vulnerable.

He said, 'Thanks for coming to see me,' and fidgeted in his chair.

Libby thought, I don't think he wants to see us at all, really. He thinks he's failed us. He's embarrassed. She took his hand and tried to cheer him with tales of the latest antics of the evacuees. He smiled dutifully, but only with his mouth. His eyes roamed around the room, as if searching for something. Once or twice they looked vague, and she knew he had not been listening, and had lost the thread of her narrative.

His father, meaning well but misunderstanding, thought that Jamie wanted to talk to Libby alone, and, after a few minutes, mumbled something about checking that the car was not parked in the way, and lumbered out. Uncle Gerry would get it wrong, all with the best intentions, thought Libby.

Now that they were alone, however, Jamie seemed to stir and to have something of his own that he wanted to say. She asked him if he needed anything they could send, or bring next time. But he leaned forward, ignoring her question, and blurted out, 'I'm sorry it had to be me. That I flew him in.'

'That wasn't your fault,' she said awkwardly. He still looked miserable, so she went on energetically, 'Look, it was what he wanted to do. He trained for that. You took him in safely, that was the best thing you could do. You helped him. You should be thanked for that, not blamed!'

'You don't blame me?' he asked, rather doubtfully.

'No, of course I don't!' Then she realised that he must know all about it, about her and Marius. She blushed, and added in some confusion, 'We didn't mean it to happen that way, you know. It just did. We didn't mean to hurt you, Jamie, and I'm so sorry if we did.'

'It's all right,' he said. 'You were never that keen on me, not in that way, so sooner or later you were always going to meet someone else. It might have been better if it hadn't been him, but I ought not to say that. He's everything I'm not, I suppose. Perhaps I'm jealous of that, not of the fact that you fell in love with him.'

'How can you say such a thing?' she cried. She seized his hands, and shook them. 'Jamie, you're not well, and you're feeling down, but it's temporary and you'll get better. You have nothing to be ashamed of. You are also very brave, and have done your duty. No one can help being ill.'

'I'm not ill,' he said stubbornly. 'I've cracked up inside. I'm useless.'

'Rubbish!' she stormed at him.

'They have fellows in this place who have gone completely off their rockers,' Jamie said calmly. 'Sometimes at night I hear them laughing, or crying. I don't sleep much.'

'I'll tell the nurse.'

He shook his head. 'No. They come along with pills. I don't want to go to sleep. I have this fear that I might not wake up. Sometimes, though, I think it might be good to go to sleep and not wake up.'

'Jamie,' she said urgently, 'you are sick. But you will get better. You must believe you will get better.'

'I suppose so,' he said, 'but I'll always be suspect. They will always look at me, and think, he might do it again. They'll ground me, of course. I shall sit out the war behind an office desk. Meanwhile, over there, your friend Marius is virtually taking on the Third Reich all by himself. It must be nice not to have any doubts.'

'Marius has his doubts,' she said. 'He wouldn't

talk about them, but he has them, I'm sure of it. He's not superhuman. He is really very human.'

'Hope he comes back,' Jamie said.

She was spared having to find an answer to that one. The door swung noiselessly in the way of hospital doors, letting in a draught and a distant clatter. Libby thought it would be Gerry Daventry, but it wasn't. It was Evangeline Watts.

Jamie looked up and said in quite a different voice, 'Oh, hullo, Eva. There you are.'

'Here I am!' announced Evangeline, bouncing in cheerfully. 'I'll sit on the bed, if you don't mind. Not on a chair. I've got a bruised backside. Sabre threw me, rotten animal.'

'Whoever calls a horse Sabre, for crying out loud?' Jamie asked her seriously.

'He's got ruddy great teeth. If you saw them, you wouldn't ask.' She leaned forward and dug Jamie in the ribs. 'How are you doing?'

'Bloody awful,' Jamie said, and smiled wanly.

Libby got up. She had recovered from her initial shock, and now felt angry. Evangeline behaved as though Libby just weren't there. She said starchily, 'Could I have a word, Eva? Just for a minute. You'll excuse us, won't you, Jamie?'

Outside in the corridor, she demanded furiously, 'What are you doing here, Eva? The last thing he needs is you bounding about, making familiar remarks and flashing your underwear.'

'Honestly,' Evangeline replied, not in the least offended, 'I know you're a lot cleverer than I am, and all that. I mean, people usually say I'm dim. I am pretty dim in most things. But I'm brighter than you in one way, at least. Of course he needs me. He's always got to pretend with you. You make him feel he's got to live up to expectations or something. You and his father and that frightful mother of his. The poor bloke isn't perfect, you know. Neither am I. He doesn't have to pretend with me. I just accept him the way he is.'

Libby stared at her. She wanted to deny it angrily, but even as she opened her mouth, she recalled Jamie's face when Evangeline had entered, and the expression of relief in his eyes.

'Anyway,' said Evangeline in practical tones, 'it was all arranged while you were fooling about with that Belgian. I mean, anyone could see poor old James was falling apart.'

'They could?' Libby whispered. 'I didn't.'

'Bless your cotton socks, of course you didn't. Never bothered to look. But I did. So I told him, then, I'd look after him and,' finished Evangeline with a slightly pugnacious expression entering her features, 'I'm jolly well going to do so, so there.'

Libby walked out of the hospital and towards the car park. She moved as slowly as possible, but she still met Gerard before she had worked out what to say. He was ambling along, with his hands in his pockets, his expression dogged and frowning. He looked for all the world as if he was debating how to present the case for the defence.

'I came away,' Libby said, meeting his enquiring gaze, 'because Evangeline is there. It's all right . . .' she added hastily, marking his open dismay. 'He was pleased to see her. I think we've all got to get used to Evangeline.'

'Heaven forbid!' Gerard burst out angrily.

'Heaven doesn't interfere. Free will and all that. Uncle Gerry, I may have to go away. Not yet, but eventually. This seems a funny time to tell you. Don't ask me about it.'

He hardly seemed to have heard her. 'The sooner James is out of that hospital and home, the better,' he said vehemently.

But he'd lost the battle, and he knew it. All the love in him had belonged to his son. Yet, for that son, it wasn't enough. He turned away and walked off back to the car, looking smaller and older—a weak, elderly man.

'Let them send for me!' Libby prayed. 'Don't let them turn me down.'

CHAPTER EIGHT

MARIUS STRUGGLED out of his parachute harness, dragged in the silk, and bolted for the cover of nearby trees with it bundled in his arms. The drone of the aeroplane was already faint, as it headed back towards the coast. He hoped Jamie got home safely, and that Libby would at least have someone.

After that, he had no time to think about her. He plunged into the dark mass of trees, his feet sinking into the leafmould. There he paused, panting and listening. He was not really out of breath, just tense, which made normal breathing difficult. The sudden snap of a twig to his left caused him to hold his breath altogether and freeze into immobility. There came a low whistle and a voice called softly, 'Over here!'

Marius moved slowly in the required direction. Suddenly, as from nowhere, a darkly silhouetted figure emerged from the undergrowth and a light shone briefly in his eyes, blinding him. He threw up his arm to shield his face, and the torch was switched off again, leaving him in total blackness. Any alarm, however, was instantly dispelled by a chuckle and a familiar voice, which said, 'They've sent us *you*, have they? I was wondering when you would turn up.'

'Harry?' Marius tried to peer into the gloom.

His arm was grasped. 'Come on, time for reunions later! Let's get out of here. That plane will have been spotted, and they'll know he's dumped someone. Place will be swarming with grey uniforms in ten minutes.'

They plunged through the trees and out the other side, running, bent double, keeping to the shelter of hedges and bushes. Eventually, they came to a halt before a low dark building, and Marius sniffed the air. There were cattle nearby.

'This is Wouters' farm,' he whispered.

'Right. You can lie up here for a day or two. There's a hidey-hole up in the roof under the eaves.'

Marius followed his guide down to the farmhouse. A tap at the door led to their being admitted by a burly man, who peered at Marius in some surprise and exclaimed, 'It's you, is it, Mijnheer van Malderen?'

'Go to bed, Jan,' Harry said quickly. 'I'll get him upstairs and hidden away.'

When at last they were ensconced in the tiny living space constructed up in the eaves, they settled down uncomfortably, and Harry lit a cigarette.

'I'd offer you one, but I suppose you still don't smoke? You were always so keen on keeping fit.' He grinned. 'And look where it got you!'

'I need to be fit, to keep jumping out of blasted aircraft!' Marius moved awkwardly. 'How long am I to be shut up here? I hate cramped spaces.'

'What do you expect, a hotel?' Harry indicated the curtained-off gap in the wall behind him. 'Good view of the main approach to the farm, which is the way any vehicle would have to come. You can see anyone coming a full four minutes before he gets here. I've timed it.'

'What about the bridge?' Marius asked in a businesslike voice.

'You'll have to be a magician to make that disappear. That's my opinion. They guard it round the clock.' Harry reached up into a space above his head and dragged out a rolled sheet of paper. 'Fortunately, you are an engineer and I am an artist. This, if I say so myself, is a very accurate, not to say first-class, drawing of your target, and not unpleasing to the eye.' He spread it out on the floor between them and pushed the paraffin lamp towards it, so that its dull yellow glow fell across the paper.

Marius scowled at it, and then pointed. 'Here. That's where I need to fix the explosive. It will bring both piers down. We'll have to bring it up from below. Do they still sell picture postcards of the bridge area around here?'

'A few. I'll see what I can find. They flew in the necessary the other night, by the way, by Lysander, and we picked it up all right. It's hidden out in Jan's cowshed. The Germans could send dogs all over that place, and they wouldn't smell a thing for dung. Useful stuff, manure.' Harry paused. 'But things are getting difficult around here. It's nothing I can tell you of, nothing specific. It's a crawling feeling I get in the back of my neck. I feel as if they—they tolerate us, just giving us a little push from time to time to show who's boss, you know, like a cat plays with a mouse? I feel almost as if they are waiting to see just what we can do, and how we set about doing it, and when they think it's time, they'll pounce.'

'Are you trying to tell me I've been set up?'

'Hell, no, Marius! At least, not by *us*. Not at this end.' He shrugged. 'Maybe my nerves are just shot to pieces. Now you're here, I feel a whole lot better.'

Marius lay back against the wall. A scattering of claws nearby indicated he would have mice for company. He hoped he was not going to be shut up here for long. It was too much like that damn cupboard. He asked, with elaborate unconcern, 'How is everyone?'

Harry gave a brief account of mutual acquaintances, then, after a perceptible pause, added, 'Annette is living here at the moment, over at the old château.'

Marius stiffened. 'I thought she got away to Switzerland?'

'Change of plan. Her husband—you know she married, don't you?—well, he's doing good business with the Germans. Stinking collaborator. Never mind,' said Harry comfortably, 'we'll get him. Perhaps not tomorrow or the next day, but we'll get him.' He examined the glowing end of his cigarette. 'He's afraid to come down here himself, hides out in Brussels. He knows how we feel about him here.'

'What about Annette?'

Harry shrugged. 'As far as I know, she hates the sight of him. Nothing to do with his being a traitor. Just simple dislike. They have a sort of unofficial separation. She won't go to Brussels; he can't come here. She tried to get a divorce but he wasn't having it, and both families were horrified. They put the pressure on, and she had to give up the idea.'

Marius closed his eyes. 'Annette never gives up if she wants a thing.' It was a last, unwished complication, as if the situation were not bad enough. Annette here! Annette separated from her husband. Annette changed?

Harry, as if reading his mind, said, 'She's still in love with you, you know. She always was.'

'She wouldn't know the meaning of the word. You're a sentimentalist, Harry. She made a bad marriage and she wants to get out of it. That's nothing to do with me.'

'She's older, and wiser, and still good-looking. Whatever she did to you, Marius, it was four years ago. That's a hell of a long time, and she's sorry for it. It's a tough world where no one can ever make a mistake.'

'It's a tough world,' Marius said harshly.

'Be kind to her, Marius,' Harry said gently. He paused and added with a touch of resentment, 'You could at least have brought me some decent cigarettes!'

Libby had never felt so completely in limbo. There was no going back, and until—and unless—she received the telephone call from London, there was no going forward. Frustration gnawed at her and made her restless and impatient.

Miss Biddle watched her with a satisfied smirk. 'Gone off, has he, the Czech? That's the way of these foreign fellows. All promises one day, and gone off and left you the next.'

'Mind your own business,' said Libby wearily.

Even the matter of Jamie had been taken out of her competence. Turning that over in her mind, she realised that Jamie had guessed what effect Marius had on her from the first. Good grief, she thought, I must be pitifully transparent. What kind of agent would I make? Jamie, in their moonlit conversation on the staircase, had tried to warn her what she was getting into, but after that he had not tried again, nor, as she now realised, had he ever again tried to kiss her on the mouth. Jamie knew, she thought. Jamie knew before I did. Jamie understands me so much better than I ever understood him.

She hated the thought of him in the spotless clinical confines of the hospital, lying awake in the night, listening to the distant manic laughter of those for whom there was no hope. She and her Uncle Gerard began to agitate to get him home. In Gerard's natural wish to have his son under the family roof again was, no doubt, mingled a plot to exclude Evangeline. Considering all their motives with a new, cruel clarity, Libby thought: What we're really trying to do is to prove that we never really neglected him. To make up for our failure to see what was happening. To show that he doesn't need Evangeline more than he needs us. We say we are thinking of Jamie, but really we're thinking of ourselves.

Was poor Jamie now destined to be tugged back and forth between a guilt-ridden family which loved him, and the girl who, it seemed, would after all be his life's mate? They must not allow themselves to fight over Jamie like quarrelling hounds over a rabbit. It is the rabbit which is torn in two. 'Me Tarzan—You Jane', that's what mattered in the end. Jamie had surrendered her to Marius, albeit with a heavy heart. They must now surrender Jamie to Evangeline. Loving him meant letting him go.

Loving Marius meant the opposite. It meant never letting go. Never letting the obstinate flame of hope expire in her breast. Never letting a treacherous thought of failure enter her mind.

Whatever her own hopes and plans, life intruded in its insistent, mundane way. They all had to turn to and help bottle the runner beans for winter. It meant slicing up mountains of beans grown by Farley the gardener. Then great blocks of rock salt were laboriously crushed and the beans packed into jars, layer of beans, layer of salt, repeated until the jar was full. As a preserving method, it was not entirely successful, but it served well enough. Wasn't it the ancient Egyptians, thought Libby, hammering an awkward block of salt with a rolling-pin, who buried the bodies of their enemies with salt, to prevent decay and obstruct the release of the soul?

The call came on a Monday evening just after six o'clock. It was raining, and Libby had been to visit two host families, riding her bicycle, and becoming thoroughly drenched. A quarter of a mile from home, the chain slipped again, and although she had crouched in the mud, cursing the recalcitrant metal, she could not get it back, and broke her fingernails while water poured steadily from the overhead branches down the back of her neck. She was forced to trudge home, pushing the bicycle, cold, wet and thoroughly fed up. She left the bike in the garage and entered Merriton House through the kitchen, leaving her wet shoes in the outer scullery, and her dripping mackintosh to be dried by Mrs Hills.

'We could do with a drop of water,' said Farley, who sat in the kitchen by the Aga, drinking tea out of an enamel mug. 'No harm in a drop of water.' He nodded portentously at the streaming windowpane.

'You haven't been out in it,' muttered Libby fiercely, plodding across the stone-flagged floor in stockinged feet, leaving a trail of wet footprints like those patterns designed to teach the latest dance steps.

Farley's deafness was of the variable kind. 'Oh, ah, can't be digging in the wet. Can't get out there.'

Neither could he get out there when it was hot, dry, frosty, windy or had snowed. The number of days in the year when Farley could 'get out there' was limited. Most of his time was spent in Mrs Hills's kitchen, when she allowed him in—or in his potting-shed. There he fiddled about the earthenware pots, puffing happily on villainous Woodbines and reading the *News of the World*, occasionally aloud, with comments. 'Vicar and choirmistress e-lope. Oh, ah—hee hee!' Cough, cough. 'I forgive him, sez wife—' cough, cough '—be waiting for 'un with a rolling-pin, more like'—snigger, wheeze, clouds of smoke.

As Libby reached the hall on her way to take her regulation-permitted, two inches of water, bath, the telephone rang. She snatched it up and said crossly, 'Merriton House.'

'Miss Sherwood?' Van Malderen's careful, cultured tones echoed faintly down the line, touched with doubt.

'Oh, yes,' Libby pushed back a lock of wet hair. 'I'm sorry, I just got in, and it's raining.'

'I shall not detain you. I ring only to ask if you can come and take tea with me this Thursday. About three-thirty?'

'Yes . . .' She wanted to say more, but words deserted her.

'Very well. Till Thursday, then.'

She put down the receiver. At least they were going to take another look at her. She had not been rejected out of hand.

The train was very crowded, and had the smell of many damp bodies crushed together. A number of merchant seamen were on board, and their kit encumbered the corridors. Outside it was misty, and when she tried to read her newspaper, Libby found that it lurched about as the train rattled over the points, and gave up.

At Micheldever, a man got on and took the seat by her. He was forty-ish, with a moustache, and a pin-stripe suit, and pale, prominent eyes. His knee rested familiarly against hers.

'Going up to London for the day, shopping?' he asked affably.

Libby gave him a cool stare. 'No.'

'Oh, you live in London?'

'No.'

He was not deterred. One of the merchant seamen gave him a jaundiced look in which scorn was writ large.

'Mind if I borrow your paper?'

'Yes, do.' She passed it across thankfully. Perhaps now he would keep quiet.

But he didn't. He used it as a springboard for conversation. 'Not much war news.'

'Course there ain't, mate,' said the merchant seaman with derision. 'No point in telling everyone what you're doing and get blokes blown out of the water.'

'Careless talk costs lives!' said a lady in the corner sharply.

Her acquaintance changed tack. 'Not much fun for a pretty girl, these days.' He sneered at the lady in the corner. You look like the back of a bus, said his look, so it's not a problem for you. 'Difficult to get clothes, stockings, all that. Perfume, and so on.'

Possibly he was a black-marketeer, sounding out a possible customer. He had an attaché case at his feet, and for all she knew it was stuffed full of cigarettes and chocolate.

Libby did not deign to reply and stared out of the

window at the cotton-wool fog which had developed. He continued to make this one-sided conversation all the way to Waterloo. She had hoped, when she got to the station, to lose him, but he stuck to her side as she walked briskly down the platform.

'Care for a cup of coffee or something? Warm you up? Nasty day—touch of winter in the air.'

'No, thank you,' she said, 'and I really wish you would go away.'

'Don't be touchy. I don't mean anything. Just being friendly. Times like these, we don't have to be stand-offish.'

They had reached the barrier and she handed over her ticket. 'I'm being met, so there's no point in your hanging about.'

He smiled. He didn't believe her. He went to the news-stand and began ostentatiously to turn over magazines. Lord, what was she going to do? He obviously meant to wait for as long as it took for her lie to be shown for what it was.

Then, unexpectedly, she saw salvation. It came in the unlikely form of Colonel Watts. He was proceeding down the concourse, spine rigid as a ramrod, his shoes polished like mirrors and wearing a bowler hat. Eva's father had obviously come up to town the day before and spent the night at his club. He was on his way home. Libby ran to meet him.

'Oh, Colonel, there you are!' He looked startled, and she hissed, 'Please look as if you've come to meet me. I'm trying to get rid of someone.'

'What's that?' demanded Colonel Watts, grasping his brolly. 'Some blackguard makin' passes? Where is he? Damn impudence. Wouldn't have happened to a decent woman in my young day! Ruddy socialists!'

Libby turned. Her unwanted admirer had disappeared, melting into the crowds.

'He's gone,' she said with relief. 'Thanks, Colonel—sorry if I gave you a shock.'

'Glad to be of service, m'dear. Want me to escort you to wherever you're going? I can catch a later train.'

'Thank you for your offer, but it's all right now.'

'Hum,' he said. 'My girl says she's going to marry young Daventry.'

'I know.'

'Glad she's marrying someone,' he muttered. 'About time, too. How is the boy?'

'Doing as well as can be expected.'

'Bad show, bad show,' he muttered. 'Won't be fit enough for a guard-of-honour and marquee-on-the-lawn do, I suppose?'

'Lucky to get as far as the local register office, I think.'

'Save a bit of money,' said Colonel Watts, a practical man.

The episode had shaken Libby's confidence badly. It was such an ordinary, everyday occurrence, and not the first time someone had tried to pick her up. But she had not been able to handle it without the help of Colonel Watts. Across the Channel, she would not have a friendly face appearing unexpectedly to save her. As Count van Malderen had warned, she would be on her own. Supposing, travelling on a continental train, a similar thing occurred? And supposing the Colonel had insisted on accompanying her to van Malderen's doorstep? She must be utterly self-reliant, and had wanted to convince van Malderen that she was. Yet, at the first small test, she had failed.

When she reached the street where van Malderen lived, she received a further jolt to her peace of mind. The house at the end of the row was gone. Just gone. What had been a white-painted Victorian family residence was a levelled field of broken bricks. The end wall of the adjoining house was shored up by a cat's-cradle of buttressing timber beams.

'Incendiary,' said a woman walking past, pushing a wailing infant strapped in a perambulator. 'Burned out. They knocked the rest down because it was dangerous. Stop grizzling, Rosemary.'

Libby hurried along the row of houses, but the one she sought was untouched. Had the Angel of Death simply spared this one as at the Passover, because righteousness dwelt in it? Was it just a matter of luck? She could equally well have arrived to find this one flattened.

Count van Malderen was not alone. He was accompanied by a small, spare, middle-aged man in a pre-war brown suit. He had a bald head which shone as if it were polished walnut, and eyes like two bright buttons.

'Mr Smith,' said Count van Malderen gravely.

They shook hands. 'Good of you to come, Miss Sherwood,' said Mr Smith. 'Trains all at sixes and sevens these days.'

Libby mumbled something about it being a good journey, adding that she was sorry about the incendiary at the end of the street.

'Why?' asked Mr Smith disconcertingly. 'Not your fault.'

'No,' she said lamely. It occurred to her that she would do best to say nothing at all. She had dressed very carefully in a Harris tweed costume and sensible shoes, in the style of Aunt Jennie. She wanted to look reliable. But she was wearing a precious new pair of silk stockings she had been keeping for a special occasion. This was it.

Mr Smith's bright little marmoset's eyes twinkled at her. 'I was briefly in Canada before the war. Toronto.'

They made desultory conversation as the tea arrived, brought by the same, dour, competent woman.

'I believe your father founded one of North America's largest passenger-carrying air companies.'

Libby started. She had not told van Malderen this. They had done their homework and researched her background. They probably knew all there was to know about her. It was an uncomfortable thought.

'Dad always loved aeroplanes,' she said. 'He was a pilot in the last war.'

Mr Smith knew that. He was nodding. 'Yes. Army man myself, but I've spoken with people who knew your father.'

Some kind of signal, unrecognised by her, must have passed between the two men. Van Malderen rose to his feet and murmured, 'You will excuse me . . .'

When he had gone out, Mr Smith stood up, put his hands behind his back and proceeded to the window. 'Whatever I say to you, Miss Sherwood, must not, of course, be repeated outside this room.'

'Of course not. I do understand,' she said, faintly resentful.

Disconcerting her again, he began to hum, '"Take a pair of sparkling eyes . . ." I'm fond of G and S,' he said apologetically.

G and S? She sought frantically for a clue to the

initials. Gilbert and Sullivan, of course. 'I've only ever seen *The Mikado*,' she confessed, afraid, although it seemed crazy, that this admission might somehow bar her from a career in espionage.

'"I'm the Lord High Executioner . . ."' carolled Mr Smith softly. He swung round to fix her with his bright gaze. 'I am, too, in my way. But I don't like losing agents. We don't aim to lose 'em. But it's a risky business, and if you think you might like to try your hand at it, you have to understand that.'

'Yes, sir,' Libby said obediently.

'Hm. Women agents are useful. In some cases they're a distinct advantage. The Germans are less suspicious of women. *Kinder, Kirche, Kueche*, you know—Children, church and kitchen. They expect women to be at home, breeding the master-race, not facing them as active opponents. Besides, any young man travelling in occupied territory is likely to be stopped and asked automatically why he's wandering around. So many have been taken away for forced labour, you see.'

'I see.'

'Right. We'll get you down to one of our training bases and see what you can do. Officially, you're doing clerical work—tell your family and friends that. No one, repeat no one, is to be told what you're really up to!' He glared at her fiercely.

'No, sir.'

'Hm,' he said again. 'Might have to rush through your training a little. But you look fit. Things are hotting up over there and we've had a few losses recently. Need replacements.'

He was certainly spelling it out, Libby thought ruefully. He wanted her to understand just how dangerous and possibly short-lived a business it was.

'I can leave for the training base straight away,' she said.

Her basic training was certainly taken through at a brisk pace, the normal period halved, and she was allowed none of the—as she afterwards learned—usual initial time to settle in. In at the deep end, seemed to be Mr Smith's attitude towards her, and she quickly learned to shut up and listen.

'Firearms . . .' began the relevant instructor.

'I can fire a gun,' she offered brightly, interrupting. 'My father taught me . . . I'll be all right if I have to fire the gun I shall be carrying.'

Frozen horror crossed the face of her controller. 'Carrying?—*Carrying a gun?* Are you out of your mind? Do you think you won't ever be stopped and searched? How do you propose explaining a concealed firearm to the Germans? You will not—*not*—carry a gun! You may, however, find yourself required to operate an automatic weapon in, for example, an ambush situation.'

'Ambush situation' sounded distinctly unpleasant. 'How am I supposed to defend myself at other times?' she asked rather snappishly.

He stared at her. 'Got hands and feet, haven't you?'

So that was how she found herself in the gym, facing, across a none-too-well-padded mat, an army unarmed combat instructor who, if he could not have doubled as Tarzan, could certainly have turned in a fair performance as one of the apes. He had a shaven bullet head, a broken nose and missing teeth. Hair grew profusely, not only under his arms, but all over them, across his chest and shoulders, and as far as a sweaty singlet revealed, all down his back.

Libby speculated idly about the rest of him. He leered at her unpleasantly.

'Right. I'm attacking you, see? Like this . . .' He moved like lightning and put a stranglehold on her neck. Libby saw stars and choked. Through them, she heard his voice ask, 'What you going to do about it, then? Hurry up! If this was real, you'd be dead by now.'

Libby tried jabbing an elbow in his stomach, but it was like jabbing at cast-iron. She tried stamping on his feet and kicking his shins, all with futility. He released her before she blacked out completely.

'Oh, Gawd . . .' he said resignedly, as she sat on the mat, gasping for breath.

His open scorn stung her to scramble up and snarl, 'Well, if I don't know, *tell* me what to do!'

He smiled sadistically. 'Attack *me*.'

'What?' She peered at him mistrustfully.

'Go on, have a go! See what damage you can do.'

Libby circled warily round behind him, and his bloodshot eye rolled round in its socket, watching her contemptuously. She had not the faintest idea how to attack anyone with her bare hands, and unwisely attempted to use against him the move he had used against her.

The world turned upside-down, there was a shattering crash, and every bone in her body jumped loose—or that was what it felt like. She stared up at him from the mat.

'Try again,' he invited. 'Only you got to learn you won't get any second chances, see? Not like I'm giving you now, on account I'm a kindly soul, see?'

'Like hell . . .' thought Libby, struggling to her feet once more. He clicked his tongue sorrowfully and held out his hand to help her. She took it, and found herself back on the mat again, sprawled inelegantly, and with bruises rapidly forming on the bruises she already had.

His battered face leered down at her. 'And another thing you got to learn: You haven't got any friends. Remember that. You ain't got *any* friends. No one is going to help you—and anyone who offers to, well, if you can't do anything else, kick him in the goolies and run.'

'And that,' thought Libby, 'is what I'd like to do to you.' But she didn't do it, because by now she firmly believed he would quite happily murder her.

Despite all this, they made progress. Every night she crawled into bed wanting to die, and every morning she crept out from the sheets, gasping with pain. But they made progress.

The last time she ever saw him, at the close of their final violent session together, he leaned forward and urged, 'Now you remember everything what I taught you! Never mind what your old mum taught you—you forget all that. You remember what *I* taught you, see?' He glowered at her, and for the first time the naked sadism in his face was replaced by concern, and she realised with surprise, and even with some amusement, that he was quite worried for her.

Other necessary skills were rushed through, but fortunately, she was not entirely a novice, being already familiar with Morse code, if rather out of practice since girl scout days, and handy at reading a map. Committing a map to memory, however, was something else. 'Anyone can read a bloody map,' said the instructor. 'You have to see it, up here . . .' He tapped his forehead.

However, in one skill she proved surprisingly

adept, the all-important parachute jump. She was fit and naturally athletic, and unafraid of heights, not hesitating to leap off a beam high above the floor while trusting to a frail-looking harness. Above all, she was used to aeroplanes, and knew their limitations and their possibilities, the problems of the pilot and his navigator, and hence the significance of her instructions. This was because, as she explained to her instructor rather diffidently, her father owned an air company, and she had been around aircraft all her life.

The instructor said, 'Oh, yes? How many planes has he got, then?' obviously under the impression that she meant her father operated two or three ramshackle second-hand transporters over short-haul trips. When she told him, she had the satisfaction of seeing, for the first time ever, someone's jaw literally drop. His mouth fell open, his face paled, and he gasped, 'Blimey!' His next question was an incredulous, ''Ere, does he know what you're about?'

'No,' confessed Libby. 'But I think he'd understand.'

'I hope nothing happens to you,' said her instructor gloomily. 'I'll have the Canadian government on my neck, I can see it. Still, I'll say this for you—you are one of the best I've had through here.'

Libby treasured this compliment with forgivable pride. Between achievement and failure, she continued to progress, and every day brought her nearer to her goal. The thought drove her on. It took pain away from aching limbs and bruises, and it dulled the humiliation from scornful instructors, because all these things, the progress and the failure worked to one end.

To that one end her life now was totally dedicated: to that night-time leap from an aircraft into unknown and enemy territory.

CHAPTER NINE

MARIUS CRAWLED through the bushes in the darkness, the wet peaty ground soaking the knees of his trousers and brambles scratching his face. Finally he stood upright among the trees and called softly, 'Jan?'

'Is it all fixed up right and proper, Mijnheer van Malderen?' came Jan Wouters' hoarse whisper.

'A work of art,' said Marius modestly. 'If I say it myself, Jan.'

'Beats me how you handle that stuff,' Wouters mumbled. 'Brings me out in a sweat, just looking at it. I thought you'd be heard for sure, out there, crawling among those girders. Sentries parading up and down over your head and everything. If you weren't heard, I was sure you'd lose your grip and fall off.'

'I'm glad you didn't express this lack of confidence in my abilities before!' Marius remonstrated mildly. 'You get along home, Jan. I don't need you any more.'

Wouters shuffled his feet in the leafmould. 'Don't like to leave you. Doesn't seem right. Filthy night, too.'

'There's no sense in risking two men when only one is needed to blow the target. Go on, Jan, for crying out loud!' Impatience broke through Marius's voice.

Reluctantly, Wouters made off into the darkness. Marius sat down on a tree-stump and peered at the luminous dial of his watch. He had an hour. It was, as Jan rightly said, a filthy night. It had rained earlier, and towards evening a swirling mist had enveloped everything, enabling Jan and himself to bring themselves and their deadly consignment close to the target without being detected. Now, although the evening mist had cleared, the night was dark, damp, gloomy and cold. For Marius's purpose, ideal. The sentries up there, patrolling one from each end of the bridge to a central rendezvous and back again, were far more concerned with their own misery than with anything else. Probably the poor wretches reasoned, wrongly, that on a night like this any sensible saboteur would be snug in his bed. It took the sentries a quarter of an hour to complete their dual manoeuvre, but occasionally they varied it when they took time for an illegal cigarette, out there in the middle of the central span. Marius knew they were there now, because he could pinpoint the glow of twin red lights. Occasionally one spiralled down like a shooting star, as a stub was tossed over the edge. One had even fallen past him, earlier, when he was up there, crouched under the bridge among the girders. Little had the sentries known, as they puffed furtively on their forbidden cigarettes and whispered together, that beneath their feet Marius worked patiently, fixing his explosive charges. It had been dry under there, drier than here among the trees—Marius shivered. But the wind had been more unpleasant there, and quite a problem, threatening to numb his fingers and make him clumsy. But he could work in all weathers. It was his job, after all, and he'd trained for it.

It seemed odd, in a way, to be planning to destroy a landmark he remembered from his boyhood. He did not feel guilty, but he felt a responsibility to do the job extra well. Even if he had not remembered the bridge, Harry's meticulous drawing of it was fixed in his brain. He had studied it closely, back at the farm, and had always been blessed with a near-photographic memory. He knew the position of every metal strut out there. Strange, too, to think that, in something under an hour, the whole lot would come crashing down.

Marius turned up his collar, pulled his cap down over his eyes, and settled back uncomfortably against the tree-trunk. Having Harry was a godsend. Harry knew exactly what was required and was a hundred per cent reliable. If Harry drew a diagram and marked a measurement as one metre twenty, that was what it measured and not a millimetre more or less. Marius smiled. Harry was asleep in his tiny flat above his shop, little knowing that the plan they had hatched together was being put into operation tonight. They had intended to wait another two nights, but the hiding and waiting had been so irksome to Marius that when the weather had turned in his favour he had made a split-second decision to move tonight. It needed only Jan's help to transport the stuff. The rest was his job. As he had pointed out to Jan, you didn't want too many bodies blundering about in the dark. That was how operations were put at risk. One man working on his own, with another backing him up if necessary, was virtually undetectable . . . if he did his job properly and Lady Luck smiled on him.

Marius reckoned he had done his job properly. He took pride in all his work. Every mission was more than a patriotic duty, his part of the Allied war effort; it was a personal challenge. He calculated it out beforehand, chose his moment, worked carefully and thoroughly with no cut corners or easy dodges, and he knew that bridge was going to come down. He put out his hand to touch the side of the detonator, and then peered again at his watch. Thirty minutes.

Jan ought to be well on his way back to the farm and safety. He, Marius, ought to be able to make his getaway, too, in the confusion following the explosion. Sitting here in his damp hiding-place, he felt almost happy for the first time since his arrival, tense and jubilant with the anticipation of success.

Sometimes he thought that what he experienced now was almost akin to the moment when he took a woman. The blood raced through the veins in the same way, the body came alive and the moment when his hand struck that detonator came as the moment of relief.

In the darkness, he smiled, because sitting here made him remember prowling through the shrubbery in the Daventrys' garden to toss a handful of gravel at Libby's window, and afterwards, in the air-raid shelter. He stirred slightly on his tree-stump at the memory. Consciously he tried not to think about Libby, although sometimes she emerged from the recesses of his subconscious, as now. But, at this moment, all that really mattered was to complete his task. That was why the physical emotion these missions roused and the physical satisfaction they gave him were so important. They replaced all else for him. Once started on a mission, he could no more abandon it, no more walk away from it unfinished, than from a half-completed act of love.

'God knows what makes a good saboteur,' his

controller had once said to him. 'Being a single-minded blighter helps!'

Marius was a single-minded blighter, as he admitted to himself. Once he had started on a job, he thought of nothing else. He lived it, ate, drank and breathed it, and all led towards the moment—now only minutes away—which saw the culmination of his dedication. A gigantic roar, a rending of wood and metal, the awesome power of the blast and complete and utter destruction.

'But neat,' said Marius to himself firmly. 'A neat, tidy job. No unnecessary mess—even in this. Not a blade of grass crushed which isn't unavoidable. Mess is for amateurs. I'm not an amateur, I'm a professional.'

This very professionalism acted, of course, as a trademark. As soon as that bridge went up, the Germans would suspect—and inspection of the wreckage by daylight would confirm it—that they had a trained saboteur in their midst. Not a slap-happy, enterprising local hero, but a man sent on a mission from London. They would move heaven and earth to find him.

'But I'll move heaven and earth first!' thought Marius with grim humour. His fingers grasped the plunger and he thrust it down. In the same movement, he flung himself full length on his face, folding his arms over his head, as the monster he had unleashed opened its mighty jaws.

When Marius got back to the farm, it was after two in the morning. The countryside was alive with trucks and other motor vehicles, as the Germans scurried round like a disturbed nest of ants, swarming round the heap of twisted metal he had left in his wake. He paused, panting at the edge of the farmyard, to ease his aching lungs. He put out a hand to steady himself on the gatepost, and as he did so, he heard the sound of an approaching motor engine, while the twin yellow beams of headlights split the night.

'You have four minutes,' Harry had warned him precisely. 'From when they turn into the track to when they reach the front door.'

Marius turned and bolted back into the night. He scrambled across a pile of midden, choking in the released gases which would serve to baffle any dogs, and made for the nearest trees. He grasped a low branch, and as the truck disgorged its cargo of armed men before the farmhouse, scrambled up into the heart of the tree. If the English king Charles II could hide in an oak tree from his enemies, it was good enough for him. From his perch he saw them ransack the farm, and saw the Wouters taken away. He had sent Jan back from the bridge to protect him, but, by a bitter irony, had sent him back in time for this . . .

When the Germans had searched through the buildings, they left. But they would be back. They would not just give up. Marius had been in his tree for about an hour. He was numb, wet, stiff, and he stank. He cautiously dropped down to the earth beneath and set off. When he reached the river, he washed his face and hands. Somehow they had broken the network. The Wouters had been arrested, but who else? Everyone, for all Marius knew.

For the rest of that day he hid, moving from place to place like a hunted animal. They saturated the countryside. He could hear their voices as they criss-crossed the land methodically. They knew he was here somewhere. The bridge told them what kind of man they sought, and they could not afford to leave a skilled saboteur at liberty.

By nightfall, his situation was desperate. He had not eaten all day, but worse, he was now so cold and wet through that he would succumb to pleurisy if he didn't find cover and dry clothes. He emerged from a ditch and came to a decision. It was the only one he could reach, but he had never made any decision so reluctantly. He set out again, across country, jumping ditches, scuttling bent double across roads, until he reached a high stone brick wall. He collapsed against it for support. He had a painful stitch in his ribs and every breath was agony, but he had to summon just a little more energy. He gathered himself together, jumped up, grasped the top of the wall and scrambled over it to drop down on the other side, trusting that, in the blackness, he would land safely. There was little moon in the night sky heavily shrouded by scudding cloud and threatening rain again. Not that he could get any wetter. He moved forward.

The last thing he would ever have wanted, and in other circumstances the last thing he would ever have considered, was just what he was about to do now—to go to her. But since the network would seem to have been broken wide open, there was nowhere they would not look for him, except under the roof of the wife of a collaborator.

He moved slowly towards the mass of the château, his heart thudding painfully because he had been running, and sweat bathing his body uncomfortably inside the rain-damp clothing so that he experienced the paradoxical sensation of being both hot and cold at the same time. The building loomed up, stark and forbidding, a blacker shape against a grey-black backcloth. A setting for *Macbeth*, or *Hamlet*. The wind soughed dismally in the trees, and he stopped to take stock of his surroundings.

All kinds of large houses are called châteaux. This one had been built by a successful industrialist in the middle of the last century after a visit to England. There he had become enamoured of Gothic castles, and returned dreaming of living like a medieval baron. Unfortunately, as his architect pointed out, medieval living conditions showed a distinct want of comfort. The house was basically a large northern-French-type country manor, but had been decorated with an incongruous profusion of turrets and battlements. The architect was reputed to have considered suicide when he viewed the probable damage to his professional reputation, but settled for an exorbitant fee instead. The rich pay for what they want, and they get what they want. It was too much to expect them also to have good taste. Over the years, succeeding generations had added modern sanitation and electric wiring. Ugly lead pipes now swarmed up the sides of the house. Marius, looking up at it in the darkness, could not see the details, but he knew them, and even in his predicament smiled faintly as he recalled its grotesque fantasies.

One of the ground-floor windows was unshuttered, and a light shone from it, cutting a narrow swath into the darkness. He moved cautiously towards it, and flattened first against the wall, slowly craned his head round the stonework and peered in. The sight hit him like a blow to the diaphragm, and he cursed again the malignant fate which had brought him here. The room was the drawing-room, unchanged and achingly familiar, and sitting in it, before a roaring fire—*she* had no trouble in getting fuel—was Annette. Exhausted, desperate and hungry though he was, it was the sight of her, and not his present troubles, that set his stomach churning with a sea-swell of old emotions.

She was reading, and as far as he could see, she was alone. Marius waited for a little, but no one else passed across his line of vision, nor did she raise her head and either look or speak to anyone else. He raised his hand and tapped urgently on the pane.

She looked up immediately, towards the window, wary and suspicious. Then she put down her book and got up and came towards him. She was older, but as beautiful and elegant. He did not like the current women's hair-style, the hair rolled round into unflattering sausages round the face, but on Annette it displayed the fine bone-structure and unwrinkled brow. She wore a couturier gown, cut on the bias to emphasise her slim figure, with wide, padded shoulders, and the material cleverly draped over one hip. It was in a pale, smoky-grey colour which would contrast strikingly with her green eyes and auburn hair. As she reached the window, he moved out of the shadows and into her line of sight, a ghost from her past, trusting she would not cry out.

She started, but only very slightly. In no way could she be said to look surprised. For a moment, he wondered if she were the bait in a trap and they had, after all, calculated what he would do—but she had already opened the window and it was too late to flee.

'Hadn't you better come in?' Her voice was low, even, faintly sarcastic.

He relaxed. She was amused, damn it! She had him again in her power, and she knew it. He stepped through the open window and into the room. Behind him, she leaned out to unhook the wooden shutters and close the window and latch it. Then she drew the heavy velvet curtains.

'I left it unshuttered,' she said, 'because I thought you might turn up.'

'How the hell . . .' he exclaimed, startled, because he had not thought Harry would be so unprofessional as to tell her of his presence in the country.

'Old Jan Wouters,' she said. 'He came and whispered the news that you'd dropped in from the sky to me in the strictest confidence. He thought I ought to know. I'm sure he still remembers the time—years ago—when he discovered us in his hayloft. Do you remember? I shall never forget him standing there with a pitchfork in his hand, trying to pretend he couldn't see us.'

'Wouters and his wife have been arrested,' he said sharply.

She bit her lip. 'Yes, I know. I heard they had rounded up a lot of people. I was afraid they'd caught you. I'll see what I can do about Jan and his wife. I can't promise anything, but I'll try. Being the wife of a collaborator has its uses—unexpected uses, I mean.'

A bitterness had entered her voice, and he saw, now that he was accustomed to the light, that there were faint shadows beneath her lovely eyes. 'It wasn't I who betrayed Jan or anyone else,' she said suddenly, 'in case you're standing there wondering whether I can be trusted.'

'I think you can be trusted,' Marius said hoarsely, 'or I wouldn't have come.'

'You came, because you had nowhere else to run to, Marius. Otherwise, you would avoid me like the plague. Well, you had better sit down. You look as if you need a drink.'

He moved across to the fire and threw himself down in one of the high-backed tapestry chairs. The room was expensively but oddly furnished. There was an Aubusson carpet on the floor and a set of three Sèvres vases on the mantelshelf, the mere fact that they were still here and on display showing the political hand their owner played. Other people hid their antiques. The other furniture was heavy, ponderous late nineteenth century, and the family portraits around the walls stiff and unappealing. Even the Germans wouldn't want them. They had enough Biedermeyer monstrosities of their own.

There was a chink of glass and Annette moved towards him, holding out a goblet of brandy. He took it and cupped it in his hands, leaning back to stare up at her.

'How do I look?' she asked, mockingly.

'Good.' His voice sounded thick and awkward.

'You look a hell of a mess—but still attractive. It's been a long time, Marius.'

'Yes, a long time.' He sipped at the brandy. Training, confound it, training. Use your brain, man, and try to forget your loins. 'Are you alone in the house?'

'Yes, apart from the elderly couple who work here and look after me, and my simple needs. You want a bed, I suppose?' Her eyebrows twitched. 'Not mine, of course. But there are plenty of rooms, and you're quite safe here. Louise and her husband are very old, deaf and loyal. You're not to know it, but only this room and the dining-room are in use on the ground floor, and the kitchens, naturally. Upstairs, just my bedroom and my bathroom are used. All the rest of the house is shut up and dust-sheeted. You can have the run of the place. You'll have no company but mice.'

'Your husband doesn't come here?'

She winced. 'He wouldn't dare.'

Marius set down his glass on the floor by the side of his chair. 'I might be here some time. The whole network is torn apart. I don't know at the moment how or when I can get away.'

'Stop worrying,' Annette said carelessly. 'Be like me, just—just opt out of the war. It's quite easy.'

'Not for me!' he said in a hard voice.

'No, not for you,' she said, and sounded sad. The beautiful mask cracked very slightly. 'I haven't just opted out of war, Marius, I've opted out of life. I don't care about anything any more. Sometimes, I don't think I'm even alive.'

Her full lower lip trembled slightly and his insides turned to water and he thought: Oh hell, no!

'I hoped you might come here, despite everything . . .' she said, almost humbly. 'I almost went to Jan's farm. Knowing you were there, I wanted to see you—just for old times' sake.'

She stooped over him as she spoke, and as she finished speaking, pressed her warm, moist scarlet mouth over his. Despite himself, despite all he knew of her, all that had happened since he had left, and all that was happening now, he felt himself respond. His hands slid automatically round her slim waist, and he felt old desire return.

But it was not the same, and she knew it. She

broke away and stood, looking down at him with sadness. 'You don't love me any more, do you?'

Yes, she knew. She could still arouse the old physical desire, but not light the flame.

'I shall always have a special corner for you in my heart,' Marius said truthfully. 'You can be sure of that. And I would be the first man to admit you're a very desirable woman. In that way, I love you. But I'm not *in* love with you, Annette, you're right. Not any more.'

She moved away, her face averted, and sat down in the other chair. Staring into the fire, she asked, 'Because of my marriage? I didn't know he'd prove a traitor.'

'I don't suppose you did. No, not because of that.'

She looked up, the mask intact again, the green eyes gleaming. 'Then there is someone else. You've met another woman. It must be in England. Good God, displaced by a flat-chested Englishwoman with a cardigan and brogues!' She burst into laughter. 'The humiliation—you can have no idea, Marius!'

'She isn't like that!' he burst out angrily. 'And she isn't English, anyway, she's Canadian . . .' He broke off.

'Ah, so I'm right! Well, no woman likes to think she's lost her hold on a man, Marius, but I'm fair-minded. Not a fool, at any rate. I never thought you were off to enter a monastery when you left here. I'm glad you have someone to love. Yes, truly. Tell me, do you carry any pictures of your lady fair about with you?'

He stared at her for a moment, and then unwillingly pushed his hand into the lining of his jacket and took out a crumpled snapshot. He passed it across and she studied it carefully.

'Yes, she has style. Dreadfully badly dressed, of course. But, with a little effort, she could be quite *comme il faut*, even Parisienne.'

'Don't be so damn condescending!' he snarled, snatching back his precious photograph and returning it to its place. 'Not every man wants a fashion-plate at his side.'

'Or in his bed. Quite right. We do, after all, take our clothes off for the important matter. Don't be cross with me, Marius. I haven't changed, you know. Did you think I had? My poor love, no one ever *changes*. We learn a little from experience. We get a little wiser—not much. We get a little more tolerant with age—although, sometimes, that's just laziness. But we don't change. You haven't—you're the same old noble Roman. My country, my honour, my family name! I wonder if she knows you as well as she thinks she does, this girl.'

He said evenly, 'I don't intend to discuss her with you any more, Annette.'

Her full, scarlet lips made a moue at him. 'Yes, you are a man of honour, Marius; you always were. I was always a bit of a whore. But you were always so honourable, and it's your blind spot, the weak link in your armour. If they ever catch you, it will be because of that. Remember, I've warned you! It makes you predictable, you see. I don't believe—for all your war record—that you have it in you to do a really rotten thing, and if you want to survive, you have to do rotten things. I do, all the time.'

He said sincerely, 'I'm sorry you're unhappy. I'm sorry about your husband.'

'Oh, I never liked him—even before he sold out on his country. He was always a stupid bourgeois pig.'

'Then why did you marry him?' Marius asked in an unexpectedly savage tone.

She hunched her shoulders expressively. 'Dear Marius, I'm not exempt from humankind. For the oldest reason in the world. I knew I was pregnant.'

'But if . . .' He broke off, and the full implication of her words struck him like a thunderbolt. He saw the truth then, in her mocking, haunted eyes. 'My child?' he asked hoarsely.

'Of course yours, damn it!' The green eyes glittered at him. 'Who else's, for heaven's sake?'

Marius pushed a lock of dark hair away from his forehead and forced himself to think rationally. He was perspiring again now, but not from the heat of the fire, which had already set a steam rising from his drying jacket and trousers. A dull anger like a smouldering fire, the unquenched ashes of his old passion, perhaps, flaring up as old, dead fires do. It gathered strength in the pit of his stomach and turned to resentment. 'You should have let me know, told me . . . I wouldn't have abandoned you.'

'Marius! Stop being so confounded heroic! You were all set to go to England. What good is a dead hero as a father? Don't tell me you wouldn't have taken to the Resistance anyway?'

His self-control snapped. 'A dead hero is a hell of a lot better than a stinking collaborator!' he yelled. The sinews in his neck swelled with rage, and round his mouth the colour had drained away, so that beneath the weathered bronze and the grime the skin was marble white. 'Don't you realise, when this is all over, the situation you'll be in? The child's situation?' He got up and stumbled blindly towards her and she threw up her arm to protect herself.

Then they both stopped, frozen in their respective attitudes.

'Where is—the child—now?' Marius muttered huskily.

'With his grandparents, in Brussels.' She lowered her arm and stared at him with a new defiance blazing in her eyes.

A son, then. He had a son. 'Grandparents?' he muttered.

'My parents. And there he stays! No one is going to have him but me, do you understand? Neither you, nor that fat coward I married. He's my son, mine alone!'

There was something purely animal about her maternal savagery, the power of her possessive passion for her young.

Panting, and eyes blazing like green fire, she gasped, 'He's all I have—*all*, Marius! All I'll ever have. He's the only reason I'm still living. I don't want you to be his father, because you'll never change, Marius, just as I said. We don't. Always the hero! Well, heroes can be very boring, Marius. Go on blowing up bridges and playing your war games. What use is that to me or to Francis? You and my husband, you're more alike than you would like to think. It's a game of chess to you both—he took the black chess-pieces and you took the white. You both think, don't you, that you can win? Neither of you ever—not once—has stopped to ask, what about those who get caught up in your manoeuvres?'

He made no answer, and she went on more steadily, but with her voice still shaking, 'Listen, I mean to get that divorce. After the war, it will be easy—any woman will be able to divorce a collaborator without shame. I'll be able to get rid of him, and Francis will still be legitimate. Supposing I told my husband now that Francis isn't his child. He'd divorce me at once. But that would make Francis a bastard and shock my family to the core. They don't like my husband, but they accept Francis, because he was born in legal wedlock. Don't misunderstand them, Marius. A bastard, the discovery that *j'avais fait des folies*, and they'd reject him at once. They're old-fashioned. In their day, no one flaunted an illegitimate baby. It was sent out to the country to a peasant nurse, and discreetly paid off when and if it grew to the age of twenty-one.'

'If that happened, I'd . . .' Marius broke off.

'Marry me?' she asked, raising a delicate eyebrow. 'Yes, you would offer that, wouldn't you?'

He drew a deep, shuddering breath. 'I—can't. I can't marry you, not now.'

'Oh, yes, of course. How silly of me, the Englishwoman—sorry, Canadian—with the dreadful summer dress. *Si enfantine!* I wouldn't marry you, anyway, Marius. I'm going to do things absolutely my way and no other. I'll sit out the war, and then I'll divorce him immediately afterwards while all the recriminations are flying about and even my so-traditional family will want to be rid of an alliance with him. Then Francis and I will go away, and start again somewhere. Without *any* of you!'

She shouted the words at him in a kind of triumph. His son was lost to him; she would never let the boy near him. Probably, after all, it would be for the best. All the same, he said obstinately, 'I want to see a picture.'

She hesitated, then shrugged. 'Well, you showed me your Canadian . . .' She stood up and walked over to the far table, and picked up a photograph in a silver frame. Coming back, she handed it to him. 'First birthday, and not a tooth in his head. Late teether. Got all his teeth now, of course. He's three and a half.'

As old as that. Had he been away so long? War made them forget time. They were all forgetting that the years, and their youth, flew by. They would emerge at the end, fancying themselves the same as when they began it. But they would not be the same. They would be older, sadder and robbed of their youth.

Marius took the picture frame, his hand shaking slightly. The baby looked like any baby, round and jolly, a Breughel infant. Not much hair, and encased in some sort of knitted outfit like a Polar explorer's underwear. One chubby hand grasped a rattle with a cheery confidence that suggested, in years to come, that it would grasp a beer-mug as heartily. The original black and white photograph had been hand-coloured by an artist. The baby's cheeks were improbably pink and the Polar outfit a curious green. It did not look much like him, but then, neither did it look much like Annette.

'My father,' Annette said, reading his mind. She took the photograph back, firmly. 'He looked a lot like my father then, being bald. Now he has hair—it's red, I'm afraid—he looks rather different. I've other photographs upstairs, and I'll show you tomorrow.'

Marius sat back and said nothing, filled by a great sense of pity. The child looked like neither of them, because he was—other than biologically—neither of them. He was himself. He was an independent unit who, later in life, would make his own decisions without regard to them, or anyone else. If he was indeed all that Annette had, then a greater tragedy awaited her. That adored baby would grow to manhood, and walk away—even worse, he would do so hand in hand with some girl.

He stirred and said, 'I don't suppose I could have a bath? I couldn't at Jan's farm.'

'Yes, of course. You can use my bathroom. There's a gas geyser and it's eccentric, so I'll light it. I'll get rid of those clothes, and find you others. There are some here, my husband's, which he left behind. Yes, get out of those damp things before you get rheumatics.'

The bathroom was delightfully feminine. Its shelves were crowded with talcum powders and perfume, body lotions, hand-cream and make-up. Yes, being married to a collaborator obviously had its advantages. Marius picked up a bottle of genuine eau-de-cologne and his expression grew sombre. But the bath was inviting. He shook the eau-de-cologne over the bath, climbed out of his clothes, suddenly realising how weary he was, and slid into its warm, soapy depths with a feeling of luxury. The scent of Attar of Roses from the soap filled the air as he rubbed it between his palms, and he thought humorously: If they pick me up outside here, they will think I've been hiding out in a brothel!

There was a tap at the door, but she didn't bother to wait for him to answer. She walked in with clean towels and hung them on the rail. Perched on the end of the bath, she surveyed his naked, soapy figure and observed, 'You're not going to turn modest on me, are you?'

For a moment, he was almost betrayed into saying, 'Join me, if you like.' Instead, he said, 'Where's my bed?'

'Once upon a time you would have said: Where's *your* bed?'

'I wasn't so damn exhausted then.' That was true. He had not realised how tired he was, how tense the muscles, until he got into the bath.

She flicked soap at him and went out.

Later, Annette found him a dressing-gown. It was a flamboyant affair in peacock-blue silk. 'What the devil do I look like in this?' Marius asked, raising his arms and surveying himself with disgust.

'Like an ageing matinée idol.' Annette bent her face close to his, and sniffed. 'And you smell like one! You've been wasting my soap.' He was still tugging disapprovingly at the dressing-gown, and she added, 'My husband's mother gave it to him one Christmas. She's the most vulgar woman you could hope to meet. She buys ready-made skirts and wears jewellery in the mornings.'

'You really are the most perfect bitch,' Marius said suddenly, and with great satisfaction.

She burst into laughter, and they both laughed, until Marius unexpectedly sneezed.

'You've already caught a cold,' she said reproachfully.

'No, I haven't.' He glanced wildly about him. 'There it is! Get it out of here!'

Annette turned in surprise and saw that he was pointing at a large tabby cat slumbering peacefully in the depths of a canework chair. 'Oh, Minou—how on earth did she get in here?'

'Throw it out, for goodness' sake! I'm allergic to the brutes!' Marius rubbed his nose and gestured furiously at the somnolent animal.

'All right, don't go quite mad.' Annette scooped up the cat, which allowed itself to be borne out, still curled up in a sleeping position, like a fur cushion. 'She creeps in and finds places to hide,' she said, returning. 'We sometimes lose her for days.'

Marius was contemplating the bed, a large, four-poster monster with brocade hangings. 'I am, you know, a hunted man. You are offering me the trappings of an Eastern potentate.'

'Make the most of it.'

'Better than sharing living-space with Jan's cattle, anyway.' He climbed into the bed and settled down on the pillows.

She watched him with folded arms. He didn't move, and she saw he had fallen asleep instantly. Just passed out from exhaustion. She picked up the peacock-blue dressing-robe from the floor where he had dropped it and hung it over a bedside chair. Then she stooped over his recumbent form and lightly kissed his forehead.

'Goodnight, Marius, and damn you. You're the only man I ever loved. And I can still get you back, you know. You have me lodged under your skin like a poisoned dart. I'm part of you, Marius. Sweet dreams, my darling.'

She paused by the door to switch out the light, and set off quickly along the corridor to her own room, her step brisk and light. The cat had been waiting at the corner of the corridor, and bounced along behind her in anticipation of supper.

Jamie was allowed home. He was forbidden radio and newspapers, and they were not to talk of the war in his presence. He seemed listless and apathetic, and he had lost weight. In appearance he looked a sicker man, now, than during the worst moments of his breakdown. He concentrated with difficulty and was apt to lose the thread of a conversation, simply because he had stopped listening.

The only time he brightened was when Evangeline came, her hearty voice booming through the house. 'Come on, old chap. On your feet. Walk round the garden.'

Libby came upon them once, in the garden. They were sitting on the ramshackle bench by the tennis court that none of them used any more. Jamie was huddled over, bent almost double, and Evangeline had wrapped her arms round him, nestling him against her ample bosom, rocking and crooning softly like a nursing mother. With her vivid carrotty hair and statuesque build, together with the maternal attitude, she looked like the Earth-Mother herself. Primitive man would have worshipped her, thought Libby. Garlanded her shrine with flowers and begged her protection. Her protection she had granted to Jamie. In her arms, he was safe.

The rest of the time Jamie spent on the sofa in the drawing-room. It was never a warm room, getting little sun, and now that the days were cooler, it was dark and chill. They had to light a fire for him, not only for warmth, but to cheer the place up. There was no question of using precious coal, as that had to be kept for winter. So Farley was hauled out of his potting-shed and sent foraging for firewood on the heath. He threw himself into this with surprising gusto, alarming Gerard's tidy, legal mind. It was all very well impressing on the gardener that wood already fallen from the trees might be picked up, but wood must not be cut from trees. Farley returned in triumph, laden with bundles of faggots like King Wenceslas' peasant.

'Lord knows where he's getting it from,' groaned

Gerard, the possibility of writs dancing before his eyes. 'Trespassing on everyone's land, no doubt. Pinching it from other people's wood-piles, and I'm not blind. I could see the fresh axe-marks on the last lot!'

Libby, on a week-end pass, tried to recommend prudence to Farley, who leered up at her and tapped the side of his nose. 'Don't you go fretting, miss. I knows what I'm about. And don't worry I'll let the young gentleman suffer cold. Ah—I'll see he's kept proper warm.'

'He's not very well,' Libby tried to explain. 'And feels the cold.'

'Oh, I knows what ails him,' said Farley unexpectedly. 'Seen it afore—seen it happen to my own liddle brother in the last war. Come back from the trenches with his mind clean gone. Never recognised none of us no more. Fair broke Mother's heart. Never fear. I'll see the young feller is comfy.'

He hobbled away, a gnarled figure in ancient corduroys, a Fair Isle pullover full of holes, a coat with no buttons and a trilby hat green with age. His hobnailed boots scuffed along the path and struck sparks off large stones.

Libby stared after him in despair. How ignorant she was about people, about life. Even Farley had his history, his tragedies, his loves. It was a shattering revelation to know that the gardener saw in James, not the son of his employer, but a beloved, shell-shocked younger brother with the twitching limbs and vacant eyes of those who had not been able to cope with the horror of the Somme.

'War, war! I hate war!' shouted Libby aloud in the garden, and a pair of wood-pigeons flew up from the trees as her words were whirled away on the wind with the first falling autumn leaves.

CHAPTER TEN

THE TIME had come for Libby to leave. She was being sent on a mission across the Channel, but even she did not know where as yet. She was to go to London and report to Mr Smith, who would give her the necessary details. Standing in her bedroom, she packed her case, not knowing what she should put in it, apart from basic essentials like a nightdress and toothpaste. When they sent her in, everything she wore would have to be French or Belgian. Every detail would have to be taken care of. There must be no makers' or laundry marks. Every item would be taken from her in England, even lipsticks and underwear, and replaced. She would take on a new, fake identity. She would have identity documents to prove it, and even fake letters from non-existent relatives in her handbag. She would step into a new skin and become someone else, a new person.

Libby frowned down at the open suitcase. Suddenly, it was all very real. Could she do it? She had expressed unhesitating confidence to Mr Smith, so anxious had she been to be chosen one of the selected few. But had she, after all, bitten off more than she could chew? A knock at the door made her swing round.

Jamie wandered in, and stood with his hands in his pockets.

'What's wrong?' she asked lightly. 'Book no good?' She had lent him her stock of Agatha Christies.

'Always guess who dunnit,' he mumbled. 'Woman never varies her technique. Just pick on the least likely person—kid, maid, chap telling the story—and you've got your murderer.' He sat down on the end of the bed and glanced at the open suitcase. 'I know what you're up to as well, you know. I mean I know I'm cracked up, but I'm not cracked in the potty sense. I'm not daft.' He stared at her with some of his old aggressiveness, lower lip jutting, and hair tousled and untidy.

Libby froze. 'I'm just going to stay with a friend for a week or two.'

'No, you're not,' he said obstinately. He looked up at her, his pale face twisted in agony. 'For God's sake, don't do it, Libby! You don't know . . . *They* won't have told you everything. If you get caught, it's not like a captured serviceman in uniform. You're a spy, and they can do what they like with you. You've no uniform, no rules of war, no Geneva Convention, nothing to protect you.'

'I have to do it,' she said quietly.

'You don't! Velden was different. He had proper training and could look after himself. Just physically he was stronger than you and could put up a fight.'

'Don't talk about him in the past tense,' she said tightly.

'Why not? He's probably dead. Face up to it, Libby. I'm sorry, but I did tell you—they don't last long. What you're proposing to do isn't just dangerous, it's a waste of time!'

Libby sat down on the bed beside him and grasped his hands which were shaking. 'I'm sorry, Jamie. I can't do anything else.'

'I blame those ruddy nuns!' he muttered fiercely.

'They filled you with ideas of holy martyrs winning crowns of glory.'

'They didn't. I'm not after a crown of glory.'

'Then what are you after?' he challenged her.

She paused. To be spiritually with Marius, even if she could not be with him physically? To share something with him, even if only death? Or perhaps just an end to the unbearable not-knowing? 'I think, the truth,' she said.

'Nobody wants to know that,' he muttered, and she shivered.

'We had intended to send you into France,' Mr Smith said. He stood by the window-pane, which was streaked with rain. It was a cold, blustery day, a first harbinger of winter. 'The idea was to send you over by Lysander, landing you and picking up returning agents. But events have overtaken us somewhat and we've had to scrap that idea for the moment. We're dropping you into Belgium instead. It will be a parachute drop, by the by. For reasons you'll understand in a moment, we can't land a Lysander there just now.'

'Belgium?' Libby whispered. Her heart gave a little skip. Was it possible, against all the odds . . .

Mr Smith was talking again, marching up and down the little room as if on parade, hands clasped behind his back, and casting sharp little glances at chairs and filing cabinets as if he suspected them of unpolished buttons and dirty rifles.

'The group young van Malderen, to give him his right name, parachuted in some time ago to join has been broken up and dispersed. Some people have been arrested . . .'

'Marius has been captured?' she interrupted, her anxiety breaking discipline.

'Not that we know of but, frankly, we are not sure where he is. We need desperately to know how many members of that Resistance network are left free and to what extent the network can function, if it's still able to at all. They don't make radio contact, possibly because their code is broken. It could also be, of course, that the equipment has been discovered, or the wireless operator picked up. We hope not. The operator is a local chap, name of de Vries, active in the local Resistance since the beginning, and very experienced. He may have judged it expedient to sit tight and wait for us to send out a new code. The point is, we have to send more than that: we have to send in someone to have a good look round and report back. We haven't used a woman agent in that area before, and the Germans won't expect it. We'll have to drop you away from the district, and you'll travel there by train. You'll have all the necessary documents. Think you can handle it?' He swung round and glared at her ferociously.

'If I can't, it won't be for want of trying,' said Libby sturdily.

'Good girl. Now I don't want to lose you, too. I'm planning on using you again. Look upon this as a test run, if you like, though it's deadly serious. I want you back in one piece, and we'll do our best to get you out, but it's never a promise, understand?'

'Yes, sir, I understand,' Libby said. 'What about Marius?'

'Oh, young van Malderen,' Mr Smith said, and his abrupt tones became somewhat wistful. 'Yes, see if you can locate him. If he's still at liberty, he will be trying to re-organise something on the ground. He's a methodical sort of chap. He won't want to cut and run and leave everything in disarray. But it would certainly be nice if we could eventually get him back.'

'Yes, sir.' Oh Lord, just like that? It would be nice—*nice!*—to get Marius back? Don't you understand, if Marius never comes back, the heart is torn out of me?

'"Here's a how-de-do . . ."' hummed Mr Smith. '"Here's a pretty mess . . . If with you I am united . . ."' His bright little eyes winked at her. 'Run along then, Sherwood. Jump to it! Now's your chance to show we haven't wasted all time and effort on you!'

Marius awoke the next morning to a strong smell of coffee and a sense of ease that was almost deadening, like a drug. He moved slightly on the pillows, opened his eyes and squinted up and into the light which had broken in a bright shaft across the bed from one window. He struggled upright, and saw Annette standing on the far side of the room, her slim figure framed in the window embrasure. She leaned out, and pushed open the shutters.

He muttered hoarsely, 'What time is it?' and rubbed at his unshaven, bristly chin.

'Just after eleven.'

'What!' He threw back the bedclothes. 'Why didn't you call me?'

'What on earth for?' She came back towards the bed and automatically he retrieved the sheets to save his modesty.

'Don't be silly,' she said mildly. 'You don't have anything there I haven't seen before.' She stood at the end of the bed, arms folded, watching him. She was wearing a silk shirt and dark skirt and her hair was lying loosely curling on her shoulders. 'You were sleeping like a baby. Anyway, I've been doing your job for you: I've been into town. It's market day, so there's nothing in that to arouse anyone's suspicions, and I called on a few friends. Drink your coffee and I'll tell you my news.'

Marius struggled into a more comfortable sitting position and saw that she had set a tray by his bedside. Steam gently wafted from a coffee-pot. He mumbled, 'I'm not used to feather beds. I ache.'

'That's because you got so wet and hung about in damp clothing.'

'So, tell me the news,' he growled, drinking his coffee noisily.

'You look a complete lout,' she told him severely. 'You've been associating with the wrong people. I knew it would come to that. Anyway, so have I.' She sat on the edge of the bed and surveyed his naked torso. 'You can't go wandering about the place, Marius. You're far too well known. Every farmhand around here could recognise you. None of them would betray you, not consciously, not a van Malderen, but they would tell their families, and their friends, and eventually it would leak out. The English shouldn't have sent you.'

'They sent me because I know the terrain. Stop beating about the bush, woman, and tell me what's new, if anything.'

'Well, the Germans are looking for you. I do mean *you*, Marius van Malderen.'

'Damn,' he said softly. 'My own name hasn't been used in any of this.'

Annette gave a snort of derision. 'It didn't make any difference. I was trying to tell you—you're just too well known. Somebody, somewhere, saw you and recognised you. It was enough. Van Malderen is back, someone said. Didn't he go to England? asked someone else. I told you they ought not to have sent you. However, besides my marketing, I took one of those horrible family portraits from the drawing-room to be cleaned.'

Marius put down his cup. 'You mean you went to see Harry? He's still free?'

She nodded. 'He's back at the shop in the market square. He doesn't think they're on to him, and he won't bolt, because it would draw attention to him. The Germans have certainly cracked the code, and no more radio messages can be sent until London sends a courier with a new one. If they do. Although the network is all but smashed, Harry thinks it can be rebuilt, but it will take a little time. Just wait, is his message to you.'

'Can't sit here doing nothing . . .' Marius muttered discontentedly. 'That's not what I'm here for.'

'Could be worse. You're safe, you're unharmed, you're comfortable. Life could be—very pleasant . . .' She stretched out one languid hand and ran her index finger across his chest, disturbing the tangle of dark hair.

'No,' he said firmly, catching at her hand, and pushing it away. But the old Adam had been set stirring by the action, and she knew it. He saw the amusement in her green eyes, and the triumph.

'Don't be such a prude, Marius. I've been living down here like a nun, and I can tell you it's very boring.'

'Find yourself a lover. Other women do. I'm not a bloody gigolo. Keep that cat here for company, not me.'

'Other women's families don't watch them like hawks, as mine do. They know I want to get rid of my husband, and in their minds that can be only because I want to marry someone else. They're so bigoted. They can't imagine I just want to be free. They think a woman should have a husband, and therefore must want a husband. If the husband she has is less than perfect, it's better than no husband at all. That's how they reason. Both my sisters are married to the dreariest men, you can't imagine, but both would fight tooth and nail to keep their marriages intact.'

'Perhaps,' said Marius thoughtfully, 'they have weighed up the alternatives, for themselves, I mean, and being alone isn't so attractive, either.'

Her fine eyes glittered at him, and she pushed her lovely face close to his. 'Listen to me, Marius, there is nothing—nothing—more disgusting for a woman than having a man she loathes and despises in her bed! Can you imagine what it's been like for me? Have you the faintest idea? That—That creature, pawing at me with his sweaty palms, panting over me. He rolls about like a walrus when he makes love. He's utterly disgusting.'

'He does, then,' said Marius, eyeing her speculatively, 'still want you. Isn't that going to make him difficult to get rid of?'

'He doesn't *want* me!' Annette burst out impatiently. 'He gets a thrill out of humiliating me. He knows how I feel about him. Knowing I shudder when he touches me, it acts on him like an aphrodisiac.' She sighed and added resignedly, 'I haven't had a lover in the last twelvemonth. Before that, when I was in Brussels, I used to go out and just pick up someone—a stranger. It had to be a stranger, of course. Even so, it was risky. Things happened to make me think I was being watched. Whether my husband, or my family, had set someone to follow me about, I don't know. But I was frightened, I admit, so I came down here. He wouldn't let me bring Francis, but he did agree that my parents could have him with them. That's how it's been, for nearly a year. Marius—*please* . . .?'

She grasped at his arm, her voice becoming pleading. 'Men make jokes about women who are desperate for it. But I'm desperate to have someone love me—someone who isn't him. I want someone to touch me as if I were a woman, not a—an object for his own gratification. They are all against me, Marius, all of them. My parents, my sisters, the whole sanctimonious tribe. Don't push me away; you have no idea how cruel you're being.'

'I don't love you, not in that way, Annette,' he told her gently, 'I told you so last night. Nothing can change. I can make love *to* you, but not love you as you want. You must find someone else.'

'There is no one else. I'll settle for what I can have. I'm not asking for your heart. I've long ceased to be a romantic. Just take me in your arms, touch me, kiss me, love me . . . I don't ask anything else.'

When he hesitated, she breathed softly, 'You do still want me, don't you? Even if you don't love me?'

He avoided her eye. 'Yes, I suppose I do.'

'You know you damn well do!' her voice said almost viciously, but husky with her desire. She got to her feet and began to take off her clothes, her fingers moving rapidly and tearing impatiently at the fragile material of her blouse.

Marius watched her in silence. Whether she was telling him the truth, he had no idea. But it had always been impossible to know when she lied in order to get what she wanted. Perhaps she used him as a means of revenging herself against the man she hated. Whatever the rights and wrongs of it, she had won this particular battle. He couldn't send her away. He did want her, and when she slipped into the bed beside him and wound her lovely arms round his neck, his own arms clasped her fiercely, hating himself, despising his own weakness, but caught up in the flame of his own desire. She knew every trick in the book, but it was not necessary. The blood was pulsating through him and throbbing in his loins. He could hear himself panting and moaning, and though he wanted to delay the climax, to prolong this moment of delicious torment and of passion, he could not, and took her quickly and violently, so that her hands gripped his shoulders, and her long fingernails scored long red scratches in his perspiring skin.

With the release, and the tension drained out of his body, he rolled over on his back and stared up at the brocade hangings of the bed, his nerves still quivering from his victory, his mind already despising his weakness. He muttered thickly, 'You're right. I shouldn't have come here. I should never have come back.'

Annette's hand slid across his stomach and rested in his groin. 'But you are back again, Marius. Back where you were before.'

'And I am back where I was before,' she exulted in her heart. 'I am back in your mind, your heart, your soul. You'll never dislodge me. Forget your Canadian, Marius. Forget your virgin in her flowered dress. You'll never free yourself from me.'

* * *

For Marius now, the enforced inactivity to which he was temporarily condemned, as a virtual prisoner in this house, was a greater enemy than the military machine outside. He could roam freely indoors, open up the disused library, blowing dust off books not touched in years, and work out chess problems for himself on the antique board with the ivory pieces. But he was not doing the job he had been sent to do, and was out of touch with London. Kicking his heels was as alien to his nature as was the idea of making for Spain and leaving a shattered network and no effective local opposition on the ground to the Germans.

Sometimes he thought about Libby, but tried not to, because it hurt. He should never have embarked on that foolish romance. He must have been out of his mind. He hoped he hadn't wrecked the girl's life, but perhaps that was a conceited fancy on his part. She was young. Marius fiddled with the chessmen, picking up the White Queen. She would go home to Canada when the war was over and be reunited with her family. With luck, she would meet someone eminently suitable, marry, raise a brood of healthy infants and, in years to come, look back on the war years as an interlude. He would never forget her. But he had indeed forgotten too many other things. Marius turned the White Queen in his fingers, and set it beside the Red one. He had deluded himself in thinking that there were no ties left to bind him to Annette.

Somewhere a telephone was ringing, and he could hear Annette's voice, answering. A little later, her quick step could be heard on the parquet floor, approaching the library. She threw open the doors and appeared, flushed and unusually agitated.

Marius threw down the chess-piece and pushed back his chair, expecting disaster, and prepared for flight or a desperate resistance.

'That was my father,' she said, speaking in a low, abrupt voice. 'He phoned through from Brussels to say my mother has influenza. She's not seriously ill, but they could do without having to worry about Francis at this moment. Father proposes to send Francis down here for a few days. He thinks my husband would not object, if it were only for a short time and I returned the child after, say, a week or ten days. He intends to send Francis off today on the train with a friend, and I'm to collect him at the station early this evening.'

'You mean the kid is going to be here?' Marius demanded sharply.

'I can't help it!' She twisted her hands together and began to turn rapidly up and down the room, against a background of dusty bookshelves, her emotion contrasting starkly with this pedagogic setting. 'He's my child! They know I miss him terribly, and if I start making excuses—saying I can't have him here just now—they will immediately think I'm down here with some man, a lover.'

'You are,' said Marius drily.

Her face hardened. 'Now, you listen to me, Marius. Francis must not see you. Do you understand?'

'For heaven's sake, he's—what—three?'

'Marius, little children may not always understand what they see—but they do know what they see, and they can describe it very accurately. If Francis saw you here, when he got home, one day, in all innocence, he would say that there was a man living in the house with Mummy. Well, I suppose I don't have to tell you how that would set the cat among the pigeons? If he tells my parents, his grandfather will be down here on the next train to investigate. If he tells his father . . .'

'I'm his father,' Marius corrected quietly.

'He must never know it!' she shouted, whirling round, and stamping her foot on the parquet. She drew a deep breath. 'If he tells—my husband—then I'll never see Francis again, I know it.'

There was a silence. Marius swept the chessmen off the board and began to return them tidily to their box. 'What do you want me to do, then?'

'Stay upstairs in your room. There is no reason why Francis should find you. Most of the house is closed off and not used, so no one goes there. I'll smuggle up your food, or Louise will. Just keep out of the way.'

He sighed. 'Shouldn't be impossible, I suppose. I would quite like to get a glimpse of the kid, you know. I can, I suppose, peer out of a window when he's in the garden?'

'Only if you can't be seen.' She paused and added grimly, 'Don't get any ideas, Marius. He's never to know about you, and you'll never have him.' She turned and marched out, head held high, that old, arrogant Annette he remembered so well.

Marius heard her arrive with the child as the last daylight was fading. He meant to ignore the whole thing, but was irresistibly drawn to the window and stood at the half-closed shutter, peering down through the narrow gap and squinting into the dusk. His first sight of his son was a brief glimpse of a small, stocky, lively body hurtling from the car to the front door. It gave him a curious feeling, and one akin to disbelief. His mind would not accept it. So, he was a father. It made little difference. He would never act as one with regard to Francis. Francis would grow up to be whatever Annette made of him. She seemed to be a devoted mother and he would have to trust her to do her best. There was, in any case, nothing he could do about it, whether he wished to or not. It made him feel uncomfortably superfluous, and ask himself whether he was destined to spend his whole life lurching from one situation, about which he could do nothing, to another. The war, of course, had provided him with a situation about which he could do something. He messed about with explosives and wrecked things. It was a pretty effective way of doing something, but Freud might have made something else of it. A disturbing thought.

He kept his word and stayed in his room, spending the time trying to concentrate on working out some route of escape. He could sit here on his backside indefinitely, with the Germans getting closer and closer, waiting for London to make a move, of course. But it went against his instincts. He hated inactivity, being cooped up. Besides, it was a long time since he had felt so isolated. The child's arrival strengthened the feeling. He was isolated also in what ought to have been a family setting. Harry was his only link with London, and Harry's situation must be perilous. So many people had been picked up that, sooner or later, one must talk. After that, Harry's life would not be worth, as the American gangster movies put it, a plugged nickel.

A faint creak from the door caused Marius to turn his head. A small figure stood there staring at him, not curiously, but directly, almost appraisingly.

'Who are you?' Francis asked in a clear childish treble.

A thousand million curses, thought Marius ruefully. Annette will never believe I didn't contrive this. He tried to ignore the irregular thud which his heartbeat had become. In some ways, he would almost have preferred to see a field-grey uniform standing there. At least he would have known what to do. He had no answer to the question, and avoided it by putting one of his own. 'What are you doing here?'

'I'm looking for Minou. She hides in here and sleeps.'

Betrayed by the wretched cat! Marius watched his small visitor come nearer, still studying him, suspiciously now. Marius understood what Annette had meant about little children remembering what they saw. He had the feeling that the hairs on his head were being counted. There was nothing about him that Francis would not have noted.

Marius returned stare for stare, sensing instinctively that Francis would not mind this. They were on the basic, simple level of a child's social stratagems. You are a stranger, I am a stranger. We check each other out. His son was a stocky child with carrotty curly hair and a pugnacious expression. He watched as Francis climbed into the canework chair and sat there with his short plump legs stuck out straight in front of him. He had white socks and red boots. With his red hair and red boots, and a sort of navy blue jersey outfit in between, he presented a colourful picture. Marius smiled.

'What are you doing?' asked his infant interrogator, with the same calm persistence interrogators always used and fixing him with an unnerving stare.

He had to answer something this time, and said the first thing to come into his head. 'I've come to do some work. Your mother wants this room painted. I'm just looking to see what's needed.'

He had no idea whether this explanation was above the child's head. He had no idea how on earth one talked to a very small child, any small child, let alone this one. Older children he rather liked, and found they responded well to being treated on an equal level, but toddlers were completely outside his experience, and none more so than this one, his own child. Francis further demoralised him by leaping to a completely—as it seemed to Marius—new subject.

'Have you got a boy at home?'

'What? No . . .' Francis was frowning disapprovingly. That was not the right answer. Marius sought for a better one, and remembered Tommy Ryan. 'I do know a boy, but he's older than you. He collects things, and keeps them in a tin box.'

'What's a tin box?' asked Francis, with a faint air of cunning.

Trying to catch me out, thought Marius. The kid is smart. 'It's like a wooden box—you know, the same as you put toy bricks in—only, it's—tin . . .' he finished lamely. He felt like an idiot child before a stern schoolmaster.

'What things?'

'Eh? Oh, stones, funny-shaped stones, sea-shells, anything he finds and likes.'

Francis turned the idea of being a collector over in his mind, examining it from all sides, before accepting it, but only after pin-pointing a major flaw. 'I haven't got a box.'

'You'll have to ask your mother, or Louise in the kitchen.'

'I've got a tricycle,' Francis informed him. Beats a tin box any day, so there! 'Only I had to leave it behind, because they wouldn't let me take it on the train.'

'Bad luck.'

'Tell me a story,' Francis ordered suddenly in a peremptory way. It might have been Annette speaking. Francis was settling down in his cane chair, waiting.

'I don't know any.'

Francis directed a withering look at him. Obviously Marius was a wash-out as new acquaintances went. He was spared further embarrassment by a step at the door and the appearance of Annette.

'Run downstairs and find Louise,' she said calmly, but her eyes glittered at Marius over the child's head, like a tigress. If she could have torn him apart, she would have done. 'Your supper is ready.'

Francis slid off the chair, said 'Goodbye' very politely to Marius and trotted out of the room.

'I didn't entice him in,' Marius said defiantly. 'He came looking for that dratted cat. And in case you're worrying, I can assure you I made a thoroughly bad impression, and I don't think he likes me much.'

'He's not the sort of child who likes people,' Annette said calmly, sitting down in the cane chair their child had vacated. 'I mean, he doesn't cuddle people or kiss them. But if he talks to you, then he thinks you're all right.'

'I couldn't tell any stories.'

'You could show him how to wire an explosive device together, I suppose,' she said spitefully.

'Very funny,' he said coldly, turning away. 'I need to see Harry.'

'None of my business, of course, but you'd be stupid to put your nose outside this door.'

'Harry's right, the network must be rebuilt. I can't do that here, on my own. Harry can't do it on *his* own. The sooner we put our heads together and set something up, the better. Harry's cleaning that picture of yours. You can go there any time and tell that sour-faced girl he employs that you want to see him, and no one will question it. Tell him you have other paintings needing restoration and will he come out here and give a professional opinion. Make sure the girl hears you. Just get him out here.'

'Why?' she demanded angrily. 'Both you and Harry have done more than enough to win your share of medals when the war is over!'

Marius swung round on his heel, his eyes gleaming at her. 'That's not why I'm doing it! Nor Harry!'

'Heroes, bloody heroes,' she said bitterly. 'Just a pair of schoolboys playing cops and robbers, the pair of you. You and Harry, you always led one another on, I remember.'

Marius's angry expression faded into a rare smile. He said reminiscently, 'We all three used to walk to school together.'

'You and Harry used to quarrel over who should carry my books for me,' she reminded him.

'A long time ago.' His eyes met hers. 'Things change.'

Annette folded her arms, her own green eyes malicious. 'Not everything.' Her manner became abruptly businesslike. 'I'm not fetching Harry out here until Francis has gone home. The fewer people the boy sees, the better. I'll hide you, Marius, and won't betray you. But I never was part of your network, and I'm not about to become a heroine of the Resistance now. I'll take messages to Harry, but that's all I do. Remember that! I don't want to finish against a wall facing a firing-squad.'

'You'll do that, if they find me here,' he reminded her. 'You're already in, my dear, and you can't opt out.'

'Like hell I'm "in"!' she told him sweetly. 'My sole interest is *you*.'

CHAPTER ELEVEN

No matter how well prepared Libby felt herself, the moment of truth, when she stepped out on the tarmac in the cold, dark night, came as a moment of stark realisation and, despite herself, panic. She forced it down. Too late, now, to back out. The pilot smiled at her in welcome. He was very young, like Jamie, and, like Jamie, he didn't like flying in female agents, especially pretty ones.

'All aboard for the *Skylark*,' he said, but his voice croaked in his throat.

'This . . .' thought Libby, crouched in the darkness on the shuddering floor of the aircraft, and waiting, her body shot through by vibrations and the sombre droning filling her ears, 'This is what Marius experienced I don't even know how many times.'

It was also Jamie's experience. She had stepped into their man's world and a sphere of activity in which women were still an unwelcome novelty. Literature was full of beautiful spies with pearl-handled revolvers in their garters, but this was real life. No one liked sending women in: instructors didn't like it; pilots didn't like it. It wasn't the training they disliked, nor was it entirely the delivery of her like a parcel floating down through the sky. What they hated was the moment when they went home and looked into the faces of their own wives or girl-friends, knowing that, only hours earlier, they had been instrumental in dropping into enemy territory and untold danger a girl just like that.

The flight over the Channel went smoothly, but considerable flak came up over the continental coast and the plane lurched and bucketed. Then came a few moments' respite, seeming very few indeed, before a voice by her ear said brusquely, 'One minute . . .'

After that, she felt surprisingly cool and in command of herself. Training had taken over, but also an acceptance of fate, and knowledge that if you can't go back, you must go forward. 'Or in this case,' she thought with morbid humour, 'down!'

She floated down through the velvet black sky to make a perfect landing, briefly regretting that her instructor wasn't there to see it. She buried her parachute in soft soil, prepared herself in her new identity, took her bearings, and, satisfied that she was just where she should be, waited patiently until the dim light of dawn. Birdsong heralded the new day, the grass was wet and sparkling with dew. Somewhere in the distance a church bell tinkled melodiously. And she was alone in a strange country.

Nerves led to impatience, but she knew she had to do exactly as she had been taught. She stayed hidden until she had just enough time left before setting out to the small town, and its tiny station.

Nevertheless, as she walked across the station yard towards the entry to the booking-hall, she felt more vulnerable than she had ever felt before in her entire life. It was a little before eight in the morning, and the train, she knew, was due out at ten past. It gave her time to buy a ticket, and meant that she did not have to wait about too long on the platform, where, for any reason, she might be noticed. She felt as though it must be screamingly obvious who and what she was. The nape of her neck prickled, and she had the horrid feeling that at any moment a hand might fall on her shoulder or catch at her arm, or a voice shout, 'Stop!'

Fortunately there were plenty of people about, hurrying to catch the same train, so few were interested to look at the slim girl in the drab coat and slightly scuffed shoes. Libby had spent much time speculating on where these clothes had been obtained for her. All were worn, not too much, but enough to be part of someone's daily wardrobe. They were clean, neat, serviceable and not too fashionable. She looked what she was supposed to be—a young working-class girl of decent family. She touched her handbag nervously, as if to reassure herself it was still there and, with it, all her papers, naming her as Marie Gérard, a dressmaker. Even the name 'Gérard' had been chosen with care, because of its resemblance to Gerard Daventry's name. 'It's a name you know,' said Mr Smith, 'and will instinctively recognise. It will show in your eyes. If we gave you a name you'd never heard of, you risk looking blank if someone calls it out. Give you away.' Marie Gérard was travelling to visit an elderly and infirm relative, about whom the family was much concerned. She carried letters in her pockets from members of it, discussing whether or not Aunt Thérèse should be persuaded into an Old Persons' Home and, if so, what to do about the cats and the canary to which the old lady was devoted. Libby liked this touch. She clutched her cardboard suitcase and stepped out purposefully.

Just inside the entry to the booking-hall she saw her first German soldier. It came as a jolt, and her heart leapt up painfully. To walk past him naturally seemed impossible, but she must neither scurry nor loiter. Either might look suspicious. All their careful planning, all her dangerous journey so far, might be brought to nothing by a foolish, simple mistake now. To be sure, he did not look much of a threat. He was a gangling youth, with a rifle slung over one shoulder, who slouched by the door and watched people enter and leave with a bored eye. As Libby passed by him, a flicker of interest showed in his expression, but it was of a purely personal nature. He was not impervious to pretty girls. But this one had a businesslike air about her and, anyway, he was on duty. The brief curiosity in his eyes was extinguished. So what . . . said the twist of his discontented mouth. Just a girl. He was obviously thoroughly fed-up. Perhaps he had been here since early morning, and awaited his relief. Libby almost felt a spasm of sympathy for him.

She took her place in the queue and waited her turn to buy her third-class ticket. The people around were drably dressed, and their complexions were waxen and drawn. They all looked tired and irritable. She was uneasily aware of her PT instructor's warning—that she had no friends. His voice rang in her ear. If she were forced to turn for shelter or help to any of these people, would they be prepared to take the risk? Would they slam the door in her face? Would they betray her? Ahead of her, a short, stocky woman was arguing with the clerk. Behind, the rest of the queue grew impatient. One or two voices were roused in protest at the delay. By the time it came to Libby's turn, the clerk was brusque and harassed. He pushed the ticket towards her and motioned her out of the way. Thankfully she grasped the slip of paper and hurried out on to the platform.

The slight delay meant that the platform was crowded and she had only a few minutes to wait. When the train drew in, she pushed her way on with assurance, and claimed a seat in a stuffy compartment already nearly full and soon packed. A whistle blew, and they drew out. Marie Gérard was on her way. Thus far, so good. Libby tried not to give way to a glow of satisfaction. It would be a mistake to be over-confident. The more difficult part of the journey was still to come.

It was a slow train, and she was seated in the middle of the compartment. As far as she could see, they were passing through an industrial suburb, and unpainted warehouses lined the track. Most people were already at work, and the landscape seemed deserted. Perhaps, she thought with a sigh, everyone was on this train. She wriggled in her seat, trying to obtain a little more room, and was rewarded with a glare from an elderly man next to her. Don't draw attention to yourself, Libby! she lectured herself in her head, and settled down, her eyes on her knees, to spend a long, tedious journey. She would, in fact, be more than grateful if nothing happened to disturb it. They rattled over the points and rocked along in a dull, oppressed silence. A fug had settled over the compartment, damp clothes, stale cigarette-fumes, the effluvium of human bodies not long out of bed and crushed in uncomfortable proximity, each striving to maintain a tiny closed area of privacy, drawing up invisible barriers.

Libby had rehearsed her story a dozen times, and what she had to do on arrival at her destination. Lacking any better occupation, she began to rehearse it all again, and to search for the weaknesses. In her mind, she turned over and over everything she had been told.

Before leaving, she had been given all available details on the network as it had been, and ordered to memorise two addresses. One was that of the wireless operator de Vries, who, it turned out somewhat surprisingly, kept an art studio and small gallery. The other was that of a man named van Leeuwen, who was a watchmaker and jeweller by trade. Both of these had been members of the Resistance from the very beginning in that district and, if still at liberty, would be her very best bet.

'You will not be met when you drop,' she was informed. 'In the first place, we can't inform them by radio safely. Secondly, agents were formerly met by a farmer and his wife, name of Wouters. But we have very good reason to believe they have been picked up, and we cannot risk dropping you in the actual area, knowing as little as we do about what is going on there. Van Malderen was probably hidden at Wouters' farm for a while, but where he is now, Lord knows. Take a good look around before you try and communicate with anyone, and do so indirectly on some excuse which will leave you a way out, if things go wrong. For example, you will have a broken wristwatch with you. If you do decide to try and establish contact with van Leeuwen, it will be your excuse. If you're searched and they ask you why you have two watches, don't forget that the broken one was a present at your confirmation, and you're carrying it around, hoping to get it mended one day. The one you are wearing, and which works, is much more ordinary. Sort of thing any young Belgian or Frenchwoman might wear, cheap and serviceable. It won't let you down.'

Too many people picked up, thought Libby uneasily. Those presumed left, de Vries and van Leeuwen, might now be too frightened to help her. As the PT instructor had warned, she had no friends. Every attempt at contact she made was a risk.

Libby tried to concentrate her mind on something else. This was less difficult than it might seem in the circumstances, because, shortly before she had left England, she had been able to obtain permission for a snatched lunch in London with Aunt Jennie. Apart from that, she had not been able to visit the family again, and had not even been able to attend Jamie and Evangeline's wedding. Aunt Jennie had brought along the photographs to show her.

Libby could see them clearly in her mind's eye. In many respects they were like all wartime wedding photographs. The groom was in uniform, the bride in a coat and hat, not in white lace (a little inappropriate for Evangeline anyway), and attendant relatives on the female side wore obviously refurbished finery. Jamie had looked quite well in the photographs, if a little tired. Evangeline had dominated the entire wedding group, looking resplendent. She wore a mauve dress and matching coat, and grey suede peep-toe shoes, the first time Libby had ever seen Evangeline in high heels. A felt hat with a narrow brim and high tapering crown surrounded by a band and a buckle, of the type once sported by Regency bucks, crowned her red hair, which had been ruthlessly tamed for the occasion. With this outfit, she wore a necklace of three rows of pearls and pearl drop-earrings. Libby recognised this finery as heirlooms in the Watts family and traditionally presented to the eldest daughter on her wedding day. As such, Evangeline—who was twenty-six—had been in expectation of them for some years, and had tended to refer to them disrespectfully, and somewhat prematurely, as 'my beads, when I get 'em'. Well, she had got 'em now, and Jamie along with them. Libby hoped she was satisfied.

It was no use pretending she was not slightly jealous—not because she wanted to marry Jamie herself, but because Evangeline had somehow snatched him away from them all, and would make sure they never got him back. 'I hope James will remember to write home,' had said his mother, as she put the photographs back in her handbag. 'Gerry does so wait for his letters. I do hope he doesn't quite forget us.'

Libby had hastened to assure her aunt that Jamie would be the last son to forget his parents. But she couldn't be sure. Lord, she thought now, suppose Eva gets pregnant? I can't imagine her with children. Poor old Jamie couldn't cope. All the kids will be strapped into the saddle as soon as they can toddle, and grow up bandy-legged.

The train had halted and the old man next to her got out, replaced by a thin, nervous woman and a small girl with a cold who sniffed lugubriously. They trundled across the countryside and Libby glanced surreptitiously at her watch. They were running very slightly late, hardly surprising at the rate this train was travelling. It was a wonder they would ever get there. But, even so, another quarter of an hour should bring her to her destination. But they had stopped again. This time, a ripple of movement ran through the compartment, hardly visible, but communicating itself from one passenger to the next like the flow of an electric current. Imperceptibly, there had been a heightening of tension.

The door slid back with a grating sound, and a tall figure in a grey uniform appeared. Libby glanced up at him curiously, because he was the first officer she had seen, and he presented quite a different appearance from the slipshod sentry at the country station. He took off his cap, and glanced round. The compartment had seemed full, but he was not discouraged and came in, making for the seat opposite Libby. It had been occupied by the sniffing child, but the mother reached out and dragged her on to her lap. The child uttered a squawk of protest, which was cut off in the midst as the thin woman slapped her legs and muttered, 'Shut up!' Even the child sensed this was not the time to protest, and fell silent, sucking the corner of a handkerchief and glowering.

The officer sat down and crossed his booted legs, apparently quite heedless of having caused any disruption. Then he looked across to Libby, and smiled.

Too late she realised her mistake in staring at him so curiously. She swallowed, and wondered what she should do. Was this to be her nightmare of being accosted by some oversexed lounger, as she had been on the London train not so long ago? But this man was a major. A prickle ran up her spine. He ought not to be travelling third class. He ought not to be in this compartment at all. Yet he was still there, and smiling boldly at her.

'This train is very slow,' he said, in passable French. He leaned forward and addressed the words to Libby.

'Yes,' she muttered. The rest of the passengers were looking elsewhere and appeared to have all gone deaf. She was on her own.

'It is also very crowded, I could find a seat only in here.'

'Really?' It was such a palpable lie that she could hardly keep the scorn from her voice. Surely he didn't think her that stupid? She knew well, as did all these other people, that all trains had seats reserved for German officers, and she had been well warned before leaving England not to sit in one by mistake. She gave him a quelling stare.

He was not put off. Men never were. If they had the nerve to speak to a strange girl in the first place, their skins were as thick as hides. Her throat suddenly felt constricted, and she had to force the saliva down which gathered in unwished quantities in her mouth.

'You travel on this train very often, *mademoiselle*?'

'No—I'm on a visit.'

'Oh? To family?'

Wretched man! Why was he so interested? How rude could she be without being dangerously so? 'Yes. A family matter.' That ought to shut him up. How useful was that phrase, '*une affaire de famille*'. It could mean almost anything, and no one could be expected to discuss it further with a stranger.

'Indeed? Where do you descend?'

Libby sighed, and named her station. Useless to lie, and if she got off at a different station from the one she intended, she would be hopelessly confused and might have difficulty getting to her destination.

'You have somewhere to lodge, *mademoiselle*, I hope? It is very difficult these days.'

'I'm all right,' she said a little sharply. 'I shall find somewhere.'

Had he noticed something odd which led him to question her, or was he just fishing for her address? He was not very old, perhaps thirty and a year or two. He had no wedding ring. He was reasonably good looking. He was a fancy-free bachelor. Passing down the corridor towards the first-class seats, he had glanced into this compartment and spotted a pretty girl, apparently alone. Just her lousy luck!

The train seemed to put on a spurt and then slowed with a jerk, sending them all pitching forward. The major put out a hand to save Libby, who mumbled her thanks. They had drawn into her station at last, and she got up in a hurry, hoping to be free of her new admirer. But as she stretched up for her suitcase on the rack, he stood and reached over her to take it down. 'Allow me.'

'Thank you,' Libby said coldly, removing it firmly from his hand.

But she wasn't free of him. He also got off there, and walked beside her to the barrier, where there was a sentry, and a second man, checking papers. The major had allowed Libby to go in front of him, not without purpose. Over her shoulder, he was able to read her name on her identity papers. The man checking glanced briefly at her papers and at her, and then at the major. The two uniformed men exchanged salutes. Libby walked on quickly with an uncomfortable feeling she was somehow being channelled along on a sort of conveyor belt. Probably it was all her overwrought imagination, but the major was still there.

'I have a car waiting for me. I may perhaps offer you a lift, *mademoiselle*?'

She had to get rid of him, once and for all. Perhaps it was her turn to do a little organising. 'Oh no,' she said, admonishingly, 'that would not be correct.'

He had not expected that and looked taken aback.

He was not nonplussed for long, however. He rallied, and said, 'It would not be seen as an impertinence, I am sure. It is not intended as one.' He pulled on his gloves. 'But as you wish. I am Major Dettmar. You can find me at the Kommandantur. It is located in the Mairie. If you should run into any problem during your stay, please do not hesitate to contact me. I should be glad to be of service.'

'You are very kind,' Libby said, tempering her refusal with graciousness. 'But I'm sure I shall be quite all right. Goodbye.'

She marched off at a great rate before he could reply. For a moment or two she had a horrible feeling he might come after her, but she was not pursued, and when she finally ventured to glance furtively over her shoulder, he was nowhere to be seen.

Breathing a sigh of relief, she allowed herself to relax and take an interest in her surroundings. It seemed odd to be back on the continent. She stopped and peeped into a window of a grocery store. The brand-names were familiar, recalling old memories. The shelves were sparsely stacked, but there were plenty of seasonal vegetables on the stalls in the market square. Old ladies in black crouched suspiciously over potatoes and onions, and canny housewives snapped carrots in two to make sure they were fresh, in a manner which would have given an English greengrocer apoplexy. Libby moved on slowly past the lines of stalls and turned a corner, and there, staring straight at her, was Marius.

It was as if she had received a violent blow. She literally felt herself stagger. For a moment she even thought she might be hallucinating, and then she recalled herself to her situation. The wretched thing was a poster tacked up on a wall between two others. She pulled her jolted nerves into some semblance of order, and walked forward casually, pausing before it, and glancing at it with what she hoped looked like passing interest. Too much curiosity might be noticed. Above all, she must not look as if this poster in particular meant anything to her. She stared deliberately at the two pictures on either side, and then returned to the one which mattered.

They must have used an old photograph of Marius, because in it his face looked fuller and younger, despite the blurred image created by magnifying the original snapshot. The legend, printed both in French and in Flemish, gave his name and age and indicated a reward for information leading to his discovery. Libby's instinct was to tear it from the wall before someone, who might be tempted by the reward, saw it. But she forced herself to walk on, turning down a side street, and trying to make sense of what she had seen.

The poster looked relatively new. Those on either side of it were begrimed and tattered at the edges, but this one still had a pristine crispness. It could not have been tacked up there so very long, unless it was a replacement, and it indicated that Marius was still at liberty and being sought. Whether he were still in this district was another matter. But he was alive! Libby's heart leapt in exultation.

Walking along, buried in her speculations, her footsteps had brought her to the end of the street and out on to a tree-lined boulevard running alongside a canal, and separated from it by a strip of grass. There was a wooden seat there, and she sat down. Her knees buckled as she did so, and she realised that she was still suffering from the shock of seeing the poster. She clasped her hands tightly on her lap and concentrated on the green, murky canal water. Refuse floated on it, cigarette packets, bits of paper, oily cotton-waste. A little further down was a barge, moored against the bank, but it seemed to be deserted. Her earlier emotion of joy that he was alive was now replaced by depression as her spirits sank into her boots. The poster had named him correctly, which meant he had been seen and recognised and reported. The occupying powers had their petty informers and sneaks. The word had gone round among this unsavoury fraternity, any one of whom would be happy to turn him in for the small cash sum involved. It would be very difficult now for him to remain hidden for long, unless he were somewhere exceptionally safe, and it was hard to think that such a place could exist. But he might, he just might, still be in the area, since to travel out of it would be awkward with his face plastered all over the walls, and it was not impossible that they would meet.

Libby's fingers tightened spasmodically in her gloves. She had to locate one of the Resistance members still at liberty. Thinking it over, she decided to start with the watchmaker, van Leeuwen. She got up, picked up her case and retraced her steps to the town centre. She located van Leeuwen's watch repair and jeweller's in a side street, and strolled casually past it. The blinds were down, and a note on the door read 'Closed'. The closure had a permanent look about it.

However, despite the finality of the notice on the door and the desolate appearance of the shop, someone was in there. Through the dusty glass, Libby spied a movement. She shaded her eyes and peered in. It was difficult to make out much, but the figure inside was that of a woman. Libby raised one hand and tapped on the window. The woman's head snapped round, startled. Libby had a fleeting impression of a pudgy, white face, and open mouth. She tapped again, and beckoned.

The woman hesitated, then moved unwillingly towards the door. There was a sound of bolts being drawn, and the door opened some three inches, held there by a stout chain. The woman pressed her face against the opening, appearing grotesquely to Libby only as a nose, lips and gold-capped teeth.

'Go away, we're closed!'

'But I have a watch to be repaired.'

'I can't help that. We're closed, can't you read? Take it somewhere else.'

'I don't know anywhere else. I'm new in town . . .'

'For God's sake!' the mouth hissed. 'Go away, and don't come here again!'

The door slammed, the bolts rasped home, the woman was gone. Van Leeuwen was, indeed, out of circulation. The other address given to her was that of de Vries. He kept some sort of art business, and she decided to try to find it.

The shop was on the far side of the market square. Above the door stood a legend reading 'H. de Vries—Art Gallery'. The window was curtained and empty, apart from a notice informing passers-by that cleaning and restoration were undertaken at reasonable prices. Libby glanced around. Just alongside was a café. She took a seat outside, although it was a little chilly, and ordered coffee. When it came, it tasted peculiar and was not any kind of coffee she could remember, but it served its purpose. Though she watched the shop and everyone who went by carefully for fifteen minutes, everything seemed distressingly normal. Libby paid, stood up, and walked into Harry de Vries's shop.

The bell jangled, and a sharp-faced damsel in a purple blouse looked up and eyed her sulkily.

'May I look around?' Libby asked her.

The girl was Flemish and disliked having to speak French. She said sullenly, 'If you like.'

The building was very old and the shop space cramped. There was a narrow stairway at the back, which hugged the wall and disappeared through a hole on the low, uneven ceiling. The treads appeared to slope, and there was no handrail on the right-hand side. Like so many old continental buildings, this one showed no sign of any attempt at fire precautions. The whole wooden structure of the staircase would flare up in seconds in a blaze, effectively cutting off the escape of any people on the floor above. The sagging plaster of the ceiling also probably covered ancient, dry, timber beams. In fact, the whole place had an improvised and slightly crazy look to it. There were some pencil sketches hanging on the walls, showing other old buildings, probably in the town. Harry doubtless did quite a trade selling them to the Germans as souvenirs. He was a competent artist. That the works were his she knew, because he had signed them. Whether he had higher aspirations than views of his home town, and picture restoration, she had no idea.

Libby peered at one or two of the sketches. The sulky girl continued to read a paperback book, leaning her elbows on the counter, and ignoring Libby completely. But suddenly there was a noise and movement from the floor above. Voices sounded, a man's and a woman's, and a door slammed. Libby debated whether to make a rapid exit, but the sulky girl had already thrust away the paperback and straightened up, and footsteps sounded on the rickety wooden stair. Curiosity kept Libby where she was.

The two people who came down did so, from Libby's viewpoint, very curiously. Because of the layout of the staircase and the way it disappeared through the ceiling, they appeared feet and legs first, followed by torsos, and finally heads. The man ran down first, a little ungallantly, thought Libby. But he wanted to tell the sulky girl something, and a brief conversation ensued in Flemish, which she didn't understand. Glancing carefully sideways, she saw that he was a very tall, thin man with greying hair and rimless spectacles. He was not old, the hair had greyed prematurely, but the hair and glasses gave him an ascetic appearance, so that he looked vaguely like a Victorian curate.

A lighter footstep on the stair caught her ear and her attention. First appeared very good quality kid shoes, and a very shapely pair of legs. A fur coat, and then the woman's head, crowned with a fetchingly tilted toque hat. She was extraordinarily beautiful, and Libby quite forgot caution and stared at her openly. In Marie Gérard's drab clothes, she could not help feeling frumpish by comparison, and in addition very young and naïve, a real provincial. But her open curiosity was her undoing. The woman seemed to be aware that she was being stared at. She turned her head and returned Libby's stare coolly. Initially, the look she gave her was designed to set down this impertinent young woman who gaped at her. But then the woman's whole expression changed. Only briefly, but quite definitely, a light showed in her eyes which indicated recognition. Almost as soon as it had appeared, it was gone. The woman turned her head away regally.

Libby realised that she had lingered too long, and turning, made a precipitate exit. Her heart was pounding painfully in her chest, and she forced herself not to hurry, but to walk naturally. That woman—whoever she was—had recognised her. It wasn't possible, but it had happened. A cold finger of fear touched her heart. Could she have been betrayed already? But by whom?

It was possible that the whole plan that she should observe surreptitiously before contacting any member of the network was in jeopardy. But, above all, she must not panic. She couldn't cut and run, not at the first obstacle. The best thing to do would be to get under cover. Find a place to stay and keep out of the way for a day or two. She walked slowly along, scrutinising the exterior of any place which resembled a small hotel or lodging-house. As she did so, a car drew up at the kerb beside her. Private cars were few, that she had seen already, and so instinct made her hurry her step. Petrol was not available except to those on good terms with authority. But the door on the kerb side had already been flung open, and a curt voice ordered, 'Get in!'

CHAPTER TWELVE

THE VOICE was female, sharp and peremptory, and spoke in French. Libby did not need to look into the car to know it was that of the woman in Harry's shop. Her first instinct had been right, and the woman had recognised her. She stopped and, standing well back from the open car door, said, as firmly as possible, 'I think you've mistaken me for someone else, *madame*.'

'Like hell I have!' came the crisp reply. 'Get in, damn it, before some snooper notices us and picks up the phone!'

It was a blunt reminder that here, in the open street, she was vulnerable. To attempt to run away would attract even more attention, and anyway, be fruitless. The woman's brusque reference to 'snoopers' sent a shiver up Libby's spine. Suddenly the quiet street seemed full of unseen, prying eyes peering from behind lace curtains and blank shutters. The urge to be out of their sight was irresistible. She scrambled into the car, pushing her suitcase down by her feet, and the unknown woman pressed a foot on the accelerator. The car leapt forward, and they drove off, hardly giving Libby time to close the door.

'Who are you?' she gasped as they jolted along.

'You don't need to know that just now,' was the tart reply.

Whoever she was, thought Libby, putting out a

hand to steady herself, she was a good, but risk-taking, driver. They rounded a corner at speed, narrowly missed a cyclist and avoided running over an aged mongrel dog, which walked stiffly down the middle of the road, only by a stomach-churning swerve.

'All right,' Libby said, as soon as she could, 'so where are we going?'

'Somewhere quiet, to talk.'

That had the ring of truth to it and was reassuring. The car sped out of town and finally turned off the road down a track into some trees. There they stopped. The driver turned in her seat and put one arm along the back of it, leaning against her door. Her fine green eyes sparkled at Libby in a sharp, hostile fashion. She could hardly be categorised as 'friend', but what, then, was she?

'London sent you, I suppose. What do you want?'

It was, of course, the classic ploy of an *agent provocateur*, but one of these would have shown more overt friendliness. Nevertheless, Libby decided to keep silent.

A humourless smile touched the woman's lips. 'Don't worry. If I'm not exactly on your side, I'm not on anyone else's, either. I'm on mine, if you see what I mean. But we have a friend in common.'

'I doubt it,' Libby said at last.

'He carries your photograph. He showed it to me. You're wearing a very drab summer dress, and there's an old-ish man in the picture, and two dogs. There, convinced?' The arched eyebrows rose.

The photo she had given Marius! Libby's first reaction was one of anger. What did he mean by showing it to anyone? The next feeling was a highly critical professional one. What on earth was an experienced agent like Marius playing at, dropping in with genuine personal documents of any nature on him, documents which might lead either to his being correctly identified, or, as indeed had happened, to her being identified? There was, however, another question to be asked. Libby asked it.

'You could have come by that photo anywhere. Taken it off a dead man.'

'He's alive,' said the woman drily. Genuine merriment showed in her green eyes and Libby's heart leapt with an entirely new emotion: jealousy. Was this what he had been doing while she had been agonising over his fate—playing Don Juan? If so, the showing of her photo to this woman took on the character of a despicable and unforgivable act.

With barely suppressed fury, Libby demanded, 'Where is he?'

'Safe.'

'I need to contact him. Can you take me to him?' Despite herself, her voice shook slightly on the last word.

It did not pass unnoticed. A faint frown crinkled the smooth brow beneath the toque hat. Slim, kid-gloved fingers tapped an impatient rat-tat on the rim of the steering-wheel. 'I dare say.' She sounded reluctant. 'If you need to see him. I told you he's safe. Unless you need to contact him, you'd do better not to do so.'

'I have my orders,' said Libby starchily.

'They don't apply to *me*!' was the swift retort. But then the woman heaved a sigh. 'All right, I'll take you. He's going mad, anyway, out of touch with everyone, and driving me insane with him. What name are you using, and when did you arrive?'

'I've only just got here. I'm using the name "Marie

Gérard".' For better or worse, she had to trust this woman. 'I have identity papers showing I'm a dressmaker.'

'Ye gods,' said the other, 'how delightfully plebeian! I'm Annette de Jong. I'll take you to Marius. Hold on.'

The car was backed swiftly and as straight as a die down the track and out on the main road. There was little other traffic, probably a good thing, thought Libby, as Annette was not one to wait and see if there was anything coming before reversing at top speed into what would be the line of traffic if there were any. They drove on in stony silence for another two or three miles, and then Annette turned onto a side road and, shortly after that, through an imposing, if weather-worn, pair of gateposts. With a flourish she drew up before one of the gloomiest, and least welcoming, Gothic mansions Libby had ever set eyes on.

She had little time to view it, however. 'Out!' ordered her companion tersely.

Libby got out and followed Annette into the house. There was nobody about, but a child's coloured ball lay in the hall, abandoned and seeming incongruous in this setting. A child? Whose? Annette's? Where was the rest of the family?

Annette did not volunteer any answers to any of these unspoken questions. She merely said, 'You can wait in here,' and threw open the doors of a large salon. Libby walked in, and the door slammed behind her. For a moment, she half expected Annette to lock it, but there was no sinister click. Libby found the woman's whole attitude infuriating, and her barely-concealed contemptuous manner. 'As if I were a servant!' Libby thought mutinously.

She turned restlessly up and down the room, taking little notice of its furnishings. She disliked this house, this situation, and more than anything resented bitterly that her longed-for reunion with the man she loved—incredibly, to be granted to them—would be soured by a meeting with a spoilt and beautiful woman. Not just any woman. There was another reason for feeling resentment towards Annette. Libby had always suspected that in Marius's past there had been someone else, someone he had loved, and who had either betrayed him or from whom he had been somehow parted. She did not need anyone to tell her that Annette was that woman. She knew it. She knew it with every fibre of her being.

But then she remembered that, at any moment, she would see Marius again, and chided herself for a foolish and unworthy jealousy. As if anything could spoil that! I can't wait, she thought. I can't wait to see his face when he sees me . . .

She felt herself trembling with anticipation, and had to struggle to stop her hands shaking. To stand still was an impossibility and she walked quickly up and down, experiencing a scarcely to be repressed urge to go to the lavatory, not knowing whether this was due just to nerves, or a sexual anticipation which set the whole area between pelvis and thigh twitching. The door creaked, and her heart leapt up into her throat. She turned towards it and whispered, 'Marius?'

He was standing in the doorway, looking at her as if he truly couldn't believe what he saw. His expression was pale and shaken, and she knew that Annette had not forewarned him of her true identity. At the same time, she knew that this reunion was not to be the one she longed for, and had dreamed of so often. There was something in his face which struck fear into her heart. Rather there was a lack of something in his eyes as they stared at her. There was no joy. Realising it, the joy in her own heart withered and died.

Marius came into the room, closing the door behind him in an automatic gesture, his eyes still fixed on her. 'Libby?' he said incredulously.

She managed a wan smile. 'Afraid so.' She took a step towards him, and then pent-up emotion spilled out and washed away any doubts or reservations. She flung prudence to the winds and ran to him to throw her arms round him, sobbing, 'Oh, Marius! I've imagined so many things—the worst—I was afraid I'd never see you again, never find you . . .'

He caught at her shoulders and pushed her roughly away from him. He had recovered from his initial shock, and his pale face was contorted with anger. 'What the hell are you doing here?'

'London sent me.'

'They had no bloody right!' he shouted, the words ringing round the room and making the chandelier sing.

'They didn't come to me, I went to them.'

'You stupid bitch, then you had no bloody right! What do you think this is? Some blasted game?' He was shaking her now violently, so that her head bobbed backwards and forwards and she had to fight for breath.

'S-Stop it, Marius . . .' she gasped, and he released her and stood glaring at her. 'I thought,' she whispered, appalled, 'that you'd be pleased to see me . . .'

'Well, I'm not pleased to see you!' he snarled at

her. 'You're the last person on earth I want to see here!'

'I am perfectly capable, you know!' Libby snapped, suddenly angry. Humiliation surged over her.

'Sure—perfectly capable of getting yourself shot!' was the biting retort.

'Well, Count van Malderen, you don't seem to be doing so well—your Wanted poster pinned up all over the place like some Western film! Dead or alive. Bounty-hunters apply to the Kommandantur!'

'I know my business,' he said tightly, 'and this is *my* business, and not yours!'

'Wrong. It *is* mine now, and you'll have to get used to the idea! Of course,' Libby added sarcastically, 'when I said you weren't doing so well, I was speaking purely professionally. On a personal plane you seem to be doing very well indeed.'

He took a step towards her, his fists clenched, and demanded, 'What the devil is that supposed to mean?'

'I'm not stupid, Marius!' Libby exploded. 'The only reason that woman hides you is because you keep her happy in the sack! Well, you may fancy sitting out the war playing stud here—but London wants this network re-formed. They've sent me to see what's left of the original. It seems to me, pretty little.'

She was about to add that she also carried the new code for operating the hidden radio, but some instinct made her keep this knowledge to herself for the time being. She had yet to speak to Harry de Vries.

Her accusation had stung Marius, whose white cheeks glowed with two spots of scarlet. 'I take it you mean that as an allusion to Annette's role? She has taken a considerable risk in hiding me here!' he snarled.

'And got quite a lot out of it . . . What *she* wants, anyway! I've met the type before. Hates all women and can't get enough from the men—any man. She's kept you busy, I bet!'

'Stop this filth and shut your mouth!' Marius hissed and, to her absolute dismay, reached out and slapped her face.

Libby stared at him, stunned. He had not hurt her. It was not a particularly vicious slap. But it was a slap, and he was very, very angry.

'I didn't hit you very hard that time,' he said brusquely, 'but another time I might do. You know nothing about it.'

Libby drew a deep breath. Suddenly she felt quite calm. She was playing her cards all wrongly. But, from now on, she was going to be in charge of this situation. Libby Sherwood had been pushed around enough.

'Hit me again, Marius, and whatever new network is set up here, you will definitely not be a part of it. You can stay here and stew with your mistress. The Resistance doesn't need bedroom athletes. It needs men whose minds are on their work. Whatever happened between us in the past, ours is now a professional relationship, and it has to be based on mutual respect. Your precious Annette would like to treat me like the maidservant, but I'm not the maidservant, and don't you forget it. Tell her the same.'

Marius had been listening to her in silence, and silence followed now, as she finished. Then he gave himself a little shake and said coolly, 'Yes, you're absolutely right. I apologise for striking you. Unforgivable in any circumstances, and certainly between colleagues. Where are you staying?'

'Nowhere, as yet.'

He frowned. 'I'll talk to Annette. She said something about your having identity papers for a dressmaker. Can you really sew?' Briefly, as he asked this question, he sounded mildly amused, and so like the old Marius that her heart gave a painful lurch, despite her new, enforced, dispassionate calm.

'No,' she said crisply. Ruthlessly, she dragged conversation back to the matter in hand. 'Tell me, how many reliable members of the old network are left at liberty?'

He shrugged and went to sit down in a nearby chair, stretching out his legs and glowering at his toes. 'Apart from myself and Harry? Not many.'

'London gave me the address of a man named van Leeuwen, but when I called at the shop, a woman wouldn't let me in.'

Marius gave a mirthless bark of laughter. 'Ton van Leeuwen is a good fellow, but he had a bad fright when he heard the Wouters had both been picked up, and he's gone to ground. It's understandable. Ton has more reason than many to fear arrest. His wife has no doubt insisted that discretion is the better part of valour. She's a forceful woman. But he'll come back. Give him time.'

'He doesn't sound very reliable,' objected Libby doubtfully.

'He's useful. He's handy around anything mechanical and knows how to operate the radio. He's a funny sort of chap, but you can rely on him in his odd way. He wouldn't talk, if that's what you mean.'

'And Harry de Vries?'

'One of the best. Known him all my life. Harry's held this network together. You'll have to talk things over with Harry.'

Libby paused. 'And . . . Annette?'

Marius scrambled to his feet, his jaw thrust out aggressively. 'Don't start that again!'

'I do have some reason to feel aggrieved,' Libby told him. 'That was a pretty fine story you spun me in England.'

'I didn't spin you a story!' he shouted, his hair falling over his forehead in the way she remembered.

'So what was it? Or were you just bored, and passing the time with me?'

'I was not passing the time with you . . .' Marius hissed with suppressed vehemence.

'So who the hell is that woman?' Libby suddenly yelled at him.

'She's an old friend!' he shouted back.

'You don't sleep with her, of course? You're going to put your hand on your heart and tell me that, I dare say?'

'I'm not going to tell you a damn thing,' he panted, his face pale again. 'Some things are your business. That one is not.'

'Which means you have and you still do. Where's her husband?'

'Not here; he doesn't come here. They're separated . . . unofficially.' Marius hesitated perceptibly, then added unwillingly, 'He's a collaborator. That doesn't make her one.'

'It makes your association with her unwise. Does she have children?'

'One,' he said stiffly.

'Then this husband has a hold on her. Try remembering that the next time you get the urge. A cold shower might do more good than sprawling on top of her! What's the matter? Aren't there any girls like me around here? Simple types whom you can persuade to drop their knickers? Just so you can keep in practice. We wouldn't like you to get rusty in such a vital department.'

'It's not like that,' Marius said wearily. 'Of course you mistrust her, but I came here because I had nowhere else to go at the time. The very fact that her husband is so friendly with the Germans makes this the last place they'll come to look. Yes, we were once lovers. Yes, I have been to bed with her since then, since coming here. It didn't mean a damn thing. It was a simple case of lust. I'm not Don Juan, but I am normal. She is extremely talented in that way. I'd be a fool, knowing her as I do, to consider it anything more than an erotic exercise, and I don't consider it anything more. Does that satisfy you?'

'You miserable louse . . .' Libby whispered. 'What are you trying to do to me? If you don't want me, say so. But don't make me feel such a damn amateur. Fumbling around in an air-raid shelter might not equal grand passion in a mausoleum like this place, but I don't have her talents because I don't have her free and easy attitude. It wasn't an erotic exercise for me. I did what I did, I let you do what you did, because I cared for you and I wanted us to be one . . .'

Words failed her, and she turned away so that he could not see the tears which flooded into her eyes. 'Damn, damn, damn!' she muttered, rubbing them away.

Marius took a step towards her and put out his hand, but let it drop by his side when she threatened, 'Don't you dare to touch me ever again!'

'Listen, Libby,' he sounded less sure of himself, 'I had no idea London would send you. It was a hell of a shock to see you standing there.'

'I bet it was!' she interrupted, eyes flashing dangerously.

'Listen, will you? You can't possibly expect me to be pleased to see you in this situation. I thought you were safe in England, and whatever happened to me, you were well out of it. I still wish you were safe in England and well out of this. As for Annette, I don't expect you to like her, but I don't apologise for her. Whatever she is, she isn't going to betray me, that I do believe, and it's all that matters.'

'All that matters,' she returned, 'is that the network is re-formed and working again. I need a place to stay.'

'I'll speak to Annette.'

'Not here, damn it!' she blazed. 'Haven't you got any sensitivity? Or does it seem amusing to you to have all three of us cooped up here together? Do you suggest we share an extra-large bed?'

'You gave me a lecture on not getting private and professional business mixed up!' Marius said sharply. 'You were right, but the rules apply to you, too. If you don't like her, too bad. We need her. So do you. Wait here.'

He stalked out and slammed the door. He was gone some minutes, and eventually Libby grew rebellious. Damn it, they were *not* going to decide what was to be done about her without her being present! Angry as she was about Annette, there was no doubt in her mind that Annette was equally angry about her. Marius was caught in the middle, and he didn't like it. 'Serve him right!' she muttered. He was probably, even now, trying to placate Annette.

But he could not exclude Libby, even so. She pushed open the door of the salon and stuck her head out into the hall.

Voices sounded from a short distance away. The hall was still empty, so she made her way cautiously towards the sound, and traced it to another closed door. She put her ear to the panels.

'I am not going to have your tart staying here!' Annette was shouting. 'She can lodge in town. Harry can look after her!'

'This place is safer!' Marius argued.

'I told you before, I'm not one of your machine-gun-carrying Resistance fighters! You're here because of what we once were to one another, because I'm still fond of you, and because I still know what makes you tick, Marius! I'm not a fool. I brought that girl here because I didn't really know what else to do with her, and she might just have found her way here by herself. She wanted to see you, and she's seen you. But she doesn't stay under this roof!'

Wryly Libby considered that at least she and Annette were agreed on something. She opened the door and marched briskly in. Both whirled round and stared at her, equally flushed and angry.

'So long as you're going to talk about me, I think I should be here,' Libby announced calmly. 'Don't worry, Annette, I've no intention of staying here. If you think it's safe for me to go to Harry de Vries, I'll go there.'

Marius gave a kind of growl. 'I have to be in touch with you. You'll have to come out here to meet me. I can't go into town. My face is known.'

Annette's brain was obviously working at lightning speed. 'You're supposed to be a dressmaker.'

'I've already told Marius I can't sew,' Libby interrupted, 'before you suggest I alter your entire wardrobe.'

Marius gave her a hunted look, Annette only shrugged.

'A pity. I do have a length of jersey silk. I've had it since before the war and I need it made up into an afternoon dress.'

Libby, her face burning scarlet with fury, snarled, 'I'm not here to sew superfluous gowns for you!'

Annette smiled at her unexpectedly. 'Of course not, my dear. But if you are to come out to the château, you must have an excuse. It's a pity you can't really sew, but it might not matter. You can come out anyway, as a dressmaker, and we'll fiddle about with the length of cloth if anyone calls by snooping.'

'It's a long way out from town; she'll have to take the bus,' Marius said bleakly.

'I can't send the car for a dressmaker. Harry can organise a bicycle for her. I dare say she rides a bicycle?' The green eyes rested on Libby's flushed face.

'Yes,' she said tightly, between gritted teeth. So help me, I'll hit this woman in a minute. I'm being treated like a servant again. She hasn't the courtesy to address me directly.

But Marius, who until this moment had been looking increasingly embarrassed by the tone of the acrimonious exchange between the two women, startled both of them by chuckling in unfeigned mirth. 'Oh, yes, she rides a bicycle, all right . . .' he said.

* * *

Eventually, Annette agreed to drive Libby back into town and introduce her to de Vries. By the time they got there, it was getting dark, and the shop was closed. Annette knocked at the door, and a window above their heads opened.

'Only me, Harry,' Annette called softly.

'Wait . . .' ordered a man's voice.

After a few minutes, there was a scraping noise at the door and it opened to admit them. De Vries closed it. They must have interrupted him at work, because he held a paint-stained rag in his hand, and began to wipe his palms slowly with it, as he looked enquiringly from one to the other of them.

'London's sent you this one,' Annette said without preamble. 'Keep her out of my hair. Marius has seen her. She'll tell you what we decided. You'll have to lodge her here. It's all right. She's got papers.'

Annette turned on her heel and let herself out of the shop without further ado. Harry contemplated Libby.

'You'd better come upstairs, then.'

She followed him up the rickety staircase. At the top, a door stood open and from it came the unmistakable smell of an artist's studio. It filled her with an almost unbearable home-sickness, because her mother was an artist, and at home in Canada, at the top of their house, was just such a studio, muddled, cluttered, a workroom and a refuge.

Libby put down her case and walked into it. Harry followed her. 'My mother is an artist . . .' she faltered, turning to him.

Harry took off his glasses and squinted at her, then began to polish the lenses in a way which reminded her of Uncle Gerry. 'Want to see what I'm doing?'

He led the way to the easel and she saw he was working at cleaning a nineteenth-century canvas, a not very flattering portrait of a plump lady who appeared to be wearing every piece of jewellery she possessed.

'The flesh tones are coming up well,' said Harry. 'And she has plenty of flesh.'

The humour was unexpected, and Libby suddenly found herself liking him. 'She's a little overdressed,' she said, relaxing.

'Only got her portrait painted once, I suppose, and wanted to make the most of it. The painting belongs to Mrs de Jong. I'll show you where you can sleep.'

He led her out of the studio and along the corridor, pausing at midway to point up to a trap-door in the roof. 'Emergency exit.' The vulnerability of the staircase had not gone unnoticed. Libby began to feel a greater confidence in her companion, who seemed, at first sight, rather too mild and academic for such a dangerous occupation. He had opened the door to a tiny room at the end of the corridor. It held a bed and a washstand and very little else, and was little more than a large cupboard. 'Not the most comfortable in town,' he apologised, 'but the best I can do.'

She turned to thank him, and saw he had pushed his spectacles up on top of his head, and was staring at her appraisingly. Tall, thin and stooping slightly, with a prominent nose, he reminded her faintly of some sort of large bird of prey. He had grey eyes, and they were surprisingly sharp for someone who needed spectacles. The restoration work, of course, required detailed observation. He nodded, as if satisfied, and she had passed the test. She was reminded of her first meeting with Marius, when she had had the same sensation of being subjected to some sort of test.

'I live through there . . .' He pointed. 'I'll make supper in about twenty minutes.' He shambled out of the door, bending his head beneath the lintel.

Libby put her case on the bed and glanced around. She wasn't lodged like Marius, in the luxury of the château. However, even given one or two unpleasant upsets, things had not gone badly. She wondered whether she ought to offer to cook the supper for herself and Harry. It seemed odd, in their situation, to be worrying about a mundane task like getting meals. But, she thought ruefully, for these people, Harry and those like him, this is a normal situation. This is how they live. Their Resistance activities are part of their lives. They don't think of themselves as incredibly brave, just as doing their job. And now it's my job, too.

Harry lived in a tiny sitting-room *cum* bedroom with a complete disregard for what most people would call the basic necessities of comfortable living, in a way which only writers or artists can. It didn't worry him that one had to clear stacks of cartridge paper from the table before one could put down a bowl of soup. Or that the sofa obviously doubled as his bed, that the kitchen was only just big enough for one person to squeeze into and all the saucepans had lost their handles. Libby let him get their modest supper, after all, as only he knew where everything was—which was never in the obvious place. The discovery of a pair of socks among the potatoes did not come as a surprise. Certainly not to Harry, who observed absently, 'I wondered where those had got to,' and put them in his pocket, where they were instantly forgotten again. He nevertheless produced thick vegetable soup, coarse bread and quite good cheese. Harry was not a man to be underestimated.

They sat in the cluttered bed-sitter while he explained those details which she had not gleaned from Marius. It was quickly apparent that the muddle which surrounded Harry applied strictly to things he did not consider important, like day-to-day housework. The things which mattered to him—his art work, the Resistance, her presence and the necessity of re-establishing the broken network—all these were discussed lucidly and with objective clarity. Harry spoke very good English, and as he spoke, gesticulated with long, thin hands, and fiddled constantly with his spectacles. He had also tried to contact the jeweller van Leeuwen, and, as had others, failed to get round the barricade of his wife. But, like Marius, he was of the opinion that he would emerge in his own good time. 'Or we'll eventually flush him out,' he said, 'when we need him.' On the subject of Annette de Jong, Harry was cagy. He trusted her to hide and help Marius, but she would not willingly do anything else. Besides, there was an added complication. Her child had recently arrived and presented a problem.

'Children notice things,' said Harry, absent-mindedly eating Libby's piece of bread. 'I think it's best you stay here and not out there. I don't know how she's explained Marius away, but she couldn't explain you away, too, not if you were sleeping there.' His sharp grey eyes flickered over her. 'You're pretty friendly with Marius, are you?'

'I knew him in England,' she said stiffly. 'That's all.'

It wasn't all, and Harry wasn't deceived, but he let the subject drop. 'Did London send a new code out with you?'

'Yes,' she admitted cautiously. 'But what about the radio equipment?'

'It's quite safe.'

'Where?' She looked about the cluttered room. 'Here, in this building?'

'Good God, no!' he exclaimed, shocked. 'As a matter of fact, it's still out at Wouters' farm.'

Libby frowned. 'But I thought the Wouters had been arrested.'

'So they have. But the Germans didn't find the radio. It's behind some false panelling in Jan's cowshed. The Germans crawled all over the house, but were less enthusiastic about the cowshed. Oh, they looked it over, but the smell of Jan's cattle and getting themselves covered in manure made them hurry it, and they missed the hiding-place. Marius got away from there by the skin of his teeth. The Wouters were sitting ducks. We've lost them for good.'

There was a terrible, practical tone to his voice. No use crying over spilt milk. Wouters and his wife had paid the ultimate price for their loyalty and patriotism. Others would have to see the job through, and make sure they had not died in vain.

'Who is at the farm now?' Libby asked.

Harry pursed his mouth. 'No one. Wouters ran the place single-handedly—with his wife. They had a son, but he was taken for forced labour. A neighbouring farmer took over the cattle and other livestock. The farm itself is abandoned.'

'So,' Libby pursued, 'I—and Marius, too—could if necessary move back there?'

He shook his head. 'The place is empty. An empty place looks empty. There's a sort of feel about it. If you or Marius were there, even if you kept under cover, sooner or later someone would spot you, or a sign of life. Marius is better off with Annette, and you're all right here for the time being.'

Libby nodded, but it was comforting to think there was another possible bolt-hole. She said no more about it to Harry. He hadn't asked her for the code, so she stretched her arms, saying, 'I'm dog-tired. I spent last night crouched in an aeroplane.'

'So you did,' said Harry. He paused. 'So you did,' he repeated. 'Sorry you weren't met, but that was Jan Wouters' job. I met Marius—but that was because Marius was a special visitor.'

'Yes,' Libby said. 'Marius is special.'

CHAPTER THIRTEEN

DESPITE HER brain buzzing with so many new experiences and information, Libby slept like a log. Harry woke her in the morning with a cup of tea, and said he had borrowed a bicycle for her, if she wanted it.

Later, primed with directions for finding the way out of town, she set off. It was a grey day and the long, country road exposed to the weather. She pedalled resolutely along, buffeted by wind and her face wet with rain. The wheels creaked a little, but at least this bicycle was an improvement on the one she rode in England. 'How did you spend the war, Libby?' she imagined her parents asking when at long last she got home to Canada—if ever she did. 'Well, Mother and Dad, I rode a bike round England, and then I rode a bike round Belgium. You don't know anyone who needs a peacetime lady cyclist, do you?'

A car was coming up behind her and she wobbled slightly as she steered into the edge of the roadway. It passed her with a flurry of grit and drew up a little way down the road, waiting. It was a German staff car, and her heart sank as she saw a familiar and rather dashing figure get out and wait for her. Libby slowed down and put one foot to the ground.

'Good afternoon, Mademoiselle Gérard.'

'Good afternoon, Major Dettmar.'

'A bicycle ride in the country?' He raised his eyebrows. 'In such bad weather? It is not a day for this sort of exercise.' He frowned disapprovingly at the rainspots which had begun to stain his sleeve. He was actually, now that she could study him away from the crowds of the railway station, a very handsome man. A lady-killer. He automatically made conquests as he proceeded through life. She was a stage on his journey. One day he would tell his friends about her, 'I knew a little dressmaker in Belgium . . .' followed by some salacious detail of her performance in bed.

Not a chance, Major, thought Libby, eyeing him. Slip your hand up some other girl's skirt. Try it on me, and I'll ruin your chances of fathering any contributions to the master race. Aloud, she said, 'I'm on my way to see a client—or someone I hope will be a client. I'm a dressmaker.'

'Indeed? Who is the lady?'

'A Mrs de Jong, she lives in the village just ahead, at the château.'

A flicker of recognition passed across the grey eyes watching her carefully. His manner changed, becoming almost confidential. 'I have met Mrs de Jong. A charming lady. Of very good family. Always very elegant. To sew for her must be an honour. You will be so good as to pass her my regards?' He leaned forward anxiously.

'Yes, all right,' Libby said, looking at him curiously. She decided to take this as a parting phrase and settled back on the saddle of the bicycle.

'It is a great pity,' Major Dettmar said, with every sign of real regret, 'that I did not know you wished to call at the château. I could have taken you there.'

Libby smiled glacially. He gave her a debonair salute, got back into his car and roared off. She pedalled on slowly, the wind blowing into her face and chafing her skin.

The rain had stopped by the time she reached the château, and as she rode up and dismounted before the house, a small child in coat and gaiters ran out, obviously just released to play in a gap between showers. He chased round the corner in pursuit of a large, fat tabby cat which moved just fast enough to keep ahead. That must be Annette's child. She had not struck Libby as the maternal type, but there was no accounting for the way people behaved.

The house looked even more unattractive than it had done the previous day. Water dripped from its battlements, and its turrets looked indescribably mournful. Whoever had built this place must have been a manic depressive. But there was a huge log fire burning in the drawing-room, and she was glad to see it. She held out her chilled fingers to it, and felt life returning. Studying it more closely than on her previous visit, she thought what a perfectly awful room it was. There was a pale square on one wall where the picture Harry was cleaning had hung. The other portraits were similar to it. On a table a length of material was spread out, together with scissors, pins, and various pictures of model gowns torn out of magazines. The dressmaking. A click at the door led her to straighten up and turn round in nervous anticipation, but it wasn't Marius—it was Annette.

'Filthy day,' her hostess offered by way of greeting. 'I set the sewing out.' She gestured towards the table with one elegant hand. Her manner seemed marginally more friendly than the day before. At least, more co-operative. That was not kindness. Libby was not deceived. Annette had no unselfish motives. If she had changed tactics, it was because she wanted something herself.

'I noticed the needlework,' Libby said, nodding

towards the table and the length of cloth. She expected that Annette might suggest fetching Marius now, but instead, the other woman took a seat by the log fire and leaned back, as if prepared for a heart-to-heart talk. Libby sat down too, warily.

Annette stretched out slim fingers with red-varnished tips for a silver cigarette-case. 'Marius doesn't. Do you?'

'What? Oh, smoke, no thanks.' Libby watched her light up.

'How did you make out with Harry?'

'All right.' Libby flushed, as it struck her that some double entendre might lie in this question.

But Annette had other things on her mind. Without further preamble, she went on, 'That photograph of you which Marius carries around, next to his heart—romantic, if you like that sort of thing—it's not very good, but that's just my opinion. Marius handles it as if it were framed in diamonds. When I first saw you in the flesh, in Harry's shop, I must admit you looked just like the photograph, and I couldn't imagine what on earth Marius saw in you, unless he had suddenly developed a penchant for schoolgirls, as some men do. But you're not really like that, are you? You're not the girl in the snapshot, I mean. You're rather remarkable. I just wonder if Marius realises it.'

Not yet, thought Libby. I've destroyed that old image he had of me, but I've yet to persuade him to accept the new. How much of an obstacle is this woman going to be? Ask her, why don't you? She likes to be direct. Serve her up a dose of her own medicine.

'Do you want him?' Libby asked, staring directly

into the green eyes regarding her from the other side of the fireplace.

'Do you think I do?' The pencilled eyebrows rose fractionally, the red mouth repressed a smile.

'I don't think you love him,' Libby told her bluntly. 'I think you don't want to give him up to someone else—because that hits your pride. You're lonely here, your marriage has failed, you need someone there to admire you. I also think you're acquisitive. Marius is an acquisition. You're not generous by nature and you don't give anything away, certainly not Marius.'

Annette, who might have been expected to be angered by this speech, took it calmly. 'That's very shrewd of you, my dear. I knew I was right in deciding you were brighter than you look. You, I suppose, do want Marius, for keeps.'

'Yes,' Libby agreed calmly, 'but I know no one can go back, put the clock back, to something which existed before. Marius and I have to start all over again. We can't pick up from where we were, as I believed when I prayed we would one day be re-united. I believed that until I came here, but now I know it's not so. I think Marius saw me as a sort of symbol, before. The opposite to war, and what he had to do here. But I'm not a symbol, I'm flesh and blood. That's what Marius doesn't realise.'

Annette was watching her speculatively. 'He does, then, want to pick up where you left off?'

'I don't know. I don't know what Marius wants or thinks.' She frowned. 'I used to think I knew what he thought of me. I thought I understood what he meant, even if he hadn't said it in so many words. But now I'm not so sure.'

Annette drew on her cigarette, blue smoke curling

into the air. 'I was like you once, young and naïve, believing in love. I thought I could change the world, and any man in it I fancied, to suit me. I found I couldn't, and you'll find you can't. You won't change Marius. He and I get along together so well because we're so alike. We're both selfish, we're both pretty ruthless and we understand one another. You say you don't understand him now. You never will understand him.' There was a silence, and the ticking of a clock seemed abnormally loud. Annette rose composedly to her feet. 'Marius was probably attracted by that porcelain exterior of yours, but that kind of thing bores men after a while. They go back to what they know.'

'Are you always so rude to people?' Libby asked seriously.

'Always, my dear. I can't help it. I have a spiteful nature. I'll fetch him.'

Left alone, Libby wandered to the window. On a ledge was a wooden train engine, painted red and blue. She pushed it back and forth idly. The child, Harry had said, presented problems. Problems for Annette, too. The collaborator husband from whom she was separated, the child she presumably loved, Marius whom she was hiding . . . Annette was performing quite a juggling act. It could not go on. Sooner or later she would have to let one of the skittles drop. Which one? I suppose, she thought, it's just as well I'm not pregnant. I could have been; we never worried about it, that night in the air-raid shelter. It's a piece of luck that I'm not—or I wouldn't be here now. No jumping out of aircraft in those circumstances.

She put down the toy train, folded her arms and stared morosely out at the denuded formal garden which graced the front of the house. It had a grey-black winter look to it, in the dismal drizzle which had begun again. No one had planted late flowering bedding-plants such as Farley tended at Merriton House, and these neatly-raked but bare beds looked uncomfortably like graves.

She sensed Marius come up behind her, rather than heard him, and shivered as his breath skimmed the lobe of her ear. 'Don't stand so close!' she muttered.

She heard him hiss with annoyance. 'You're being stupid, Libby, and pig-headed.'

'Makes two of us.'

'What do you want me to do? Grovel? Well, I'm sorry if I didn't dance with joy when I saw you yesterday. But I explained that, and I explained Annette, and I can't help it if you choose to make yourself judge and jury and crown yourself with self-righteousness!'

'Don't attack *me* because you're in the wrong!' she snapped.

'Damn it all!' he burst out resentfully, 'I'm human and I make mistakes. Since when has it been a crime? Am I now to be a permanent outcast because I experience all the normal physical reactions when a woman strips off her clothes and gets into bed with me?' When she didn't answer, he added irritably, 'For pity's sake, you must know it doesn't mean I don't still want you!'

He slipped his arms round her waist and drew her back towards him, and at that, she drew a sharp breath, and reminded him, 'I told you, don't you dare to touch me!'

'Why not?' He sounded obstinate now. He held her pressed against him and she could feel the heat of his body through her clothing, feel too, his own mounting desire. 'You had a choice,' he said huskily. 'You chose to come here. You could have stayed at home in England.' One hand slid across her hip and thigh and the other tightened on her breast. His mouth pressed against her neck at the point of her jaw. It was an absolute claim for possession.

Libby shuddered and bit her lip to stop herself screaming. Every nerve in her body was jangling at his touch, and a pulse leapt in her groin. She knew that if he attempted to take her now, she could not have resisted, not with every fibre shrieking, 'Yes, yes!' She jerked herself resolutely free and spun round to face him.

'We can't just go off to bed, Marius, which I suppose is what you want, and pretend nothing has happened since we were together in England to change the situation between us. I asked you once, then, to make love to me. But I'm not asking now.'

'Because of one meaningless episode with her?' he demanded, pointing towards the closed door of the room.

'Marius,' Libby said steadily, 'I was lucky enough to have parents who really loved one another. They would never have betrayed one another, *couldn't* have betrayed one another, because it wasn't in them. They just believed in one another.' She saw his mouth open to interrupt again, and said fiercely, 'Don't—let me finish! I don't blame you for going to bed with Annette. You think I'm angry about that. But I've met Annette now. She's beautiful. She obviously finds you attractive, and sex is important to her. She needs that. You knew her long before you knew me, and she was your mistress then, so I shouldn't be angry, or even surprised. Of course, I don't *like* it. No woman would. But there's something far more important, which can't be explained so easily.

'You wrote me off, Marius. That's what I don't forgive so easily. I never did that to you. Not when you left, not when Jamie told me he had flown you into occupied territory and how unlikely it was that you'd ever come back. Not when Mr Smith told me you were on the run, and the network had been smashed. Not any of those times, not *ever*. I never gave up on you, but you gave up on me!' Her voice had become louder, and her face flushed. Her blue eyes sparkled at him.

'I'm sorry,' he said after a pause. He moved away from her. 'It didn't seem, to me, I'd done that. I always tried to be fair, to be honest. I told you there wasn't any future for us. Not because I didn't want there to be, but because I couldn't see any. You call that lack of faith. But I didn't see it as giving up, only as being realistic. I still know there's damn little chance of either of us getting out of this.'

'Was it being fair to me, to use me as an escape from the war? I know you tried to be honest, but you weren't being honest with yourself.'

He made a gesture of impatience. 'This is getting us nowhere. Say what you like, believe what you like. The fact is, we haven't time to argue over what I or you should have done or didn't do. That's the way it is. You can't make the situation change because you want it to, Libby.'

'Yes, you can!' she said energetically, angered by the way he seemed to echo Annette's words. He looked towards her and twitched one eyebrow. 'You can make things whatever you like, inside yourself.

No one outside can stop that happening if you really want it to happen.'

'It isn't true, Libby,' Marius said obstinately. 'I wish it were.'

'It is true!' she stormed at him.

He didn't answer. Libby drew a deep breath and began, 'Harry says the radio equipment is still safely hidden, and in working order. It's still out at Wouters' farm, behind some panelling in the cowshed. The Germans didn't find it because it's behind a muck-heap or something. It sounded pretty disgusting.'

'It's all a disgusting business, dirty all round,' Marius said moodily. He twitched his shoulders. 'Even if it's safe, we can't use it. We've every reason to believe the code has been broken.'

'I've brought out a new one.'

Marius's eyes sharpened. 'You've given this code to Harry?'

'No, not yet. He knows I have it, though.'

Marius muttered, 'Good, good . . . At least we can get in contact with London again. Look, try and dig out Ton van Leeuwen. That battleaxe of a wife has to go out shopping, or something. Go round the back of his shop. There's an alley, all drains, smells and rubbish-bins, but there's a wooden door into his backyard.'

'I'll try . . . but I'm blowed if I can see why you have such faith in him. He sounds a regular mouse.'

'He's not a mouse; he's a frightened man, and has good reason to be. Reasons you don't know about.' Marius hesitated. 'No need for you to know, but take my word for it. You can count on Ton to hold his tongue.' His manner brightened. 'Things aren't so bad, after all. There's you and Harry and me—

and Ton, with luck—a radio safely hidden and working and a new code so that we can begin sending messages. With a bit of organisation, we'll get this network working again pretty soon.'

On the way home, the borrowed bicycle developed a slow puncture. There was a repair kit in the saddle-bag, but light was fading, and Libby made a poor job of mending it by the roadside, and finished up pushing the bicycle for the last mile of the way.

Had Dettmar appeared again now, offering a lift, she might even have been tempted to accept. 'They're never around when you want one!' she observed with wry humour to herself as she trudged through the mud.

When she reached Harry's shop, she was footsore, tired and worried that she might fall foul of some curfew. All the shutters were up and she had to rattle at the door for admittance. It seemed an age before she heard Harry running down the rickety wooden staircase and the rasp of the bolt being drawn.

His tall, gangling figure loomed over her in the unlit doorway. 'Where the hell have you been?' he demanded.

'Pushing the blasted bike!' she snapped. She had had enough. She shoved her way unceremoniously past him, bicycle and all, and propped the machine against the wall in the shop.

Harry muttered, 'Just a moment!' He locked up again carefully, and tugged at the heavy curtains. Only then did he switch on the light and turn towards her. The bulb flickered erratically. 'We had a power cut this afternoon,' he said. He peered down at her in the yellow glow. 'What's wrong with the bicycle?'

Libby sat down and pulled off her headscarf. 'Puncture. I tried to mend it, but I didn't do very well.' She slipped her feet out of her shoes and inspected her right foot gloomily. There was a large blister on her heel.

Harry stooped over the machine, and grunted, 'I'll fix it in a minute.'

Libby eyed him curiously, while he prodded at the soft rubber tyre. He must have been at work in his studio when she hammered for admittance. The paint-rag hung out of his pocket and his sleeves were rolled up. Despite his spidery frame, he had strongly muscled forearms. She wondered whether in his youth he had been some kind of track athlete. He had the build of a runner. On an impulse, she asked him.

He turned round and stared at her in surprise. 'No—Marius was the sportsman. I used to skate a little in winter. Why?'

'Oh,' she was suddenly embarrassed. 'You're fit but skinny, sorry if that sounds rude.'

Harry grinned. 'I always was thin. Probably from living off my own cooking for so many years.'

She smiled back, and wished she did not like him so much. Liking people was bad in this game. She was uneasily aware that she was learning what it was like to live with the constant possibility of discovery. You didn't know whom to trust. You spent your life looking over your shoulder. Aloud, she said, 'I'm dog-tired.'

'Go upstairs. I'll see to the bicycle.'

There was soup in a pan in the kitchen and a dirty plate, so Harry had eaten. Libby heated the rest of the soup, even though she did not feel very hungry, and poured it into a bowl, retreating to the sitting-room. The heating in there came from a pot-bellied iron stove. She opened the little door with the hooked implement provided and rattled around in the stove's innards to encourage flames. It seemed to contain a lot of ash. Harry had been burning paper. When he came in, she said over her shoulder, 'You ought not to put too much paper in this stove, it puts the fire out.'

'Teach you that in the Girl Guides, did they?' Harry went into the kitchen and could be heard washing his hands in the sink. 'I was burning rough sketches, ideas which didn't work out. The bicycle is fixed.'

He continued rummaging about in the kitchen, and Libby picked up a poker and pushed idly at the unburnt scraps of paper. As a child, she had always been fascinated by the gardener's bonfires and tried to poke flames from smouldering rubbish. Her prodding now brought to the top a scrap of card, half-burned, but with printing on it. No sketch. Curiously, she fished it out, blew on it to rid it of ash, and handling it carefully because it was still warm and very fragile, bent over it.

There was a movement from the kitchen. Harry was coming back, and it wouldn't do to be seen investigating the contents of his stove, like a real Paul Pry. Guiltily, she thrust the scrap of card into her pocket out of sight.

Harry appeared before her, holding a cup and saucer. 'This will set you up and get the damp out of your bones. Mint tea.'

She peered suspiciously at the brackish liquid. 'In England, they eat mint with lamb and new potatoes.'

'Well, I make it into tea instead. It clears the

head. You look as though your head needs clearing . . . No disrespect. I fancy you have a problem?'

'Is that what you call trying to reconstruct the network?'

'I mean,' Harry said mildly, 'you have an extra problem. A personal one.' He sat down on his sofa *cum* bed, pushed his spectacles on top of his head and rested his long thin arms on his knees, like a waiting stick-insect.

'Nothing I can't handle,' Libby said sturdily. 'I made a mistake, that's all. I wanted to know the truth. Before I left England, someone warned me about that. I should have listened. But it's nothing to worry about, Harry.'

Harry stirred his tea and the smell of mint filled the air. The aroma of the tea was penetrating Libby's tired brain and, as he had promised, clearing it.

'What did Marius have to say?'

'Not a great deal. We talked about the network. He's pretty optimistic. He wants to find van Leeuwen.'

Harry snorted. 'That little rat?'

Libby got up and wandered over to a work-table in the corner covered with sheets of paper. After a moment, she sat down, picked up a piece of charcoal and began to set on paper a rough representation of a flowerless geranium plant in a pot on the rough window-sill. It was a distraction and a way of calming her nerves more than anything, but after a few moments she became interested and began to improve on her drawing. She hunched over it, her hair falling over her forehead, the tip of her tongue protruding between her teeth in concentration. It was a little while before she realised that Harry had come to stand behind her and watch over her shoulder. She glanced up a little guiltily and saw that his grey eyes were narrowed in a critical appreciation of her work. Libby set down the charcoal, beset by shyness.

'That's very good,' Harry said slowly. 'You've had art lessons.'

'Only from my mother.'

'Oh, yes, you told me . . .' Harry wandered away a little. 'But you have talent, too.'

There was something of a new note in his voice, which she could not quite identify, and she watched him a little curiously. He seemed about to speak again, then to think better of it, and went back to his sofa, where he settled down full length, with his back propped up on a pile of cushions against one arm and his knees crooked up in front of him, his feet on the seat. He rested his arms on his knees and interlaced his long, slender artist's fingers. Without looking towards her, he said, 'It's difficult, living in an occupied country.'

'Yes, I realise that,' Libby replied awkwardly.

'Do you, I wonder?' Harry's grey eyes shot their surprisingly sharp glance in her direction. 'People like Marius—or even like you—run great risks in getting here, staying here to do what you have to do—and getting away again. But there's a time limit on it. One operation, beginning, middle, end. The rest of us, we're here all the time. We don't jump out of aeroplanes or blow bridges . . . and we don't get away again, back to England. We just stay here, day after day, night after night, listening for the knock on the door. After a while, your nerve cracks. It doesn't do it because something has happened. It does it because *nothing* has happened. You begin to wish that something, anything, would happen. It's the waiting . . .' He fell silent.

'You're a brave man, Harry,' Libby told him earnestly. 'And London knows it, and appreciates it.'

'I'm not the heroic kind,' he said curtly. 'Marius is. Marius is born out of his time. He would have done well in the seventeenth century. A swashbuckling musketeer in ruffles and thigh boots, rescuing fair damsels and defending king and country. Are you in love with him?'

The question came unexpectedly. Because it was so direct, and because she was not prepared for it, Libby could not think of any way of avoiding it. 'Yes,' she confessed. 'That doesn't mean everything is all right between us. In fact, it's all wrong. But one doesn't stop loving a person just for that reason.'

'Hm, don't ask me; I'm no expert! Why are you in love with him? Because he's a handsome, dashing fellow with a heck of a reputation in love and war?'

'No!' she said vehemently. 'I could do without the reputation in love and war: it's the cause of all the trouble! I love Marius because—because he just is—Marius . . .' she finished feebly. 'I can't help it. I feel—incomplete—without him. I don't think he feels that way about me. Sometimes he retreats into some sort of private shell and locks the door against everyone else. It's as if he doesn't *need* anyone else. Just when I feel I'm beginning to understand him, I find I don't. I'm not a *femme fatale*, you know. I don't understand men very well. I haven't known very many that well.'

Harry wriggled his back against his cushion support as if afflicted by a sudden itch, and scowled into the empty space in front of him. 'I'm not the person to advise you on affairs of the heart, but you're going to get hurt. I'm sorry.' He turned his head to look at her, and she was surprised at the sincerity in his face. 'I'm sorry you'll be hurt. I'm sorry you're an artist, too.'

'An artist? Why are you sorry about that?' she asked in surprise. 'What difference does it make?'

'It makes a difference to *me*!' he muttered. He swung his long legs off the sofa and jumped up, scooping up his empty cup and hers, and disappeared into the kitchen, where he could be heard washing up with a great clatter.

Libby frowned, then shrugged. She had enough troubles. If Harry had problems, and certainly he must have, it couldn't be helped. All the same, something had clearly upset him. She glanced thoughtfully towards her abandoned drawing. A shared artistic talent had more than surprised him: it had distressed him. It seemed that Harry was another one she did not understand.

He had come back into the room, and was carrying a bottle. He held it up.

'Apricot liqueur, and it's pre-war. Kicks like a mule! It's the only cure for love-sickness I can offer you, but it's a good one.' He opened a cupboard, rustled about inside for glasses, and produced two after rejecting three or four as insufficiently washed.

'You ought to get food-poisoning,' she chided him. 'That kitchen is a disgrace.'

'My stomach is used to it.'

'Mine's not.'

'You are not supposed to be staying very long,' he reminded her. 'Not that I'm trying to be inhospitable.' He poured out a glass of the pale yellow liqueur and handed it to her.

She did not really want it, but she drank it to please him. It did, indeed, kick like a mule, and molten fire coursed through her veins. Harry refilled her glass, holding the bottle to the light and peering at the amber glow.

The liqueur had reached her brain and was undoing the good work of the mint tea. She was beginning to feel distinctly fuzzy. She put down the glass, and when Harry stretched out his hand to the bottle, signalled to him that she did not want any more. 'I'm not a drinker, Harry.'

Harry had thrown himself full length on the sofa, and was nursing his half-empty glass on his chest. 'When this war is over, I shall go and live in the south of France, and paint seascapes and torrid landscapes which I shall sell to rich Americans.'

'You should do well.'

'Van Gogh didn't do very well.'

'He had problems.'

'Who hasn't?' said Harry.

Curious, she asked him, 'Your art, it means a great deal to you? I'm not talking of the shop. I'm talking about real painting. That's what you'd really like to do? Give this up and go and be a full-time serious painter somewhere?'

'A man knows his limitations. I don't deceive myself I'm a great artist. I'm a capable artist. I have an eye for a view. I'm a pretty fair draughtsman. I have a sympathy for old paintings so that when I restore one, I do it with tact. No one is ever going to remember me as a great artist.' He did not sound so regretful; more practical. If he had regrets, he had learned to live with them. If there was bitterness in Harry, it didn't show. He turned his head, and his sharp grey eyes rested on her slightly flushed face.

He took off his spectacles and reached out to put them on the table. 'Come over here.'

There was an audible change in his voice, something in it which had not been there before. He looked less harmless and relaxed lying there, and indefinably more masculine and unpredictable. Libby looked at him, startled. 'I most certainly will not! How much of that stuff did you drink before I came home?'

'One glass.' He held up a forefinger solemnly. 'One glass. Because I was worried about you.'

'Don't worry about me. I'm fairly well able to look after myself.'

'No, you're not . . . At least, I don't think so.' Somehow, he managed to make these confidence-sapping words sound quite friendly. 'Why did they send you, for goodness' sake? Because you were buddy-buddies with Marius?'

'I suppose so. They didn't tell me much.'

'They ought to have sent a man. Girls get into trouble when they're left on their own. Pretty ones do, anyway. You're pretty. I shall sketch you.'

'Thanks.'

'You're in love with Marius, you say.' He drained the last of his apricot liqueur and put the glass on the floor by his sofa. 'Wasting your time, Mademoiselle Gérard or whatever your real name is. Marius has been in more beds, as the saying goes, than most people have had hot dinners. Of course, Annette was something special. There he really fell hard. He wanted to marry her, you know.'

Libby shifted uneasily in her chair. She did not want to listen to this, but knew she had to. She was not quite sure why he was telling her. Warning her?

Trying to stir up dissension? 'Why didn't he marry her?' she asked, trying to sound nonchalant.

'She wouldn't have him. Turned him down. Quite a shock to Marius at the time, I fancy. He isn't used to girls rejecting his advances.' If Harry was aware of her evident distress, neither his voice nor his expression showed it. 'I think she realised she couldn't control him. Annette likes to get her own way. Marius, even head over heels in love, is always damn difficult.'

'He's not in love with her now!' Libby heard herself say, unwisely and with more force than was strictly necessary. The apricot liqueur had released the brakes she had put on her tongue. Careful! she thought. I must watch what I say.

'Who knows? Who cares?' Harry smiled at her. 'You do, I dare say. Forget him. You can have me. I'm not second-rate at everything. In my own modest way, I make love rather well.' He meant it. She could see it in his eyes, in which she glimpsed briefly an animal and predatory glow.

'I don't doubt it, Harry, but there's a time and a place . . .' Libby got up. 'I'm going to bed—all on my own! I don't want to have to bar the door. I can rely on you not to lurch in in a haze of alcohol and lust, I hope?'

Harry chuckled and waved a long, thin hand at her. 'I like you, Marie Gérard.'

'I actually like you, Harry,' Libby said seriously. 'And I'm relying on you.' She stood over him and looked down into his face.

Harry crooked his arm under his head and smiled up at her. 'Trust old Harry . . . He's everyone's friend.' He winked at her.

Libby retired to her tiny bedroom with a sigh of

relief. As if there weren't complications enough, she could do without Harry getting amorous. He was, however, a little under the influence of demon drink—or at least, she gave him the benefit of supposing that it was the apricot liqueur which had propositioned her, rather than cool intention on the part of the man.

She took off her clothes and hung them up carefully. Her identity papers she put on the bedside washstand, and as her fingers searched in her pocket, they closed on another small scrap of paper. She drew it out. It was the piece of card rescued from Harry's fiery furnace, and which she had quite forgotten. In the uncertain light of the bare electric bulb swinging from the ceiling, she studied it. It had been a piece of stiff card, and had once borne a photo, but that had been torn away. At the top, before the burned edge, she could read part of a word, 'Auswei . . .' Beneath that was illegible, except for the numbers '1.85'. At the very bottom was a fraction of the rubber stamp with the letters '. . . andantur', and the remains of a signature, '—ttmar'.

Jamie was awake. He spent most of most nights awake. He was, so they said, cured, but they couldn't let him go back on active duty again. At the moment he was attending a rehabilitation centre as an out-patient twice a week and, the rest of the time, holding down a desk job. He supposed he was as cured as he was ever going to be. But he still didn't sleep. On good nights, he managed as much as three hours, on and off. But that was seldom and usually it was nearer two. Sometimes he cat-napped in the afternoon, but not for more than ten minutes. He didn't miss his sleep. He was not tired, or didn't feel so. He just felt wound up, like a watch spring. The pressure was always there and was never released.

He moved on the pillow, but carefully, because he did not want to wake up Evangeline, who slumbered peacefully alongside him, snoring gently from time to time. It was difficult to make out the time even on the luminous dial of the alarm clock, because the black-out curtaining made the room so dark. He could not even make out the shapes of the furniture. It was like being buried alive. What he really wanted to do was get up, go downstairs, and either make a cup of tea or help himself to a glass of his father-in-law's whisky, and sit and read till morning. But when he did that, Evangeline had a way of knowing. He could leave her sleeping like a log, but when he'd been away a few minutes, some instinct woke her up and she would come looking for him. Eva meant well, but there was a limit to what she could do, and sometimes her sheepdog tendencies, as he privately termed them, only served to remind him how much he depended on her. All the same, she was a good old girl, and he was fond of her. He owed her his sanity, after all.

Jamie turned over on his side, propped his head on his folded arm, and wondered what Libby was doing. Of all the problems he mulled over in these sleepless nightwatch hours, this was the one which tormented his brain most frequently. He didn't even know where she was. If they had dropped her into occupied territory . . . Jamie tossed over on his back. She might be a goner, for all he knew. She wasn't the type. She was too trusting. She was too frail. Couldn't fight her way out of a paper bag. It was all on account of that wretched Belgian. Not his fault, poor devil . . . but Libby had fallen for him like a ton of bricks and was prepared to follow him to hell or high water. What's more, she'd done it.

'Jamie?' whispered Evangeline in the darkness. She rolled over in her seal-like way and prodded him. 'You awake?'

'I am now,' he said.

'You were before. Can't sleep, I suppose. Want me to get one of the pills?'

'No, I don't. Go on back to sleep, Eva. I'm OK. I don't need much sleep.'

She put her arm round him and he patted her hand. 'Are you thinking about Libby?'

He was surprised, but Eva was smarter than most people thought. 'A little,' he confessed.

'Pushed off on some hush-hush mission or other, I suppose? I know you can't answer that. She'll be all right, you know.' He gave a snort of disbelief. 'She will, honestly,' she insisted. 'Libby has that sort of innocence which protects. You know, bad things sort of bounce off her, and bad people, if she ever meets any, will be afraid of her.'

'That's a deep and rather Victorian thought!' Jamie exclaimed, surprised. 'You never cease to amaze me, Eva.'

'I'm a sort of carthorse,' said Evangeline slowly, 'and Libby is a thoroughbred. We've both got staying power, only she looks better.'

'Dear old thing,' he said, amused. 'You are *not* a carthorse!'

'Well, slim and lovely I never was. I love you, Jamie.'

'I know. And I love you, Eva. Honestly.' He turned over towards her and put his arms round her. She rested her head on his chest, and he kissed the top of her head. 'I wish I wasn't such a crock,' he said.

'I don't mind,' Evangeline said frankly, her voice sounding rather muffled from beneath the blankets. 'If you weren't, you'd be off somewhere and I'd never have got a look in.'

'You make me feel like a heel,' he said after a while. 'I'm sorry I moped about sighing for Libby for so long, like some sort of love-sick owl. It's not that I've latched on to you because I need something from you. I mean I do need something from you: I need a rock to cling to, and you're it. But I always did like you, Eva, even when we were kids, although you always seemed to be glued to the back of a smelly horse.'

'You liked Libby more. I'm not jealous, or anything, but I ain't daft, either.'

'That was just one of those things,' he protested. 'She's a cousin, and I'm fond of her, and worried about her—yes. But I've got over the crush on her. Adolescent infatuation, you know.'

'My Aunt Fanny,' said Evangeline inelegantly.

'Why is it that gently-bred gals like you always cuss like old salts and call a spade a bloody shovel?'

'Gentility is for the middle-classes. They can't afford to be vulgar. That's what my old Ma used to say.'

'I never really knew your Mama.'

'She was a decent sort,' said Evangeline. 'Daddy thought the world of her.'

'Eva,' he said seriously, 'I really do think the world of you.' He fiddled with the buttons on the jacket of her pyjamas. 'Why do you insist on wearing these peculiar male garments?'

'I'm not the frilly nightie sort. I only wear the

pyjamas in the winter. In the summer I sleep in the buff. Only we haven't been wed long enough for you to find that out.'

'Ah, the prospect of nude frolics in the summer!'

'Frolic now,' said Evangeline. 'I'll take 'em off.' She sat up in bed and divested herself rapidly of them and threw them over the side of the bed.

Jamie began to laugh. After a while he put up his hand and pulled her over on top of him. 'Bless you, Eva, you really are the only person who can make me feel life is worth living.'

'You bet I can,' said Evangeline. 'I'll show you.'

Marius, too, was awake. He got out of bed, put on the dreadful peacock-blue dressing-gown and went downstairs to the library. There he pushed open one of the shutters and sat in the gloom, looking out into moonlit gardens. It had at least stopped raining, and, with luck, Libby had got back to Harry's without getting wet through. He wrote 'Libby' invisibly on the window-ledge with his forefinger. He supposed everything she had said to him was true. He had not wanted to love her and leave her, but that was just what he had done. Old Adam, that was the trouble. He was not the platonic type. That was where Annette understood him so well. He knew that Annette didn't love him, and never had—not in any way he would have recognised. She might have come near to it at some time. But she was a person who saw everything from her own viewpoint outwards. Sometimes, he thought she had the instincts of a female spider. She sat in the middle of her web and manipulated all the radiating threads. Any fool creature that fell into her toils was lost. As for the male spider, he got eaten up, of course.

Libby was different. She was not only different from Annette, she was different from any girl he had ever known. He sat and thought about her now, and wondered at the complexity of the emotions she aroused in him. Above all, he felt responsible for her. It was, after all, because of him that she was here. There was no way she would have undertaken this job, had he not been involved. The thought did not flatter him; it worried him sick. Somehow or other, he had to get her to safety. It didn't matter about himself. About his own prospects, he had become fatalistic. But he knew he could not go on with Libby's capture, and quite possibly her death, on his conscience.

He turned his head, listening. From somewhere in the house came a faint mewling noise. Francis was crying. He sat listening for a while, but it went on, so Annette had not wakened up. He walked to the foot of the stairs, and after a moment's hesitation, climbed them and opened the door at the top.

'Mama?' asked the small voice hopefully.

'No, it's me,' Marius went across to the bed and squatted on his heels by the side of it. 'What's wrong?'

'Minou is lost.'

'She'll come back. Cats do that—They go for long walks and come back days later.'

'Do they?' Francis asked doubtfully.

'Absolutely. I'm sure of it. But if she doesn't, it will be because she's happy somewhere, and your Mama will buy you another kitten.' He put out his hand to pull the eiderdown up over the child. 'Go to sleep now, or you will wake your Mama. She loves you, you know.'

Francis mumbled sleepily. He rolled over into

Marius's arm and settled down, not unlike a somnolent cat himself, and went back to sleep, as bidden, just like that. Marius stooped to kiss the tangled curls. 'I love you too, little man,' he said softly, 'but much good it will do you. You won't remember me, but I'll remember you, and perhaps, one day . . .'

One day. Marius fell silent and reflected bitterly on the sheer, hopeless brevity of life. You had to seize what you could, while you could. Even then, it got torn out of your grasp. He sat there, cramped, chilled and uncomfortable, until the dawn, cradling his sleeping child, with an odd, haphazard sort of prayer running through his mind. 'O God, let me come out of this with something. Don't take everything away.'

CHAPTER FOURTEEN

IT WAS barely dawn when Libby slipped out of bed and dressed as quietly as she could. She took pencil and paper and carefully wrote a note for Harry: 'Will be back in twenty-four hours. Don't worry.'

She scrutinised it carefully. She could only hope he accepted it at face value. She would leave all her Marie Gérard change of clothing and her suitcase here, and there should be no reason for him to suppose that the note didn't mean exactly what it said. She slipped it under his door and crept away. The narrow stair creaked beneath her step and it seemed it must waken him, but she reached the ground floor and let herself into the tiny yard behind the shop where the bicycle was kept. Wheeling it out into the street, she set off.

She had been worried that she might attract attention, out and about at this hour, but she had overlooked how early in the morning continental Europe sets off to work. Despite the hour, several people were scurrying along the pavements, their faces still puffed with sleep, or cycling, as she was, slowly and resignedly to work.

She left the town and pedalled briskly through the countryside. There had been a heavy dew overnight, and it had left the grass and foliage silver. But the sun had come up, pale and watery, and at least, thank goodness, it wasn't raining again. She passed only two farm carts before reaching the turn-off to the château, and wheeled in through the gates.

No one seemed to be stirring behind the tall windows, but Louise, the old housekeeper, was already about, and opened the door to her, peering up at her suspiciously.

'It's very early. The mistress isn't dressed yet.'

'I know,' Libby replied impatiently. Louise hadn't a clue about what was going on. As far as she was concerned, this young woman was the dressmaker. But Libby trusted she could count on the housekeeper's blind loyalty to her employer. 'I need to see Mrs de Jong immediately. Also, I'd like this bicycle to be put away, out of sight.'

The faded eyes blinked at her, peasant shrewdness gleaming briefly in their watery depths. 'Then come in, *mademoiselle*. Someone will take care of the machine.'

She was conducted into the hall, and left there. After a few moments, a light footstep sounded on the stair, and Annette appeared, wearing a wraparound morning coat. At the sight of Libby, she demanded immediately, 'What's wrong?'

'I'm not sure, but I need to see Marius at once.'

Annette frowned. 'He's not here.'

'He's gone?' Libby exclaimed, dismayed.

'No, no!' Annette waved her hand irritably. 'But this is the only time of day he can get out for any exercise. Since he has to keep under cover the rest of the time, early in the morning he goes and runs round the grounds.' She glanced at her watch. 'He'll be back in, say, a quarter of an hour.'

Libby sighed. It was not long to wait, but time suddenly seemed precious. Annette, watching her face, offered, 'You'd like breakfast, I suppose? If you go into the salon, Louise will bring you something. I have to go and see to my child.'

Libby had forgotten the child. She mumbled thanks, and went to sit in the salon, as bidden. She had not given any thought to hunger, so intent had she been on getting here as soon as she could, but now she realised that the early morning ride on an empty stomach had left her ravenous. When Louise brought a tray with coffee and rolls, she fell on it, and demolished the lot. She was just finishing when she heard voices in the hall. The door flew open, and Marius appeared.

He looked hot and flushed and was wearing a disreputable sweater with holes in it, which she presumed he'd borrowed. His trousers were equally old and work-worn, and he hadn't shaved. He lacked only a villainous-smelling cigarette clamped between his teeth to be the perfect farm labourer, early about his work.

'What the hell is going on?' he demanded immediately, not bothering with the formality of greetings. 'What are you doing here? Have they picked up Harry?'

'No, and it's about Harry that I'm here. Oh, do sit down, Marius. I want you to listen to me, and *carefully*.'

Marius sat down at a small table, leaning his elbows on it, and said, 'Well?'

Libby drew a deep breath, knowing that her first words would bring forth an explosion of protest. 'How sure are you of Harry de Vries?'

For a second or two he just stared at her as if he hadn't understood the question. Then his face darkened angrily, and he burst out, 'I've known Harry all my life, and that's what I'd trust him with—my life!'

'I know.' She had to keep calm. She had to get

him to listen. 'And that's just what we are doing, trusting Harry with our lives, and the lives of a lot of other people.'

Marius pointed an accusing forefinger at her. 'Now you listen to *me*, Libby. You don't know this country, you don't know these people. I do.'

'But that's the problem!' she argued. 'You do know them so well that you don't stop to think whether they've changed at all over the years. You've been away, and you don't really understand the constant pressures they are under, even though you think you do! You don't stop to think things odd, which you would notice if you weren't so close.'

'Go on,' he said dangerously.

'Right. Doesn't it strike you as strange that so many have been arrested, but Harry is never touched? He's been active so long, since this network was first set up, and his cover ought to have been blown by now, if anyone's was. But they never touch him. Nor do they try very hard to find that radio equipment . . . equipment on which he continued to send out messages in a code we now know was broken long ago.'

'Harry didn't know that, any more than we did!' Marius said tightly.

'How can we be certain? You talked of trusting Harry with your life. Perhaps Jan Wouters and his wife also trusted Harry, and where are they now? And what about Ton van Leeuwen? He's keeping out of sight and out of touch. He's frightened, all right, but of what, exactly? Maybe he doesn't trust Harry either, but he can't prove anything.'

'Can you?' asked Marius bluntly. 'The points you've made are fair enough, but Harry has been the mainstay of this operation, and if you're going to cut him out, you have to be sure of what you're doing.'

'All right. I think the last thing Harry expected was that Annette should show up the other night with me in tow, and ask him to lodge me. He couldn't refuse. But that's a very small apartment he has above the shop. I think he decided that if he had anything compromising around, he should get rid of it, in case I took to snooping around. When I got back yesterday, he'd been burning papers in the little stove. Old drawings, he said. I poked around in the ashes, and I found this.'

She put her hand in her pocket and pulled out the fragment of charred card. 'I know what this is. It's the remains of an official pass. See, it says "Ausweis" at the top, or it did, but the "s" has burned away. The photograph is gone, but there's the height of the holder—1.85. I'd say Harry was a metre eighty-five, wouldn't you? Here's the stamp of the local Kommandantur, and the signature, I'd bet my bottom dollar, is that of a Major Dettmar who works, I know, at the Kommandantur, because I've met the man and he told me so. He tried to pick me up on the train. This is Harry's pass—and it isn't a Belgian one, it's in neither French nor Flemish, it's in German. It gets Harry past German patrols or out of round-ups, or it did—till I showed up, and Harry decided it was too hot to keep around.'

Marius sat studying the scrap of card for a minute, then he crashed his fist on the table, swore and jumped to his feet. He began to pace up and down. 'I'm still not convinced. Harry helped me blow the bridge, damn it! He reconnoitred the area and made a precise diagram of the target which he put into my hand himself! He wouldn't have done that on

German orders, and they certainly wouldn't allow things to go as far as blowing it, even if he is working for them—which, I repeat, I doubt!'

'He offered the diagram as a sprat to catch a mackerel! Once he gave you that diagram, you trusted him implicitly. It was his sign of good faith. Whatever happened after that, the last person you would suspect would be reliable old Harry! Almost certainly you weren't supposed to be allowed actually to blow the bridge! Something must have gone wrong for them. Either you were too efficient, too damn good at your job, or Harry failed to stop you because of some mix-up. I don't know, no one does. I like Harry, too, Marius, even thinking what I do about him. But it doesn't make me trust him. Being your old friend doesn't automatically qualify him as trustworthy, either. Napoleon thought he could trust his marshals because they had been boyhood pals, but they deserted him in the end. All I'm asking you is, can you absolutely trust Harry beyond any doubt?'

Two nights too soon, Marius was thinking dully. I blew the ruddy bridge two nights too soon . . . Suddenly he felt physically sick. Betrayal was something he had long lived with, but not from someone so near, or so well trusted, or for whom he had entertained such genuine affection. His mind, as well as his stomach, rebelled at the idea. No, no, *no* . . .

Seeing the mulish set of his features and guessing something of what was going through his mind, Libby went on earnestly, 'Let me tell you how I read this situation. The raid on Wouters' farm was meant to net *you*. Jan and his wife could have been picked up at any time, but you got away. It left Harry in a pickle, especially when he learned you were here with Annette. If he put the finger on you here—and you got away again—you'd know *he* had sent the Germans here. It could only be Harry. So he left you here, knowing that he could keep tabs on you, that you still didn't suspect him, and wouldn't make any move without telling him. He sat quiet and he waited for the new courier to come out with the new code and instructions for reconstructing the network. Now he means to continue to sit back while you and I set up a nice new organisation to replace the old one. We'll recruit new people. We'll start sending messages in our nice new unbroken code. And then, hey presto, Harry pulls the rug from under the new network, just as he did from under the old one! He doesn't net just one fish; he nets a whole bagful, and throws the whole notion of an organised Resistance force in this area into such disarray that it's unlikely anyone will try to set up anything for months, perhaps ever.'

Her voice and manner were growing more and more heated. She tossed a lock of unruly hair out of her eyes. 'You know how they hunt the tiger in India, Marius? They tie a buffalo or goat to a stake, and wait. You and I are the sacrificial bait, Marius. As secure from Harry's viewpoint as if we were tied to a stake. They don't want us—well, they do, but not only us—they want the whole spirit of Resistance in this area. That's the tiger they're trying to bag.'

Marius turned away, his hands thrust into his pockets, and was silent. Libby held her tongue, too, knowing he was turning over in his mind everything she had said. Eventually he swung round, and observed, 'If you're right, I'm not safe here, and you're not safe at Harry's. He might decide to pull that rug earlier than we anticipate. You can't go back to his place, but if you don't, he'll smell a rat.'

'I left him a note saying I'd be away for twenty-four hours, and not to worry. He won't know what to make of it, but if he is playing some kind of double game, he won't want to show his hand too soon. He'll wait, I guess, the twenty-four hours before he makes his move. He's got to take the gamble. At the moment he doesn't have anything but you and me, and he'd like a lot more. Especially, he'd like the new code, and that,' she smiled triumphantly, 'he doesn't have.'

'You refused to give him the code? That's bad. He'll be suspicious.'

'No, I just forgot to hand it across, last night. He decided to play safe and not push me for it. That was his mistake.'

'Right!' Marius said briskly. 'Then the first thing we have to do is to move that radio equipment out of Jan's cowshed. Put it somewhere Harry can't get at it, and then we can use it. We *have* to dig out Ton van Leeuwen. The devil of it is, neither you nor I can go boldly into town now, and we daren't risk the phone. But we'll tackle that one later.' He paused and walked across to stand before her, surveying her thoughtfully. Unexpectedly, he smiled and reaching out his hand, pinched her cheek. 'Good girl,' he said.

Her heart leapt up, but she kept her voice steady. 'I know I can be wrong, Marius. But I don't think I am. I think I'm right.'

'Yes, you probably are. I don't know why Harry . . .'

Marius broke off, and Libby said awkwardly,

'That's the funny part of it. I think, last night, in a strange sort of way, he tried to explain it to me. Somehow or other, in his heart, he wanted to make a confession, but he knows he can't do that. He told me how difficult it was, living under occupation, and waiting for the knock on the door. He kept telling me he was sorry. He produced a bottle of liqueur, real fire-water, and got us both a bit tiddly. I thought first of all he was trying to seduce me, but now I think he was trying to console himself, and build up his courage for what he was going to do.'

Marius grunted and turned away again. He wandered over to the window, and stared down at the ledge on which the toy engine still stood. He picked it up and spun the wooden wheels with one finger. Certainty closed over Libby's heart like a steel shutter.

'The child—he's yours, isn't he?'

'Yes.' He did not look towards her and continued to spin the wheels of the toy engine. 'She doesn't want it known. She has her own plans for him, and they don't include me. Maybe, when this is all over, she might change her mind. After all, it won't be good for Francis to be thought the son of a collaborator. A Resistance fighter, dead or alive, will be better.'

'You—You would like that, for her to change her mind? Yes, I suppose you would.' Perhaps he did still love Annette in his heart, after all, she thought sadly. Perhaps he still hopes.

'Don't misunderstand me, Libby,' he said firmly, putting down the toy. 'She might want to quote my name one day—but she'd never let me have that child. She thinks I might contaminate him.' He glanced towards her. 'I'll have to tell her I'm leaving.

I can't just walk out. That's not just sentimentality on my part. I know Annette well enough to be aware that if I simply left, she'd think it was something to do with you, and she has to know it's more than that. She has it in her to be spiteful. What's more, she has to be warned about Harry.'

'You'd better go and tell her, then,' Libby said. 'I'll wait here.'

Annette was in the kitchen, supervising Francis's breakfast. The boy was dunking lumps of bread into a bowl of warm milk, intent on watching them sink. She glanced at Marius's face, and got up. 'Just watch the child, Louise.'

As the housekeeper moved towards the table, Annette turned and accompanied him into the library. There she folded her arms and her green eyes glittered at him. 'What's that shrinking violet had to say for herself?'

'Shrinking violet isn't how I'd describe her,' Marius said mildly. 'Listen, Annette. We've good reason to suppose Harry isn't all we thought him.'

Her eyelashes flickered, but she was not one to show surprise. 'You've got your reasons, I suppose. The girl doesn't want to go back there, I take it. I can't hide her.'

'No, and you can't hide me any longer. Harry knows I'm here. It's a risk to you, and a risk to Francis.' The mention of the child was a low blow, but he had to use it. He had to believe the child's safety meant more to her than his.

She was silent, thinking it over. At last she said, very quietly, 'So where will you go?'

'The only place I can think of at the moment is Sophie's.'

She twitched an eyebrow. 'Very apt. Will you take Miss Virtue with you?'

'I'll have to.'

'Explained to her, have you, exactly what Sophie's is?'

'No, I haven't mentioned it yet.'

Annette stared at him, then observed crisply, 'May you rot, Marius! I suppose you'll come through it with your skin intact. You generally fall on your feet. You'll be in more trouble, if you tie the rest of your life to that sweet innocent with the penchant for jumping out of aircraft, than ever you're in now. Don't say I didn't warn you.' Annette gave an unexpected peal of laughter. 'Good grief . . . How I wish I could be there to see her face when she realises what sort of place you've taken her to!'

They took the bus back towards town, boarding it separately. It was a country bus, very old and jangling, and it bounced over the ruts in the road. The driver crouched over the wheel with a set and manic expression, his brawny arms akimbo, shovel-like hands gripping the wheel. Libby was glad to get off, which she did at a signal from Marius, at the last stop before the town buildings began in earnest.

Marius pulled his hat down over his face, and they set off through the dusk.

'Where are we going?' she whispered.

'You'll see.'

They had entered narrow streets and seemed to be in a seedy suburb on the outskirts of town. The houses here were very old, and the drains, to judge by the smell of the gutters, even older. Eventually Marius stopped before one of the more dilapidated houses, a tall narrow affair with a raucous bar on the ground floor. Libby peered in, through a haze of smoke. It seemed to be filled with unprepossessing men and blowsy girls. Marius put his hand in the small of her back and pushed her through the door, across the floor, and through another door into the back of the building. Libby found herself standing in a grimy office.

A small bird-like woman in a frilled georgette blouse, with a grotesquely painted face, peered up suspiciously at their entrance, and then, seeing Marius, gave a sudden cackle. She came towards them, and plucked at his sleeve. 'So it's you, then, is it? Thought they'd have caught you by now.'

'I'm pushing my luck, Sophie, and we need a place to stay tonight.' He gestured to include Libby.

'The girl, too, eh?' The painted face peered up into Libby's, treating her to a sharp, professional scrutiny. 'She's young. Pah!' She shrugged and turned to unhook a bunch of keys. '*Alors, suivez-moi*. Mind the stairs; some of the treads are loose.'

They followed her down a dingy hall, past a closed door into the bar, through which came the sound of ribald laughter. Laughter, too, could be heard from behind some of the closed doors they passed as they began their climb to the uppermost floor.

'Marius!' Libby hissed, as she accompanied him up the winding staircase behind the decrepit little madame. 'This place is a brothel!'

'You shock me! Don't let it worry you. Sophie is absolutely reliable.'

They had reached the top of the stairs and the old woman was unlocking a door. '*V'là* . . . It's comfortable and it's quiet, and no clients climb up the stairs this far. They like to save their strength . . .' Her sharp eyes twinkled up at him beneath painted black eyebrows. Libby realised that she was extremely old. Marius stooped and kissed the raddled cheek, and she chuckled and patted his arm with one wizened claw-like hand. Glancing past him towards Libby, she croaked, 'Don't waste your time, make the most of it! He's a fine young fellow—and you'll be my age soon enough!' She gave Libby a smile which was supremely wicked, and turned her witch's stare back to Marius. 'Do you need anything done?' she asked briskly, as if this were a matter of business.

'Yes, but I don't know if you can do it. First of all, I want some radio equipment retrieved. It's out in the country at a farm belonging to a couple by the name of Wouters. They've been arrested. The place may be watched to see if anyone goes near it, so whoever does it will have to go at night.'

Sophie turned and pursed her lips. 'Maybe, I say maybe, I can arrange that, but where is this radio to be taken? I don't want it here. The Germans, they have machines . . .' She gestured vaguely. 'They can trace the waves or whatever they're called.'

'I understand. I just want it moved for the moment and hidden somewhere safe.'

'I'll see what I can do. Anything else?'

'Yes, I want to reach a man called van Leeuwen, who has a jeweller's and watchmaker's business in town. His shop is closed up and his wife won't take messages. I don't how it could be managed.'

Sophie gave a shrill cackle. 'Van Leeuwen the jeweller? You want him, you shall have him, my dear.' She patted Marius's cheek. 'Nor do you need to send for him. He'll come here, anyway. He's an old customer, is van Leeuwen. When his wife goes out visiting, this is where he skips off to.'

'Good Lord!' said Marius, truly surprised.

'It has a good reputation, has my house,' said Sophie severely, taking his tone as criticism. 'I'll see about your radio . . .' She scurried away.

Libby pushed her way into the room, switching on the light. 'That old woman is disgusting! What do you mean by bringing us here?'

He shut the door. 'Because it's safe. I told you Sophie is reliable.'

'Because you are an old and valued customer? Is this where you mis-spent your youth? Don't answer that!'

'I wasn't going to,' he informed her. He took off his coat and hung it on the hook behind the door. 'Sorry it's not the best in town, but it beats sleeping rough.'

'I'm not so sure!' she returned crossly. The room was depressing in appearance. The patterned wall-paper was faded and torn beyond recognition, but once it might have had flowers on it. The floorboards were bare, not parquet, but plain wooden planks which had been stained and polished—although certainly not polished recently. In places there were holes in the wood. By the bed lay a strip of thread-bare carpet. The bed itself was enormous, resplend-ent with brass knobs, and a satin quilt which had seen better days. A cracked washbasin hung crazily from the wall. There was a rickety table and a chair, and a wardrobe of a size to match the bed, a Second Empire monstrosity in dark, carved wood. Libby slipped her hand beneath the satin quilt.

'This is damp.'

'Probably just cold.'

'Damp, I tell you—and I'm not sharing it with you!'

'You're going to sleep on the floor?' Marius enquired, twitching an eyebrow at her.

'No, you are!'

He shook his head. 'I am not, you know.' He took off his jacket and tie and hung them on the back of the chair. 'I'm getting my rest while I can, and in the best comfort I can, and I recommend you to do likewise.' He pulled his shirt over his head.

Libby sat on the edge of the bed and watched him, glaring belligerently. 'You think I'm going to turn in with you, is that it?'

'I told you, please yourself.'

'If I do—*if* I do—stay on your side of the bed!'

'Libby,' Marius said wearily, 'this may come as a surprise to you, but at this moment, sex is the last thing on my mind.'

She flushed. 'Just keep it that way.' She glanced round. 'Where is the bathroom?'

'There's a WC on the way down to the floor below, on the mezzanine, if that's what you want. If you literally mean a bath, I doubt this establishment runs to those.'

Libby put on her coat again, and made her way down to the lavatory on the mezzanine. It had a huge walnut seat, meant, she could only assume, to accommodate not only a bottom, but a bustle. The pan itself was patterned with blue flowers, and on the wall hung a cheap printed version of a Toulouse-Lautrec, showing a black-stockinged dancer.

Libby made her way back, and found that Marius was already in bed, rolled up in the quilt on the far side. There was no bedside lamp, so she put out the light by the door, undressed in the darkness, felt her way across to the bed and climbed in beside him.

It was very cold, and damp, and she did not

suppose the sheets were very clean. That Marius could settle down in them without a moment's hesitation was beyond her comprehension. She curled up into a ball, and wondered whether she would freeze to death before she got pneumonia. The pillows smelled frowsy. Despite this, she dozed off. It had been a long, tense and exhausting day. After about an hour she woke up, and realised that in her sleep she had automatically moved closer to Marius for warmth. She was now nestled up against him. Their damp warm skins stuck together like adhesive, and the mattress had sunk under their combined weight so that they lay together in a kind of depression in the middle. She tried to move away without disturbing him, but was unsuccessful. He stirred and rolled over and put his arm round her.

'Libby?' he whispered in her ear.

'Yes,' she muttered fiercely.

'What's the matter . . . cold?' His voice vibrated against her neck.

'No. Would you like to take your arm away?'

'You realise this could be our last night together?' he said. 'Come to that, it could be the last night either of us spends with anyone.' His fingers caressed her breast, and as they ran lightly over the surface of her skin, it became ultra-sensitive beneath his touch.

'Yes, I know.' Libby moved uneasily. Don't touch me, don't touch me . . . I ache for you, a voice in her brain begged. You set my body on fire, don't you know it?

He moved his hand to caress her hip, and she quivered and pushed her face into the pillow. He paused and whispered, 'You don't want me to?'

She could lie to him, and say 'No', but he would

know it wasn't the truth. Of course she wanted him to, but it was still all wrong. 'This is such a horrible place,' she whispered, 'and this bed is horrible, and it never seems to work out for us, Marius. Air-raid shelters, sleazy beds in houses of ill fame. It was all a mistake, right from the beginning.'

'You blame me for it?' he asked her seriously.

'No, it wasn't your fault, or my fault, or anyone's. It was just wartime, and everything being wrong. I thought we could make it right, but we couldn't.'

'I'm sorry,' he said. He kissed her shoulder, the print of his lips burning on her skin like a branding-iron. 'Can you not stop worrying about the rights and wrongs of it for a while?'

It was, after all, the only thing to do. Libby turned towards him and put her arms round his neck. He stooped over her and kissed her mouth.

It was a crazy situation, but he was right. They had little time left. Life had turned into a crazy game. She stroked his face with exploring fingertips, feeling the roughness of the skin that had not been shaved since that morning. Sliding her hand away, she let it creep over his shoulder and down his chest, brushing the tangle of hair and pausing at his stomach. There it touched against his aroused manhood and she drew in a sharp breath and stopped in her exploration.

He muttered, 'Libby . . .' pressing her back into the pillows.

If she had had any doubts, they had gone. If they were hunted, in danger, possibly living out the last hours of their lives, that, too, was as nothing. All was forgotten in a primeval longing, a sense that nowhere in the world was there anyone else, and they existed in a private, dark, warm world in which nothing mattered, nothing but their need for each other. The urgency of that need increased. She felt her body arch to meet his, and her lips parted in a moan of pleasure, of longing, and of fulfilment.

When she went to sleep at last in Marius's arms, she knew that she had no regrets, could never regret this moment, whatever the truth of it. Whatever happened now, this was a moment and a memory no one could take away.

The following morning they breakfasted with Sophie in her private rooms. They were surprisingly cosy. There was a fire, a canary twittered in a cage at the window, and the smell of coffee filled the air. The old woman stood at the bird-cage and talked to her pet as her two guests ate, interspersing her words with asides to Marius.

'Do you want to stay longer? Pretty fellow, sing for Maman . . . You can, it's safe. My girls won't give you away. Chirp, chirp. Sing for the lady and the gentleman . . .'

'For the time being, at least,' Marius said. 'Eat up, Libby.'

'I'm not hungry,' she said. Reaction was setting in. I shouldn't have been so weak last night. I should have summoned the courage to push him away. She toyed with a tartine of bread, watching him wolf down his share. Whether a successful night in bed made him hungry, or whether he just lacked her sensibilities and had a cast-iron constitution, she had no idea. She managed to drink her coffee, real coffee. Sophie had access to the black market.

The old woman turned away from the canary's cage now, and her eyes sparkled at them both maliciously. 'Your radio was moved last night.

There's a timber-yard not far away, and it is hidden there. But only for the time being, mind! It will have to be moved again. The owner of the yard, he owes me a favour, but a man's memory can be short and his gratitude run out. Two or three days at the most.'

'Find me van Leeuwen, and it will be long enough,' Marius promised.

'All in good time,' she said.

In fact, they had not so long to wait. They spent an exhausting day, arguing what they should or should not do, should Sophie fail to produce Ton van Leeuwen. In the early evening, when they had exhausted their joint ideas, their attention was drawn by a commotion on the staircase outside the room. Marius jumped up, grabbed Libby, and pushed her behind him. The door burst open, but it was no uniformed figure which burst in but a totally incongruous and unexpected one.

It was a small, slight, sallow-complexioned man wearing a pair of long woollen combinations and socks. He was held firmly between Sophie on the one side and a buxom girl in a dressing-gown on the other. He was putting up violent resistance and swearing vehemently. At the sight of Marius, however, he stopped wriggling and trying to shake off the pair of harpies who had him in their grip, and said wearily, 'Oh, hell!'

'Good evening, Ton,' Marius said politely, and Libby emerged from behind him, doing her utmost not to laugh. Despite the seriousness of their situation, the unfortunate van Leeuwen could hardly be viewed with a straight face. 'You seem to have lost your trousers.'

Van Leeuwen shook off his captors with some disdain, and marched to the nearest chair with considerable dignity in the circumstances. He sat down and glowered at them both. Sophie and the girl retired tactfully.

'We've tried to reach you, Ton,' Marius said, 'Mademoiselle Gérard here tried. She didn't get past your wife.'

A lugubrious expression crossed the watchmaker's face. 'She's a good woman, my wife. But strong-minded, very strong-minded. Not that she isn't scared. She is. She's gone to see her sister . . .' he added, inconsequentially, as if he felt he ought to explain his presence there tonight.

Briefly, Marius explained what had happened, their fears about Harry, and the removal of the radio to safety, while van Leeuwen looked increasingly mournful on his chair, and shuffled about as if his woollen combinations irritated.

'Sophie can tell you where the radio is, and there's no reason why you shouldn't go there and operate it, Ton, in perfect safety.'

'Huh!' exploded the hapless van Leeuwen.

'Listen, man! We need you. Marie Gérard here has brought out a new code. Where is it?' he turned abruptly to Libby.

'Concealed in the sole of my shoe, between two layers of leather.'

'Fine, go and get a knife and give me the shoe.'

He levered busily at the false sole, watched with some trepidation both by Libby and the underwear-suited Ton, who scratched his groin absent-mindedly. Libby felt herself blush unexpectedly, and looked away.

'Right,' said Marius briskly at last. 'Listen, Ton, you must go there tonight, do you understand? There must be no delay. Call up London and let them know we have a traitor in our midst. On no account are they to act on any signals received in the old code, which is the only code Harry has. Tell them that Marie Gérard and I are safe for the time being, but await instructions. Got all that?'

'All right, all right,' mumbled van Leeuwen. He looked up. 'I know you think I've been running scared, but I had my reasons. I never liked Harry, nor he me. He always was an arrogant bastard, and I suspected him long ago. That's why I kept clear. I didn't want anything to do with him, not after Wouters got picked up.'

'Then why the devil didn't you say anything to me of your suspicions?' Marius demanded in some exasperation.

'Didn't know if I could trust you, either,' came the devastatingly simple reply. 'You were Harry's dear old pal, believed his every word. Even if you were on the level yourself, you wouldn't have believed me instead of him, not unless I had some proof—which I didn't. But after you managed to get away from Wouters' farm, I wasn't sure about you. I thought maybe Harry had set that up, too. I didn't know what to think!' Ton's voice grew louder and more aggrieved.

A tap at the door heralded the buxom girl carrying Ton's trousers, shirt, jacket and shoes. He snatched them from her and began to dress. 'I'll go and find the ruddy radio,' he muttered at them, standing on one foot, the other in his trouser-leg. 'What do I do about Harry?'

'Not much you can do at this moment, except warn London—and any other of our people you can find.'

'I'll take care of it,' van Leeuwen promised. 'I'll take care of everything.'

Libby glanced up curiously at the note of resolution in his voice. It held more than determination. It held hatred.

CHAPTER FIFTEEN

LOUISE, HAVING announced the visitor, withdrew and carefully closed the doors. They could both hear her shuffling progress down the hall towards the kitchen.

'Come in, Harry,' Annette invited him.

She was sitting before the fire, with the child on her lap. It was early evening, and dusk, but although the light had not been switched on, her pale, beautiful face was clearly visible in the fire-glow, watching him a little sardonically. She had been reading to her son, and the book, of the kind printed on linen pages for small children, lay on her lap. Francis twisted in her arms and stared curiously at the visitor.

Harry came into the room and stretched out his arm to switch on a table lamp, illuminating all three of them in a golden capsule.

'Make yourself at home,' she said drily.

He had not said anything so far and did not say anything now, only stood observing her. The firelight gleamed on the lenses of his spectacles, so that she could not see his eyes, and her own expression became more wary. Then Harry strolled over to her, and stood with his hands clasped behind his back, looking down at mother and child.

'A charming scene, very domestic. Where are they, Annette?'

'You mean Marius and the girl, I suppose?'

'Don't play games with me!' His voice grew

sharper. The calm façade cracked a little. 'The girl took off on her own, leaving all her kit behind and a note telling me not to worry! That was almost thirty-six hours ago. I've searched all round town. The girl hasn't been arrested. She's just disappeared.'

'How do you know she hasn't been arrested?' Annette asked him. 'Or do you have a private source of information about that, Harry?'

He took the chair opposite hers and leaned forward, with his hands clasped on his knees. 'How I know, is no concern of yours, Annette. The girl can't have vanished off the face of the earth. If Marius is here, bring him in.'

She hesitated. 'He isn't here. Neither is the girl.'

'So I was right.' He drew a sharp breath. 'Now listen to me carefully, Annette. You are a far from stupid woman. I know how you feel about Marius—and I've a shrewd idea how you feel about the girl. But you have to tell me where they are, now, without any more beating about the bush.'

Francis slipped off his mother's lap, realising that the arrival of the visitor meant no more story. He wandered over to the other side of the room, and began to push his toy engine up and down the floor. The noise of the wooden wheels rattling along over the polished parquet blocks seemed to annoy Harry, who glared in the child's direction, and then took off his spectacles and made an impatient gesture with them.

'I'm Marius's contact, for crying out loud. He can't just make arrangements and not let me know!'

'Of course he can, and he has.' Annette settled back in her chair, putting the child's book on the table beside her, and searching for a cigarette in the silver case. 'You do smoke, don't you, Harry?' She extricated a cigarette and tossed it across to him. He caught it, but did not put it to his mouth. 'Oh my,' she said. 'You are in earnest!'

'Yes, I damn well am!' She had succeeded in irritating him at last, and cracking open the assumed air of composure. He started forward in the chair and said angrily, 'Listen, Annette, we're old friends, and I don't like to spoil an old friendship! I don't want to see you in any trouble. But you are in trouble, and it's going to get worse if you don't tell me where they are!'

She had lit her cigarette while he spoke, but her hand trembled very slightly. Harry did not miss it, and a muscle twitched at the corner of his mouth. She was not as tough as she seemed. He allowed himself a smile. 'Come on, Annette, stop playing the heroine. You're not the stuff of heroines. Stalling me isn't going to make any difference, you know!'

She blew a cloud of blue smoke into the air. 'Why did you send Marius to me, Harry? Because you thought I could keep him here safe for you? That he wouldn't be tempted to cut and run? Or perhaps you thought I might provide sufficient distraction to stop him getting suspicious about you?'

'I didn't send him to you,' he said curtly.

'Yes—you did!' She leaned forward, and spat the words at him with such venom that he automatically recoiled. 'Oh, I know you didn't say, "There's Annette, go and stay with her"—but you told him I was here, I was alone, possibly you let him know I was lonely, that I'd be overjoyed to see him . . . Whatever you told him, you knew that, sooner or later, if he slipped through their fingers, he would come here, and having him here was as safe as having him locked up in a cell. That's what you thought, isn't it, Harry?'

'If I understand you right,' he said slowly, 'you are suggesting that I meant to betray Marius. You're wrong. It's a crazy idea. Why should I do it? Marius was always my friend.'

Annette got up and began to turn up and down the room with her arms crossed, the smoke from the cigarette curling into the air. 'Don't talk to me about friendship, Harry. One thing I never was, and that's a hypocrite. I know we all go back a long way, but my memory is better than yours.' She came to a halt by her chair and leaned over the back of it, so that she looked down on him. 'I remember, one day, you and I were watching Marius play tennis. I suppose you and he were about sixteen, and I was fifteen or so. He was a very good tennis player. He kept winning things, cups, championships, anything he entered for. That day, he played one really superb shot and I turned round to you to say something about it. But I didn't say a word, because I saw your face, Harry, as you watched him. You'd forgotten me, and you'd forgotten to keep up the pretence. You were watching Marius as he stood there the victor, sweating and handsome like a young warrior. I don't think I ever saw such hatred in anyone's eyes in my life, as I saw in yours for Marius, Harry. Not even since. I saw, then, what you really thought of him. Did you always hate him as much as that? Or did you ever like him, once?'

Harry lit the cigarette now, bending his head over the task, so that she could not see his face. 'Marius isn't always the easiest person to have around, you know.'

'Certainly not. But that isn't a reason to hate him. Were you jealous?'

Harry leaned back in the chair. Something about his manner had changed and she realised that he had decided on a new tactic. Meet bluntness with bluntness. 'All right, let's say I hate his guts. Why not? He was always so damn good at everything. As if he needed to be! He already had everything. He had money, good family, good looks, any girl he wanted—including you, my dear, though you weren't the only one. You were, however, his principal conquest, I suppose.' He saw the angry flush darken her pale cheek, and chuckled. 'But you've lost your hold on him, haven't you? That girl has him firmly in her toils. She won't let him go. She's young, she's pretty, she has a quality of innocence. You can't hope to fight off a rival like that.'

Annette had regained her calm. 'You're wrong in thinking I still want him, Harry.'

'But you won't tell me where he is?'

'No, I won't. And before you start saying that's because I still carry a candle for him, let me put you right. It's not because of him, and it's not because I'm sentimental about any relationship he might have with the girl. It's because of *you*.'

He was startled and looked at her enquiringly. 'Yes, you,' she said softly. 'You tried to use me, Harry. You sent Marius here so that I could do your dirty work for you. You made me Marius's keeper, safely stowed away here while you set up whatever plan you and your German friends have hatched. But I don't like being used, Harry. And certainly not by a miserable little scribbler of bad drawings like you! Sure you envied Marius his abilities—because you never had any. You're second-rate,

Harry. A second-rate artist, a second-rate businessman, probably a second-rate agent—I bet, even in bed you're second-rate.'

She had picked the words deliberately, knowing what their effect would be, but she realised even as she finished speaking that she had overplayed her hand. She had underestimated him. Harry's lean features twisted and became ugly. The grey eyes looked as merciless as a bird of prey's.

'That was a mistake, my dear,' he said softly. 'I tried to help you, Annette. I tried to make it easy. Don't think you can fool with me, because you can't. I know a lot of things about you, more than you imagine.' He swung round on his heel and walked over to the playing child.

'Get away from him!' she shouted, scrambling away from her chair and darting forward.

But Harry squatted down on his heels by Francis, and said amiably, 'That's a nice engine. Did you come here on the train?'

'Yes, but I didn't like it,' said Francis simply. 'There were a lot of people.'

'I said leave him alone, Harry,' Annette whispered.

'Give me your hands,' Harry said to the child, grasping the small fingers in his. 'Hang on tight!' He stepped back and swung Francis off the floor and round and round in a circle. Francis screamed with delight, and when Harry put him down, shouted, 'Do it again!' Harry obliged, and finally set the child down, to wipe his own brow. 'Go and find Louise now, go on, run along!'

When the child had gone, he turned back to Annette. 'I know Marius fathered that kid, Annette. Your family doesn't know it, but they can be told.'

'I'll kill you!' she threatened, eyes blazing.

'It wouldn't help to turn murderess. They'd lock you up and take the kid away for good.'

Annette whirled round. The table with the sewing-materials still stood behind her. She made a lunge towards it and snatched up the scissors and came at him, springing at his throat like a wounded tigress.

She only just missed him, the steel blades of the open scissors grazing his chin. He grasped her wrist and twisted it hard. She shrieked, and the scissors clattered to the floor. Harry gave her a violent shove and she sprawled back and lost her balance, falling down by the table and striking her cheek against the solid oak leg. Harry bent down, grasped her shoulders and dragged her roughly to her feet. He pulled her across the room and threw her down in her chair. She lay there, panting, and staring wildly up at him. A crimson stain showed where her cheek-bone had struck against the table-leg and where, tomorrow, a purple bruise would disfigure her face. Harry stooped over her and put his arms on either side of her, imprisoning her where she lay.

'Now listen to me, my dear. I can do one of two things. I can go to your family and tell them the kid is Marius's brat, and let them disinherit him and disown him. Or I can go to your husband and tell him you've been playing around down here, and he can divorce you and take the kid and you'll never set eyes on him again. Either suits me. I don't care which. Either way, I wouldn't give a cent for the kid's future. So, don't try any more silly tricks like that one.'

'You wouldn't have the nerve!' she gasped. 'Why should anyone believe you? If you tell my husband I've had a lover down here, you'll have to name the man! You can't name Marius without tipping your own hand. Whom will you tell him I've been sleeping with?'

Harry grinned down at her. 'With me, of course, my dear.'

She stared at him and then gave a peal of hysterical laughter. 'With *you*? You think anyone would believe that?'

'Sure they will, if it's true. And it will be true, Annette . . .' He stretched out his hand and grasped the neckline of her dress, wrenching it away and tearing the fragile material down to the waist. 'Don't screech, my dear, and don't bother to put up a fight. It's not as though you had any virtue to defend. I'm not the first, and I'm sure I won't be the last.'

He stood up, dragging her out of the chair and hurling her down on the Aubusson carpet. She rolled over away from him, but he threw himself down on top of her and pushed her over on her back, gripping her wrists with his sinewy hands. She brought up her knee, and swore at him, but he caught at her long hair and jerked her head so that it cracked on the parquet.

'Don't try it, Annette. Just show me a few of the tricks I'm sure you showed Marius!'

'You're out of your mind if you think I'm going to co-operate!' she spat up at him.

'Please yourself.' He smiled down at her.

She turned her head aside and closed her eyes, her bright red lipsticked mouth twisted in a grimace. She didn't put up any more fight, but lay motionless under him, moving only when he pushed and pulled her about to suit his own needs, and only when he finally rose from her and moved away did she open her eyes, and roll over and sit up.

Harry was a few feet away, tucking in his shirt and fastening his trousers. He ignored her until he was tidy again, and then went to fetch his spectacles from where he had left them, and put them on. Only then did he turn and look down at her, where she still sat on the parquet floor, in her shredded dress, her face blotched and bruised, and her green eyes gleaming at him like a demon's.

'Now, my dear,' he said mildly, adjusting his spectacles and peering down at her, 'tell me where I can find Marius and the girl.'

'I want a promise,' she articulated hoarsely. 'I want a guarantee from you that you will do nothing to harm Francis.'

'Of course, my dear. I'm very fond of you, and the kid is a nice little chap. You see? We can help one another. I'll be nice to you—if you're nice to me. Now then, Marius . . . and the girl.'

She gave a deep sigh which seemed to rise up from the depths of her being, and bent her head forward so that her tumbled hair fell over her face, both hiding her from him, and shielding his cold grey eyes with their implacable gaze from her. 'All right,' she breathed, 'I'll tell you.'

Lothar Dettmar walked slowly round his desk, passing the mirror on the wall as he did so, and casting an automatic glance into it. A faint frown crossed his brow, and he smoothed an unruly lock of hair with his palm. In fact, it was not this slight imperfection in his appearance which annoyed him, so much as being hauled away from a rather pleasant little dinner with a very charming lady, in order to come into his office, summoned by a man for whom he felt nothing but contempt.

It was difficult not to show that contempt. In the mirror, he could see Harry's reflection. The artist was watching him with some apprehension. Dettmar had always found Harry useful, and easy to manage. But it was this very lack of backbone, as the major termed it to himself, which brought forth his scorn. The man was a miserable traitor to his own people, and much as it might serve German purposes, Dettmar himself had great difficulty in repressing the urge to boot the fellow down the stairs.

All the same, they had gained considerable success in disrupting criminal activity in the area since Harry had been recruited. Dettmar always referred to the Resistance as 'criminals'. They had had their setbacks, of course. The blowing of the bridge had not been well received in Berlin. The major had personally given Harry a very bad time over that, put the fear of God in him.

But lately Dettmar had begun to mistrust Harry, especially since the episode of the bridge. Not that he had ever genuinely trusted him. Who could trust a man who so easily betrayed his own? But Harry had been decidedly shifty these last few weeks, and Dettmar suspected he was holding out on information. The question was, was Harry now more afraid of reprisals from his fellow-criminals than he was of Dettmar? The major placed both hands, palm downwards, on his desk, and asked severely, 'Well? And it had better be good, bringing me out at this hour!'

Harry cleared his throat and rubbed his hands together. It made a scraping noise and caused Dettmar to frown again. Harry noticed it, and stopped. 'You want to catch van Malderen? I can tell you where he is now.'

Dettmar gave him a jaundiced look. 'I have an idea you could have told me long before now, Harry. Why are you suddenly so anxious to divulge this information?'

'I haven't been holding out on you.' Harry sounded briefly aggressive, but Dettmar was not convinced. Miserable rat had been holding out, playing some devious game of his own, most likely. However, here he was now, offering information Dettmar dearly wanted.

But if you want something very badly, you don't let it be seen. Dettmar spread his hands dismissively. 'Is that all?'

'No. He's got a girl with him. She's a courier sent out by London. You can pick her up as well, if you move quickly.'

The major's eyes narrowed at the faint reproach in the last words. 'Tell me about this girl.'

Harry shifted his feet on the waxed linoleum of the floor. 'She's going under the name of Marie Gérard, and carries papers showing her to be a dressmaker.'

Susceptible as he was to the major's moods, Harry noticed every flicker of emotion to cross the other's face, and he would have had to be blind not to see the momentary surprise which showed in Dettmar's eyes. Then the German leaned back and sighed.

'*Ach, so* . . . Well, well . . . Such a pretty girl. A pity.'

Dettmar was an officer of the old traditional Counter-Intelligence Service and inclined to view the Gestapo as Johnny-Come-Lately thugs, thoroughly unprofessional and socially barbarian. Besides which, they were irritatingly inclined to pry into the affairs of other departments. He communicated with them only when he had to, and then by telephone. But they were efficient, they knew every damn move he made, they would put in an immediate claim for such significant captures as van Malderen and the woman Gérard, and he would not be able to keep the girl out of their hands.

Harry flinched. His mind and the major's had moved momentarily on the same track. Once she was captured, Marie Gérard would soon cease to be pretty. Soon cease to be recognisable. Dettmar, that connoisseur of pretty women, regretted the loss as he would have registered the breakage of a piece of Meissen porcelain. Broken, and no longer of value. To be thrown away. Marie Gérard, once broken and valueless, would be dispatched to that human dustbin, Ravensbrück.

Harry had not the same dispassionate view. At the thought of the girl in the hands of her captors, he wanted to throw up. He turned his head aside, and when he looked back, Dettmar was watching him sarcastically, with open dislike in every line of his expression. 'Where, Harry?'

Harry mumbled the required information.

Dettmar stretched out a hand to the telephone, but half-way there paused, with his fingers hovering above the receiver. 'You had better be right, Harry, because I'm fast losing confidence in you. If you're wrong, *I* shall deal with you. If you are right . . .' Dettmar smiled at him glacially, '. . . I dare say your criminal colleagues will deal with you.'

Harry swallowed with difficulty. 'They know about me; they must do. The girl . . . I don't know how she did it, but she worked it out somehow. I've been useful to you, and I still can be . . .'

Dettmar shook his head regretfully. 'No, Harry, not any longer. To be frank, your usefulness always had its limits. Don't try and play me for a fool. You've tried to stay on both sides. A little information for me, a little work for them. You're lucky I don't hand you over to the Gestapo.'

'I don't know any more than I've told you now!' Harry burst out, his voice cracked with fear.

'You're a stupid man, Harry, who fancies he's a clever one,' the major told him. 'And I have no time for stupid men. You've bought all the time you could buy. You've run out of currency, Harry. I'm not about to play banker. You're on your own.'

Dettmar no longer troubled to hide his contempt. The wretched fellow was green with fear, he observed, shaking in his shoes quite literally.

'You should protect me . . .' Harry whispered through dry lips.

'Get out!' Dettmar said brusquely, and picked up the telephone.

Libby lay awake. It was well past midnight, and rolling over carefully so as not to disturb Marius, she managed to make out the luminous dial of her watch. Ten to two. She sighed. Marius slept like a log. It irritated her, as she listened to his deep, regular breathing, that he could sleep like it while she lay awake, her mind teeming with a hundred possibilities. Supposing Ton van Leeuwen had not been able to make the radio contact with London? Supposing he had, what would London ask them to do? What about Harry? He must have realised by now that she wasn't coming back. Thwarted and cheated, he would be furious, wild with frustrated anger, and capable of anything.

She sat up and swung her legs out of bed. It was cold in this unheated room, but it was no use lying there sleepless. She pulled on her sweater and skirt and pushed her feet into her shoes, one repaired in haphazard fashion by Marius with a hammer and tacks after the hidden paper with the code had been retrieved. That was another thing. She had kept that code successfully from Harry, but Marius had handed it over to van Leeuwen without a moment's hesitation. Marius had been wrong about Harry, and it was to be hoped he wasn't going to be proved wrong about Ton as well.

Poor Ton, what a funny little man he was . . . and how he hated Harry. For all the little watchmaker's apparent insignificance, and his awe of his fearsome wife, Libby sensed that Ton was a bad enemy to have. She prayed he would prove equally as good a friend.

There was a muffled noise from the bed, as Marius stirred, throwing out an arm across the adjoining pillow. Sensing it vacant, he awoke, sat up, and whispered, 'Libby?'

'I didn't mean to wake you, but I can't sleep,' she answered from the darkness. Despite the shuttered window and the lampless street outside, enough silver moonlight slithered through the slats to allow her to make out the even darker silhouette of Marius sitting up, with his forearms resting on his knees.

'There's nothing to be gained by worrying,' he said reasonably. 'You might as well come back to bed. Besides, you need your sleep if you're to keep your brain alert and working.'

'Yes, I know . . .' She wandered to the shutters and peered down through the slats. In the distance, she could hear an engine. A car? No, too deep, a lorry. Lorry? Lorries didn't travel at night, not commercial ones, not in wartime. 'Marius!' she exclaimed sharply.

But he had already heard it, too. He leapt out of bed, dragging on his clothes, as running feet sounded outside and someone pounded on the door. It flew open, and one of the girls burst in.

'*Réveillez-vous!* Stinking Boches on their way! Sophie says to come with me to the cellar!'

They stumbled helter-skelter down the uneven staircase behind her. The whole house was awake now, people running back and forth, girls shouting. As their guide threw open the door to the cellars, a blast of dank, earthy air hit them full in the face, and their ears were assailed by a thunderous hammering at the front of the house.

'This way!' The girl was already half-way down the steps, her voice floating back to them. Marius and Libby stumbled after her.

At the bottom, the girl grasped Libby's wrist and set off into pitch blackness. Libby grabbed Marius's hand and they could only follow, the blind leading the blind . . . the macabre thought flashed through Libby's mind. Like Breughel's painting of the blind beggars. If this girl falls or gets lost, we're all lost.

The girl didn't get lost. As she dragged them along, she panted, 'These houses are old—cellars even older. They all inter-connect, *vous savez*? All the length of the street. If you know the way, you can go down in the first house and come up in the last one . . .'

'Germans will have blocked both ends of the street!' Marius gasped. 'We'll have to stay down here!'

Libby cannoned into something, badly bruising her shoulder. She stumbled, and Marius hauled her upright. Crash, she cannoned into something else, stone and solid. These cellar vaults were supported on ancient Gothic stone pillars. It was like a descent into the grave. Like early Christians fleeing into the catacombs, they groped their way through ancient crumbling masonry and shuffled over packed earthen floors. From time to time a little moonlight filtered down from a slit, an air-vent at pavement level on the street high above. At last the girl pulled them into a niche behind some firewood. They helped her to pile up the short lengths of log to form a screen between themselves and possible searchers, and crouched in the darkness, waiting.

It seemed very quiet. Water dripped near by, and a sudden scattering of claws made Libby jump. Rats. She had always had a terror of them. Beside her, Marius gripped her shoulder in warning and in reassurance. Beside her, the girl muttered unexpectedly, 'Hail Mary, full of grace . . .' There was a sound of voices, and approaching footsteps. 'Pray for us . . .' The girl fell silent.

The footsteps came closer, slowly and hesitantly. A yellowish light bathed the area. It was a soldier with a torch. He wasn't sure where he was, or of the way. The gloomy surroundings made him nervous, and he was more afraid of someone finding him, a desperate Resistance fighter, than of finding anything himself. On the far side of the cellar, something fell and claws scrabbled. They heard him swear. The light disappeared as he swung his torch in the direction of the sound, and they heard him kicking objects out of the way and cursing, as he searched in that area.

'*Was denn?*' shouted another voice, more distant.

'*Ratten . . .*'

'*Ist was da?*'

'*Na, nichts . . .*'

He began to move away, not wanting to linger down here. The light disappeared, and silence fell over the cellars.

The three of them remained in their hiding-place, it seemed to Libby, for an age. Her imagination ran riot. Had everyone in the house, from Sophie downwards, been arrested?

No. New, lighter and more sure footsteps hurried towards them, and a girl's voice called, 'Yvonne?'

'Here!' The girl beside them stood up, and pushed aside their wall of logs. They emerged stiffly from their shelter into the glare of torchlight. Libby could see now where they had been sheltering. Ancient stone walls rose, damp and greenish with some kind of mould, and met above their heads in shadowy arches. Barrels, boxes, woodpiles filled the area haphazardly. Some looked as if they had not been moved in a century or more. Perhaps they hadn't.

'Sophie says you can come up again now. They've gone. Didn't find anything.'

They made their way back upstairs. The girls were sitting about looking grumpy and dishevelled in a variety of night attire, one or two with their hair pinned up in curlers. They had probably only just gone to bed when the search-party arrived. Or got to bed alone, thought Libby, wondering what time the last customers had left. Not too late. Anyone making his way home too late would be arrested by suspicious patrols. Business must be badly affected by the petty restrictions of wartime, unless any of the soldiers found their way here bent on pleasure. Perhaps the house was off-limits. The Wehrmacht was probably allowed only into approved houses of ill repute.

'Ah,' said Sophie, sighing, 'in the old days, when

I first set up business and hadn't got myself properly organised, the police used to raid us all the time. I've always made sure my girls know the way through those cellars. Insurance, you might say.'

Marius was sitting on the bottom stairs, his hands clasped, and staring straight ahead with unseeing eyes. 'I never thought she would . . . But she must have done. She was the only one who knew we had come here . . .'

He was thinking of Annette. Libby touched his shoulder. 'You don't know what happened. Anything might . . . I expect Harry decided to do something. He must have realised I wasn't coming back. He'd have gone to Annette straight away. He might have tricked her, or found some way . . . Don't forget her son.'

She bit back the words, but too late. Annette's son. His son!

Sophie pattered across, a puce satin gown wrapped tightly about her wizened body. '*Alors*, are you staying here? They won't come back tonight.'

Marius shook himself and looked up. 'No!' he said briskly, 'we're moving out. What about that timber-yard? Is it far away? Tomorrow—that is, today . . .' he glanced at his watch, 'is Sunday. There won't be anyone there. Thank God we got hold of Ton earlier, and he was safe out of it. Let's hope he was able to raise London on that radio.'

'As you like. I'll send word to Emil—that's the owner of the yard. He's a good man, he'll see you're all right.'

Musical chairs, thought Libby, remembering the old children's game. Marius and I, we move along the chain of safe houses, one to another . . . until the music stops. It stopped tonight, but we were lucky, we had a chair. Next time perhaps we'll be the ones caught 'out'.

Harry made his way through the dark, deep in thought. He knew the district well; he could, if necessary, have found his way home blindfold. The familiarity enabled him now to walk briskly along, without putting a foot wrong despite the absence of street lighting. His thoughts concerned his situation and his very problematic future.

He was not a traitor from conviction, he was one from necessity, or that was how he explained it to himself. It had all begun nearly a year before when they had quietly picked him up, and explained, very politely, that he had a choice. He could help them, or he would go the way of all the other Resistance operatives. Instinct for survival dictated his response. Harry saw no advantage in finishing up being shot in the head in some scruffy backyard, or starving in some camp. He did see the advantage of playing for time, and opted for helping his captors.

It had not, at the time, seemed very serious. He had thought—wrongly—that he could play it cleverly and avoid giving them any information of real importance. Eventually, he trusted, he would find the opportunity to give them the slip.

In reality, he soon found that unless they received a steady stream of information of a useful kind from him, they grew suspicious. Nor was it possible to give them the slip. The information he had already passed on precluded his turning to his fellow Resistance workers for help or begging London to get him out. These last months, he had gone half out of his mind trying to allay the suspicions of his Resistance colleagues on the one hand, and those of his

German masters on the other. He was sick of it, and frightened, and desperate. If he had known a way of getting out of it, he would have done so. There was no way, and his flounderings had become an increasingly vicious and self-centred fight for sheer survival.

The arrival of Marius had been the catalyst which had precipitated the situation he was in now. It had been one thing to sacrifice people like the Wouters, simple country folk of no account, but Marius van Malderen? The van Malderen family being what it was around here?

Harry did not suppose that Germany would ultimately win the war. There was just too much stacked against it, and the more intelligent German generals had been well aware of the fact since 1941. Whatever Hitler and his more fanatical adherents thought they were doing, shrewder minds saw Germany's battle now as a means to obtain as strong a position as possible, from which to negotiate a peace advantageous to the Fatherland. It was wishful thinking, by desperate men. In order to hang on to that hypothetical advantage, Germany had to fight to keep every inch of conquered territory, and resort more and more to the methods which ensured that, after the war, vengeance would be exacted. The Allies would crush Germany. Peace would return, and, with it, the hunt would begin for those who had supported a vile regime.

Old Count van Malderen was in London, and as soon as the Allies liberated Belgium, the old man would reappear here. He would return with powerful friends in the new postwar government, perhaps even be a part of it. The first thing he would do would be to set about finding the man who had betrayed his son, and he would have the whole apparatus of police and intelligence services to help him. As a result of this reasoning, even resenting Marius as he did, the thought of betraying him, and the consequences to himself if he did, had frankly horrified Harry long enough to make him desist from any such idea until now. And then, the more he had thought about it . . . and he had spent many a sleepless night mulling it over . . . it had seemed a very good thing to leave Marius at liberty, for the time being. Harry knew where to find him—with Annette—and sooner or later Marius would get things reorganised here, and Harry would have a really fine bag to offer Dettmar. Either way, Marius was an ace in his hand, and the only ace he was ever likely to hold. He had to play it wisely. He could either be the man who protected Count van Malderen's son, which would put him virtually in the clear when inevitable enquiries were made about informers, or he could offer Marius to the Germans in return for some guarantee of safety and protection. Only the whole blasted thing had gone wrong, with the arrival of the girl. As for protection, that bastard Dettmar had virtually laughed in his face. Harry's precious ace had been played—for nothing.

Harry shivered, and not altogether from the night's chill. He thrust his hands into his pockets and strode on, not noticing that a small, slight shadow followed behind him, dodging in and out of doorways. Harry was at the door of his shop before he realised that he was not alone. His ear caught the scrape of a shoe on cobbles and he whirled round, peering into the darkness.

'Who the devil is there?'

'Only me, Harry . . .' Ton van Leeuwen slipped

out of the shadows and scurried up to him. 'I was waiting for you. I must talk to you. Can I come in?'

Harry hissed with impatience. 'Oh, very well!' He unlocked the door and refastened it behind them both. He did not need a light to climb his rickety stairs, and took a perverse pleasure in hearing van Leeuwen stumble uncertainly up the treads behind him. At the top, however, he switched on the light.

Van Leeuwen blinked in the sudden glare and looked about him. 'I've been meaning to come . . . but I wasn't sure what was happening.' He sidled towards Harry's studio and peered through the door.

'Of course you weren't. You haven't put your nose outside your own front door!' Harry said curtly. 'What do you want now, you gutless wonder?'

Like a folktale in which the master kicks the butler, and so on through descending pecking order to the scullion kicking the dog, Harry, having been metaphorically kicked by Dettmar, itched to kick the watchmaker.

Van Leeuwen, in an irritating way, had wandered into the studio and was fiddling with the tools used by Harry when framing pictures. 'Been doing a bit of framing, Harry? Is this it? Nice job you made of that.'

'Get out of there!' Harry snapped. 'If you want to talk, come into the other room!'

He walked off into his sitting-room, van Leeuwen following. It was as Harry stretched out a hand to switch on the light in this room that he realised how close behind him van Leeuwen stood, and some instinct made him turn.

But he did not turn quickly enough to avoid the blow from the hammer which van Leeuwen had abstracted from the studio.

CHAPTER SIXTEEN

MARIUS SWARMED up the fence round the timber-yard with alacrity and hauled Libby up after him. They both dropped down onto the ground on the other side and stood there, panting, in the darkness. It had begun to drizzle, a chill wind blew round the stacks of timber, the air smelt of wet wood-shavings and creosote and there was a feeling of mournful desolation all about them. Libby peered at her watch with difficulty, because the rain-clouds had obscured the earlier clear moonlight, and decided it was a little before four in the morning. It was the hour of the night when human resolve is at a low ebb, and she gave vent to a dispirited sigh.

Marius, hearing it as he turned up his coat-collar against the breeze, stretched out his arm to hug her shoulders in consolation. 'Cheer up. It will look better in daylight.'

'Don't say anything,' she warned him resignedly. 'Especially, don't be optimistic. I don't think I can take it. As far as you and I are concerned, standing about in a woodyard at four in the morning in the rain is about par for the course.'

'I daren't show a torch light,' Marius muttered. 'I don't know if it can be spotted. Someone might just be looking out and decide the yard has been broken into and pick up a phone. I wish I knew the layout.'

They sheltered as best they could until daylight, and then emerged, damp and aching, from under a pile of planks. There was a hut in the corner of the yard, but the door was securely padlocked and the begrimed window did not open. As they turned away from this, they heard a rattling at the main gates.

Marius pulled Libby back behind the pile of planks again, and peered through a chink in the stack. Someone wrestled irritably with the lock, managed to open it at last, and a body squeezed in through the narrow opening. It belonged to a large, burly man wearing overalls, a vast, shapeless jacket that would have done credit to a clown, and a peaked cap. He locked the gates again behind him carefully and walked slowly into the middle of the yard.

'If you're there,' he said, apparently to no one, 'you can come out. Sophie sent me word. I'm Emil, the owner of this yard.'

He watched them appear from behind the wood-stack without the slightest change of expression on his flat, pudgy-featured, unshaven face. He stared first at Marius, then at Libby, and then turned back to Marius. He was obviously used to dealing with men, and plainly meant to keep discussion between men now.

'Best come out of the rain,' he said.

He led them over to the padlocked hut and produced a key. The interior was dusty and cheerless. It was stacked with boxes, on the top of one of which stood a small spirit-stove, a saucepan with no handle, and two tin mugs. Emil went to the end of the hut and dragged aside some of the boxes. 'Your wireless,' he said laconically.

'Good God, is it all right there?' Marius exclaimed.

Massive shoulders shrugged. 'As all right as anywhere. I run this yard with my brother-in-law. No one else. No one comes in this hut. My brother-in-law isn't very bright, you understand, but he keeps his mouth shut.' Emil dragged the boxes to conceal the radio equipment again. 'There are some blankets up there.' He pointed to a shelf above their heads. 'A few months back we had a break-in, and my brother-in-law and I took to sleeping down here in turns for a week or two. You'll be all right. The little chap said he'd be back again tonight, and you should wait for him.'

'Van Leeuwen got here, then,' Marius said *sotto voce* to Libby, who had not followed much of this conversation, conducted in Flemish. 'It's something to be thankful for.'

Emil was delving into one pocket of his voluminous jacket to produce a paper-wrapped parcel. Then he delved into the other, and a bottle of beer appeared. 'Thought you'd want some breakfast,' he observed. 'You won't be troubled today. Sunday, see? Day off.'

'Will neighbours think it odd that you're here, in that case?' Marius asked sharply.

Emil shook his head. 'No . . . Often come down on a Sunday to make sure no one's been messing about overnight—since we had our break-in, see?' He went outside and began methodically to check round his yard.

'He doesn't think we've been spending our time off-loading a few lengths of timber onto the black market, does he?' Libby, watching him through a crack in the door, muttered resentfully.

'Let the man go through his normal routine, can't you? It's the best thing.'

Emil plodded back, stared at them thoughtfully, and announced, 'I'll be off. You'll be all right, see? I'll lock the main gates. Can't no one get in.'

'How about Ton?' Marius asked him.

'Little chap? He don't need a key, he told me,' Emil sniffed disapprovingly at this ability to deal with locks in unorthodox fashion. 'But I gave him one, anyway. The spare. It usually hangs up there . . .' He pointed to a vacant hook in the wall. 'So you don't have to let him in, and if anyone else comes trying the gates, you just climb over the wall at the back, and you'll drop down on a bit of a path along by the canal. We got another gate there, but it's mostly kept locked unless we're loading or unloading, and it's best left that way, because you might get a bargee coming up to look round. Bargees, they come and go. Might be one there overnight, might not. They mostly keep themselves to themselves, and you don't have to worry about them.'

Emil appeared to recollect Libby's presence, and gave her a farewell nod. She smiled at him and said, 'Thank you,' but he only mumbled disapprovingly and plodded away homewards.

'He thinks women ought to be at home, cooking meals and having babies,' said Marius.

'Sorry he disapproves of me. What's in that package?'

Marius unwrapped it. 'Bread, salami, cheese. Here, sit down over there. Might as well eat while we can.'

Libby found herself to be starving, and devoured her share with enthusiasm. Well fed, she felt much more optimistic. 'When will Ton come back, do you think?'

'Oh, as soon as it gets dark, early evening. I wish I knew whether he got through to England.'

'The Germans can pick up that broadcast, can't they?' Libby said thoughtfully, glancing towards the boxes which hid the wireless. 'It wouldn't be difficult to trace it here.'

'No. We shall have to move the radio after today. Emil must have transport of some kind. Actually . . .' Marius grew thoughtful, 'he was talking about barges on the canal. The canal runs behind this yard. Now, if we could get the radio equipment onto a barge . . .'

'It would keep moving, and the Germans would go half crazy trying to locate it!' Libby anticipated him. 'Hey, that's very good!'

'Thank you! I get the occasional brainwave, you know. I'll talk to Emil about it.' He got up and dragged the blankets from the shelf. 'Here you are; better make ourselves comfortable. You can wrap a blanket round yourself, or sit on it, as you wish.'

Libby inspected the blankets. 'Thanks, I'll sit. I bet they have fleas in them.'

'Why the hell should they have fleas in them? Don't be so damn fussy! They're only damp.'

He packed the blankets into a seat against the wall, and they sat down, side by side, leaning back against the wood.

'If I sit here all day,' she said, 'my legs will go as stiff as bits of wood themselves, and I shan't be able to get up, much less make a run for it if we have to.'

'True. We'll have to get up and do a few physical jerks. We had better not go out in that yard in the open daylight.'

'What,' asked Libby, struck by a practical thought, 'do we do about calls of nature? I'm not a camel.'

'You'll have to go over there in the corner. Earth floor, no problem.'

'One can take togetherness too far, you know,' she grumbled.

Marius chuckled and put his arm round her. After a moment, she rested her head on his shoulder and his hand caressed her tangled hair. After a silence, he said, 'I'm sorry I got you into all this.'

'I got myself into it. Contrary to what everyone likes to tell me, I did have some idea what I was about.'

There was another pause, and then Marius spoke again, his voice sounding unlike its usual self, halting and awkward, rather as though he tried out words new to his vocabulary. 'I do love you, Libby.'

Her heart gave a little skip, and the discouragement fled from her. 'I always loved you, Marius.'

'You make that sound as if I didn't always love you. But I fell in love with you in England. I didn't want to. I did my best not to. In the end, I wasn't able to stop myself. I wish I could have told you before, but it wasn't the right time. I dare say it isn't the right time now, but it's the only time we have . . . and I want you to know it, in case . . .'

'In case we're caught.'

'Yes.'

Libby turned towards him and put her arms round his neck. His own arms encircled her, drawing her close to him, and his mouth closed over hers.

'We always seem to be making love in such damn awful places, Libby. I know you don't like it, neither do I. One day, who knows, we'll get into a proper bed with clean sheets.'

'And nice soft pillows,' she suggested, wriggling uncomfortably on the rough blankets.

'Feather pillows.' His fingers ran along her cheek and across her lips. 'When we get back to England—if we do—we'll get married, and then we can tell everyone else to get lost. We'll lock the door and climb into our nice comfortable bed, and make love.'

She whispered, 'Oh, Marius . . .' and pressed her head against his chest. 'We'll have children, Marius. I know how you feel about losing Francis, but we'll have children of our own.'

'Sure.' His mouth was pressed against her ear, the words vibrating in the flesh. 'You were always different, and something special, Libby. I'd known other girls before I met you—and of course there was all that business with Annette, before the war. I thought, at the time, it was love, but I know now it wasn't. It was just sex. Annette knew that, even then. She laughed at me. It made me mad as hell at the time, but she was quite right to laugh. I was pretty angry with you when you turned up here. It wasn't because I didn't want to see you again . . . it was because I knew what a dirty business this is, and what it does to people. I hate it. Some men love it: war. It releases all their inhibitions, and gives them an excuse to live out what otherwise would be fantasies. Lord knows what they will do when peace comes. For me, it's been a job, and a duty. You don't have to like your job, and you don't have to like your duty. But you do have to do both.'

'I understand,' she said softly. 'But you've done your duty, Marius, and you can be free now. I know we're hunted and don't have much chance, but, in a funny kind of way, we're free. It's all finished. We can just be ourselves.' She put her arms round his neck. 'Make love to me now. Then nothing else will matter.'

Marius got up and took off his overcoat, to spread it out on the floor. 'Better than the blankets, but still not a feather bed.'

'We don't need that feather bed.'

Marius lay down beside her and put his arm across her pliant form. She turned towards him, pressing into the warmth of his body, threading her hand through the tangle of clothing until it touched the warm, soft skin. Marius moaned and she felt the increasing tension and the power of that muscular body. He had some trouble with her underwear, and in that she had to help him, wriggling out of the satin knickers trimmed with lace which London had so thoughtfully provided for Marie Gérard, and kicking them away. After that, they took their time, because it was possibly the last time, certainly the most important time, and the one which, come what may, they would remember. Their bodies moved in unison, a unity both physical and spiritual, a harmony of mind and of desire, until the desire grew too great to be contained and she gasped and clutched at him, hearing the deep ragged breaths which he took with each convulsive movement until the final low cry of triumph.

Marius turned away from her, and they lay silent in the darkness for a while, side by side. Then he stretched out a hand and touched her shoulder. 'Was it good?'

'It was very good,' she said.

He turned back towards her and caught her chin in his hand, twisting her face gently towards his, so that he could kiss her. 'No one can take this away from us, whatever happens.'

'No one,' she said softly.

* * *

Ton returned at nightfall, bringing more food. Despite Marius's confidence in him, Libby had secretly doubted that the little man would come. But van Leeuwen seemed completely to have recovered his nerve.

'I raised England all right,' he said. 'Told them what you said to tell them. They'll come back tonight with instructions for you.'

'What about Harry?' Marius asked. 'What's he doing?'

Van Leeuwen's gaze slid away from his. 'Nothing. Won't do anything, not ever again. I took care of it. Said I would.'

There was a long silence. Marius asked, a little hoarsely, 'No one can connect you with it?'

'Don't worry. I chucked the . . .' van Leeuwen glanced at Libby. 'I chucked the weapon into the canal. Before that, I emptied his cash register and broke the lock on his door. There's been quite a bit of burglary in town. With no street lighting, it encourages anyone to take a chance. If they don't believe it, they don't believe it, but they can't prove anything else.'

'I suppose . . .' Marius said slowly, and broke off.

'Oh, it was Harry, all right,' van Leeuwen, reading the unspoken question in Marius's mind, spoke with assurance. 'Last night, after I'd finished here, I was on my way home, and I had to go past the Kommandantur. As I did, who should come running out but Harry himself. Saw him clearly in the shaft of light, when they opened the door for him. He'd gone to tell them what he knew, see . . . and I don't mind telling you, I was glad to hear from Emil today that you and the girl were safe. Well, I followed behind until he got to the door of his shop, and then I stepped up and asked to have a private word. He wasn't keen, but he never thought much of me. He certainly wasn't scared of me. His mistake, that.'

Libby drew back into the shadows in the corner of the hut. They had blacked out the window with one of the blankets and lit a paraffin lamp, but they kept its light low, and it did little to dispel any but the immediate gloom. They crouched there like the assassins they were. They had murdered a man. Between them, they had done it. She had named Harry, put the finger on him; Marius had agreed, van Leeuwen had struck the blow. It was not sufficient to say, 'Us or him,' even if it were true. Yet Harry could not be left to continue his treachery. By it, he could be argued to have encompassed his own death. But it didn't help now. Libby shivered in the darkness. She remembered Jamie saying of Marius that he had 'the mark of Cain on him'. And now, she thought, perhaps people will say the same of me. Perhaps it will show in the way I look at people, in something I say. When I go home again, if I ever do get home again, I shall be a different Libby, and perhaps they won't like it, won't like me.

Marius and Ton had dragged away the boxes in front of the hidden radio equipment. 'I'll go outside and stand guard,' Marius said, and slipped out of the door.

Libby sat and watched van Leeuwen fiddling with the radio. After a moment she got up, because she didn't want to remain hunched in the dark corner, on her own with her dark thoughts. She went to stand beside Ton's crouched figure, and he glanced up at her, and gave her a crooked, shy sort of smile.

'Can't make me out, can you?'

'No,' she confessed frankly. It was disconcerting

to think that her mistrust of him had been so obvious. At least it did not seem to have offended him.

'Have to watch my step a bit, see?' He moved a knob slowly and carefully. His hands on the radio were gentle and sensitive, the hands of the craftsman and watchmaker. 'But you can rely on me. I won't let you down.' He bent his ear close to the transmitter, and frowned as he tried to catch a sign of life.

'Why not?' she asked calmly.

He gave her that odd, shy look again. 'I'm a Jew,' he said. 'Married to a Christian, so they haven't rumbled me yet. When they do, they'll pick me up anyway. So, while I can, I do what I can. But I can't go calling too much attention to myself. That's why I have to hide out in my own house. After Wouters was picked up, my wife got scared. So did I. I expected them to come for me then. I don't know why Harry didn't split on me. It wasn't because he gave a damn about me, but I think because it might have been traced back to him. Or maybe he was saving me for the next time they asked him for a name. He was an odd one, Harry. He did some really good work for us, you know, before they got to him . . . Anyhow, you don't have to worry about me. Even if I was picked up, I wouldn't tell them anything. I wouldn't . . .' He twiddled a knob and bent his head close to the set, '. . . tell them if it was raining.' The radio emitted a sharp crackle. 'You go outside,' Ton ordered. 'Watch the back.'

Libby stood in the darkness, pressed against the back fence of the yard. Now that she knew the canal ran along the other side, she could distinguish the slap of water, and wondered whether a barge were moored there. If so, she hoped Emil was right about the bargees. She glanced apprehensively towards the hut, but there was no sign of light from it. A slight clatter from the darkness heralded the appearance of Marius, who came up and whispered, 'All quiet?'

'I think so. You should have told me Ton was a Jew. I would have understood why he was behaving so oddly, hiding out like that in his own home.'

'Better you didn't know; then you couldn't tell anyone else.'

'I wouldn't have told anyone!' she said indignantly.

'Don't bet on it. They can be very persuasive.'

The door of the hut opened slightly, and a low whistle was heard. They hurried back.

'London wants you out of it and back,' Ton said, as he neatly stowed away his wireless equipment again. 'Sending a Lysander for you, next clear night. Tomorrow, if possible. If it's cloudy, night after. Same field as before.'

'We'll have to organise reception on the ground!' Marius exclaimed. He turned to Libby. 'When the Lysander comes in, we'll signal a recognition sign, a Morse letter . . . What will it be, Ton?'

'G,' he replied.

'OK. The Lysander will signal back—we hope, correctly—and then we light a flare-path for him, but that takes men on the ground.'

Van Leeuwen began to calculate, ticking off names on his fingers. 'Emil and his brother-in-law. Farmer next to Wouters' land, and a couple of old chaps who work for him—they've lent a hand before. We can do it. I'll fix it. You just get yourselves out to the field before two in the morning. The Lysander can't wait. If you're not there for the pick-up, he'll go.'

'What about the field itself?' Marius asked, sounding worried. 'Is it still clear? The Germans haven't been out there and stuck obstacles all over it to stop a plane landing?'

'Not that I know. If they have, we'll just have to move them.'

'I'd feel happier,' Marius muttered, 'if some of those men were armed.'

Van Leeuwen shifted his feet. 'We hid a couple of machine-guns and some ammunition at the other farm, next to Wouters', before Jan and his wife were picked up, and stuff was still being dropped from England. Harry wasn't involved in that drop, and he never knew about some of the guns being moved. I already suspected him, and I persuaded Jan not to put all our eggs in one basket, as a matter of principle. Should still be there.'

Emil arrived at dusk the following evening, and opened the back gates on to the canal path. The water slapped eerily in the darkness and they could see the long, low dark shape of the barge a little further down. He led them towards it and, as they came up, Libby saw the dark silhouette of another man, presumably the bargee, detach itself from the bulk of the barge and sidle along the narrow catwalk running its length. He and Emil exchanged a few low words, and then all three climbed aboard. Neither Marius nor Libby was introduced to the bargee, so they were not to know who he was or see his face. It was a simple precaution.

There was not much room in the living quarters of the barge, certainly not with Emil's vast bulk squashed in there with them. The barge slid away from the bank and began to putt-putt softly through the night. Quiet as it was, it seemed unbearably loud to Libby. But it was safer, whispered Emil, than going through the streets. There were extra patrols out. Having missed their quarry at Sophie's, the Germans were casting a wider net. Marius was silent, and she knew he was worried about Ton, and whether he had been able to organise the reception committee at the field.

The barge drew into the bank again outside the town, and they clambered off, whispering their thanks to the unseen and unknown bargee. Marius was their guide after that, because he knew the way across country. Libby and Emil blundered along behind him. Twigs scratched her face and caught at her hair, and brambles snagged her skirt and stockings. Emil followed behind, wheezing noisily and crashing bodily through obstacles regardless. But then the moon came out clear and bright, bathing everything with a silver sheen, and they were better able to see where they were going.

'He'll come tonight, all right,' Marius muttered, his face a curious pale grey, and seeming to shimmer. They must look, thought Libby, like three spooks. Well, perhaps not Emil, a little too substantial to be taken for a ghost. 'We have to be there—get a move on, Libby.'

After about an hour, they emerged from a thicket and were unexpectedly confronted by an unknown man cradling an automatic weapon in his arms, who rose like a phantom from the ground. Libby let out a startled squeak, but it was one of Ton's reception committee. The field, silver in the moonlight, lay before them. Equally without warning, Ton materialised at her elbow.

'Germans had been here and stuck poles all over

the place,' he said. 'The farmer says they did it after the raid on Wouters' place. But we dug them up all right, and the Lysander will be able to land. When you're away, we'll put the poles back and the Germans will be none the wiser. Can use the field again, then.'

'You should think about coming with us, Ton,' Marius said abruptly. 'You'd be better off in England.'

Van Leeuwen shuffled his feet. 'No . . . Better leave me here. Someone has to operate the wireless. London will send in someone else, I suppose, and there will have to be someone here, or there will be no one to contact. I'll get something fixed up and working, don't worry.'

Faintly, in the distance, came a drone of an aeroplane.

'The Lizzie . . .' Marius muttered.

The drone came nearer, lower now, as the Lysander came in to land, waiting for the signal from the ground. Ton stepped out on the field and flashed the code letter with his torch. Answering lights flickered from the sky. 'Now!' called out van Leeuwen into the gloom, and the men stationed with torches lit a flare-path to guide the plane.

Libby could see the Lysander now, with its distinctive wing design, coming down towards them like a great black moth. It landed bumpily and rolled to a stop a short distance away, the engine still ticking over. The hood slid back, and an English voice yelled, 'Get a bloody move on! There's a whole lot of cars or lorries coming this way . . . Flew over them, saw the headlights!'

'Come on!' Marius grabbed Libby's arm and they both sprinted towards the Lysander. Glancing over her shoulder, she saw the sweep of headlights appear in the near distance, and heard the crackle of automatic fire, as the men Ton had stationed on watch saw the approaching danger. There was a sudden increase in the firing . . . It was being returned. Something soughed past her ear, and, beside her, Marius grunted and seemed to stumble. They had reached the Lizzie now and somehow scrambled aboard. It was already moving, taxi-ing down the improvised runway and gathering speed. Abruptly it lurched, bumped, lurched again, then rose steeply, banking, and she clutched at Marius.

He gasped and struck her hand away, and at the same moment, to her horror, she felt the wet warm blood ooze stickily over her palm.

'You're hit!' Libby exclaimed.

'Shut up!' he muttered. 'The pilot has enough to worry about. Give me your scarf.'

She dragged off the headscarf and folded it hurriedly into a pad with shaking, clumsy fingers. She reached out and pressed the pad against the wound in an attempt to stanch the flow. Inside her head, a dull refrain was beating: 'No, not now, not at this stage . . . Not now . . .'

'Are you all right back there?' crackled the voice over the intercom.

Marius gasped, 'Yes, we're fine.'

'Good show. Sorry about the bumpy take-off,' apologised the voice, 'but I didn't fancy hanging about. Bit too lively down there.'

'Ton and the others . . .' Libby whispered, suddenly recalled to the plight of those who had covered their own escape.

'It's dark. They should have a good chance . . .'

Marius's voice broke off. 'You haven't got anything else, have you? I'm bleeding like a stuck pig . . .'

The pad was sodden. He was losing blood at a frightening rate, and soon, she knew, would pass into unconsciousness. She ripped a strip off the hem of her petticoat and bound it tightly round his ribs in an effort to maintain the pressure on the wound. The Lysander droned on through the night.

'Might be a bit bumpy over the coast!' advised the disembodied voice.

Marius muttered drowsily. His head was propped on her shoulder and he seemed to be falling asleep. Not sleep, she thought desperately. It isn't sleep . . . She shook at his arm. 'Marius! Try and stay awake!'

'All right . . .' he said indistinctly.

'Listen,' she said urgently. She had to keep talking, she had to keep him talking, about anything. 'You remember Tommy Ryan? You remember him, don't you?'

'Mmm . . .'

'He gave me a piece of heather—he said you'd given it to him, for luck.' She shook him again, almost angrily. 'Damn it, Marius, answer me!'

'Yes . . .' protested his voice, sounding blurred. 'Skinny kid . . .'

'That's right. He gave me the heather, and I kept it. It's at home at Merriton House, in my room. I didn't bring it because, if I'd been searched, I would have had to explain a sprig of heather. Marius, listen to me! I know it's lucky, and it will bring us back home!'

'What's going on back there?' demanded the voice in her ear.

'He's hurt . . .' she gasped.

'Tell him to hang on. We're coming up to the

coast. I'm switching off the intercom . . . Too many uninvited listeners . . . Tell him to hang on, and he can have breakfast in England . . .'

There was a rattle, as if someone had thrown a handful of dried peas against the Lizzie. The plane banked again and swerved. Lights flashed and the distant fire crackled again. Flak. They were over the coast. The powerful beam of a searchlight suddenly illuminated them, exposing them in all their vulnerable nakedness. The Lizzie swooped down and banked again, and the light disappeared.

Silence fell, broken only by the drone of the engine. They were over the sea. 'Marius!' Libby hissed, shaking his shoulder again. 'Marius?'

His head fell forward, and he slumped over sideways into her arms.

CHAPTER SEVENTEEN

'GOOD TO see you both back again,' said Mr Smith. 'Good piece of work on the bridge.'

This last was addressed to Marius, who said, 'Thank you, sir,' and shifted awkwardly in his chair.

Libby glanced at him apprehensively. Two weeks had passed since their escape by Lysander, two busy weeks which Libby had spent between putting in reports and answering questions, and visiting Marius in his hospital bed. A hospital bed, moreover, where she strongly suspected he still ought to be. But that, after all, was only her opinion, and he thought differently. He had a half-healed flesh wound in his side and two cracked ribs, but obstinately refused to be an invalid. Though bandaged up like Pharaoh's mummy, as he himself described it, he insisted on being discharged from hospital and moving around slowly under his own steam. If he was in pain, he wouldn't admit it.

'You ought to be in bed!' she had told him repeatedly.

'Only if you come with me.'

'I wish you'd be serious.'

'I *am* being serious.'

Libby realised that Mr Smith was looking towards her.

'Well done, my dear. Well done, in fact, to both of you. At least our wrong 'un has been well and truly nailed, and we'll be able to send in someone to re-establish that Resistance network.' He paused, and added apologetically to Marius, 'Sorry it won't be you, lad, but your days of leaping out of aircraft are over. You're too well known.'

'I'm not finished!' Marius said sharply, adding 'sir', belatedly. 'If I'm no more use as an agent, there must be a regular unit somewhere which can use me.'

Libby turned her head away, and stared at the opposite wall on which hung, inappropriately, a printed copy of Constable's 'The Haywain', which surely couldn't have any connection with anything done in this office. But it was something to pretend to look at while she fought for control of her features. Although she should have expected this: it would be foolish to imagine Marius would ever settle to or even accept the idea of a desk job. Besides, he had specialist skills of the sort needed in the field. Yes, they'd find a job for him. No doubt of that.

She turned her head back and met Mr Smith's eye, treating him to a frosty gaze of her own. 'And me?' she asked calmly.

From the corner of her eye, she saw Marius wriggle, wince and pull a face. He didn't like her asking the question, but, too bad, she had specialist skills of her own.

Mr Smith pursed his lips. 'Pleased to continue to have you with us, of course, my dear. But take some leave, and some time to think it over.' His sharp gaze flickered towards Marius again. 'You need to be fully committed to the job, you know, not worrying about anything left behind.'

There was a silence, and Mr Smith got to his feet and walked to the window, his hands clasped behind his back. He stood, staring out between the criss-cross of tape across the panes. 'Nasty raid last night,' he said. 'Blew a ruddy great hole in the bus depot. Buses never on time before. Don't turn up at all now.'

'I dare say they'll organise something,' Marius observed, stony-faced.

'Oh, yes, we British always organise something. Great organisers, we are.' Unexpectedly he burst out, '"I've got a little list!"'

He turned round apologetically. '*Mikado*,' he explained. Unexpectedly he smiled, and added, 'Well, at any rate, the fighting is over for you two, so to speak, for the time being. Get yourself fit, lad. Don't worry. You can leave here confident of a job well done. Go away, both of you, and relax for a spell.'

Marius struggled out of his chair and reached for Libby's hand.

Mr Smith cleared his throat. 'Just one word more, van Malderen . . . If you don't mind, Sherwood?'

'I'll wait outside,' Libby said, wishing she could get used to being addressed by her surname.

When she had gone out, Mr Smith avoided Marius's enquiring look and turned away, hands clasped behind his back. He went over to his desk, unclasped his hands, fiddled with the blotting-paper and said, 'Harr-ump! We have been in touch with the wireless operator you left behind.'

'Van Leeuwen,' Marius said. 'We ought to get him out, sir.'

'Not possible for the time being. He reports a good deal of German activity on the ground, which is only to be expected in view of your slipping through their fingers. But all our remaining operatives are safe. Including, van Leeuwen reports, the lady. He says you will know who that is.'

Marius heaved a deep sigh. 'Yes, sir. It's Mrs de Jong, sir. I'd like it on record, in case anything happens to prevent either Libby or myself from testifying after the war. She hid us both—well, hid me principally, but picked up Libby after she'd dropped in and brought her to me. Her husband is a collaborator and I shouldn't wish her to be accused of the same thing.'

'I'll make a note of it. What brought her to risk her neck?'

'I knew her before the war, sir,' Marius said expressionlessly.

His bleak tone was not lost on Mr Smith. 'Could have been tricky, that,' he said musingly. 'Female of the species, you know, deadlier than the male . . . My father knew him.'

'Who?' asked Marius, startled.

'Kipling. Rum things, old love affairs. Never get 'em quite out from under your skin,' Mr Smith cleared his throat again noisily and looked embarrassed. Marius could have sworn he blushed.

'No, sir.' Marius hesitated. 'They always linger on, in a corner of your mind. I don't mean you're still in love with that person, but you can't forget you once were. Whether it's a bad memory or a good one, it stays.'

'Simple chap, myself,' said Mr Smith. 'Got a couple of girls, giddy young idiots. Lost the boy, of course . . . Submariner. Ruddy tin cans, submarines. Wanted him to go for the army, but he fancied being a sardine. Said he didn't mind the smell. Get a spot smelly, submarines, when they've been at sea for a bit.'

Marius said awkwardly, 'I'm sorry . . .' but the other did not appear to have heard him.

'Talking of Kipling,' said Mr Smith, causing Marius to make another mental leap. 'I don't know if you're acquainted with the *Just So Stories*. '"The cat walked by himself and all places were alike to him . . ."' I've always thought that described your job rather well. Make the most of what you've got, won't you, lad? Don't keep the lady waiting.'

'Yes, sir—I mean, no!' Marius let himself out of the room and found Libby pacing up and down impatiently outside. 'It's all right. He hasn't posted me out. He wanted to quote Kipling at me. Come on.' He smiled at the relief in her eyes, put his arm round her shoulders and guided her towards the exit.

From his vantage-point at the window, Mr Smith watched them leave the building and walk off together down the road, the young man moving awkwardly because of his damaged ribs, the girl trotting alongside, chestnut hair bobbing, holding protectively onto his arm. They might have to send the girl over to France, but not yet. Give the youngsters some time together. War or no war, some things don't change . . .

'"Take a pair of sparkling eyes . . ."' hummed Mr Smith quietly to himself. '*Gondoliers* . . .' he explained automatically to the empty room.

To Libby, walking down the cool, sunny London street with Marius, everything around her seemed unreal. Even after two weeks back in this country, her nerves were still strung like violin strings and she had to repress the instinct to look over her shoulder. One of the strangest things was to think that she had actually been over there, in enemy-held territory, so recently. It would have seemed incredible to those people scurrying past them along the pavements, going about their usual business. But usual was an odd sort of thing these days, and the war wasn't simply something over there, across the Channel. It reached out here, too. It came from the skies above, with little warning, in a torrent of flame and destruction. Two streets further on, they came across men struggling to clear the débris from the previous night's raid. Bricks were piled up anyhow, and beams, snapped like matchsticks, protruded at crazy angles. On top of one pile of rubble stood a chair, quite intact; how it had got there, and why it had survived unscathed, a total mystery. The workmen had paused for a break and stood about singly or in silent, exhausted groups.

'Office block,' said the man nearest to them, seeing them pause and stare curiously. He wiped a sweaty face with a grimy hand, leaving a trail of black across his nose and cheek. 'Or more would have copped it. Casualties not too bad this time.'

This time. Wait for the next. There would be a next, perhaps tonight, or tomorrow or next week.

'My missus,' said the man, accepting a tin mug of tea from a stout lady in brogues and a WVS uniform, 'she's moved us all down the tube, whole bloomin' family.'

'Down the tube?' asked Libby, momentarily puzzled. Ridiculously, the words of the old Cockney music-hall song rang in her ears: 'My baby 'as gone dahn the plug-'ole, My baby 'as gone dahn the plug. The poor little fing was so feeble and thin . . . it oughta bin barfed in a jug . . .'

'Yus . . . down the underground. Any number of folk sleeping down there on the platforms. If nothing else, it's safe, that's what she says. Don't reckon much to it, meself. Bloke's entitled to the privacy of his own home, even if Jerry is chucking ruddy bombs at it every blooming night.'

He moved away, and they walked on in silence. After a while, Libby said quietly, 'It isn't really over for us, not yet, is it? I'm beginning to think it's never going to be over. We'll never get a chance to be together, left in peace.'

'Of course we will,' Marius said robustly. 'We may have to wait a little, that's all.'

'There's nothing I want more than peace,' she said sadly, 'and for us to be together.' She glanced at him. 'Will you really go off to the army or something, when you're fit?'

'Can't sit around on my backside, waiting for peace in our time to catch up with me. I might not be any more use jumping out of aircraft, but a chap who can blow up bridges and railway lines and so on is always useful somewhere.' He frowned. 'When I trained to be an engineer, I always imagined I'd be building things. Instead of that, I keep destroying them. Odd, that.'

'After the war, there will be a lot of rebuilding to be done.'

'There will be time for us, too.' He squeezed her hand.

After a few moments, Libby observed briskly, 'I dare say they will want to send me in again. Not to Belgium, of course, but perhaps to France. I know Mr Smith left it all vague, but they can't have that many women agents, and if they lose a few here and there, they'll want me.'

That got a vigorous response. 'I don't think you should. For one thing, you're too squeamish. Yes, squeamish. Don't look at me like that! I know you don't like what Ton did to Harry, but it was unavoidable . . . And another time—if you do go back—you may have to do the messy jobs yourself. I don't think you could. It's not a criticism. It's a simple fact.'

'I never thought I'd ever go jumping out of aircraft in the first place, but I did. One can get used to anything.'

'Sure you can do anything. But afterwards you have to live with it.'

Marius hunched his shoulders, and then swore, because the movement tugged on half-healed skin. He didn't want her to go. His reasons were of the most obvious kind. Yet they seemed purely selfish in the light of events, and he hesitated, even now, to admit to them. These weren't the days for selfishness, he thought sadly, and then reflected that he could string together a dozen good sound practical reasons why she shouldn't go back, but he still hesitated to say, 'I want you to stay here, in safety, because I love you, and when I come back, God willing, from wherever I go next, I want to know you'll be here . . .' He hesitated to say it, because for so long now, duty had come first and duty had been all, until he had been in danger of turning into a robot.

Drawing a deep, determined breath, he stopped in the middle of the pavement with such abruptness that Libby bumped against his injured side, and he exclaimed, 'Ouch!'

'Oh, Lord, I'm sorry!' She put out a consoling hand. 'I didn't mean to do that, but you didn't give any warning.'

'I want us to get married!' Marius said bluntly.

'What, right now?'

'Yes, now! Right now!' His voice took on a tone of anger. He forced it back and added stiffly, 'One can get special licences or something in this country, can't one?'

'Sure.' There was a warning sparkle in her blue eyes. 'I guess so. But why are you so keen? It wouldn't be, by any remote chance, a ploy to stop me being sent back over there?'

'No—well, yes and no. Of course I want you still to be here when I come back from wherever I go next. And if they send you in again, you might not be. How many successful pick-ups do you think any one agent can hope to make? This time you were lucky, and next time the Germans may get there first.'

Her gaze moved away from his flushed face, and she stared away down the road towards an oncoming red double-decker bus. 'Jamie said something, once, about being afraid he'd come back and there'd be nothing and no one here.'

'We all fear that. But it's not the only reason. You know I love you. And you love me, and I thought it's what you wanted: for us to be married.' Despite his efforts to sound persuasive, he was sounding increasingly cross and even petulant. 'I promised you, anyway,' he said firmly, 'when we were hiding in Emil's shed. I said we'd get married.'

A mischievous smile unexpectedly touched her lips. 'I don't hold you to that, you know. It was rather like a death-bed promise. I mean, words spoken on a death-bed are legally binding, aren't they? In common law, anyway. I mean, if you make a statement believing you're dying, it's acceptable in a court of law? You thought we wouldn't get out of it alive, so I guess it applies to anything you said then, too. But I'm not about to sue for breach of promise!'

'I think,' said Marius slowly, 'I'd like to push you under that bus. Stop tormenting me, will you?'

Sorry for her teasing, she took his hand. 'You know I want us to be married, Marius. There's nothing I want more. But my bosses, and yours, might object.'

He thrust out his chin pugnaciously. 'Listen, I'm no John Doe or Tommy Atkins. If Smith tries to be awkward, he'll find me damn awkward, too. If all else fails, I'll get my father to support us. They won't want to upset him.'

'Perhaps your father wouldn't want me as a daughter-in-law.'

'Yes, he does. I already told him.'

She felt vaguely ruffled that he seemed to be taking it all so much for granted. 'Heck,' she thought, 'I trained damn hard to be an agent!' The memory of all those bruises and of sadistic instructors came back. Mr Smith, and all the others, hoped a lot from her. They counted on her going back again. Other people had to make sacrifices. If she had not been prepared to do that, she ought not to have volunteered in the first place. Marius had put his duty as an agent before all else, but he seemed unwilling to accept that she should do it. Of course he was right in what he said. The dice were loaded against continual safe return. Some agents crossed to and fro from France as many as three or four times by night-time Lysander flights, or by parachute drop. But they were few, and she had never met anyone who had made more. Some got picked up within hours of landing. If she were afraid, she thought, this was a chance to opt out, and perhaps her controllers would see it so. Yet she didn't want to opt out, for all the risks. She wanted to do the job she had been trained to do.

But she did want to marry Marius, too. A conventional happy ending to their joint adventures? It seemed too much to ask for, a temptation to fate. As if they asked for a reward they had not earned. *She* had not earned, at any rate, even if he had. An irrational fear gripped her. 'Can I think it over . . . please? I know it seems superstitious and foolish, but I'm afraid to think about our getting married.'

'Think quickly, then!' he said sharply. 'If they give you two weeks' leave, they mean two weeks!'

They went down to Merriton House, because it was the best place Libby could think of for Marius to recuperate. They were met on the station platform by Evangeline, wearing slacks and what looked like one of Jamie's pullovers. She was a big girl, and it fitted tightly enough over her bra-less bosom to appear incredibly indecent. Many a Windmill girl looked more respectable in a G-string and a couple of gilt stars. Startled passengers, clambering down from the train, stared at her in wonderment. Evangeline waved both arms above her head and bounced towards them.

'You look a bit dodgy,' she said cheerfully to Marius by way of greeting.

'Healing nicely, thank you, only a flesh wound.' Strictly out of a sense of humour, decided Libby, he picked up Evangeline's hand and kissed it in a continental way.

'Lawks,' said Evangeline, gazing at her fingers. 'I saw Charles Boyer do that in a film. I usually get my backside pinched.' She waved a hand in the general direction of Marius's upper body. 'Bet those busted ribs slow down the action, though!' She chortled merrily, and dug Libby in the ribs. 'Glad to see you in one piece. We all thought you might come back in a box.'

'Eva,' said Libby seriously, 'you are the most tactless person I ever met.'

'Don't mind me. I'm chauffeur today, because Jamie got himself posted up to Scotland. Perishing Scotland, I ask you!' She shunted them towards the car, which proved not to be the Riley but an incredibly battered pre-war shooting-brake belonging to Colonel Watts. 'Sit in the back, both of you, you'll feel safer,' said Evangeline.

They got in, to find themselves sharing space with a saddle with a broken tree, and a mud-caked pair of wellington boots. The interior stank of dogs, and the seats were covered in hair and grit. Evangeline slammed her door, and set off with an excruciating grinding of gears.

'I mean, Scotland! A desk job, of course, so why couldn't they find somewhere nearer than the bally banks and braes? That's what I want to know. I'm going up to join him as soon as he can find me somewhere to live. I don't know what I'm going to do about the mare. I can't crate the poor brute up and ship her north. Have to sell her, I suppose. Daddy's got enough to do, keeping Sabre, and I won't be there to lend a hand, mucking-out.'

Libby repressed an almost hysterical desire to giggle. She had been afraid that, when they got home, everyone would want to know what they had been doing, and ask all manner of awkward questions they couldn't answer, such as how Marius came to be injured, and press for details they couldn't give. But that was to misunderstand human nature. People are primarily interested in what touches their own lives, however mundane and humdrum, and not really so very interested in other people's problems. Nothing either Libby or Marius had done worried Evangeline half as much as what to do about a horse superfluous to requirements.

She nevertheless made a heroic effort to cater for her passengers' interests. She had, after all, been properly brought up. 'Your uncle is OK, Libby. Jamie's mother is away somewhere doing her good works, and won't be back for a week.'

The shooting-brake rattled merrily along, and Marius muttered softly, because it jarred his injured side.

'Have a good swear, old chap, and get it off your chest!' advised Evangeline over her shoulder. They rounded a bend, and she added in a musing tone, 'I was going to drop that busted saddle off at the saddlers'. But I don't suppose I shall be needing it much more if I'm going to sell the mare.'

Gerard Daventry looked old and tired, but obviously pleased to see them both. He greeted Marius with old-fashioned courtesy, and hoped they could make him comfortable, insisting he stay as long as necessary or he liked. That evening Libby walked round the gardens with her uncle, the dogs running ahead. The gardens were bare and wore their winter aspect. When they turned a corner and the sharp wind from the sea struck them, she felt Gerard, who held her arm, stagger and check, and she realised how frail he was now. He had always been such a robust man, large, portly, hale and hearty. Now the winter bareness of the gardens seemed to echo his whole condition.

'We'll go back to the house,' she said in concern.

'Not just yet.' He stopped and turned them both so that they faced out to sea. They were standing at the far end of the gardens, above the strip of private beach. The sea was grey, and the white horses of foam showed where the wind whipped up the water.

'Is your young man badly hurt?' he asked unexpectedly.

'Marius? No, not as badly as I thought at the time . . .' She broke off hastily.

'I know you can't talk about it,' he said, 'but the chap is obviously in some pain. One can tell by the way he moves. Seeing him like that, I remember going with your mother to see your father, as he was to become, in Paris, after the Great War, when he was barely recovered from his injuries.' He fell silent again, and Libby did not interrupt his thoughts. 'I was a non-combatant in the first lot,' Gerard said. 'I volunteered, but they wouldn't have me . . . Bad eyesight, they said. Now, in this lot, they even send the girls into action, it seems.'

'You don't approve,' Libby said ruefully.

'I don't approve, but I'm still very proud of you, Libby, and so will your parents be—when this is over and you can tell them about it all.' Gerard walked slowly towards a garden seat and lowered himself stiffly onto it, resting his walking-stick against the arm. 'Leave me here, my dear. I'll just sit for a while and watch the sea. I do that a lot these days.'

'It's very cold, Uncle Gerry,' Libby said doubtfully.

'No matter, no matter. Go on back to the house. The young man will be wondering what's become of you. The young man is the one who matters, not me. I'm yesterday's news, as they say.'

She walked slowly back the way they had come down. At a bend in the path, she turned her head and saw that Gerard was sitting quite motionless. The dogs were digging at an old rabbit-hole. Libby walked on. As she neared the house, she saw Marius standing just outside the french doors and looking about him, obviously for her, and she thought she understood what Uncle Gerry had meant. 'Life goes on. It doesn't go backwards, it goes forwards. The future, whatever it holds, that belongs to us, to Marius and to me!'

She called out, 'Marius!' waved, and ran towards him. He looked at her enquiringly as she panted to a halt, chestnut hair tumbled over her rosy-pink, flushed face. 'About that special licence . . . and our getting married. I've made up my mind!'